Driftless GOLD

SUE BERG

Best Wishes

Sue Berg

2022

LITTLE CREEK PRESS®
AND BOOK DESIGN
MINERAL POINT, WISCONSIN

Little Creek Press®
A Division of Kristin Mitchell Design, Inc.
5341 Sunny Ridge Road
Mineral Point, Wisconsin 53565

Book Design and Project Coordination:
Little Creek Press and Book Design

First Printing
April 2021

Printed in Wisconsin, United States of America

For more information: downadriftlessroad.com
To contact author: bergsue@hotmail.com
To order books: www.littlecreekpress.com

Library of Congress Control Number: 2021905702

ISBN-13: 978-1-942586-96-8

Cover photo:
Grandad's Bluff overlooking La Crosse, Wisconsin
© **Phil S Addis**

ACKNOWLEDGMENTS

To Alan:
always the wind beneath my wings

To MF:
you fanned the ember into a flame

To my kids and grandkids:
You make me sing with joy.

To Kristin Mitchell and the team at Little Creek Press:
This is a dream you helped make a reality. Bless you!

To my first readers:
Thanks so much for all your encouragement.
In a day when electronic communication governs our lives,
we still need readers. Without you, books make no sense
and authors lose their purpose.

Thank you for your encouraging comments.

To the Lord:
Without you, I would be nothing.

PRAISE FOR DRIFTLESS GOLD

Deeply engaging and absorbing. A thrill ride of twists, turns, and romance at the same time. When I finished reading *Driftless Gold*, I was ready to read the next book in the series.

~Bill, southwest Wisconsin

An interesting and captivating mystery set in La Crosse and surrounding southwestern Wisconsin. The story is centered around missing 1866 gold coins from Prairie du Chien, a couple of murders to cover up the recently discovered treasure, and a love story between two characters. The third-person perspective reveals the killer's side of the story. I am looking forward to the second book in the series based on the character Jim Higgins.

~David, Eau Claire

I found *Driftless Gold* to be a very intriguing and enjoyable mystery with a little romance thrown in. Anyone who has lived or spent time in the Driftless area will find familiarity with the setting and the interesting, hard-working main characters. I give Sue Berg's first novel two thumbs up!

~Mary, Viroqua

Sue Berg's *Driftless Gold* takes us to the bluffs, coulees, and winding roads along the Mississippi River in western Wisconsin. The dramatic landscape is blended into an irresistible tale of lost treasure and the scoundrels who will do anything to get their hands on it—even murder.

~Jeff Nania, author of the best-selling Northern Lakes Mystery series and 2020 Midwest Book Award Winner, Portage

Murder, hidden treasure, and a side of good old-fashioned romance make *Driftless Gold* a delightful read. Berg does a superb job of developing her characters and creating a sense of place. I felt like I was traversing the La Crosse area and the Driftless region along with Lt. Higgins and his team.

~Leah Call, Westby

Set in midwest Wisconsin, this suspenseful mystery intertwines with a love story and takes you through the dips and valleys of the Driftless region while solving a murder. As the book unfolds, it keeps the reader guessing and in suspense. With each page, more is revealed about the characters and who they are, helping the reader understand their journeys. A must read!

~Kara, Viroqua

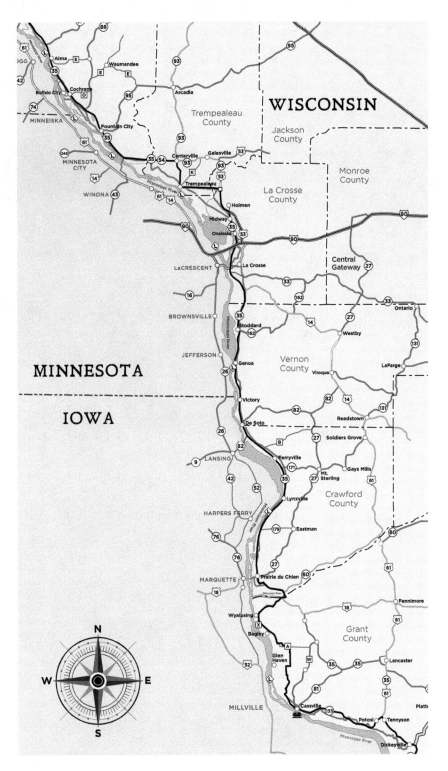

PROLOGUE

His years of searching for the lost gold shipment had been an obsession. It kept him from developing close relationships with others, and he'd neglected to make friends. He was what some would later describe as a true loner. Most people didn't know enough about him to realize that he spent every spare minute planning, hiking, and climbing the bluffs. They just thought he was an exercise freak. He'd been in every known cave between La Crosse and Prairie du Chien. The discovery of the unknown lost cave was pure luck, with a little help from a savant named Jamie Alberg. When he'd had the courage to enter the small opening of the rock shelter, his curiosity had been his greatest reward.

He remembered the smell of the damp earth in his nostrils and the cool, moist feel of the limestone floor. Chilled, he crawled on his belly, wondering how much farther he should go before easing his way back. As long as he could see the opening, he knew he was safe. You had to be careful and keep your bearings since some caves had multiple rooms and small ponds. Worming along, he'd spotted the glistening metallic sheen along a wall of the cave in the dim ray of his flashlight. It was so out of place that, at first, it didn't register. He squirmed closer and sat up where the cave opened to a small room. Collapsing, he shed tears of pure joy. After a few moments of disbelief, he began sifting the gold coins through his hands. Unbounded jubilation washed through him.

Back at home, he meticulously documented his discovery on the map he'd hidden behind the fuse box in the garage. On it, he had recorded every cave and its contents, plant life, insects, rocks, and traces of animal that he'd identified. It was a paper shrine to his effort, intelligence, and persistence that no one would probably ever see but him. But it was enough.

It took him a few days to decide how to handle his tremendous good fortune in discovering the cache of gold coins. Later, in hindsight, he realized he hadn't spent nearly enough time planning the removal of the gold from the cave. It was just the first of many blunders.

He hadn't meant to kill the Mexican. It all began as a simple business deal. The gold needed to be removed from the cave to a safe place, but just getting in and out of the cave above the Mississippi River was treacherous and steep. Lugging the bags of heavy, cumbersome coins on his back was exhausting. Besides the physical challenge, he'd had to confront his inherent dread of snakes and bats. Both were probably in the cave somewhere. He'd spent many moments cowering and shivering just thinking about the dark dampness and what might be lying in wait. His skin crawled when he recalled the whole experience.

The Mexican's offer of help had been too tempting to turn down, especially after they'd both smoked a couple of good doobies. Jorge claimed his experience in the drug cartels in the mountains of Mexico was an advantage. Climbing steep, difficult terrain in his home country made him physically fit and strong. But when the work began, and the Mexican realized what was at stake, he wanted payment—in gold coins. He wanted *in*. Now it was too late. All his years of work, crawling over rocks, taking dangerous chances made him realize that he should have done the hard physical work alone. Their argument above the quarry had quickly turned ugly, and in the scuffle that followed, the Mexican slipped and fell over the edge. What was that old saying? *Fear is temporary, but regret is forever.*

Most nights, he slept well, secure in the knowledge that no one else knew about the gold. But infrequently, he would dream that he was falling, the air rushing past his ears. Screaming, he would wake with a thud and sit up suddenly in bed, drenched in sweat. And then he'd remember—*I am a murderer and a thief.* He would stare at the ceiling, willing himself to calm down, waiting for the terror to pass until morning. Regret didn't come close to describing how he felt. ⊙

SUE BERG

1

FRIDAY, JUNE 4

As he left his house, Jim Higgins was already mentally reviewing his day as chief investigating officer of the La Crosse County Sheriff's Department. Jim sighed, ticking off his responsibilities in his head.

He liked these quiet hours before the world intruded. As he climbed into his Suburban for his morning commute up the Mississippi River, the birds were just starting their raucous morning litany. Though quiet is almost nonexistent in modern life, it can be found along one of the famous Wisconsin trout creeks that run through the valleys and ravines near La Crosse. Now that is quality, quiet time.

He turned onto Chipmunk Coulee Road, driving quickly on his way to U.S. Highway 35.

The drive this day up the Mississippi was especially beautiful. In his job, a typical day could be shattered in an instant by anything from a missing teenager, a drug-induced rampage of assault on a wife, a senseless robbery, a mindless shooting, or a family shattered by dysfunction that had turned violent. That old hymn came to mind. *Whatever my lot, thou hast taught me to say, "It is well, it is well with my soul."* Many people need a little peace in their lives—something for the wounded soul—but so few seem to find it.

He came to the intersection with U.S. Highway 35, otherwise known as the Great River Road. Traffic at this time of the morning was still relatively light. His cell phone buzzed.

"Hey, Chief. Saner here. We just received a phone call from the Knutson crew at Chipmunk Coulee Quarry. The guys found something very interesting down there while one of their operators was loading some screenings.

"Oh, yeah. What's that?" Jim asked. He thought about the major road construction projects recently halted by MVAC (Mississippi Valley Archeological Conservancy). One project was interrupted when pottery shards and bone fragments were unearthed. They were believed to belong to a pre-Columbian Indian tribe that had inhabited the Mississippi Valley area thousands of years earlier.

"It's not what you're thinking, sir," Officer Saner continued as if reading Jim's mind. "No old bones this time. Just a real dead body."

Jim sat up in his seat, his curiosity stimulated.

"How long has it been there, do you think?" he asked.

"Not sure, Chief. Probably no more than a week or so. I can meet you at the quarry if you're on your way in. Save you a trip back this way later."

"Sounds good. I'm heading there now. I'll meet you there. Call the coroner, too."

"Right, I'll get on it. See you in half an hour." Saner commented.

Jim replaced his cell phone in his jacket pocket. He mulled over the prospects and information while he swung his Suburban around, drove through the Kwik Trip parking lot, and headed back south to Chipmunk Coulee Quarry.

As Jim sped along, the shadow of the trees that hung over the road made the morning seem cool. He tried to imagine who would deposit a body in a gravel quarry. Murder? Suicide? *Actually, it wasn't a bad place for either,* he thought. Gravel quarries were quiet during the winter months when road construction came to a halt.

The entrance of the quarry came into view. On either side of the

SUE BERG

gravel road, huge boulders had been pushed up next to two swinging steel gates. Sand and gravel trucks had access while keeping out rock hounds and teenage kids looking for a cool place to have a beer party. The gates were wide open now, and a nervous, slender man paced anxiously back and forth, puffing on a cigarette.

Jim swung the Suburban into the entrance and stopped near the gatekeeper. He flipped open his badge, and the young man flagged him through the gate. Officer Saner wasn't here yet.

Charles Knutson, foreman of the gravel crushing crew and heir to the Knutson gravel fortune, approached the parked Suburban just as Higgins was climbing out. They shook hands. Jim could feel the man's calloused palm grip his own.

"Mornin', sir. Charles Knutson. I'm the day foreman. We've got a problem." His eyes held Jim's in a steady gaze. A mop of unruly brown hair flopped over his forehead. Jim guessed he was thirty-something.

"Yes, Officer Saner called me on my cell while I was on my way into work. He tells me you've discovered a body. Who found it?" Jim asked, his eyes scanning the quarry.

"Everyone was confused, and no one really knew what to do," Charles stammered.

"Just tell me who discovered the body, and we'll go from there," Jim said patiently, his blue eyes locking on Charles.

"Well, not me. Nate Leland, our loader operator, dug it up from a pile of crushed gravel over by the west wall. Do you want to talk to him?"

"Sure. First, show me what you found," Higgins replied as he followed the foreman across the hard-packed limestone floor of the huge quarry.

The walls of the quarry had been dynamited many times. They rose to a height of 150 feet and enclosed a blasted area about five acres in size. The heavy dump trucks and earth-moving equipment seemed dwarfed by the huge stockpiles of limestone gravel that rose from the quarry floor like miniature mountain ranges.

As the men crossed the quarry, they fell into an easy stride. Knutson offered more information as they walked. Scattered pieces of gravel made crunching noises under his feet.

"So you've been working in this quarry about a month?" Jim asked.

"Yeah, more or less. No weekend work—a few days of rain here and there but pretty much steady otherwise."

"How many men on this crew?"

"A crew of five right now."

Jim nodded. Slowing his gait as he approached the gravel pile, he watched the loader operator jump down from his perch in the driver's seat.

Jim shook Nate's hand, noticing the gritty, rough skin. They were like pieces of abused sandpaper. Working man's hands, as his dad used to say. Jim thought they were more like the casualties in a war with sand, gravel, and rocks.

"Let's see this body," Jim said, noticing the other workers edging closer. He suddenly felt as if he was in an ancient amphitheater, and a play was about to begin. A chill ran up his back.

"Sure, it's right over here. I lowered my bucket and was turning the pile when I noticed a shoe. Thought that was odd. Didn't know if I'd seen it for sure, so I used my bucket to gently lift some of the gravel, and a body slowly rolled out. Didn't move anything more," Nate explained.

Jim knelt by the body. Although gravel was dispersed in the folds and creases of the clothing, it was remarkably well preserved. A strong odor of decomposition drifted in the air. He spent time looking the entire body over from head to toe, at times kneeling and getting uncomfortably close to the body. A man, about six feet tall with a lean build, stared back at him, his eyes cloudy with horror. He was wearing jeans, a T-shirt, and a denim jacket. The gravel, acting as a preservative, had probably insulated him from the wind, rain, and snow. He'd been dead a couple of weeks at the most. Facial features made Jim think he might be Hispanic. Migrant or construction worker? La Crosse and surrounding counties relied heavily on Hispanics to milk cows at the large area dairies and also to pick apples in the nearby orchards south of La Crosse. *It wasn't apple season now,* he thought. *So where did he come from?*

Jim stood up, wincing a little. He brushed the gravel dust from his dress slacks. "I'll make some calls. We'll have an investigative team here in less than an hour."

Turning to Charles, he said, "I'm afraid your work in this quarry will have to stop until we can establish whether a crime has taken place here." Bodies buried under gravel piles were not normal under any circumstances. Was it transported here and then buried? Or did the victim fall from the cliff, and someone covered him up?

"Not a problem. We've got plenty of other work elsewhere," Charles responded.

Jim's gaze traveled up the rock wall of the quarry to the tufted grassy area above. "One more question. Do you know whose land this quarry is on?"

"Yeah. A guy named Andy Straken owns all the land above and around it. A bluff rises to the south behind the quarry." He pointed as he spoke. "That land is rough and pretty much wasteland. You can't farm it. Andy probably owns 200-plus acres. Milks a herd of about sixty Holsteins. Has beef cattle, too."

"Thanks." Jim wrote the name in the little lined memo book he always kept in his pocket. "I'll be in touch and give you the all-clear when we finish here."

"Sounds good."

As the crew walked away, Jim noticed the dust raised by a Ford F-150 pickup entering the quarry. Detective Paul Saner slid out of his seat and sauntered toward Jim across the quarry's hard gravel floor. He stopped short of the body in the gravel and knelt next to it.

"What have we got, Chief?" he asked, gazing at Jim with a set of curious, hazel eyes.

The sheriff's crew privately called him Piano Man. Paul started as a music major at UW–La Crosse with piano as his instrument of choice. A run-in with a chainsaw during a weekend brush cleanup had sliced his fingers on his right hand and severed a tendon, eliminating music as a full-time profession. A bright mind and insatiable curiosity mixed with a slightly funky sense of humor led him into law enforcement. He had worked under Jim now for about two years and showed promise as an investigator.

"What do you see?" Jim asked, standing with his arms crossed.

Paul knelt again and began his analysis. "Well, male victim, possibly Hispanic. Could be suicide, but since he was covered with gravel in a shallow grave, I'm leaning toward murder. We'll have to wait for the crime scene crew to get here and sweep and bag up the scene before we see what we've got."

"I agree. Looks suspicious," Jim said.

"Can't think there'd be too many other circumstances that would explain a body being hidden under a pile of gravel. Unusual circumstances for sure," Paul concluded, standing up.

Jim nodded in agreement.

"Okay, then. What do you want me to do?" Paul asked brusquely.

Jim squinted into the morning sun, his hands resting casually on his hips. "You stay here. Help the team set up and get started. I'll catch you later when we know more. I'm heading up there," Jim pointed to the land above the quarry, "to talk to the landowner. Maybe he'll remember seeing someone that might give us a clue as to how this body got here."

Using the directions from the quarry crew, Jim retraced his trip up Chipmunk Coulee, the beautiful morning marred by the mysterious body in the quarry. When he reached the top of the ridge, he turned right on Koll Ridge Road until a gravel driveway appeared. A sign with a Holstein cow on it was placed strategically next to the road and surrounded by red geraniums. "Straken Holsteins—A Century Farm." He dodged some early spring potholes and pulled up to a low-slung white pole building where the milking cows were bedded down. Attached to the large shed was a smaller area where the milking parlor and an office were located. The pungent smell of cow manure and fresh hay silage wafted on the cool mid-morning breeze.

As he approached the door of the parlor, he noticed a little girl playing in the dirt nearby. She had a toy shovel and was planting a dead dandelion.

"Hey there," Jim said. "Whatcha doin'?"

She turned toward him and stared with innocent brown eyes, sizing him up. "Just planting some dandy lions for my mommy." She spoke in a serious, no-nonsense tone.

"Well, I'm looking for a guy named Andy. Would that be your daddy?" Jim asked, grinning.

"Yes, I'll show you where he is."

"Sounds like a deal to me." Jim smiled down on her as the child grabbed his hand, oblivious of the dirt and mud.

"My name is Ruby. We have a lot of cows. My daddy works really hard. Mommy takes care of us kids." She looked up at him, then dropped her head as if she'd said too much. They turned, walking down a concrete corridor. She stopped in the door frame of what appeared to be the farm office.

Sitting at a desk, a younger man looked up from a computer monitor. A set of similar brown eyes greeted him. *Can't get away from genetics,* Jim thought. He wondered if other people saw such similarities between him and his kids.

Jim reached across the desk and shook his hand. "Lt. Jim Higgins, La Crosse Sheriff's Department. You must be Andy Straken."

"Yes, I see you've met my daughter, Ruby." The little girl, suddenly shy, ran around the desk and climbed into her dad's lap. "What brings you out here? Can I help you with something?" He was wearing a Funks seed corn hat and a red Wisconsin Badger T-shirt frayed at the neck. His neck and arms were muscular and tanned, his hands gnarled and calloused.

"Well, I don't know. I'm hoping you can," Jim explained. "We were called to the Chipmunk Coulee Quarry this morning. Charles Knutson told me that you own the quarry. Is that right?"

"Yes, I own the quarry. Knutson Brothers lease it from me."

"The crew uncovered a body that was buried under a gravel pile this morning. I was wondering if you'd noticed any activity above the quarry recently. We're not sure how the body got there or how long it's been there. Since you own the quarry, we wondered if the victim might have recently been on your land or maybe was an employee?"

Andy paused, eyes widened with shock. "Whoa! Do you know who it is?"

Jim shook his head. "No idea."

Andy's eyebrows drew together in a frown. "I don't have hired help. That's what my kids are for. Can't say I've noticed tracks or anything. I've got a really good four-strand fence around the top edge of the quarry and along the bluff to the south since I pasture my cows out there. My older kids ride their four-wheelers out to the field road. Knowing how they drive when I'm not looking, I thought I needed a really good fence."

"I hear you," Jim said. "Mind if I drive that field road out there and look around? Maybe I can spot something that will help us."

"Go right ahead. You passed the field road on your way in." He pointed vaguely in the direction of the quarry. "There's a gate you'll have to go through, but the fence isn't electrified. There's a twenty-foot buffer of weeds and stuff beyond the fence to the edge of the quarry. Let me know if I can help in any way." Jim turned and waved.

Driving down the field road to the quarry edge, he parked and climbed over the fence. He pushed his way through tall dried weeds, refuse from the winter. A patch of blackberries was beginning to bloom, and honeybees were working the blossoms. As he came out of the brush, the view cleared. Off in the distance, Jim could see the Mississippi River sparkling in the sun. In a nervous truce, barges and recreational boats avoided each other. Some headed up river and some toward the locks and dams downriver at Genoa. In the distance, the beige bluffs rose above Iowa to the south and Minnesota to the north. Bald eagles and turkey vultures made lazy circles in the cloudless sky.

Jim began investigating the edge of the quarry for any evidence of human activity. A gum wrapper, a cigarette butt, a Kwik Trip coffee cup, a beer bottle—anything. At the precipice, he knelt down and stretched out on his stomach to peer over the edge. *I would hate to fall off here and see the ground coming up. Did the guy fall, or was he pushed?* Jim didn't find any evidence on top of the quarry that anyone had been there, and the recent spring rains a few days ago would've obliterated any footprint evidence.

As he looked to the left, he noticed some gravel and dirt on the edge that had been disturbed. He walked over to the scuff marks and knelt down for a better look. He could see Paul down in the quarry working with the team. Other police vehicles had arrived. The disturbed gravel aligned with the body below. Perhaps this was where the man had been when he went over. Reaching in his pocket, he pulled out a latex glove and tied it to the top of a tall weed as a marker. Jim stood and retrieved his cell phone, snapping pictures of the disturbed ground and the quarry below him. The CSI techs would need to make casts of the partial footprints.

He made his way out to the field road. He hoped other physical evidence that might be on and around the body would help because he didn't have a clue how that guy had gotten there.

He got in the Suburban, negotiated his way along the field road until he reached Chipmunk Coulee, then stepped on the gas and headed downtown. Whatever the crime scene crew found, it couldn't come soon enough for Jim Higgins. ☉

2

Jim Higgins parked in the crowded parking lot of the La Crosse County Courthouse and Law Enforcement Center on Vine Street. The tan and brown building looked like a huge stack of children's blocks arranged in perpendicular positions. The building was punctuated with narrow glass panels that let in minimal light. It was a typical government building designed by someone who seldom saw sunlight. Squatting on Vine Street, it was a silent and imposing structure, its windows unblinking like the eyes of a big brown toad.

Jim made his way to the third floor, where the investigative team had their offices. They were in a staggered arrangement down a long corridor, within easy shouting distance of each other. The rest of the third floor was subdivided into various rooms used for data collection and analysis from crime scenes and team meetings for brainstorming. Just off the elevator, the secretaries huddled together around a group of four desks. The women always reminded Jim of a covey of quails, all pecking away at their keyboards, chattering, answering phones, and sharing an occasional coffee break in the tiny kitchenette with a refrigerator, microwave, and coffee pot. Of course, he'd never tell them that. It was just an affectionate way of thinking about them.

Emily Warehauser, department manager for ten years, had

seniority and directed the office workers, demanding high exacting standards. Like all office settings, despite their efficiency, the gossip flowed freely.

After greeting Emily and gathering his mail, Jim entered his office. He took off his jacket and draped it on the back of his black padded desk chair. Without the coat and with the air conditioning pumping, he felt cooler. His office smelled like the lingering fragrance of lilacs that had drifted through an open window the day before. A penchant for neatness was evident in the tidy piles of papers on his desk and the display of Native American arrowheads and spear points framed and hung on the wall. Various awards and photos of his career in law enforcement were assembled on another wall. His cell phone chirped.

"Lt. Jim Higgins," he said, suppressing a yawn. He plopped in his chair.

"Saner, here. Body's going down to the morgue. Luke will get started on the autopsy. Something else. The victim had an old coin in his jean pocket—I mean really old. It's going to take some research and digging, but that coin is going to cause a stir. It's dated 1866."

"Huh. No kidding. I'll take a look when you get here," Jim said dispassionately.

Downstairs, Luke Evers, La Crosse County medical examiner and coroner, would probably be starting his work on the victim. He was a quiet, unassuming guy who performed the forensic autopsy procedures for the sheriff's department. Things like blood, body fluids, broken bones, bashed in skulls, gunshot wounds, and death, which sickened Jim, didn't seem to deter Luke in the least. If anyone could find dubious patterns and trails on the human body, it was him. His work was thorough, professional, and carried unquestioned authority. Investigators and attorneys relied on his expertise in court. Jim had only seen him unnerved once when police officers had returned to the morgue with the charred remains of a four-year-old girl. Meth-addicted parents had run to Walmart and left the little girl alone when the fire broke out.

"There's nothing as sad as the loss of a child," Luke said sadly. "I've got three kids, and I can't think of a more horrible death than by fire. Parents never really recover from the death of a child. They put on a good face, but I'm sure they think about them every day. I know I would. I'd hate to have to carry around the guilt of those parents when they finally get sober and realize what they did to that innocent, precious child." Jim silently agreed.

Jim pulled himself back to the present. His favorite photo of Margie sat on the corner of his desk, reflecting the light from the window. It had been taken on their boat near one of the islands above Lock and Dam No. 8 near Genoa. Margie wore a halter top and shorts in the photo, which accented her petite, trim figure. Her dark green eyes gazed back at him, her hair windblown and tousled from a day on the river. She seemed to say, "Whaddya lookin' at?" That smile. They'd had so much fun together. *She was a babe ... had been a babe.*

The death of his wife was something he'd hoped would come later—much later. He'd pictured them accepting the joys of grandkids, retirement, and the challenges of declining health together. Being alone had not been what he thought the future would hold.

In the desperate days immediately following her death, he'd wandered from room to room like an abandoned puppy dog, head hanging, eyes sad. He'd been able to get past that, but since her death, he didn't have the punch and purpose he'd always enjoyed. He felt like someone who'd taken a surprise blow to the stomach and still hadn't gotten his wind back. The gnawing ache he felt inside didn't go away. It wasn't cancer or ulcers; it was sadness and maybe a little situational depression. At last, that was what his doctor had told him.

He missed Margie—the smell of her skin at night in bed, her cheerful voice, the sweet kisses she gave as he'd headed out the door. Their ardent, passionate lovemaking filled his mind and made the sweetness of their relationship even more intense in her absence.

SUE BERG

His phone beeped again.

"Jim Higgins."

"Jim. Carol Olstad down here at the morgue." Carol had been a good friend of Margie's and was a long-time family acquaintance. Although Margie and Carol might not talk for weeks at a time, they had a special, unassuming bond. Jim and Carol knew each other well, too. Talks on the patio after a shared meal, Carol's continuing interest in the twins' lives, and visiting Margie in her last days elevated her to a treasured friend. "Just letting you know that Luke started the forensic exam on the quarry body."

"Thanks, Carol. Any idea when he might finish?"

There was a pause. "It's eleven now. I wouldn't expect anything until early Monday morning." Carol was the coordinator, secretary, coffee queen, and general manager of the morgue department. Nobody, dead or alive, went in or out of there without her stamp of approval.

"Okay. I can live with that. So, how have you been? You know … outside of work?" Jim asked tentatively. They had been casually dating for about six months. Jim was getting comfortable with the idea of having another woman in his life, but he didn't think things were going to change any time soon. Carol was much different than Margie—an independent, working woman with a life of her own. Besides, after twenty plus years of marriage, the dating scene seemed overwhelming to him.

"Are you asking as a friend so that I can unload on you? Or should I just chirp out a cheerful response?"

Jim hesitated, but Carol giggled. He could picture her at her desk—a petite brunette with brown eyes and a gracious smile.

"Just kidding," she said. "I'm doing what a woman's got to do. Workin' every day, catching the symphony once in awhile. I'm dating a few too many middle-aged guys who have forgotten what manners are and turned into drunken bores. I spend time gritting my teeth when I hear young people who can't construct a sentence without using the f-word. Otherwise, life is great. You?"

Jim smiled. Honesty was one of Carol's best qualities, but he wasn't sure if he wanted to be on the receiving end of her candid observations. *Wonder what she thinks of me?* he thought.

"I'm okay. I'm hoping to get the boat out on the river with this glorious weather and do some fishin' and cruisin.' Hey, maybe we can have a beer sometime on the boat. Right now, though, I've got folks waiting on me. Gotta go. Let's catch up soon."

"Is that a promise?"

"That's a dangerous word, but yeah, I promise. Catch you later, Carol."

"See ya, Jim."

He clicked off. Most people didn't answer a "How are you?" with an honest response. It was always "Fine, just fine!" when you knew that couldn't always be true. Nobody was just fine all the time. At least with Carol, he'd had an honest exchange about life's ups and downs. That short exchange with Carol brought back the memory of another conversation he'd had with Margie the last week of her life.

Margie had snuggled under a comforter and was lying in a wicker chaise lounge propped up by pillows at her sides. The April sunlight was streaming into the sunroom off the kitchen, gaining strength every day. The leaves had just begun to bud, and the air was clear and hopeful. Margie had a small set of binoculars and was observing the returning spring birds at her many feeders scattered throughout the backyard.

Jim walked in with a cup of peppermint tea laced with honey. As he set it down and settled into a chair next to her, she grabbed his hand. Lately, she'd had moments of serious intensity on a variety of subjects—the kids and their careers, whether they would get married, how she'd miss out on the grandkids, where she wanted to be buried, plans for her memorial service. All the stuff Jim wanted to avoid with a ten-foot pole. Now her frail hand gripped his with surprising strength. She focused her dark green eyes on him. Her bald head, the result of chemo treatments, was covered with a beautiful silk scarf splashed with floral motifs. Even in the throes of cancer, she was still gorgeous to him.

"Jim, I have something to tell you, and I want you to listen carefully," she began. Her voice was weak and scratchy, but you couldn't mistake the seriousness in her tone. "I've been thinking about your life after I die. I know that's morbid, but I'm dying, so I get to be morbid." She smiled a sad smile. "Just hear me out. I know I have no right to make plans after I'm gone, but I am shamelessly going to suggest something to you that will probably shock you. But I want you to understand that it comes from my heart and my love for you." She stopped, winded by the effort it took to speak so many words.

Tears glistened in Jim's eyes. He stayed quiet, taking in the essence of her, knowing her final days had arrived like a stranger on the doorstep who was awaiting some silent, predestined signal. Jim was learning the value of being vulnerable and in the moment like never before. It was intensely uncomfortable, and he had a long way to go, but he was learning. Margie was a good teacher.

She started again. "I don't want to hurt you with what I'm about to say. But I want you to feel free to find someone after I'm gone." The silence was palpable. She continued, "And I think Carol Olstad would be a really good companion for you." She stopped, gasping for air, weakened with her effort, while Jim stared at her wordlessly. He gave her the courtesy of not disagreeing or arguing. *Must be the morphine the nurse had given her a couple of hours ago,* he thought.

Jim had noticed a marked acceptance in Margie the last few days. She knew her days were numbered. This was the hard work of dying that the hospice nurse had explained to him. This was Margie's last great hurrah, and she would do it in her inimitable way. He could see that happening now, and he didn't know if he could handle it. He didn't want to fail her in the last thing she was trying so hard to do right.

Margie went on. "Carol is practical, fun-loving, and she's just plain good. You've known her a long time, and I trust her completely. She's been a family friend forever. And her value system and morals are a good match to yours," she finished.

"God, you didn't talk to her about this, did you?" Jim blurted, forgetting the effort it took Margie to tell him this.

"Oh, for heaven's sake, no. No. I'm dying of cancer, but I'm not stupid. I love you too much to watch you suffer." She locked eyes with him and noticed his tears. She reached up and brushed his cheek with her fingers. Jim grabbed her hand and held it tightly. "I want you to be happy again. You've had enough sadness to last a lifetime, and you're too young to live the rest of your life alone. When this is all over, you're going to remember what I told you today."

She leaned back on the cushion, exhausted from her efforts. In a few minutes, she drifted off, snoring softly, binoculars cupped in her frail hand. Jim gently unwound her fingers and pulled the quilt up around her shoulders. He couldn't remember ever being this sad. *How am I going to go on after this?* He paused a minute, watching her sleep. *You'll do it,* a voice told him, *because you have to. One step at a time. One day at a time.*

Jim's reverie was interrupted by a staccato knock on his open office door.

"You want to take a look at that coin?" Paul Saner asked.

"Sure," Jim said, getting up from his chair. He pulled his office door shut and followed Paul down the hall to one of the evidence rooms. Beige walls, bookshelves along one wall, a variety of tools including hammers, picks, pliers, drills, and fine brushes were strewn on a white plastic oblong island. A row of generic cupboards stood against the back wall. A young woman with latex gloves was bent over the coin placed on a clean paper towel. A fluorescent recessed light illuminated the coin. Jim and Paul crowded around.

"Don't block my light," the girl warned.

"Lt. Higgins, meet Leslie Brown. She's our new detective and crime scene lab assistant," Paul said.

The girl looked up at Jim, her blue eyes and medium blond

hair a testimony to her Nordic genetics. She was dressed casually in comfortable business trousers topped with a light blue camisole and a nubby cotton sweater. Her smooth skin was unimpeded by makeup. Jim thought makeup would just detract from her stark Scandinavian beauty.

"I'd shake your hand but …" She shrugged as she held a small brush in her latex-gloved hand, then smiled. "I've heard a lot about you, sir. I'm really glad to be a member of your team."

"Nice to meet you, Leslie. U.S. Army, right? Dog handler?" Jim said, assessing her as she went on. Leslie stood straight and tall under his blue-eyed gaze. *A soldier through and through,* Jim thought. The moment of casual scrutiny passed.

"Yes, sir. I worked with dogs that sniffed out bombs and detected IEDs. I loved that job, but it did require some grueling days in hundred-plus heat. Trained in Yuma, Arizona, in a mock Iraqi village the Army has down there. So I'm loving all this Wisconsin green and the wonderfully cool weather."

"Glad to have you on board," he said sincerely. Jim got to the business of the coin. "So what do we know so far?" he asked, pointing to the specimen on the table. He leaned back, crossing his arms over his chest, and watched her as she launched into her report.

"I haven't had much time to dig and research, but I can tell you, and you can see for yourself, that the coin is in very good shape. The patterns and ridges are clear, as well as the date. I'll do some hunting and get more information to you as soon as I know something."

"Are there any coin collectors in the area that might give us some help?" Paul asked.

"Yeah, there are. We'll check that out," Jim responded. "Could be treasure, too."

"Treasure? Really?" Leslie said, her eyes widening with surprise. "You're talking lost treasure, like the *Titanic*?" Jim nodded.

"Actually, there are a number of treasure hunters in the area and even a few clubs. I know a guy in town who goes to the meetings," Jim said.

"I never knew there was treasure around here," Leslie commented.

"You'd be surprised," Jim commented. "The internet is full of YouTube videos about hunters and their finds. Coins, relics, arrowheads, pottery, that kind of thing. I've got quite a collection of Native American artifacts, some found and some purchased. I'll run over to Steve Stoner's shop this afternoon and talk to him." He glanced at the clock. "I'm sure he'll be very interested in this find, even though someone may have lost their life over it."

Using his cell camera, he snapped several views of the coin. He paused and looked Leslie and Paul in the eye. "I know this coin is a link to this whole thing."

"How can you be so sure?" Leslie asked.

"Ever heard of gut feelings?" Jim asked.

Leslie nodded.

"This is one of them." ⊙

3

Steve Stoner was the sole proprietor of Stoner's Snowmobile and Cycle Shop on the north side of La Crosse. He didn't advertise his business, and he only accepted new customers by word of mouth. His parents were deceased, and he inherited the house and the business. Steve took on jobs that allowed him to pursue his treasure hunting passion. If truth be told, the cycle shop was secondary to "shooting" with his metal detector. (Shooting is the term used by treasure hunters when searching for relics.) He was as addicted to collecting as some men and women were devoted to flyfishing, golf, or hunting.

He didn't have any real friends; he had acquaintances. Sharon Cross, his girlfriend, had no interest in marriage. She wasn't interested in treasure either. In her opinion, relics were old, dirty, and irrelevant. Steve and Sharon didn't live together. They just enjoyed each other's company, although the relationship was far from platonic. When they went out for drinks or dinner, they split the bill. It kept things uncomplicated, which was how they both wanted it. Steve liked Sharon. Sharon liked Steve. Simple, untangled, fun. That's how Steve described their friendship to those who were nosy enough to ask.

Stoner's shop was set back from Monitor Street and could only be approached by a long, narrow driveway, which led to a blacktopped parking pad behind the house. Steve's dad had the shop in the back built to match the style of the residence. The home was a Sears craftsman-style bungalow built in the 1920s. The house had a low-pitched roof and a porch that faced the street. A large fieldstone chimney gave the house a stately look with loads of curb appeal.

The yard was tastefully landscaped with a variety of soft maples and a clump of white birch next to the garage. It was a great property, although the upkeep left regular dents in Steve's budget. The Three Rivers Trail and the backwaters of the Mississippi River nearby provided bikers and hikers exercise and recreation opportunities. However, the trail was far enough from the property lot lines that homeowners could still retain their privacy.

Early on the afternoon of the discovery of the victim in the quarry, Steve was working in his shop, getting greasy and sweaty. He was trying to get a Kawasaki cycle to run smoothly, adjusting the carburetor and timing chain. Wrenches, screwdrivers, and other tools were scattered on the cement floor around the bike. He wore a Harley Davidson hat turned backward, a black T-shirt with Jackson Hole in white block letters across the front, and a pair of brown Carhartt work pants spotted with grease and oil.

Steve was about six feet tall, stocky, and in good physical shape. Keen blue eyes were set in an angular tanned face. He sported a blond cookie crumb mustache, and his hair revealed specks of gray here and there. Most people would say he was attractive at forty-two, if not downright good-looking. He was neat and fastidious by nature, which were unusual qualities for a mechanic to possess.

It was a beautiful summer day, and he was itching to get out along the Old Road Trail south of La Crosse near the village of Stoddard to do some metal detecting. He'd found some cool old buffalo nickels, wheat pennies, and just a few weeks ago, a 1900 silver dollar in good condition. But coins were just the tip of the iceberg. Two years ago, when he was slogging through the mud of the La Crosse River marsh, he dug up an actual certified Mayan jade carving. He'd also recovered two perfectly preserved tomahawks still

　　　　　　　　　　　　　　　　　　　　　　　　　　　　SUE BERG

wrapped in their leather shields along the Black River. Both of them were museum quality. He'd sold one of them to a private collector in Rochester, Minnesota, for $4,200. When he finished this carburetor job this afternoon, he planned to pack up his pails and shovels, metal detector, hightop rubber boots, and a cooler of Old Style beer and head to the river for a little bit of shooting.

He'd been working steadily for about forty-five minutes when a gray Suburban rolled quietly to a stop out on the street. He watched as Jim Higgins walked up the driveway. He laid down his screwdriver and met him outside the garage door of the shop. Steve knew Jim through his girlfriend, Sharon Cross. Sharon and Margie had served together on various civic and cultural boards in the La Crosse area, and of course, Jim was well known for the difficult cases he'd solved over his career as a cop.

"Jim, good to see you. What's up?" he asked as the two men shook hands.

"Just here to ask you a few questions about your favorite pastime."

"Treasure hunting?"

"That and other things."

"Like what?" Steve asked. He felt a twinge of anxiety, but his curiosity was aroused. Jim wore a serious look, but that wasn't unusual. As a detective, Jim was focused, thoughtful, and sober. He had that look now—like he was on a hunt—and Steve supposed he was.

"Can I get you something to drink?" he asked Jim politely.

"Actually, a Pepsi would be great."

Steve walked back into the cool darkness of the shop, grabbing a Pepsi and Mountain Dew. Jim followed him into the shop and sat on a black upholstered stool near the workbench. He propped his feet on the rungs below the seat in a casual, relaxed fashion. The smell of gasoline lingered in the air. Jim popped the top off the drink, the condensation collecting on the outside of the can.

Jim told Steve about the discovery of the victim at Chipmunk Coulee Quarry. Then he asked, "You're an active treasure hunter.

I've heard about some of your finds. Have you ever run across any gold coins?"

"No, but I have discovered coins. I have about two hundred in my collection, none of them very valuable. Are you looking for a specific coin?" He tilted his head slightly and looked at Jim with deliberate attention. Jim thought his eyes had changed from friendly to wary, all within an instant.

"Yeah, yeah, we are. Have you heard about the body we found in the quarry?"

Stoner nodded. "No, I haven't." Jim told him about the body that had been unearthed in the quarry.

"We found an 1866 twenty-dollar gold piece in very good condition on the body." He fiddled in his coat pocket and retrieved his little memo book. Referring to his notes, he said, "Went on the internet and did a quick search on a site called TJ Bullion USA. I found out that an 1866 Liberty Head $20 gold coin—that's what we've got from the crime scene—is worth from $2,100 to $2,850. That's if the coin is rated as extremely fine or uncirculated. I guess uncirculated condition is worth more because it hasn't been handled and retains its original clarity and brightness. I've seen the coin. It *glows*. The detail is very clear. Here, let me show you some images of it."

Jim pulled the photos up and handed his phone to Steve, who studied them with intense interest.

"Wow! That's awesome," Steve whispered in a reverential tone. "I'm no expert on coins, but the price sounds reasonable, and it looks like it's in great condition." He paused, handing the phone back to Jim. "So what information do you want from me?"

"We're trying to connect with treasure hunters in the area to see if anyone has come across another coin like it. Maybe they know a dealer who brought them into the area. Or maybe the coin was picked up at a trade show."

Steve looked thoughtful. Then he said, "Stoddard has a treasure hunting club that meets at the River Road Cafe once a month just to report on finds and shoot the bull. After a few beers, I'm not sure how believable the stories are. But I'm sure many of them would be willing to share what they know. The president of the group knows me. I'll contact him and see if he could set up a meeting time or give me a roster of the members. I go to meetings occasionally, but I don't know everybody."

"Thanks, that'd be great. It's a start," Jim said, handing him his card. "My office number is there, and my cell number is on the back. Call me if something comes up. I'd appreciate it." They shook hands, chatted a little more, and ten minutes later, Jim walked down the driveway. He slid into his Suburban, waved, and pulled away from the curb.

As Jim returned to his office, something was humming on his radar. He'd gotten a wary vibe from Steve, and he'd learned that feelings like that could come back to haunt him later. He tucked the thought away in his mind.

Steve Stoner stood in his driveway for a long time. What he'd heard from Jim Higgins hadn't just been interesting. It had been riveting for reasons only a treasure hunter would understand. ☉

4

Jamie Alberg pedaled furiously down Losey Boulevard. It was early evening, and a light rain began to fall. He was late for work at the Alpine Inn at the top of Grandad's Bluff—again. If he didn't get fired this time, it would be a miracle. The waiter job fueled his interest in archaeology, treasure hunting, and rock climbing, and it gave him extra cash for metal detectors, shovels, brushes, ropes, and other equipment.

He pumped his way past the Kwik Trip and the huge Oak Lawn Memorial Cemetery. The graves were colorfully decorated with red geraniums and tiny American flags. His yellow rain slicker flapped against his leg like a spent torn sail. The rain continued unabated, smudging the bluffs above the river into a misty haze of gray-blue shadows.

Jamie grabbed his phone from his inside shirt pocket to check the time. He needed at least twenty minutes to crank up Main and hit Bliss Road, which would take him up to the inn. Whether it was the distraction of taking a peek at his phone, or the yellow light at the corner of Main and Losey, or the rain-slicked street, he failed to negotiate the turn. Without warning, a furniture delivery truck barreled through the yellow caution light and plowed into him.

Jamie knew he was going to get hit, and his life flashed before him. He thought of his mom and dad. He made a clumsy inept move to get out of the way, but his reflexes were too slow. He heard the dreadful thud of the truck fender as it connected with the left side of his body. As he flew through the air like a rag doll, a horrible out-of-control feeling engulfed him. He heard the sickening crunch of his bike under the van tires and then nothingness. Velvety blackness. Jamie was out for the count.

He woke to the pulsating orange lights of a Tri-State ambulance. The brick house on the corner reflected orange blips from the windows in a sickening rhythm. An elderly lady was on her lawn, her apron covered in flour, an umbrella fanned out above her. Up and down the street, neighbors began drifting out of their houses, gathering in little groups.

An EMT hovered over Jamie, adjusting an oxygen mask. Jamie tried to talk, but the mask made that impossible. Instead, he groaned, rolled on his side, pulled the mask off, and vomited. Somebody held his head. "Stupid," he finally mumbled softly. "So stupid."

Blooming red roses climbed a wall nearby. Their ethereal beauty touched Jamie, and he began to cry. Maybe he was dying. God, he hoped not. He had so much to do, and his mom and dad would be devastated. *Please, God, not yet.* His prayer came to a halt as the attendants did the unison count and lifted him on the stretcher. He screamed, fainted, and was loaded into the ambulance.

Later, in an opioid haze, he woke up after he dreamed of crashing his bike. The events of the last few hours began to cement themselves in his foggy brain a little at a time.

Nurses walked past the doorway, scurrying around, their stethoscopes swinging to some invisible rhythm. Eventually, a nurse came in, smiled, and asked how he was doing. Stupidly, despite the cast on his left wrist, he gave her a thumbs up. That wasn't anywhere near the truth. He hurt all over. He drifted back to sleep.

Later still, his mom, Lydia, stood by his bed, gripping the side rail. She looked down at her son. He was mildly autistic and had a passion for knowledge, but relationships with people were awkward due to Asperger's syndrome. Things had improved a little since he began working at MVAC with colleagues who shared his interest in archaeology.

"What's the official prognosis?" Jamie asked softly, his eyes at half-mast. Lydia jumped at the sound of her son's voice.

His mom's eyes softened. She took in his curly brown hair and intelligent hazel eyes. "Honey, you're going to hurt a while, but you'll heal. You have three bruised ribs, a cracked bone in your wrist, a big contusion on your elbow, and a lot of very nasty road rash. All fixable," she whispered.

She leaned over the railing, her face etched with concern and worry—and plenty of frustration. He'd sure given her a lot of crap over the years, climbing the bluffs along the river, a brief but spectacular attempt at motocross, and getting his brains rattled playing football. Now this. Practically killing himself on a bike—the safest vehicle he'd ever driven. Despite his escapades, she loved him fiercely and wanted to protect him. "What do I have to do to stop the world from trying to kill you?" she asked him softly.

"I'll be fine, Mom. Really. Just give me a few days," he cautioned, but he groaned when he tried to move his legs. "What about my job at the inn? Damn! I guess my job at MVAC will have to be enough."

"Shh, shh! It's all taken care of," Lydia whispered. "As soon as the police called, I texted Jodi and told her what happened. She's rooting for you, too, like we all are." She touched his cheek, then smoothed his hair. "You rest now. I'll be here all night. Don't worry. Dad's just down the hall getting some coffee. He'll stay for a while, but he has a full docket of surgeries in the morning. They're telling us you'll be released tomorrow."

Jamie drifted off again, letting sleep steal him into another land.

Around ten that night, he was aroused by the sound of the TV. The WXOW Evening News was on. The anchor, Dan Kirchoff, reported the bike-truck accident on the corner of Main and Losey.

SUE BERG

He named Jamie as the bicyclist who was injured and hospitalized in stable condition. Jamie didn't feel stable at all—not even close. Gentle snoring caught his attention. His sleeping dad was scrunched into a lounge chair, his feet extended in front of him, his head lolling to one side.

Jamie focused on the news reporter. The image of a gold coin dominated the screen. What Jamie heard next left him speechless. Finding a remote clipped on the sheet, he turned the volume up slightly.

"An unidentified man was found this morning in the Chipmunk Coulee Quarry buried under a gravel pile. His death is being listed as suspicious by the La Crosse Sheriff's Department. In his pocket was an item of interest—an 1866 twenty-dollar gold piece. Lt. Jim Higgins is quoted as saying, 'The coin is highly unusual. Currently, there are only about one hundred known to exist in the U.S. These coins are very valuable on the collectible market. Anyone having any information about this incident is asked to contact the La Crosse Sheriff's Department.'" The reporter finished, "An ongoing investigation is being conducted."

Jamie leaned back on his pillow, a slight chill running up his spine. "Man, I can't believe that," he whispered to himself. Was it even remotely possible that someone had found the lost Fort Crawford payroll? Then another thought wormed its way into his head. Who found it? He'd have to get in touch with this detective, Jim Higgins. This was unbelievable. Just unbelievable. ⊙

5

FRIDAY EVENING, JUNE 4

Carol Olstad sat on the patio of the Freighthouse, a classy, upscale restaurant in the heart of downtown La Crosse. The establishment was housed in the original Milwaukee Road offices and was recently renovated and preserved as one of the few remaining nineteenth-century railroad depots in the country. Her date, Officer Gordy Wilson, had ordered prime rib sandwiches at the bar and another round of drinks. *I'm getting too old for this,* Carol thought. *When did I outgrow this?*

The first Friday night of the month was the night the courthouse staff socialized. Usually, the atmosphere was genial and fun. Tonight, law enforcement personnel milled around the outdoor L-shaped bar. The night air was saturated with the smells of steaks frying on an open grill, exhaust from nearby traffic, perfume, and cologne. As the evening wore on, everyone got louder. Carol attended occasionally, but tonight was becoming a big regret as the festivities reached their peak.

Why had she consented to a third date with Gordy when she hadn't enjoyed her first two? That was still a mystery to her. *What was I thinking?* Gordy had a reputation for fast women, booze, and unsolicited sexual advances. On her first two dates, he'd been charming and well-behaved, but something about the look in his eye this evening put her on edge. He'd been churlish and impatient with her. It was beginning to wear on her nerves. She looked up and smiled wanly as Gordy shuffled and pushed his way through the crowd.

"There you go, darlin'." He set a second glass of wine in front of her. He was weaving slightly, his tie askew, his face too red. Spotting another colleague from the police department at the bar, he waved enthusiastically.

"Thanks. I do have to leave fairly soon," she said, shouting over the noise of the revelers. She made a point of checking the time on her phone. "I have an early day tomorrow with a friend. We're going shopping at the Mall of America," she explained. *Liar.*

Gordy's eyes hardened with suspicion, and that look sent shivers up Carol's spine.

"Oh, sure. Just let me catch up with Bruce. I'll be right back," he slurred.

He stumbled toward the bar while Carol chatted with some of the girls from the office. She made her apologies when Gordy stopped at the table. Fifteen minutes later, they exited the bar and walked down Vine Street to Gordy's car.

The close proximity to Gordy within the car evaporated Carol's sense of security. Alarm bells were clanging in her head. She knew better than to ignore them. *Going out again with this oaf was one of your less than perfect ideas. Why do you always sell yourself short?*

Gordy rattled on about the discovery of the body at Chipmunk Coulee, slurring his words and punctuating his account with profanity. She hadn't realized how drunk he was. Ignoring his attempts at conversation, she answered in monosyllables.

Carol lived in a new condominium located around a sharp curve off Highway 14 on the south side of town. When Gordy missed the turnoff, she chalked it up to his drunken state.

"You missed my street. Where are you going?" she asked nervously. *Stay calm. Breathe.*

He drove farther down U.S. 35 and maneuvered his car into Goose Island Park. The enveloping darkness and unfamiliar surroundings tripped Carol's panic button.

"Just out for a little love drive, as my second ex used to say." He looked at her, sizing her up. "We always liked to experiment in the car." She could see the hardness in his eyes as he gazed at her with a quick, penetrating stare.

"I'm not interested," she stated firmly as he pulled the car into a darkened turnout.

He rammed the car in park and, in one swift move, grabbed the back of her neck, pulling her close. His hot, boozy breath rolled over her face. "You are one good looker, Carol. But what you need is someone who can teach you to forget the little goody-two-shoes routine," he whispered, his voice threatening.

Carol was shaking from fear and anger. "Stop it! You need to stop and take me home right now," she said loudly. Her heart was thudding in her chest. She tried to pull away from him.

"Not on your life, you little priss." He desperately grabbed Carol's arm and began squeezing. Carol winced. His grip felt like steel.

It's now or never. Surprise him. She grabbed the door handle with her right hand and threw it open. Working quickly, she jerked out of his iron grip and reached down to unsnap her seatbelt.

But Gordy had come alive. He swore a string of profanities. "Don't even think about runnin'. You're staying with me," he yelled.

He grabbed her hair and slapped her across the face. Carol was stunned with shock, but she managed to push Gordy hard. His head cracked against the window, and she escaped out the open car door. She tripped and fell on the pavement but quickly recovered. Running blindly into the woods, Carol ran several hundred feet, tripping and falling many times. She stopped and listened. Gordy was still cursing inside the car. She hoped he was too drunk to chase her.

Eventually, she hid behind an old cottonwood and waited for the engine to start. A set of headlights came on. Gordy's car slowly cruised down the road. She waited until he left the park. Walking home in the dark was the only option she had, but it was a terrifying thought. Gordy might come back for her.

Feeling around on the ground, she realized her purse was on the floor of Gordy's car. Suddenly, the tears came, and she cried in great convulsive sobs. Her arm and face throbbed with pain. In the darkness, she slid down the trunk of the tree, still crying softly. *What am I gonna do?* Panic threatened to unhinge her. *Stop. Think. Make a plan and call someone. Call?* She patted the pocket of her jeans. Relief washed over her as her fingers curled around her phone.

She sat there a while, willing herself to calm down. The night air grew chilly, and a damp fog hovered over the river. The darkness was penetrating and foreboding. Rustling grass and unseen scurrying creatures overpowered her resolve to stay calm.

She had no idea if her phone would raise a signal, but she was amazed to see three fully lit bars when she turned it on. She scrolled through her contacts, wondering who to call. She still had Margie's number. Even though Margie wasn't there, maybe Jim would answer.

She punched in the number. *Please, please answer.*

"Hello. Jim Higgins."

"Jim, it's Carol—Carol Olstad." There was a pause. "I'm in trouble."

Jim heard crying and sat up on the edge of the bed. He'd been reading a C.J. Box novel. "What's happened? Did you have an accident? Call 911 right away," he ordered.

"No, no, you don't understand. Can you help me? I need a ride home. I'll explain when you get here." More crying.

"Okay. Clam down. Where are you?"

"I'm at Goose Island Park. Drive to the first turnout in the park. I'll meet you there."

"On my way. Stay there."

Jim slipped on his jeans and a sweatshirt and grabbed his boat shoes by the back door. He tore down Chipmunk Coulee Road and traveled north on U.S. 35 two miles to Goose Island. He found the first turnout and parked the Suburban. Five minutes later, he finally saw Carol approach the car from behind. He reached over to open the front passenger door, and Carol fell into the seat.

"What's going on?" Jim demanded, his voice loud in the confines of the car. The overhead dome light provided enough illumination to see that Carol was in a world of hurt.

"Please don't yell," Carol said breathlessly. "It's a long story, and most of it is my fault. I feel so stupid and humiliated. I should have known better." She began crying softly again.

Jim touched her arm, which was beginning to bruise into a dark purple splotch. Her fingernail was ripped and bleeding, and mud caked her sandals and the knees of her jeans. She was shaking and distraught. Bits of burdock and dried leaves clung to her blouse.

"Who did this? Were you raped?" Jim could feel the anger growing in his chest like a slow burn.

"No, he didn't get that far, thank God, but I'm sure that's what he planned."

He reached over and touched her knee. "Let's get you home. You can tell me on the way." He fastened her seatbelt as she leaned back in the seat, a flood of relief washing over her.

On the ride back to her condo, Carol mentally ticked off the warning signs she'd noticed in Gordy's behavior. She told Jim about hiding in the woods without a car and her purse, beaten and petrified. He pulled into the driveway. They let themselves in the side garage door after retrieving a key from the rock garden. She continued to let off steam, upbraiding herself for failing to listen to her inner voice.

Standing in the kitchen, her injuries, though not severe, were nonetheless traumatizing. Jim encouraged her to get in the shower while he made a pot of strong coffee. She appeared a half-hour later wearing sweats, her brunette hair wet and curling around her face. Without her makeup, she looked vulnerable and scared. Jim's anger seethed beneath his calm exterior. *Damned perverts.* They sipped on their coffee in silence.

"You still haven't told me who attacked you," he said softly, watching Carol closely. "Do I know him?"

She looked at Jim over her coffee mug. "Please don't give me that look. I just need a friend. We'll get to the other stuff later." She sat on the stool by the counter and cradled her head in her hands. He let her collect her thoughts for a few minutes.

"So what's the other stuff?" he finally asked, struggling to balance his attraction to Carol with his protective sensibilities. He had an impulse to hold her in his arms and comfort her.

She lifted her head out of her hands and looked at Jim for a long moment. "Gordy Wilson took me for a 'love' drive," she did air quotes, "and fortunately, he was too drunk to take complete advantage of me." She stopped briefly. "I fought him off, but I can see you're furious. I recognize that look. Matt used to get that way sometimes." She held up her hand and said, "I just need to handle this my way."

"And what way would that be?" Jim snarled. "Gordy Wilson assaulted you. He hurt you." Jim felt himself slipping into a tirade, easy to do but not very helpful at the moment. He stopped and breathed deeply.

"Okay, you're right." Carol sighed, holding up both hands. "But I have to work with the jerk, and I see him practically every day." She felt her anger growing and her fear shrinking, replaced by outrage. "I will report this, but not tonight," she said firmly. "I promise I will do it tomorrow."

"Not good enough," Jim replied, his voice hard with anger. "The assault needs to be reported now—tonight. Gordy Wilson needs his sorry ass hauled out of bed and dragged down to the station. How many other women has he done this to?" He waited for an answer, and not getting one, he continued. "You're not the first, I'm sure. The incident needs to be reported tonight," he repeated. "Besides, even if you don't want to report it, I have to. I'm a police officer."

She gave him a look of resignation. "Okay. Call it in." She stood, wincing. "I'm going to the couch to rest. Have the officer come out here. I'll tell them what happened." She looked like she was going to cry again.

Jim helped her to the couch and gently covered her with a quilt. His eyes softened as she looked up at him. "I'll be right here. I'm not going anywhere," he said gently.

She whispered, "Thank you."

He had another cup of coffee while he waited for the officer to arrive. He'd been on many domestic and sexual abuse calls. They were always ugly and demonstrated the very worst in partner relationships. He remembered his feelings of inadequacy, anger, and helplessness in those situations. The danger to officers was a lethal possibility. The frequency of news reports about shootings and the death of police officers trying to calm a domestic situation was familiar territory to Jim. Put drugs, booze, and volatile behaviors in a bag, shake vigorously, and you'd get an explosion of rage and violence. Kids crying, hysterical women bloody and beaten, and husbands defending their actions, drunk or high on drugs, begging for mercy as they were arrested. It was all so depressing. Carol's attack brought it all back. He'd kill somebody if they'd done this to Margie. There was going to be hell to pay, police officer or not. He'd see to it.

Over the next hour, Carol recounted her story to Officer Mike Leland, including her desperate call to Jim. Office Leland took photos of her injuries. She was acutely aware of Jim's presence. He leaned against the living room wall with his arms folded across his chest. His face was tight and intent as he listened to the details of the attack. Feeling exposed and embarrassed, Carol mumbled her thanks when the interview was over. Seeing them to the door, Officer Leland and Jim left quietly. Carol locked the door of the condo, slamming the deadbolt shut. She heard the vehicles start, then drive away.

Padding down the hallway, Carol entered her bedroom and crawled between the sheets. But sleep eluded her. Lying wakeful and restless, she listened to the night sounds through her open screened window. Now she understood how devastating a sexual assault could be. Her sense of security and well-being was shattered. Although she hadn't been raped, the horror was more real to her now than ever

SUE BERG

before. As anxiety and anger rolled over her in waves, the physical assault continued to replay in her mind until she finally got up and took some Tylenol PM, washing it down with a cup of herbal tea. She slipped back into bed. *Thank God for Jim.* Just as the morning sky was beginning to lighten, her eyes grew heavy, and she slept. ⊙

6

SATURDAY, JUNE 5

Jim woke late on Saturday morning. After breakfast, he headed to the Pettibone Boat Club, where he kept *The Little Eddy*. It was a beautiful, sunny day, but the events of last night had left him in a sour mood. Driving through Pettibone Park, he eased the Suburban into a space in the marina parking lot. The Cass Street bridge stood big and blue, majestically spanning the Mississippi River. Although it was only ten in the morning, boats were already cruising in and out of the harbor.

Jim walked down the dock toward his boat. He worked for a few hours, sprucing and shining up the interior. About noon his phone beeped.

"Jim Higgins."

"Hi, Jim. It's Carol." Her voice sounded raspy and hoarse.

"Hey, how're you feeling?"

"Shaky, but I'm up and around. Stiff and sore, but I'll live. I just wanted to thank you again for all your help and support last night. I felt bad I had to call you."

"Not a problem. I'm glad you called," Jim interrupted. "And I'm glad you filed a report. It was the right thing to do." There was a pause. "So, do you have plans for the day?"

SUE BERG

"Not really. Officer Leland brought my purse back this morning. He just left."

"Good." He waited. "Listen, why don't you come down to the club at Pettibone and have lunch with me on the boat? Later we can go for a spin. What do you think? You ready for that?"

Carol's stomach clenched nervously. Being alone with another man so soon after her attack left her feeling vulnerable and jumpy. She seemed tentative, and he didn't blame her. Jim could feel her waffling. Finally, she said, "I don't know if I'm ready, but..."

"That's totally understandable," Jim said sympathetically.

"I guess my trust levels are pretty low at this moment. Not that I think you'd do—." She stopped abruptly. "Oh, that sounded terrible. I didn't mean that the way it came out," she said, having trouble expressing her fears.

"Hey, no offense taken."

There was silence for a few moments. Carol thought, *You can't sit in your apartment and sulk. Are you just going to let Gordy have the ultimate victory?* Suddenly she heard herself saying, "Just give me a chance to shower and change. One o'clock okay for a time?"

"Sounds good. I'll see you then."

He continued his work on the boat and ordered lunch and drinks from the dockside restaurant. A few minutes before one o'clock, he saw Carol walking toward him on the dock. She had fixed her hair and put on makeup. She smiled down at him, her brown eyes scanning the boat. She wore denim capris and a print short-sleeved blouse with a practical pair of gray Sketchers. Small, gold hoop earrings winked in the afternoon sunlight. He tried to ignore her bruise.

"Hey. You look a whole lot better than last night," Jim said.

"Feel better. Bruised, but the sunshine helps." She scanned the sparkling river, fighting back tears. "What a gorgeous day. Way too nice to be home working on laundry. Besides, you can't keep a good farm girl down, and that SOB Gordy can take a hike." She stepped onto the boat and sat down.

"Atta girl." He hesitated a few minutes, then he said seriously. "But really, if you're having any problems, you know PTSD symptoms. Don't ignore them. You may think you're okay when you've just stuffed it. So talk to somebody if you have trouble sleeping or you can't relax. The department has good people they can refer you to."

"Thanks, I will. This whole thing has shaken me, I have to admit, but spending the day on the river will be a really good antidote. Where are we headed?" she asked, feeling for her phone in her back pocket.

"I'm thinking Lansing. Sound okay?"

Carol nodded in agreement. "Sounds lovely."

"Ready, then?"

"Aye, aye, captain." She gave him a mock salute.

Jim grinned and steered the boat into the main channel. He knew the river well and took his time maneuvering the boat in and out of the tangle of islands that make up the backwaters of the Mississippi, working his way south toward Lansing, Iowa. Limestone bluffs soared above the riverbanks, providing a perfect backdrop for bald eagles making lazy curls on the rising thermals. A turtle splashed from a weathered log, and blue herons and egrets balanced on stick legs, poking in the shallows for fish. As they motored along, Jim could see Carol relaxing, tilting her head back, taking in the warmth of the June summer day.

Jim loved the mystery and majesty of the great swirling Mississippi. Bald eagles soaring in a cloudless azure sky filled him with pure, unbounded joy. Isolated sandbars jutting into the blue-green water invited days of leisure and nights of laughter and storytelling around crackling campfires. Weekends during the summer were magical. The days were filled with fishing and swimming. The nights were spent stretched out on an open sandbar in a sleeping bag, gazing up at the infinite black of a sky flung with a shower of sparkling stars.

From his early childhood, Jim and his father had shared a love of the water, the lapping of its gentle waves, and the tug of its strong currents. The river claimed people for life. What was it John Muir had said? "Rivers flow not past, but through us; tingling, vibrating, exciting every cell and fiber in our bodies, making them sing and glide." For Jim, the love of the river had started long ago as he'd rocked under the spell of her meandering ebb and flow in the small houseboat his father had owned. *The Little Eddy* was Jim's now. He'd had it refurbished at La Crosse Marine, and the memories with Margie and the twins were priceless.

After a while, Jim found a perfect picnic spot on an uninhabited sandy beach on one of the small islands. He ran the boat up on shore and dropped the anchor. Unloading the cooler, he brought out two low lawn chairs from one of the storage hulls. It was exquisitely quiet and serene.

"This is incredibly beautiful," Carol remarked, making herself comfortable in the chair. She kicked off her shoes and dug her toes into the sand.

"Yeah. I always look forward to my first river cruises in the spring. Being on the water is a great way to unwind. Hungry?" Jim asked.

"Starving."

"Well, you have a choice of bacon chicken ranch or buffalo chicken wraps. There are chips and a fruit salad. I have wine, beer, or soda. What say ye, madam?"

"I'll have the bacon chicken, please. And wine."

Carol took her plate. Jim poured her a glass of wine.

"Pardon the paper cup," he said. "It is what it is."

He fixed himself a plate and dug in, sipping a beer. As he sat quietly, reveling in the beauty of the natural setting, his nerves untangled. A deep sense of contentment spread over him. Lately, he'd felt like he was looking at himself from high on a perch somewhere. He'd been lonely these last months. His solution had been to wall himself off, but now he realized that wasn't working. He was a people person; that was one of the reasons he'd gone into police work.

When he glanced over at Carol, Margie's words, "You deserve to be happy," swirled in his head. Carol was a very attractive woman.

Her brunette hair was stylishly cut. Her eyes were a deep brown set in an oval face that was accentuated by high cheekbones. She was athletic in an understated, farm girl kind of way. *That's probably how she fought off that slob, Gordy,* Jim thought. Her independence and honest views sometimes rankled him, but Margie had been far from perfect. In fact, they'd fought fiercely about money and how to raise the kids. It wasn't all peaches and cream.

They chatted quietly, catching up on each other's lives. Carol talked about her ex, Matt Donavan, a guitar player extraordinaire. He was well known throughout the tristate area, and his band, Mississippi Mud, had a faithful, if not a fanatic, following. But as Carol explained, the music scene had a proven record of being tough on marriages. Too much booze and too many women added up to divorce. Matt still struggled with alcohol addiction.

"I remember how exciting the band scene was at first," she said, her voice animated. "Weekends were crazy fun. We were minor celebrities and had a good following. But it kind of went south after a few years. It seemed like Matt was always drinking, girls hanging on him all the time. He probably cheated on me more than once. I wanted something stable and reliable, and that was not Matt. It took five years before it truly fell apart."

Jim sat still, not interrupting. His experience as a detective had taught him the value of listening for the undercurrents swimming beneath the words.

"I still worry about him," Carol added.

Jim let the silence between them sit a while.

"Still love him?" Jim ventured.

It was quiet for a moment. "Still love Margie?"

"Touché," Jim said softly, their eyes locking.

The moments ticked by. A woodpecker *rat-a-tat-tatted* in a tree nearby.

"You know," Jim commented, breaking the silence, "we both have histories with people we loved. You loved Matt, and I loved Margie. That's not going to change, but love is large. And hearts can grow larger, too. People move on, adjust, reinvent themselves."

Carol looked at him over her glass of wine, her eyebrows raised. Jim shrugged. "Just sayin'."

"I hear you," she said softly. *You're more lonely than you realize,* she thought.

They sat soaking in the peace of the place. "So, how are the twins?" Carol asked, interrupting the quiet.

Jim filled her in on John and Sara's lives, their significant others, pets, jobs, and the like. The hours slipped by. Soon the sun painted the western sky with brilliant pinks and reds. Boats towing skiers and tubers zipped up and down the river. The waves lapped quietly against the hull of *The Little Eddy.* Jim stirred, uncrossing his legs.

"Ready to head out?" he asked.

"Sure. This turned out to be a lovely day. Actually, it was wonderful." She reached over and squeezed his hand. Jim pulled her out of the chair. "Thanks so much, Jim."

"My pleasure."

He began loading the chairs and cooler, and soon they were headed back to La Crosse. Jim docked the boat and secured it. Then he walked Carol to her car. "I'll see you around the office," he said as they stood by her car. "And let's do something again soon." He leaned in and kissed her gently on the cheek. She could feel his rough skin and got a faint hint of aftershave.

"Bye. See you later. Thanks again," she said as she slipped in the front seat. A thought occurred to her. *Jim fought for me. Nobody's ever done that before.* She smiled and touched her cheek where he'd kissed her. The Dixie Chicks were singing softly on the radio. "Cowboy, take me away, closer to heaven and to you." ☉

7

JUNE 7

Monday morning dawned gray with a light, steady drizzle. The landscape was shrouded in a hazy shawl of mist. Jim stood at his kitchen window still remembering the day on the river with Carol.

Margie's words encouraging a relationship with someone had seemed premature but strangely omniscient in the light of day. He could almost hear her saying, "See, I told you she'd be right for you." He had never let the thought of a relationship with another woman take root in his mind. He was one of the lucky ones. His marriage had been very happy and fulfilling, and that was unusual for a cop. Margie completed him like no one else.

But now, after her death, things were different. Margie was gone, and he felt vulnerable, lonely, and wounded. He'd learned that vulnerability could open you to the truth about yourself, your ambitions, other people in your life. He had to admit, he'd enjoyed the day with Carol immensely, but in the back of his mind, he'd felt guilty. *Should I still be grieving after all this time?* he wondered. *Is it time to move on and reinvent myself?* He sighed and put his coffee cup in the sink. *Just relax and let whatever is going to happen, happen.*

Sunday afternoon, he had received a phone call from La Crosse Police Chief Tamara Pedretti reminding him of the ugly turn of events on Saturday night. He'd been asked to give his version of the Goose Island attack during a hearing in the chief's office at nine on Monday morning. Carol would be conspicuously absent. She refused to press charges, but she had filed an in-house complaint against Officer Gordy Wilson.

Gordy had not been on duty when the incident had happened, but it wasn't a stretch of the imagination to say that his actions were unbecoming to an officer of the law. Still, the chances of serious consequences for Gordy were slim. Jim knew cops struggled with all sorts of temptations in life, but he believed they were called to a higher standard. After all, every officer pledged "to deliver a feeling of security, safety, and quality services to our community," to quote the La Crosse Police mission statement. He also knew he'd be violating The Code all policemen adhered to—protecting their own. But Jim had bucked the system before, although it had earned him a cold shoulder from more than one officer.

He'd known about Gordy from innuendo and rumors within the department. In recent years, his reputation had gone from questionable gossip to uneasy rumors to full-blown accusations of misconduct, including inappropriate sexual advances, racist language, and profanity among the citizens he served in the city.

Jim questioned Carol's decision to associate with him, even in a casual setting. Probably a slip in judgment. Sexual predators could be very charming and convincing. Few of the women who Gordy had physically or sexually assaulted had stepped forward to confront him. Jim wondered what kinds of intimidation Gordy used to keep them quiet. He remembered Carol's reluctance to file a complaint. For once, he was thankful for the policy of mandatory reporting. He would have called in the attack whether Carol wanted him to or not.

He felt like he had turned a corner in his relationship with Carol. His fondness for her was growing along with his worry. Gordy Wilson was not one to back down or admit his wrongdoing. Jim anticipated the meeting would be hostile and accusatory, with little or no action taken. The gossip mill would have some new fodder. He hoped Carol was ready for what might be coming her way.

When Jim arrived at the police station, he was informed that the meeting had been moved to a larger conference room on the second floor. The windowless room was furnished with a large table and eight well-worn cushioned chairs. Attached to one wall was a whiteboard with markers scattered in the tray. A standard office clock hung on the opposite wall ticking off the minutes. The room smelled stuffy and felt claustrophobic. Scrolling through his messages on his phone, Jim took a seat and waited.

Officer Mike Leland and Police Chief Tamara Pedretti arrived shortly before nine o'clock. Recording equipment had been set up at the head of the table. Sharon Sobokiak, a representative for the police union and public relations council, came in along with Gordy Wilson. As they found a seat, they talked and joked, giving off an air of nonchalance.

Police Chief Pedretti placed her files in front of her. Dressed professionally, she could not be described as beautiful, although she was attractive. A mane of naturally blond hair was tied back from her face, and her minimal makeup highlighted her classic good looks. Jim guessed her age to be early forties. She greeted everyone quickly and politely, pushed the start button on the recorder, and the hearing began.

"This is a formal hearing being conducted at La Crosse police headquarters on Monday, June 7, 2017. The time is 9:02 a.m. Those present include La Crosse Police Chief Tamara Pedretti speaking, Officer Mike Leland, Representative Sharon Sobokiak, Detective Jim Higgins of the La Crosse Sheriff's Department, and Officer Gordy Wilson of the La Crosse Police Department. The issue before us is an in-house complaint filed against Officer Gordy Wilson. It includes battery, a Class A misdemeanor, involving civilian Carol Olstad on the evening of June 4 at approximately 10:30 p.m. in Goose Island Park, Stoddard, Wisconsin." Chief Pedretti looked around at the participants, her eyes finally coming to rest on Gordy. She folded her hands calmly in front of her. Jim noticed her immaculately groomed nails, which were painted a pale pink. A sparkling diamond ring graced the third finger on her left hand.

"Officer Leland," she proceeded, her voice calm and controlled, "please tell us about your interview with Ms. Olstad on Friday night, June 4."

"I was on patrol and received a call about an assault that had taken place within the borders of Goose Island Park. I drove to the home of Ms. Olstad at 1695 Clayfire Road, where the complaint was filed. Ms. Olstad had been out with Officer Wilson earlier in the evening at the Freighthouse. On the way to her condo, Officer Wilson drove to Goose Island Park instead of taking her home and proceeded to make sexual advances toward Ms. Olstad. This quickly turned into an aggressive physical assault. She managed to extricate herself from Officer Wilson's car after he had attacked her. According to Ms. Olstad, Officer Wilson prevented her from getting out of the car by holding her arm. Then he slapped her across the face while hanging onto her hair. Ms. Olstad hid in the woods and used her cell phone to contact Jim Higgins, a family friend, who came to the park to give her a ride home. Despite her bruises, Ms. Olstad refused medical treatment. After taking her statement, I left her condo at approximately 12:10 a.m."

"Is that correct, Officer Higgins?" Pedretti asked.

"Yes," Jim said. Gordy and Jim exchanged hostile looks.

"Officer Wilson, is there anything you want to add to these proceedings?" Pedretti asked, her blue eyes scanning his face.

Gordy smiled at Pedretti. The charm he'd used on others fell flat with the police chief.

"First of all, let's get the record straight. Ms. Olstad came on to me. She was all over me at the bar," Gordy bragged. A hard knot of anger formed in Jim's chest, making his heart hammer.

"Secondly, I never restrained her in any way," he continued. "This whole incident is overblown and exaggerated out of proportion. I was surprised when Officer Leland came to my home after midnight claiming Carol's purse was in my car, and I was being accused of battery. Do you know how humiliating it was to come down to the station and give my version of this incident? This whole thing is a joke. She suggested Goose Island to me. When we got there, she got adversarial, got out of the car, and refused to get back in. What was I supposed to do?"

"You used the word incident," Pedretti stated. "So you do admit there was an incident?"

"If you want to call it that," Wilson responded casually. "I prefer to call it a misunderstanding."

She slid the photos of Carol's injuries across the table where they sat in front of Gordy. "How do you explain the bruises and contusions Ms. Olstad received?" Pedretti asked, her eyes hardening with anger.

Despite his glance at the obvious injuries, Gordy remained unrepentant. "She ran through the woods. I suppose she must have fallen and hurt herself," he replied flippantly. He continued to hold Tamara's gaze, but she refused to give him any ground, returning his stare with icy disdain.

Tamara turned to Jim. "Officer Higgins, would you state the condition you found Ms. Olstad in when you arrived at Goose Island to pick her up?" Tamara limited her reaction to a blink of eyes and a glance at Gordy in which she tried to hide her contempt.

"Carol was terrified. She'd been crying when she called me. Her jeans were covered in mud, her shoes were soaking wet, and her blouse had leaves and burdocks sticking to it. She had a bleeding torn fingernail, and a purple bruise was forming on her left arm where Officer Wilson had grabbed her. Her face was red where he had slapped her. She had fled before she could grab her purse from Wilson's car. Fortunately, she had her phone in her pocket so that she could call for help." Jim paused, his eyes locking on Gordy's face. Jim continued.

"She was physically assaulted as a result of her refusal to comply with Officer Wilson's sexual advances," Jim finished with contempt in his voice.

Gordy swore under his breath, and the room grew quiet. Suddenly, his eyes blazed at Jim, and he snarled, "How do you know Higgins didn't attack her? He had opportunity, too."

Jim was out of his seat before he knew what happened. He felt Officer LeLand's arm restraining him. "Easy, Chief. Easy."

"I'm going to pretend that you never said that," Jim said quietly, his eyes honing in on Gordy. "What a pathetic excuse for an officer of the law."

"Enough!" Chief Pedretti warned loudly, pounding her fist on the table. "Let's all take a deep breath."

Chief Pedretti paused, spreading her papers in front of her. After a few moments, she said, "Officer Wilson, in reviewing your work history, you have had no less than five complaints filed against you by citizens in our policing district, which range from racial slurs to excessive profanity. In addition, in the last two years, two complaints of sexual harassment by law enforcement staff have been documented. The department has provided anger management counseling and a course that reviewed our policies concerning harassment in the workplace. However, it is my judgment in reviewing your record and listening to your responses during this procedure this morning that these efforts have been largely ineffective. In my opinion, your behavior is unacceptable and unbecoming for an officer of the law." She leveled her eyes on Gordy and kept them there until he squirmed uneasily.

"Therefore, I am recommending a full investigation into all charges filed against you, past and present. The La Crosse Civilian Review board will examine the allegations against you and report their findings to me. Until that time, you are being put on paid administrative leave until further notice. Any further comments or questions?" she asked. The room was silent as she waited for responses.

"If not, then this meeting is concluded. The time is 9:46 a.m." She snapped off the recorder, gathered her materials, and swiftly exited the room. The other participants gathered their papers and reports and left.

Gordy Wilson hung his head over the table, then rubbed a hand through his thick salt and pepper hair. Jim thought he looked like he'd taken a blow to the gut and needed a stiff drink. He had no doubt that he'd be heading to his favorite watering hole after the meeting to soothe his jangled nerves and justify his actions to anyone who would listen.

Jim was relieved that Gordy had been put on leave. Obviously, the guy had some serious problems, but Jim took no joy in celebrating at the expense of another's weaknesses and faults. *Except for the grace of God, there go I.*

He escaped to the lobby and checked his phone for messages. He had three already. He made calls to his team organizing a one o'clock meeting to review the quarry case. Someone named Jamie Alberg called and left a message and a return number. He might have information about the coin, so he needed Jim to return his call. Soon.

Arriving on the third floor, Jim chatted briefly with Emily out front. Once at his desk, he returned a call to Alberg. Jamie answered, and Jim identified himself.

"So what do you know that you think will help us in our investigation?" Jim asked, sipping a cup of coffee.

"I know some stuff about the coin," he said abruptly.

"Like what?" Jim shot back.

"Well, can we meet? I'll tell you what I know about the coin you found. But I'm at work right now. Could you meet me at the Subway closest to MVAC? That's where I work," Alberg explained.

Jim glanced at the clock. "Sure, how about eleven-thirty?"

"That'll work. See you there." Jamie clicked off.

Jim kept busy at his desk for a couple of hours. He chatted with Luke in the morgue, researched gold coins, finished up paperwork and reports, and went over his notes on the quarry case for the afternoon meeting. At 11:15, he stretched and rubbed the back of his neck. Grabbing his coat, he left the office to meet with Jamie.

Since 1982, MVAC, the Mississippi Valley Archaeology Center, was located on the University of Wisconsin–La Crosse campus. The center's mission statement was to "research, preserve, and teach the archeological resources of the Upper Mississippi River Region." Their contributions to the ancient cultures that occupied the La Crosse area along the river were well known to Jim. In recent years, he had followed the center's progress in telling the story of the pre-Colombian people through their newsletters.

The Subway near MVAC was bustling with customers. Jim went inside, picked up a sandwich and soda, and found a seat on the crowded patio. Students were hurrying in and out with their sandwiches and drinks. Many of them were seated outside since the weather had cleared mid-morning. A young man with an MVAC polo shirt and a cast on his left wrist limped painfully toward Jim and held out his hand. They shook hands, and Jamie introduced himself. Jim noticed the curly brown hair that framed his face and the intelligence burning just behind his hazel eyes. A quick, hesitant smile gave Jim an impression of teenage self-consciousness.

"How'd you break the wrist?" Jim asked as Jamie joined him at the table.

"Bike accident at the corner of Main and Losey last Friday. Didn't see a furniture truck. I got smucked."

"Ouch." Jim took a bite of sandwich. "So what's this about coins? You a collector?"

"No, I'm working at MVAC part-time as an assistant while I'm working on my degree in forensic archaeology."

"Interesting. How'd you get interested in archaeology?"

"My parents are collectors of ancient artifacts," Jamie explained. "My dad's an orthopedic surgeon at Mayo, and my mom works as an anesthesiologist at Gundersen Lutheran. Their interest is Native American artifacts, particularly Ho-Chunk, Ojibwa, and Sioux. They also have a fairly large collection of native Southwest Navajo pottery. They've got money to burn, and they spend it expanding their collections. I grew up with the stuff. I guess it rubbed off." He smiled, the hesitancy disappearing as he expounded on a familiar subject.

"But my real interest is treasure hunting," Jamie explained. "I use a standard metal detector and have found some pretty good stuff. There are a lot of us in the western Wisconsin area who are all pretty enthusiastic about the sport."

"You know some of these people?" Jim asked, sipping his Pepsi, watching Jamie's facial expressions. He seemed intense, knowledgeable, and just a little bit arrogant.

"Some, but I wanted to tell you what I know about your coin," he said, ignoring Jim's question. "I couldn't believe it when I saw the coin on the evening news last Friday night. The story behind it seems crazy, but it's known to lots of hunters in the area. In fact, I'd just about given up hope of ever finding it. I've been looking for that treasure for about eight years."

Jim looked surprised, his blue eyes intense.

"Seriously!" Jamie said. "Eight years!" His eyes had that gleam of passion Jim had seen before when people talked about a cause or interest.

"When I think that the treasure possibly does exist and might be right under our noses, I just can't believe it," Jamie said, gesticulating wildly. He winced in pain and lowered his arms. His voice had gone from dispassionate to fervent, not unlike Jim's pastor when he was expounding scripture.

"Whoa, whoa, whoa. Okay, let's back up. What's this about treasure?" Jim asked, his curiosity sparked. *This kid's intense.*

"I know all about it," Jamie began. Jim nodded, encouraging him to continue.

"Around 1868, a detail of soldiers from Fort Crawford in Prairie du Chien were in La Crosse to collect the fort's payroll from a steamship called *The St. Louis,* which had traveled south from St. Paul. The gold was reported to have been in several bags, about $80,000 in all. The coins were Liberty Gold twenty-dollar pieces ranging from 1858 to

1866. At that time, Fort Crawford was still a military outpost, and Indian attacks were fairly common. Before an impending attack on the fort some days later, soldiers were sent into the hills with orders to bury the gold 'on the highest bluff across from the fort.' The soldiers who hid the gold were killed on their way back to the fort. The gold was never recovered." He stopped, watching Jim's reaction as he leaned back in his chair.

"Quite a tale. Any way to verify it?" Jim asked, his eyebrows arching in uncertainty.

"The incident happened well over 150 years ago. It's reached the level of folklore now. But there might be a record of it at Fort Crawford. It's currently a museum."

"What are the chances this gold could actually exist? Seems kind of far-fetched." Jim doubted it could be true.

"Well, finding treasure still happens." Jamie continued. "There's been a ton recovered from the world's oceans and even the Great Lakes. You know, Robert Ballard and the *Titanic* and all of that. In 2014, a California couple were walking their dog on their property, and they stumbled upon eight buried cans with gold coins inside worth ten million. The coins dated from about the 1840s. They got to keep it. You've probably heard about the old finders keepers rule. That applies in most cases to lost treasure if no living descendants are alive. Then whoever owns the property gets to keep the treasure. So, to answer your question, it does happen, but it's a pretty rare occurrence," Jamie said.

Jim thought for a moment. "Do you happen to know Steve Stoner?"

"Yeah, he's a treasure hunter like me. I told him all about the story, and he was pretty interested."

Hmm ... he didn't mention that to me when we talked, he thought. "Well, we'll follow up with the museum and see if we can verify that." Jim checked the time on his phone. "Listen. I've got a meeting at one. I really appreciate this."

Jim wrote Jamie's address and phone number down in his

notebook. He paused and then asked, "One more thing. How much would you say this treasure might be worth?"

"On the market today, each coin could conceivably be worth about $2,500. That price would be for a coin in mint or uncirculated condition," Jamie said. He frowned as he ran the number through his head. "So doing the math, I'd say if the entire treasure could be recovered, it would be worth millions."

"Really?" Jim said. He let out a whistle.

"Good enough reason for some dude to kill for it, don't you think?" He squinted up at Jim through the sunlight, his cast resting on the table.

Jim gazed into his hazel eyes. "You've got a point there."

Jim thanked Jamie again for contacting him. Strolling through the crowds of college students to his Suburban, Jim thought about Jamie. He was certainly bright but a little socially awkward. Still, the kid's information had lined up with what he'd discovered. But Jamie's final question left Jim wondering. Was the gold reason enough to commit murder? Yeah, lots of people would kill for something worth that much. But did the treasure really exist? ⊙

8

A few minutes after one, Jim began the meeting with the investigative team. He glanced around the room. Leslie, Sam, and Luke were on time, but Paul Saner had yet to arrive from Stoddard. His text said he might be late. Other officers from the sheriff's department sat on chairs and stools, while some preferred to stand. Sam slouched sloppily across a chair, texting rapidly on his phone. Leslie sat at a table and stoically leafed through her research.

"All right, let's get started," Jim began, standing in front of a conference table. He straightened his tie and began. "We need to synthesize our information and develop a timeline of dates, times, and places. We can update and share interviews, witnesses, and suspects as they become available." He paused. Everyone seemed attentive and alert. He continued.

"Before I forget, I want to introduce our newest team member." Jim held out an open palm toward Leslie. "Everyone, Leslie Brown comes to us from Decorah, Iowa. She has served three tours of duty in Iraq with the U.S. Army as an MWD—military working dog handler. She's had extensive training in protecting and retrieving ancient artifacts that have gone missing. Thank you for your service, Leslie, and welcome." He pointed in her direction, the crew clapped, and there were a few whistles. Leslie waved and smiled.

"All right," Jim said, waving the applause aside. "I want you all to report on the assignments I gave you Friday. Sam, you're my man at the board. You've got the best handwriting of any of us."

Sam Birkstein walked to a whiteboard and began constructing category headings. Jim was a visual person. When he had come to the investigative side of the force, he started this tradition. Eventually, "the board" would morph into a jumble of paper scraps, photos, handwritten observations, timelines, and questions. Arrows in various magic marker colors linked information that might suggest solutions to the crime. The board became the focal point of any case. Often during an investigation, members of the team could be found standing around it, digesting the information. Jim had seen them alone or in a group, thinking, discussing links, and making connections.

Jim began again. "We'll start with the body of the victim. Luke, you're on."

Luke Evers, La Crosse County Coroner and Medical Examiner, began rattling off the facts. "I conducted a post-mortem forensic exam of the victim on Friday, June 4. The victim was a male, approximately 35 years in age. Height 5 feet 7 inches. Weight 187 pounds. He was dead approximately 10 to 12 days when discovered in the quarry. Degradation of tissue was not as advanced as it could have been due to the cold spring."

He handed photos of the victim's face to Sam, who pinned them on the board under a rectangle labeled VICTIM.

"DNA showed the victim to be 95 percent Hispanic ethnicity. He had no alcohol in his blood, but there were traces of marijuana and cocaine. I believe the victim fell from a ledge above the Chipmunk Coulee Quarry, landing on the rock floor below where he was found. The injuries are consistent with this type of trauma. The victim may have been moved after he fell, but the fall is what killed him." Luke looked around the room, making eye contact with each person.

He continued. "Indicators to the victim include multiple lumbar fractures, broken ribs and clavicles, and a multiple-fractured left arm and leg. I believe he landed on his left side. He had punctured lungs and a ruptured spleen and heart. He suffered massive internal injuries and died on impact." Luke paused in his assessment.

"The presence of random bruises and superficial wounds to his face and upper body lead me to believe he may have been in an argument with someone. He might have been shoved from the edge or lost his balance, sending him over. Investigators are examining that upper rim. His chances of survival from a fall like this would have been close to zero. His weight plus the height of the fall at over 150 feet doubled the likelihood of death." Luke stopped and looked at Jim. Jim stood to the side, listening intently, leaning against the wall, his arms crossed, one foot crossed over the other.

Since no one interrupted with questions, Luke went on with the analysis. "He had a unique tattoo in the upper left quadrant of his chest above the nipple—the number thirteen surrounded by three dots. A quick scan of the internet revealed that this is a common Mexican mafia gang tattoo. From my research, the three dots can mean 'my crazy life,' or they could mean 'prison, hospital, and cemetery.' I'll let the rest of you decide the significance of that. We were able to get one pretty good fingerprint from his right index finger, and we're hoping to get some identification from it."

"Did he have any unique clothing, a wallet, or other paper that would help in identifying him?" Leslie ventured.

"Well, all we found was the unique coin he had socked away in his jeans pocket. The only other evidence I collected was a Viroqua Walmart receipt in his T-shirt pocket dated May 15. We also gathered some kind of pollen from his shoes and the pockets of his jean jacket. We have a professor who specializes in plant reproduction at UWL who will analyze that. We took impressions of his teeth on the chance he may have visited a local dentist. Nothing on that yet. His clothing was ordinary run-of-the-mill work clothes. Nothing distinctive there." Then he said, "That's about it."

The afternoon wore on as the team continued their reports.

When Leslie's turn came, she walked to the board and handed

enlarged photocopies of each side of the coin to Sam. He pinned them to the board under a heading labeled EVIDENCE.

"I was asked to examine the coin found on the victim. It is an authentic 1866 gold twenty-dollar Liberty coin," Leslie recited in a confident voice. She pointed to the enlarged photos. "I'm far from an expert. But as you can see, there are no scratches or signs of wear from handling. I believe the coin is uncirculated, which contributes to its pristine condition."

"This morning, I was able to get through to the U.S. Mint in Washington, D.C. They referred me to David Dushay, the current director of the San Francisco branch. An FYI. The mint in San Francisco was established in 1854 to serve the goldfields of the California Gold Rush in 1848 and still operates today as one of four mint sites in the continental United States. I sent a photo of our coin to him via email, and he believes it was minted there because of the S embedded in Liberty's hair. All coins that were struck in San Francisco use the S mark. Mr. Dushay believes our coin is the real deal."

"How'd it get here?" asked Paul Saner. "Did he have any ideas about that?" He'd managed to get to the meeting only a few minutes late.

"We discussed that briefly, but Mr. Dushay agreed it was an unusual coin found under unusual circumstances. He doesn't really have a theory about that," Leslie finished, shrugging her shoulders. It was quiet for a moment.

"Thanks, Leslie." Jim interjected, glancing around the room. His eyes wandered back to the photos of the coin on the board. "What we need to figure out is how the coin got here. Was it traded at a coin and relics show? Was it discovered somewhere else and brought here?" Jim stopped to collect his thoughts.

"And how is the Hispanic man involved? Is he a link to more of these coins?" Paul interjected.

Jim looked around the room, thinking about the reaction the team might have to what he was about to divulge. "I think I can provide one theory about this coin and how it got here. But you might find it hard to believe."

Jim repeated the legend Jamie Alberg had told him earlier that morning.

He stopped. The team displayed looks of doubt and disbelief.

"Are you serious? According to *legend*?" Sam Birkstein asked, his felt tip marker poised in midair.

"Well, Jamie told me he's spent the last eight years of his life trying to locate it. By the way, this kid is only nineteen." He let that sink in. He shifted gears, looking over at Paul. "What did you find out in Stoddard?"

Clearing his throat, Paul reported his findings. "I met with Haaken Iverson, who is the organizer of the Coulee Treasure Hunters Club. They occasionally meet at the River Road Cafe in Stoddard. I got a list of the hunters who come to the gatherings—a pretty loose group. Sometimes they can have twenty at these meetings and other times only four or five. Some of them have found coins and Native American artifacts like beads and arrowheads but nothing that would be as valuable as a lost treasure. But it does sound like something they all dream of." He ran his hand through his dark hair and scratched his ear. "Haaken said he thought the hunters would be glad to meet and assist us in any possible way. By the way, how much are these coins worth?"

"According to Jamie and the website I looked at," Jim answered, "an $80,000 cache of coins in today's money would be worth millions. We're talking about 4,000 coins, and if each coin yielded its current market value of $2,500, well, do the math. That's about ten million dollars." Sam added the incredible figure to the evidence box.

Somebody whistled in the back of the room. A wave of amazement passed through the group. Mouths hung open, and eyes widened in surprise.

Jim continued. "So to review: We need to get a positive ID of the victim and his history. We'll be releasing his profile at a news conference this evening. Hopefully, something will shake out that might help identify him."

"Paul, we're going to meet with this club. Leslie, I want you to get topography maps and books about the caves along the Mississippi and locate landowners who have caves on their property." Jim continued handing out assignments, pointing to each person as he spoke. "Sam, I want you to contact Fort Crawford. Question the curator about their archives to see if this incident about the lost gold shipment is recorded anywhere in their records."

"I'll check the tattoo parlor down on Pearl Street to see if they know more about the tattoo on the victim," Sam offered.

"Good, you do that," Jim said. "We'll meet again Friday morning at nine unless something comes up that gives us more to work with. Any other questions?"

Nobody said anything.

"Remember, jump in anywhere the trail leads you," Jim advised. "One of the ways to solve any problem is to eliminate what it isn't. Good job, everybody. Stay in touch," Jim concluded.

As the group of law enforcement personnel left the room, Jim poured a second cup of coffee. He studied the board, thinking about the ramifications of their evidence so far. The team had assembled a good amount of initial information, which was encouraging. A quiet tapping on the door got his attention. Jim turned to see Carol Olstad standing in the doorway.

"Hi. I was just wondering how the hearing went," she said. She looked worried. "I hid in my office all morning."

"Coffee?" Jim asked. Carol shook her head.

"Wilson got a grilling from Chief Pedretti. Indefinite suspension pending a ruling by the LCR. Once the board gets wind of all the problems he's had, I doubt he'll retain his position on the force," Jim answered succinctly.

"I never thought Tamara would push it that far." Carol's brown eyes searched his face for some kind of reassurance. "Her being a newbie and all."

"Hey, you did the right thing," he said softly, his blue eyes locking on her. "Tamara might be a newbie, but she was tough and professional. Just for the record, you and every other person who has suffered from Gordy's abuse deserve justice. You're worth it."

Carol stared at Jim.

"This is where you say thank you," Jim said, hiding a grin.

"Thank you," Carol said seriously. "I mean it. I probably would have let it slide."

"Yeah, and then he'd just continue whalin' on other women," Jim remarked quietly. "You did the right thing."

By late afternoon, the word had gotten out about Wilson's mandatory leave and the pending investigation by the LCR. Rumors about a woman chief of police being out of her depth were put to bed, and Carol and Jim decided on a drink after work to celebrate. ⊙

9

The news of the dead man and the enigmatic coin hit the tristate area papers on Monday evening with a special write-up in the *La Crosse Tribune* by veteran reporter Troy Fish. Jim was surprised it hadn't leaked out sooner. Facebook, Snapchat, and Twitter were in a frenzy of communication to support their incessant need for drama. Paul Saner headed up a five o'clock news conference, releasing just enough accurate information to counteract erroneous fictional concepts about the crime on social media outlets.

"We need to identify the quarry victim. We're asking the public to come forward if they can share information that might lead to his identity," Paul finished.

Jim was glad to have Saner on the team. Paul came to policing late after working as a paralegal. He had an eye for detail without coming off cocky or egotistical. His down-home appeal was contagious. Paul was the dream public relations officer, attending neighborhood block parties and going to the local schools to teach drug resistance and anti-bullying lessons. He loved taking their K-9 black Lab out in public. He had appeared as a guest on local television news shows to demonstrate some of Telly's skills. When bad news had to be delivered, he was the soft shoe they called on. He was a very versatile officer—sharp, dedicated, and consistent.

As soon as the news conference was over, Jim headed to Piggy's on Front Street. The historic pioneer foundry had been reinvented into a gourmet restaurant. It had an upscale vibe but kept its hometown feel with its fabulous barbecued pork ribs and succulent grilled steaks. With a view of the Mississippi, the Cass Street Bridge, and access to Riverside Park, it had become one of the destination dining spots in town.

It was after six when Jim arrived. Carol was already seated at a table in the Blues Lounge, texting and scrolling through her messages. Jim slipped into the chair next to her.

"No running interference with a phone." He took the phone and gently laid it on the table. He smiled and looked into her eyes. "How are you? Have a better afternoon?"

Carol noticed he liked to hook two and three questions together. Must be the detective in him. "My afternoon was busy but good. I'm just glad that meeting with Gordy is over."

"Waiting to wet your whistle?" he asked, smiling.

"Waiting for someone to share it with. I'll have a glass of pinot noir."

"Back in a minute."

Jim returned with the wine, an Old Style Light, and a basket of batter-fried cheese curds.

"Oooh, you're killin' my diet," Carol crooned. "How was your afternoon, by the way?" She pushed her hair back behind her ears and tilted her head. Jim reached for a cheese curd and dipped it in a bowl of hot sauce.

"Mmm, don't burn your tongue." He paused, relishing the snack, then took a swig of his beer.

"This case is really interesting," Jim continued leaning forward with his elbows on the table. "Never had one like this with history, antiquities, and murder all rolled together." He filled her in while she listened intently, nodding her head every once in a while. He likes the hunt, Carol realized. He seemed energized by the whole sordid affair. But she understood. Her work in the morgue was interesting and challenging, although most people turned up their nose when they found out what she did.

Carol had worked her way up the county government ladder, landing her dream job as a secretary in the coroner's office ten years ago. Luke Evers was a newbie then, and at first, Carol enjoyed showing him the ropes. But as he'd gained experience, he morphed into a real boss. The nature of their work required a compassionate yet realistic view of death. Bodies arrived at the morgue in all states of decay, injury, and termination. Medical mysteries, drownings, car accidents, murders—she'd seen the gamut of traumatic events that ended lives. Although she didn't participate in the technical aspects of autopsies, she'd seen plenty of stark, naked bodies. That no longer shocked her. Experience had hardened her to the gruesome realities of death, but she retained her sense of humor and hoped, her enthusiasm for life. All in all, she enjoyed great latitude and variety in her work, and the pay wasn't bad either.

They visited a while. Carol had never really studied Jim up close like this before. His blond hair was graying, but it wasn't unattractive; it gave him a seasoned look. His firm, tanned face framed a striking pair of blue eyes. When he smiled, a deep dimple in his right cheek gave him an impish appearance, and deep laugh lines created an overall magnetic effect. Carol was surprised he wasn't more pessimistic about the human race. But she supposed their jobs were alike in some ways. They both required a healthy dose of skepticism accompanied by some hardheaded logic and common sense. His manners were impeccable compared to some other men she'd dated, but she realized he had a penchant for perfection, which worried her. Many perfectionists she knew could be critical and harsh. Her father had been difficult in that respect, and she had no desire to repeat that history. Although she'd known Jim for years as a friend, now up-close and personal, Carol realized there was much more about him that she didn't know. Getting to know him was stimulating and interesting. He was engaging.

As they finished their appetizers and drinks, the sun began its evening descent in the western sky, setting the river aflame with pinks, reds, and purples. The river currents swirled, moving in silence. Jim noticed couples and groups of friends sitting on the patio, unwinding after a hard day's work. The jazz group Just a Minute began setting up their equipment. Laughter and bits of conversations drifted in the air.

Jim's phone chirped.

"Hello, Jim Higgins."

A moment of listening, then "Sure, why don't we plan on dinner tomorrow night?" He mouthed "Sara" to Carol. She nodded. "I'll thaw some steaks. We'll grill out, okay?" After a moment, "Love you, too. Bye."

They talked a while longer. "Hey listen, I've got to get going," Jim said, regretting the evening had flown by so quickly. "It was nice to celebrate your victory. And remember, no picking up sleazy guys in bars, especially those law enforcement types," he said, grinning, his dimple denting his cheek. He stood and held the chair for Carol, slipping her sweater over her tanned shoulders.

"Got it. Would that include you?" she said with a grin. He let his hand rest lightly on the small of her back as they maneuvered through the crowded bar.

"What are you doing Saturday night?" he asked. "The String Alongs are playing at Leo and Leona's at seven-thirty. I thought we could catch them. Wanna go?" Jim asked as he walked Carol to her car. He held out his hand protectively as a skateboarder zipped by, careening precariously down the busy street. Other pedestrians moved aside as the boarder hogged the sidewalk.

Carol stopped and turned to him. She smiled.

"Love to. How about I drive over to your place about six? I'll bring appetizers if you provide something to drink."

"Sounds great."

He opened the driver's door as she slipped in the front seat. Slamming her door, he backed up and waved. "See you Saturday night." He watched her pull out of her parking space.

She has a lovely smile, he thought. His phone beeped again. Sometimes he was tempted to throw it as far as he could—a Hail Mary into the river.

"Where are you right now?" asked Paul.

"Standing on Front Street at Piggy's."

"Just got a call from Schoep's Dairy up on Highway 33. One of their Hispanic workers has been missing for about three weeks. Hiram, the dairy owner, thought it might be the man who went over the cliff. He saw the news conference and wants to talk to someone."

That was quick, Jim thought. "Pick me up."

"Be there in fifteen." Paul clicked off.

Paul appeared in ten minutes, and Jim jumped in the truck. They wove through downtown traffic, headed out State Road up the steep hills to the northeast until they connected with Highway 33. The bluffs leveled out and gave a spectacular view of the wide river valley. The sun's intense heat was waning, and the evening rays of sunlight softened into a golden haze that blurred the distant hills. Herds of cows grazed in knee-high alfalfa. Red-washed barns whizzed by, and white clapboard farmhouses with wide rolling lawns, pristine gardens, and berry patches created a checkerboard of plenty. Paul crinkled his nose when the odor of a rotting deer and flattened skunk drifted into the truck from the roadside. Jim listened to Paul's theory of the crime, his arm resting on the pickup's open window frame.

"It's hard to put any weight in this lost gold shipment, don't you think?" he asked Jim, looking across the pickup seat, studying Jim's profile.

Jim harrumphed. "You haven't talked to one of the treasure hunters yet. They are an intense crew if Jamie Alberg is any indication. They're loners. Sometimes they seem invisible, yet they know each other well. Makes for some interesting dynamics." Jim leaned back in the seat, taking in the picturesque panorama rolling by.

"This crime could involve coin collectors or antiquity experts," he speculated. "Or it could involve the illegal trade and sale of coins. These pieces are museum quality, and if someone found the entire shipment, the gold alone would be worth millions. But the real value lies in the rarity and age of the coins. Some prestigious museum would give their eye teeth for a collection like this."

"What I can't figure out is why someone would want to hide the treasure if they had legitimately discovered it," Paul commented. "I did some research, and the old finders keepers rule usually applies to this kind of stuff."

"Yeah, Jamie told me about that, but that's only if you find it on your property," Jim said. "It might not apply if it's government property or the property belongs to someone else. Plus, the notoriety you get from becoming fabulously wealthy is not all it's cracked up to be. My first cousin won five million in the Wisconsin lottery once. Pretty much wrecked her marriage, and she constantly worried about her kids getting abducted."

"Really?" Paul said, frowning. "Hmm. Guess I didn't think of that. But still, it's good to remember that according to current law, when you buy property, you also buy anything buried or hidden on it."

Jim shifted in his seat. "True. But, here's something else to think about. What if someone discovered it, but it wasn't their property? You could offer to buy the property to get the treasure. But what if the owner didn't want to sell? My understanding of these treasure hunters is that they go to great lengths climbing hills and crawling in caves for a possible strike. So, what if some guy inadvertently discovered the treasure but couldn't claim it because he didn't own the property? That might set up a situation of sketchy moral choices," Jim said. "Talkin' about a lot of money. People have killed for a lot less than that."

They rode in silence for a while, thinking about the scenarios they'd discussed. Finally, the Schoep Dairy appeared on a rise in the land. It looked like a factory until you got close enough to see the Holstein cows dotting the surrounding landscape and smell the manure. Jim had cousins in the dairy industry, so he knew that the quaint scenario of dairy farms with herds of fifty to sixty cows had changed over the years. Now in Wisconsin, herds of a thousand cows were not uncommon. Some herds numbered several thousand. The need for Mexican workers to feed and milk cows was ongoing. Most of the Mexican workforce were here on green cards. Some were legal, but most were unauthorized by the immigration service.

Paul parked near the dairy office, and they got out. They were surprised at the scale of the operation. They strolled around the farm buildings for a while, looking for Hiram. They finally found him walking among his cows in a containment pen. He waved at them and walked over. A bunch of Holstein cows turned their dark soft eyes toward the unfamiliar pair and greeted them with hearty moos accompanied by sounds of flatulence.

After introductions, Jim got to the point of the visit. "So, why do you think the victim found in the quarry is the one missing from your milking crew?"

"Jorge has been here for two years. Rumor is that he had gang affiliations, but he's been a great worker for me," Hiram explained. "He has a wife and two small kids. He never misses work. It's going on three weeks, and there's no sign of him. It's not like him to do something like that. His wife is very worried."

"Where is she? Can we talk to her?" Jim asked, his forehead creased with a frown as he batted at a pesky fly.

"If you go back the way you came, you'll see a gravel road called Wildfire Lane." Hiram pointed to the south. "We own a couple of trailers that we provide for our steady workers. She lives in the rusty blue one. Her name's Maria. Her English isn't the best, but she should be able to answer some simple questions."

"What's the husband's name again?" Jim asked, taking out his memo pad.

"Jorge Santana. Wife's Maria," Hiram replied. Jim jotted the names down.

They climbed back in the truck and found the trailer. It was rusty. And decrepit. And old. Jim couldn't imagine that anyone could stay warm in the winter in that thing. It made him shiver just thinking about it. A small woman, dressed in jeans and a dirty yellow sweatshirt, leaned out of the crumbling metal door. Her petite face was a warm mocha brown, and her shiny black hair was pulled back in a ponytail. Two little children peeked around each leg, eyes innocent and wide.

"Ms. Santana, I'm Detective Jim Higgins. This is Officer Saner." Jim flashed his ID but didn't climb the broken-down stairs leading to the door. Instead, he stood in the dirt driveway, looking up at her. Kids' trikes and sand toys littered the base of the steps. "We understand your husband has been missing for a couple of weeks. When did you last see him?"

"He is gone now over two weeks. He does not call. I do not know where he is," she said.

"What day would that have been?" Paul asked.

She rolled her eyes upward as she thought. "I think May 16," she replied.

"Can you tell me what he was wearing when you last saw him?" Seeing her puzzled expression, Paul tugged at his shirt.

She shrugged. "Jeans, shirt, boots, maybe a coat."

"Can you tell me if he had any tattoos?" Paul questioned.

She looked over to Jim as if she didn't understand. Then after a few moments, her eyes drifted back to Paul when he repeated the word tattoo.

She said, "Tattoo? Here?" She pointed above her heart.

"Yes, did he have one there?" Jim felt a little tug of excitement.

She shrugged, then said, "He have a numero, how you say?"

Jim tore a piece of paper from his memo book and handed her a pencil.

"Draw it if you can," he said, making writing gestures in the air.

She placed the paper against the doorframe and carefully wrote the number thirteen surrounded by three distinct dots. She handed it to Jim with a shaking hand.

"Oh, boy," Paul whispered as he leaned over Jim's shoulder and looked at the drawing. "Looks like we've identified our murder victim."

Maria absorbed the looks on Jim and Paul's faces and then softly began to cry. ⊙

SUE BERG

10

TUESDAY, JUNE 8

Paul Saner rolled on his side in his darkened bedroom and grabbed his cell to check the time. 6:30 a.m. He flopped on his back, taking in the view of the ceiling. His live-in girlfriend, Ruby Irving, lay facing away from him. He rolled up next to her, wrapped his arm around her, and pulled her close.

"What?" she mumbled into the pillow. "When did you get home last night? I didn't hear you."

"I got in about eleven. Higgins and I had to interview someone way out on the ridge above La Crosse. By the time we got back, and I dropped him off at his car, it was ten-thirty. Sorry, that's the way it is," he finished, kissing her bare shoulder.

"Hmm, what time are you going in today?" she asked, turning to him. He took in her auburn hair, curling softly around her face. He loved her creamy skin and dark lashes, full lips and warm smile. *A very nice package.*

"Why? You got something in mind?" he grinned, nuzzling her neck.

"Oh, yeah. But first, I've got to brush my teeth," she said, pulling away from his grasp.

Later, he sat quietly at the kitchen table, sipping his hazelnut coffee. Ruby was in the shower. He walked to his baby grand in the corner of their Grand River apartment on Third Street. They had a great view of the river and the Cass Street bridge that led to LaCrescent, Minnesota.

He sat down at the keyboard and started with a favorite Mozart sonata. He messed around with a little Gershwin, ending his morning wake-up with the first movement of Rachmaninoff's Concerto No. 3.

Expressively, he had lost none of the music's passion and intensity, but he knew his playing would never be the same. When he hurt his hand, his career as a professional performer ended with sickening finality. Surgery after surgery, he'd waded through terrible depression, which presented itself as anger and rage. He railed against God and his family. His girlfriend could not stand up under his withering sarcasm and indifference, so she left him. Fortunately, most of his friends and family were good forgivers, long on patience and understanding. He'd had to hit the reset button of his life in a major way. It had taken professional counseling and medication to moderate his personality and ambition into something everyone could live with.

Then he'd met Ruby at a mutual friend's party, and they clicked almost immediately. Ruby did not coddle him nor tolerate his critical "artistic" spirit. Since meeting her, Paul had learned to manage his type A personality. He didn't exactly compromise his drive and determination, but he'd learned they could be useful without booze or drugs.

The paralegal work he'd done had grown boring. That's when Ruby suggested police work. Using his intellect and interest in problem-solving for the greater good appealed to his moral compass. He discovered that analyzing people's character and motivations was just the challenge he needed. Police work required persistence, grit, determination, and a healthy dose of intelligence. His natural skepticism and hard-headed realism made it a good career choice. He loved the challenge and had never looked back.

He felt Ruby's soft kisses on the back of his neck. She wrapped her arms around his broad shoulders and rested her head on top of his. The morning sunlight streamed in through the windows filling the apartment with brightness and cheer.

"How many women can wake up to that kind of music?" she asked softly.

"In La Crosse, probably only one, and you're it, babe." He stood and drew her close, kissing her tenderly.

"Are you going to be home tonight at a decent hour?" she asked, her eyes teasing. "I'll make my famous homemade spaghetti."

"The old truism at work? The way to a man's heart is through his stomach. Time?"

"Sevenish?" she asked, tilting her head, looking into Paul's hazel eyes.

"Remember that I told you if you wanted to live a predictable life, don't fall in love with a policeman."

"Too late for that. Does that mean you'll be here at seven?" Ruby asked as Paul walked to the shower.

"Count on it," he said over his shoulder.

Paul dressed and had a final cup of coffee. Ruby left for work at the Schuster, Kish, and Lancaster Law Firm down on Riverside Boulevard. Locking the apartment and walking across the outdoor patio, he descended three flights of stairs and hopped in his Ford F-150 pickup housed in the street-level parking ramp. Driving across town to the sheriff's department, he braked for a biker with no helmet and trailed a Kwik Trip semi. When he slowed down to let a car squeeze in front of him at a merging lane, someone in the car behind gave him the finger and laid on their horn. *Good mornin' to you, too. Jerk.*

At his desk, Paul opened his iPad and searched various law enforcement databases, including CODIS, which might provide details about Jorge Santana, the Hispanic farmworker. He spent time searching through his copy of *The Gang Book of 2012* published by the Chicago Crime Commission and read some stuff about Mexican gangs. On page 172, he found Jorge listed as an active member of MS-13, a notorious Mexican gang.

In recent years, the criminal gangs in La Crosse were responsible for an array of crimes from weapons violations, harassment, intimidation, car theft, drugs, sexual assault, and homicide. The latest murder of a gang member was on July 23, 2010, when Jason Sholt was beaten during a gang initiation and his body dumped in the Mississippi River. More recently, a college coed had been murdered at point-blank range on the North Side when Hmong gang members broke into her apartment and stole her purse.

Many of the gangs in La Crosse had moved in from the Milwaukee and Chicago areas. Law enforcement interacted with them on a weekly basis. Paul wondered if Jorge had played the role of counselor to some of the younger gang members. *If these kids spent as much time on their schoolwork as they do on all this gang stuff, they'd be straight-A students,* he thought.

Opening his phone, he contacted the La Crosse Social Services and asked for Lisa Timmons. He had used her translation services before when he'd dealt with people whose English was sketchy. Could she help him out with Maria? She freed up her schedule, and Paul picked her up mid-morning for a trip to the Schoep Dairy property.

They found Maria at the same rusting trailer on Wildfire Lane, except this time she was working outside in a small, well-tended vegetable garden. Paul didn't know anything about gardening, but he thought he recognized the beginnings of lettuce, cucumbers, and tomatoes. Maria looked up as he rounded the corner. She looked sad, and dark circles framed her warm brown eyes.

"Hello again," Paul said quietly.

He waited a moment. Maria held up a hand in greeting as Paul introduced Lisa.

In Spanish, Lisa said, "I am here to help you understand the questions Paul will ask. Then I can help him figure out exactly what you are saying, so we can have an honest exchange." Maria nodded her head. "Are you ready then?" Lisa asked Maria.

"Yes, go ahead," Maria said in Spanish, focusing her brown eyes on Paul.

"Okay, I have a few more questions for you," he said as he began the interview.

Through a series of exchanges translated by Lisa, a familiar story began to emerge. Jorge immigrated to Milwaukee in the early 1990s with his family from Mexico City, where they were trying to escape the drug lords and gangs that had taken over. In the beginning, his dad and mom were able to find respectable jobs in Milwaukee, which supported their family. But with welfare reform sweeping across the state, the job opportunities they had hoped would be there for their children dried up, leaving a vacuum for gang proliferation. Without a job, Jorge had gravitated toward gang life.

Maria grew up tough, living a life of poverty and neglect. Suffering from sexual abuse at home, she ran away when she was sixteen, living on the streets of Milwaukee. The local Hispanic gang embraced her, providing friendship and affirmation. The desire for acceptance overruled her common sense. When she met Jorge at a gang initiation, she soon became his girl. And very soon afterward found herself pregnant.

"Where did Jorge get his tattoo?" Paul asked after listening to Maria's story.

"He already had that when I met him in Milwaukee. I don't know," Maria said, but her eyes slid away from his. Lisa looked at Paul and shrugged her shoulders.

Maria continued her story. Jorge had a string of arrests for drug dealing and robbery. After his last stint in jail, he'd had a change of heart and wanted something better for his family. Poverty and violence in Milwaukee drove them to seek a quieter country life.

"My husband was tired of city life. A cousin who worked here helped him get this job," she explained. "He put in long hours. He was a hard worker, but we did not make much money." She hesitated for a moment as Paul waited patiently. There was more to tell he was sure.

She twirled her hair nervously. "He had a problem with drugs. So he turned to dealing to help us have more money. Sometimes there were men who came here. They were scary. I tried to talk him into quitting his drug habit. For a while, he got straight. Then he slipped and started using again."

Paul had heard similar stories so many times. Her account of Jorge's drug use confirmed the traces of marijuana and cocaine they had found during the autopsy. "So he sold and delivered drugs, too?" Paul asked.

"I think he did, even though I didn't actually see it." She twisted the fringe of her shirt, her eyes downcast.

"Do you remember any of the scary guys? Their names?" Paul asked. "Could you describe them?" Lisa interpreted.

Maria thought. "I only remember one name—a Steve somebody. I don't know his last name, but I think he lived in La Crosse."

Paul continued, his voice edgy with concern. "Your husband Jorge had a gold coin in the pocket of his jeans when we found his body." Paul pulled a photo of the coin from his clipboard and showed Maria. "Do you ever remember seeing it? Did he show it to you or talk about it with you?" he asked.

She looked closely at it, and when her eyes met Paul's, something had changed. A hardness tempered with tenacity crossed her face but lasted only a brief moment. *She knows something,* Paul thought.

"He showed me the coin. Only one time," she said.

"So you saw the coin before?" Paul asked.

"One time," she repeated, holding up her index finger. But her face had shut down. Her expression became muted; her eyes were hooded with suspicion. She had taken on a toughness. Defending her husband's actions was familiar territory.

"Do you know where he would have gotten it?" Paul asked.

"No," she said with finality.

Paul's face hardened, his voice gritty. "I must tell you, Ms. Santana, whoever killed your husband will not hesitate to harm you if you have information about this coin. Please be careful." Paul stopped and waited for Lisa to interpret. Maria's face had turned into a stone mask.

"Would you look through your husband's clothes and belongings? It would be helpful if you could find any paper, business cards, or notes. Anything that might help us find out where he got the coin," Paul said. "Or we could help you."

"I will do that myself. And I have a question. When can I get my husband's body?" Tears welled in her eyes until they spilled over on her cheeks.

"I'll check with the medical examiner's office and let you know," Paul said, easing up. He looked at the ground and let out a sigh. *Why do I have more questions now than when I started?*

Jim Higgins had been in his office studying the extensive rap sheet on Jorge Santana. His criminal activities in Milwaukee included everything from buying and distributing marijuana, gang-related activities, and a long list of traffic violations—a street-smart criminal. Jim believed his dairy-related work was only a cover for other nefarious activities. Too bad for Maria. Another innocent girl who was foolish enough to be attracted to a thug. He was sure her life had spiraled downward into more abuse, poverty, and disappointment. He paged through the information on Santana, circling facts to add to the board.

He reached for his phone and called Paul.

"Officer Saner."

"Paul, Jim here. Just pulled up Santana's rap sheet. The guy was very active on the drug and gang scene in Milwaukee. How'd the visit with Maria go?"

"Typical stand-by-your-man crap. When I asked about the gold, she became pretty hostile and answered my questions in monosyllables. Not cooperative. Which makes me think she knows something about it that she's not telling."

"Okay, we'll have to keep an eye on her. I'll catch you later," Jim said.

That same morning, Officer Sam Birkstein went to work on Santana's tattoo. He was familiar with the tattoo parlors in La Crosse. There were three. Two were located on Main Street near downtown, and another was on Pearl Street. Rather than call, he decided to visit each one. None of the owners could remember a customer who fit the description of Jorge. Another dead end.

Back at his desk, Sam called the Fort Crawford Museum in Prairie du Chien. According to the curator, the legend was a popular misconception in the fort's history. To her knowledge, there were no actual written records at the fort that would support the saga.

"So, in your opinion, the legend of the lost gold shipment is just a fairy tale?" Sam asked, staring outside at the traffic on Vine Street.

"Well, I'm not saying it *couldn't* have happened, but it seems that an incident which involved that much money disappearing would have been recorded somewhere in the historical record. I don't know of any references, although there are financial records that list expenses and payroll. I'm not real familiar with those. I could look back and see if the payrolls are listed for that year."

"Could you? And call me if you find anything? I'd appreciate it," Sam said politely.

The curator continued. "There may be something there, but I've read most of the history that's in our archives. I don't remember anything about a lost payroll, but I'll check the records just to be sure. I'm sorry I couldn't help more. You're certainly welcome to come any time for any other information you may need." She paused for a moment. "But I really think it's a dead end."

"Okay. If you find anything, please call me. And thanks for your help." Sam clicked off. *We're getting nowhere fast.*

By one o'clock that afternoon, Paul and Sam were hunched around the board adding details to what was already there, which wasn't much. True, the quarry victim's identification was a break,

SUE BERG

but unless they could hook him up with someone else and prove he had knowledge of the gold, the coin would remain a mystery.

Jim walked in at about two o'clock. He reviewed the board, read the new stuff, got a cup of coffee, and disappeared. He came back ten minutes later.

"Paul, the meeting with the Treasure Hunters Club is tomorrow night in Stoddard at seven," he said. "You can pick me up at my place. Just come in through the garage and holler. I'll be ready. Plus, I want to release the identification of the victim to the press. Stir the pot and see what happens. What'd you guys find out?"

"Not much," Paul answered. "I think Maria was honest about some stuff, like their story. She's going to look through the trailer and his truck for papers, receipts, business cards, stuff like that, but I doubt she'll find anything. When I questioned her about the coin, she admitted she'd seen it, but I got a definite feeling she was holding out. She knows something else. I just don't know what." He made a wry face. "Maybe we'll get lucky."

"Luck usually doesn't come our way. I wouldn't count on it," Jim said despondently.

Sam chimed in. "The Mexican gang symbol, although not common around here, could be done by any competent tattoo artist. That's pretty much dead in the water. I think he had it done in Mexico, not here. I had another thought, though. I don't get the impression this murder is gang-related. To me, it seems like it might have been an accident rather than murder." He looked over at Jim. When he continued to stare at him, Sam continued. "I keep envisioning a scene at the top of the bluff. Why were they there? Were they dragging out the gold? Did they argue? That seems like the most logical explanation. Those minor facial lacerations and bruises seem to indicate a fight of some kind. And the hasty burial points to someone inexperienced in getting rid of a body."

Paul nodded in agreement. "Yeah, I hear you."

"I talked to the curator at the Fort Crawford Museum," Sam continued. He glanced at his notes. "A Kelly Sanford. She thinks we're wasting our time running after a pot of gold that never existed or isn't even mentioned in the fort's archives. But she's going to check the financial records for payrolls around 1866."

"Well, looks like we're battin' zero," Jim sighed, loosened his tie, and rubbed a hand across his eyes.

"It's early yet. But without the discovery of more of the gold coins or a connection between Jorge and the coin, or records from the fort that indicate it actually existed, we've got nothing," Paul finished, his shoulders slumping.

"We gotta keep truckin'. Something will break," Sam said over his shoulder as he left the room. Paul thought about that. Dogged determination did solve crimes in many circumstances. Jim Higgins was known for his refusal to give up, and Paul couldn't imagine him throwing in the towel any time soon.

In the meantime, CSI Leslie Brown was down the hallway in her office perched over a set of maps of the Upper Mississippi River she'd gotten from the Corps of Engineers in Genoa. The maps and her morning Google searches helped her locate the known caves along the Mississippi from La Crosse to Prairie du Chien. She was working with current plat books to identify landowners who had caves on their property. There weren't too many.

She also learned that three local businesses traded in gold and silver coins and bullion. They also bought and sold collectible coins. Two were rated reputable and the other, if the Google photos and ratings were any indication, looked like a place where you might find fakes or a less than reputable dealer. The sketchy place was called Bargain Coins. Leslie planned to hook Sam over lunch and go for a surprise visit. Maybe something would shake out.

She finished marking the caves' locations on the USGS map and hung it on the wall next to the board. From her research, she knew there were more caves along the river. However, entrances to them could be concealed by erosion and the accumulation of debris that had washed over the steep slopes. There could be dozens or hundreds obscured from view, lost, and forgotten. If the gold shipment really

SUE BERG

existed, it would be like finding a proverbial needle in a haystack. Now that the vegetation was in full bloom, the chances of spotting unknown cave entries would be even more difficult. Maybe she needed to talk to Jamie Alberg. He seemed to be the most invested in the tale. *Better start looking for the needle,* she thought.

EVENING, JUNE 8

The killer was sitting in his living room in his underwear and a T-shirt eating a bowl of Cheerios with milk. The headliner for the evening news came on.

"The La Crosse Sheriff's Department announces that the victim found in the Chipmunk Coulee Quarry has been identified as Jorge Santana of rural Middle Ridge near Cashton, a farmworker at the Schoep Dairy. He is believed to have possible connections to drug cartels in Mexico and has an extensive criminal history in the Milwaukee area. If anyone has information about Santana, you are asked to contact the sheriff's department immediately."

He'd been thinking about his options, trying to make a plan since the cops had discovered Jorge in the quarry. All of his years alone had conditioned him to think of only himself. He hadn't thought about what he'd do if he found the treasure. He'd gone crazy when he discovered the stash of coins, but he'd made a terrible mistake including Jorge. Then when Jorge had gone over the quarry bluff, he'd had to haul the remainder of the gold out of the cave himself anyway.

Covering up the Mexican in the quarry had been another colossal blunder. He should have buried him somewhere else or thrown him in the river. But somebody had driven up and parked along the road by the quarry, which made him panic. Then he'd made another mistake by not checking the Mexican's pockets. How was he supposed to know Jorge had pilfered a coin and tucked it in his jeans? If they had found him dead without the coin, the police would have chalked it up to gang or drug-dealing activity. Unfortunately, he'd learned that if you wanted to cover your tracks, you had to think and plan. But it was too late now. From here on out, it was all damage control.

The killer got up and placed his bowl and spoon in the sink. He stood there for a few minutes, thinking and planning. His head began to bang with the early symptoms of a migraine. More problems. He wondered if the cops had talked to Maria yet. She hadn't seemed very bright when he met her at the trailer to pick up his dope. He didn't know how much she knew, but she was the only other possible link to the treasure. What did she know? He'd have to pay her a visit. Soon. ☉

11

WEDNESDAY, JUNE 9

Paul rolled into Jim's driveway early Wednesday evening. He got out of his truck and made his way to the garage's side door and entered the house through the utility room.

"Hey, anybody here?" he hollered, walking into the updated kitchen.

"Yeah, in here," Jim yelled. "Down the hall in my office."

Paul walked down the hall to the office and lowered himself into a winged back chair next to the window.

"Nice digs," he said, his eyes scanning the tastefully decorated room. Native American paintings and collections of arrowheads were arranged tastefully on the walls. A laptop computer and printer sat on an antique oak desk. Floor-to-ceiling bookshelves were packed with mysteries by John Sandford, Louise Penny, C. J. Box, and Tony Hillerman. There were a number of Wisconsin and American volumes of history and some religious books. Paul noticed one titled *Luther's Reformation* and another, *Imagine Heaven*.

"Didn't know you were religious," he ventured, still glancing at titles.

"In this job, having faith in God is always a plus."

"So, what do you expect from this treasure club meeting?" Paul asked.

"Who knows? I've never had such an unusual case with so many facets in thirty years on the force. Talk about feeling like the old guy. Treasure? Hidden gold shipments tucked in a cave? It's all pretty incredible. Especially if it turns out to be true," Jim confessed. "I did go over the membership list, if you can call it that. Pretty loose organization. Know a couple of names on the list. We'll see what happens when we get there. You ready to head out?"

"Yep. Let's hit the road."

The drive south along the Mississippi on U.S. Highway 35 was pleasant. After the heat of the day, the cool air from the river valleys rose in steaming pools above the marshes, providing a respite from the warmth of city concrete. Boats and barges chugged up and down the waterway.

Stoddard was a small river town with a collection of modest houses, an elementary school, a couple of bars, a Methodist and a Lutheran church, and a Kwik Trip gas station. Paul pulled into the River Road Cafe parking lot. The cafe was a simple brick structure with wide windows facing the street and window boxes filled with geraniums and trailing ivy. Jim and Paul found a booth and ordered coffees. Haaken, the owner of the cafe and the organizer of the club, approached them.

"Evenin' guys. Got a room in the back for the meeting. Good turn out." He began walking away, waving his hand for them to follow.

Jim and Paul took their coffees and walked down a short hallway to a room decorated with VFW posters and an American flag displayed on the wall. A coffee pot and cups had been set up on a side table. A collection of treasure hunters sat around tables sipping coffee and sodas. Most looked like typical farmers and laborers, the blue-collar sort, dressed in working clothes and hats to Jim.

Haaken Iverson moved to the front of the room. "Most of you probably have heard about the victim in the Chipmunk Coulee Quarry. Lt. Higgins from the La Crosse Sheriff's Department is here to ask us questions." Haaken turned to Jim and nodded. Jim stood and met the stares of the group.

"Thanks for coming tonight," Jim started, his voice dry and businesslike. He reviewed the circumstances surrounding Jorge Santana's death and the strange coin.

"What we need from you is any information or ideas about the coin that was found on the victim. I know from talking to a few of you that coins are a pretty common find in your sport. But this coin stands out from the rest by its rarity alone, to say nothing of its pristine condition."

As Jim spoke, Paul began handing out photocopies of the gold coin found on Jorge Santana. "How many of you are familiar with the lost Fort Crawford payroll legend supposedly hidden somewhere in a cave along the river?" Jim asked.

A few hands went up. Jim glanced at the small crowd and recognized Steve Stoner. He gave him a slight nod, and Steve touched the brim of his hat in acknowledgment. Jamie Alberg was perched on a chair near the front with arms crossed over his chest. He wore a brimmed MVAC hat, which shaded his eyes. Other than those two, Jim didn't know anyone else seated at the tables.

"The coin fits the description of the gold that was supposedly hidden in a cave across from Fort Crawford. But it could just as well be a stolen coin," Jim said. The room remained silent except for the swish of the overhead fan.

"Does anyone have information about the victim or the coin?" Jim asked. Many hunters shifted in their seats, and some shook their heads, but no one offered any facts. A heavy man dressed in a red Cenex T-shirt and hat tentatively raised his hand and asked, "What other kinds of information are you looking for?"

"We're in the process of locating the known caves along the river. We know about the Deep 60 Cave and Samuel's Cave, plus a few others. We're sure some are not recorded and even more that have been buried in debris and forgotten. MVAC has agreed to assist us in the cave location. We're hoping that some of you can help us with maps or your memory of the area. We need some leads on these caves. If this legend is true, the gold could be stashed from here to Prairie du Chien." Jim paused and waited.

A woman toward the back of the room asked, "So you think this legend of the lost gold could be true?" She brushed her hair away from her face and waited for the answer.

Another voice spoke up. "Are you trying to solve a murder or find a lost gold treasure? Are we paying you guys overtime for all this?" a disgruntled hunter asked sarcastically.

"Well, I know it seems crazy that these two things could be connected. But I've seen a lot of odd coincidences in my days as a cop. Right now, it's the only vein of inquiry about the murder we have, and we're running with it," Jim replied. He shifted uncomfortably on his feet and continued. "We're investigating other possible motives and connections that will lead us back to Jorge Santana. We believe the gold coin is a crucial link. We just haven't figured out where it came from or where it might lead."

"Doesn't it strike you as odd to ask treasure hunters to help you find a treasure we'd want to discover ourselves?" a gray-haired, husky man asked from the back of the room. "Why should we help you?" Several other hunters murmured in agreement.

It was quiet for a moment. Jim glanced at Paul, who had been standing next to him during the exchange.

Paul stepped forward. He tugged at his ear and hiked up his pants.

"Look, guys. We're hoping you'll view this as an opportunity to help law enforcement. I can't tell you the number of times regular citizens have given us leads that have helped solve a crime. Besides, you know this topography around here probably better than anyone." He moved his hands in the direction of the bluffs. "Any information you can provide about forgotten caves or other possible hiding places would be greatly appreciated. We need your expertise to get a lead on this case. We'll leave our cards and contact information with Haaken here at the cafe. Feel free to call or email us with anything you might know. Be cautious and smart. We might be dealing with a murder, and we don't want anyone else hurt. Thanks for coming out."

Although there were a few more questions and comments, the meeting broke up. A couple of guys talked with Jim and Paul, but they couldn't hide their curiosity about the case even though they had no clues about the mysterious coin. Most people skipped out of the door. Jim knew the drill. The meeting could yield a lead, or it could just be another dead end. Now it was a waiting game.

As he exited the cafe, Jamie Alberg sidled up to Jim. "I'm planning on spending some time this week climbing and hiking. I heard through another veteran hunter about some possible old caves near the quarry where you found the victim. I might check those out."

Jim studied him. Jamie purported a wide-eyed innocence, but in his earlier conversation, Jim knew his head was full of technical knowledge. He also probably knew a slew of odd but relevant facts about the gold and the local topography that could help them.

"By the way," Jim added through the partially-opened truck door, "whoever knows about this coin could be the killer. Don't do anything stupid. Be sure you tell people where you're going."

Jamie grinned and continued walking to his car, waving as he went. Jim waved back. *I sure hope this leads somewhere.* He worried about Jamie Alberg, though. He was just a little too confident for his own good.

Amy Bergholt wandered to her red Nova after the treasure hunter meeting and climbed in. The meeting was interesting though she hadn't learned anything she didn't already know. What had been a surprise was that the two detectives seemed to be taking the legend of the lost gold seriously. Every other person she'd ever talked to about the lost gold shipment scoffed at the tale, dismissing it as somebody's imagination in overdrive. She'd never met one person who thought the story was true—until now. Now three other people were searching for the treasure: Jamie Alberg, Jim Higgins, and Paul Saner. This was not good. She'd have to think about what she knew and how she could use that information to her advantage. *I better keep quiet about that old map,* she thought. ☉

12

THURSDAY, JUNE 10

By the time Thursday morning rolled around, the attitude on the third floor of the sheriff's department had changed. The optimism that a quick solution would be found was replaced with the realization that dogged determination would again be the deciding factor in criminal apprehension. Nothing trumped crime scene evidence and witness interviews. The grinding monotony of checking facts, movements, and alibis of suspects could quickly wear down the most enthusiastic detective. In their conversations, Jim continued to encourage his young staff. They dug in with renewed determination, carrying out their assigned duties with tenacious resolve.

Though the evidence seemed a chaotic jumble of unrelated facts, Paul remained steadfastly glued to his computer recording the day-to-day accumulation of data.

In her study of the topography along the river, Leslie had a gut instinct that finding the cave would provide crucial new evidence. Her map of cave locations had been a start, but it hardly scratched the surface when investigating the porous nature of sandstone bluffs. If the guidebooks and textbooks she'd studied were any indication, finding the cave was going to be very difficult. There could be so many more than those recorded on maps. She'd studied the MVAC website and gained some good information on familiar caves in the area. Someone from the center named Becky had given her a tour and helped her with maps of the bluffs. Becky speculated where other caves might be found.

"Come on in my office for a minute. I want to show you something," Becky said. Leslie dutifully trooped into the cramped office. Three walls of bookshelves were jammed with volumes of technical tomes on Wisconsin's geology and early people groups who once inhabited the region. On the other wall, a large hand-drawn map clung to the corkboard with push pins.

"Wow! This is interesting. Your work?" Leslie asked, scanning the homemade map.

"Yeah. I've always been fascinated by caves. My grandpa had a cave on his farm down by LaFarge, and we used to play there. I guess that's how my passion was born," Becky admitted. "But what I really wanted to point out was right along this bluff." She ran her finger along a line on the map. "The vicinity of Chipmunk Coulee Quarry, where you found your victim, is an area that we believe is geologically structured to support the formation of other caves. It's just that we've never had the manpower to search there."

"Well, we really don't either. But this helps if for no other reason than it narrows the area where we should look," Leslie answered. "This," she said as she tapped the map with her index finger, "could prove to be very helpful." She studied Becky's face. Her eyes seemed to radiate with a kind of curiosity and inquisitive fire. "Do you think the legend of the Fort Crawford tale could be true?"

"Stranger things have happened," Becky said, shrugging. "Who knows? Something occurred at that gravel quarry that needs an explanation, and the gold coin certainly adds a caveat that demands some answers. Don't you think?" She met Leslie's eyes and held them. "The story of the lost gold seems to be the only solution that meets the criteria for your specific set of facts."

"Yeah, that's true," Leslie agreed, her eyes drifting back to the map. "That's why we're continuing our search for the cave, as crazy as that might seem. There may be clues there indicating who was in the cave," Leslie finished. They chatted a little more, and Leslie turned to leave. "Thanks for this. I really appreciate it. Could I possibly take a picture of this map with my phone?"

"No problem. If you find the lost cave, it might help justify more searches in that area. And it will bring a lot of attention to MVAC. And with attention comes donations and funding for more research," Becky finished with a wide smile. "And that's a good thing in our book."

Now, as Leslie sat at her desk, she realized that other interested parties were also invested in the discovery of the cave. A lot was riding on a deep, dark, dusty cavern that no one had been in for over 150 years.

Sam had done his due diligence in learning about gang tattoos, which led nowhere. He was still hopeful the Fort Crawford curator would call with something—anything—that might confirm or deny the legend.

After visits to the two specialty coin shops, Sam and Leslie went to Bargain Coins on Gillette Street. The shop was located at the back of the house. A sign on the door said CLOSED, so they went to the house's front door and knocked. The owner, Matt Shafer, was gone, but his girlfriend, Amy Bergholt, talked to them. She gave off a free love vibe with her blue-framed glasses, camisole minus a bra, and long colorful broom skirt.

"No, this business isn't Matt's full-time job," she explained. "He works about thirty hours a week as a custodian at the university."

"What about you? Where do you work?" Sam asked, squinting in the bright sun.

"I work part-time at Subway and St. Theresa's Nursing Home on St. Joseph's Ridge. The coin business is not booming. Not surprising, eh?"

"Have you ever seen any 1866 gold coins come into Matt's shop?" Leslie asked, her pencil poised above her notepad.

"Gold coins? Not that I know of, but I don't really have anything to do with Matt's business," Amy said rudely. Her eyes turned somber as her face darkened. "I have all I can do keeping Matt's rent paid and buying groceries."

"Is there anything else you want to tell us?" Sam asked quietly.

"No, should there be?" Amy asked.

"Not if you say so," Sam answered.

"Then I say so," Amy said. They chalked it up as a dead end but added the information to the board anyway.

Photos, slips of papers, receipts, phone messages, and copies of physical evidence from the victim were clinging to the whiteboard, filling and overflowing the space. The information started in one corner and made haphazard turns when the investigators added discoveries. The VICTIM and EVIDENCE boxes were filling up, but the MOTIVATION rectangle was clearly lacking. Greed? Financial Gain? Right now, that was all up for grabs.

Midmorning, Sam showed up at Jim's office. He stuck his head in the doorway and said, "I got a call back from the curator at Fort Crawford. She said there didn't seem to be any actual financial record of the lost payroll. But in looking back, she found an odd set of numbers in the margin of the 1866 record." Sam looked down at a sticky note and read, "T15, Q18, R7W, S26 was scrawled along the side of the financial figures. Whaddya think that could be?"

Jim was hunched over his computer. He sat up straighter and looked at the numbers Sam had thrust in his face. "Not a clue," he said, shrugging his shoulders. "Ask Leslie. She might have some ideas."

Sam wandered down the hall until he found Leslie. He explained and showed the numbers to her.

"Mmm, that looks familiar, but I don't know," she said. She copied the code on a sticky note and added it to the other pile of evidence she was sifting through. "Let me think on it."

Leslie was ruminating, pondering, meditating, whatever. She found police work very interesting. She was learning to balance activity with intervals to sit and theorize. Thinking was good, and she was doing some now. She sat staring at the sticky note with the number message. T15, Q18, R7W, S26. She had an uneasy feeling she should know what that meant. Something was beeping in her brain. Was it a code or something else?

She drifted back to the meeting room. The board sat like a permanent sentinel, daring the investigators to rack up evidence. Every once in a while, the current from the air conditioner would set the papers rustling, making them look as if they were trying to escape. She looked again at the map, studying the cave locations. If she were into spelunking, the evidence she'd uncovered would be a geographical trove. But dark, damp places were just about as intimidating to her as dusty, sandy roads. Unpleasant memories from Iraq flooded back. Comrades who were injured, maimed for life, or dead. She walked back to her cluttered workspace. The counter was spread with soil samples, Wisconsin geology books, and an array of photocopied maps from the USGS.

She couldn't get the numbers out of her head. She peered at them again. They sat crouching on the sticky note like a fly on a rotten banana. What if the letters and numbers were coordinates of some kind? Surveying? She leaned back in her chair, staring at the nothingness of the white ceiling. She thought a while, her eyes closed, concentrating. Yeah, surveying used jargon like that when identifying tracts of land. *Bingo.*

She searched the yellow pages and found a company named Blackhawk Surveying on Copeland Avenue. She dialed the number and explained her problem to the receptionist.

"Is there someone there who could answer a quick question about surveying?" she asked.

"Just a moment. I'll connect you with Erik." Leslie waited impatiently on the line, rocking in her office chair, tapping the top of her desk with her pencil.

"Yes, this is Erik Lundgren. May I help you?" he asked politely.

She identified herself. "When surveyors want to locate tracts of land for land descriptions, don't they use a series of letters and numbers? Kind of a specialized language?" Leslie asked

Erik took a breath and plunged in. "Well, there are many types of surveys that are typically done when highways, bridges, or other public structures are built. You have—"

Leslie interrupted. "No, no. Sorry to interrupt, but let me cut to the chase. Do the letters S, Q, T, and R figure into land descriptions?"

"Well, yes, they do. The S is for section, Q for a quarter, T for township number, and R for range. Those are simplistic, but they still work. However, today with our technology, we can pinpoint locations much more precisely."

"Okay, now we're talking," Leslie said excitedly. "So would it be possible to get a general location using those coordinates?"

"Sure. But we have drone services that can give an aerial view of the property. Would that be helpful?"

"I'm trying to find a specific location with pretty limited information. So what you're telling me is we could get a location from these coordinates and then use a drone to get an overhead picture of the property. Is that right?" Leslie probed.

"Yes, as long as you know the county and general vicinity where you think your property is. We could definitely help with that."

"Thanks. Do you have a cell where I could reach you? I may have to contact you for some work that needs to be done for the La Crosse Sheriff's Department."

They exchanged phone information. Then Leslie walked briskly to Jim's office and tapped on the door.

"Hey, what's up?" Jim waved her to a chair, turning to face her.

Leslie continued to stand. The sticky note clung to her right index finger.

"Just got off the phone with Blackhawk Surveying. I'm pretty sure the odd numbers and letters in the Fort Crawford records are surveyor's code. I think they may pinpoint the location of the cave. Instead of entering the lost gold amount in the records, maybe they just put it in a location where they planned to hide it?" she said, questioning her assumption.

Jim looked skeptical, but he appreciated the original thinking.

"Maybe," he said. *Interesting thought.*

"Can you get a hold of this Jamie Alberg, sir? I'd like to see where he thinks this cave might be. If he's been searching for eight years, he must have some ideas."

"Sure. I'll have him call you directly. What else do you need?" Jim asked.

"Permission to contact Blackhawk's services to use their drone. If we find the cave, we can get the precise coordinates of the cave with a drone," Leslie recited.

"Actually, we have a drone. But I'm not sure it would be very helpful. The trees and undergrowth will block a good view. I'd be more interested in getting a bird's eye view of the quarry. That might be helpful later when we go to trial," Jim said.

"Okay, I get your point. Good to know about the drone. Thanks," Leslie finished.

"I'll have Jamie contact you so that you can compare notes."

Jim stayed in his office and answered his incessant emails and returned his voice messages through the early afternoon hours. He walked downstairs to Sheriff Dave Jones' office and filled him in on the specifics of the case so far. Sheriff Jones made sure Jim understood if and when to call in the feds. The U.S. Treasury people might need to be contacted if the gold stash was found. *Developments. Things were breaking loose.*

He started thinking about the conversation he'd had with his daughter, Sara, yesterday. They usually enjoyed a simple and unhurried meal together once a week. Tuesday night had been no different. Sara arrived a little before five, and over a glass of wine on the patio, Jim had grilled steaks.

Sara seemed a little quiet as they ate. Jim thought she was probably just tired from her day of teaching fifth grade at St. Ignatius School in Genoa. But eventually, she came out with it.

"Dad, there's something I wanted to talk to you about," she finally said.

"Sure, honey, go ahead." Jim's gaze met her eyes. Her blond hair hung casually over her shoulders. Her minimal makeup made her beauty all the more alluring. Those green eyes.

"One of my friends sent me a Facebook post of you on *The Little Eddy* with Carol last Saturday." She waited. When Jim remained quiet, she continued. "I admit I was a little surprised. I didn't know you and Carol were dating." She hesitated, her eyebrows in a slight frown. Jim resisted the urge to interrupt, but he was a little surprised to realize he was the subject of a romantic post on Facebook.

"I guess I'm just having a hard time thinking of you with anybody other than Mom." She stopped abruptly. "Is that stupid, Dad?"

Jim took a deep breath and dived in. "Never. With your superior gene pool, stupid does not come into the equation." He chuckled, trying to lighten the conversation. It fell flat. "So, let me get this straight. You can't picture me with someone else, especially anyone other than your mom," he asked, his tone becoming more serious.

"Yeah, that's the gist of it," Sara said tersely.

He collected his thoughts and sighed.

"I apologize for not telling you. I've been trying to come to grips with being, well, single again. For a long time, I wasn't interested in anyone." He looked out at the trees gently shifting in the light breeze, then focused his attention on Sara again.

"I think I'm coming out of my fog, or grief, or whatever you want to call it. The last few months, I feel like I'm waking up from a bad dream that didn't seem like it was ever going to end." Jim rubbed his face and ran his hand through his graying hair. "You know Carol from way back. She was one of Mom's college friends. I helped Carol sort out a tough problem recently, and it felt good to encourage her. We've been getting to know each other a little better since then." Jim gave Sara a look of reassurance. *Just be quiet and let her process all this.*

Sara nodded. "Please understand, Dad. I'm not trying to interfere." She leaned back in the chair, her eyes focused on Jim's face. She had her mother's directness. "And I promise—no Facebook.

Just for your information, I've gotten a little bored with Facebook. Too many posts that mean absolutely nothing to me. It sucks up so much time. I really don't care if Gwen went shopping at Macy's and bought a new black bra." She tilted her head at him and raised her eyebrows. "Know what I mean?"

"Got it. So you're not glued to Facebook anymore?" Jim studied his daughter. Except for the eyes, she had his looks and her mother's carefree spirit. But since Margie died, she'd become so earnest and sober.

"Nope. To quote Sister Maxine, 'I've purged my soul of things that inhibit and detract from my relationship with God.' Boy, Dad. The Lutherans got nothing on the Catholics," she finished, barely cracking a smile.

Jim grinned, took another sip of wine, then said seriously, "I see you have some ambivalent feelings about me dating someone," he continued, "but I want you to remember this. I will never dishonor your mom's memory with something cheap. She was my love for twenty-six years. That will never change. But at the same time, I'm ready to move on. You know, I'm an old-fashioned kind of guy. I'd like to have a woman in my life again. And I enjoy Carol's company. Besides, before your mom died, she gave me permission to date Carol."

"What?" Sara's eyes widened. Her mouth hung open in amazement.

"I'm serious," he said. A moment passed. "You're going to catch flies or a frog with your mouth hangin' open like that." Sara snapped her mouth shut and swallowed. "We had a talk about a week before she died. She trusted Carol and thought we'd be a good match. She said I was too young to be alone." He let that sit a while. "So, let's not complicate this. Right now, it's just a casual friendship. I can understand that this might be hard for you to accept at the moment." He reached across the table and grasped her slender hand in his. Her gaze softened, and tears pooled in her eyes.

"Boy, Mom was one incredible woman." A tear escaped and slid down her cheek.

"Don't I know it," Jim said softly. He held her hand in a firm grip. They sat like that for a few minutes. Finally, Sara cracked the silence.

"Thanks, Dad, for talking me through it." She stood up, signaling her intentions of leaving. Jim got up and stood next to her. "I get it—I really do. You, of all people, deserve to be happy again." She looked at him with those same green eyes as Margie. She attempted a half-hearted smile, but it turned upside down. She began to cry. "I miss her so much."

"Me too, sweetheart. Me too," Jim said as his eyes misted over.

Suddenly, the noise of the outer office brought Jim out of his reverie. He looked up to find Paul standing near his desk.

"Whoa," he said, "didn't hear you come in. What's going on?"

"You're not going to believe it," Paul said, resting his hands on Jim's desktop, leaning in. Excitement sparkled from his hazel eyes.

"Surprise me," Jim remarked laconically.

"Remember Luke sent that pollen dust on Jorge's clothes over to UWL to some botany professor for analysis?" Paul asked.

"Sure I remember," Jim said with a slight frown.

"Well, when the guy looked at the pollen under the microscope, he also found something else. Gold dust." Paul gave Jim a look of amazement.

He sat up and listened intently. "Tell me more," he said.

Paul began talking rapidly. "Apparently, gold's extreme softness makes it susceptible to flaking off in bits that can be detected microscopically, especially if the handlers don't wear gloves. All gold coin collectors recommend gloves. Can you believe this?"

"Well, it's about time something went our way. So Jorge had more than casual contact with the gold coin. He must have been handling quite a bit of it. There's more of it somewhere," Jim said. He was thinking about Maria. She had to know about the gold. Jim wondered, *If this is a murder, she might be in danger, too.*

"What about Maria?" Paul asked, echoing Jim's thoughts.

Jim nodded. "What do you think we should do?"

Paul reflected, worry darkening his face. "Do you think we should set up some surveillance on her?" He straightened up and crossed his arms.

"I've thought about it," Jim replied. "We don't have enough evidence yet, although we're getting closer. Let's see what develops."

Paul pivoted to leave the room, then turned back to face Jim. He shook his head. "It'd be something if this hoard of gold really existed, wouldn't it? I'm starting to get the feeling it just might."

Jim's phone chirped. He answered and held up a finger to Paul. "Hang on, Jamie. Slow down. Where are you?" Jim grabbed his memo pad and began taking down directions. "Yeah, yeah, I got it. I know that area. I don't live too far from there. We'll be there in twenty minutes. Meet us there."

Jim grabbed his suitcoat. "Let's go. Jamie thinks he found the cave where the gold was hidden." Paul followed him as they walked briskly to the elevator. "I'll be out of the office for most of the day, Emily," he shouted as the elevator door closed.

Paul turned to him. "Whaddya mean? Where the gold *was* hidden?"

Jim and Paul sped south on U.S. Highway 35 along the river. The weather had been sunny that morning, but now a dark bank of clouds was building. In the west, a cluster of supercells was morphing and mushrooming in the sky, getting larger by the minute. Humidity hung in the air, close and stifling, like sucking air through a straw. Jim leaned forward. He peered through his windshield into the growing black and threatening shadows. A streak of lightning jumped and danced amid the ebony wall of clouds that obscured the blue sky, and an ominous rumble of thunder made a deep, resonant sound that filled the cavity of the truck.

"Storm's building. You can smell the ozone. We're going to get blasted any minute," Jim commented. He stepped on the accelerator.

"Slow down, slow down! We're close to the quarry," Paul cautioned.

"Yeah, I know. This is practically in my backyard." They sped up Chipmunk Coulee Road. Jim braked around the winding curves, slowing, then speeding up, until they gradually worked their way toward the gravel quarry.

"We need to find this dirt lane, some kind of field road beside the quarry," Jim said. "It snakes along to the upper rim of the quarry. Jamie said a footpath veers off to the right following the elevation of the land along the bluff to the south. We should be coming to it soon."

More continuous and threatening thunder growled in the distance. The wind stopped. The trees were motionless, waiting in suspended animation as if nature was holding its breath. Somewhere near the bluff, a crack of lightning flashed. Then raindrops splattered on the windshield, slow at first, then pounding in torrents on the Suburban's roof. Jim and Paul strained to find the lane in the heavy downpour. The hammering of the rain drowned out the possibility of normal conversation. Finally, Paul yelled.

"Whoa, whoa! Stop! Back up a little. I think we passed it." He pointed behind him.

Jim slowly backed the Suburban down the road.

"There, I see it, and that must be Jamie's Jeep," Paul said. Rain fell in a steady downpour. Jim steered the truck onto the narrow dirt lane, which was partially obscured by tall vegetation and overhanging trees. Standing among the trees, Jamie Alberg moved from the shadows, waving and flagging the truck to a stop. He was soaking wet and cold. A coiled black tactical rope hung around his neck, and he wore a backpack stuffed with camp shovels and other equipment. He opened the back door, threw in his gear, and slid onto the seat.

"Wow. That storm came up quick," he said. His hair hung in a mass of wet ringlets, and his shirt was plastered to his skin. He was covered in muddy streaks, but he wore a smug expression like someone who had just won a game of blackjack.

Jim turned in his seat. "So, what's going on?" he asked, scanning Jamie's wet clothes.

"You really want to know what's going on? I'll tell you," he announced loudly, his voice filled with nervous energy. His clothes and hair continued to drip on the floor and seat of the truck.

He pointed to the bluff. "This is what I'm talkin' about. I've dreamt of this day even when everyone told me it was just a stupid myth. They laughed at me, looked at me cockeyed, refused to give me one shred of encouragement. Even my mom and dad gave me sideways glances when I told them about the legend." His voice changed to a whining mimic. "Get your education. Get into a field where you can get a steady, reliable job, they said. But nobody believed in the legend. Everybody thought I was just some random goofball." He stopped for a moment, looking back and forth at Jim and Paul. His eyes flashed with intensity and focus. He took a few deep breaths. Jim and Paul stared at him.

"Okay. Well, we're listening now," Jim stated dryly.

"Who are you?" Jamie asked, pointing a finger at Paul.

"Paul Saner, detective," Paul replied, extending his hand.

Jamie looked at him with wide eyes, slowly grasping Paul's hand.

"Go on with your story, Jamie. We're all ears," Jim said.

"I used to talk to this old-timer, Jake DeSmith from Boscobel, who came to our treasure meetings sometimes. He's been sick, and he hasn't shown up lately. He usually comes with his daughter. So I borrowed my dad's Jeep and went to visit him a couple of nights ago." He smiled, thinking about the meeting.

"I told him about the victim in the quarry and the legend of the lost gold. And for once, I wasn't laughed out of the room. It seemed like the more I talked, the more excited he got. And then this incredible thing happened. He told me he had something he wanted to show me. Jake disappeared in the back of his house. I thought he'd probably never return. He's what you'd call a hoarder. He came out with a really old map. All crinkled and crusty."

"A map? You mean like a surveyor's map?" Paul asked.

"Yeah, kinda like a topographical map and a mining map combined that showed claims and the names of landowners way back to the 1860s. There were geographical features drawn on the map, too, along the river. You know, like creeks, outcroppings of rock, and caves."

"Unbelievable," Paul commented. He gave Jim a look like *holy smokes*. Paul gave Jim a questioning look. *Who is this kid?*

"Were there any letters and numbers on the map, like coordinates for surveying?" Jim asked.

"Didn't notice any, but there might have been," Jamie answered.

Jamie leaned back in the seat, his hair dripping. He relaxed a little and continued his story. "So I borrowed the map from the old guy and made a transparent copy. I overlaid it on a current topographical map of this area. I had to do some finagling to get them to the same scale. I studied it practically all night, and then I decided to check it out. I came out here today, just looking around, getting my bearings. I climbed and crawled all over the bluff. Pretty steep, kinda dangerous. My mom would've freaked out if she saw where I was. But I found it! The opening was just barely visible. I used my camp shovel and started digging very carefully."

"What makes you think this is the cave where the gold was hidden?" Jim interrupted.

"Well, someone was in the cave recently and tried to disguise the opening to cover their tracks. They had shoveled dirt and leaves and stuff up against it. If animals had uncovered the cave, like a bear or something, it would have been more open and littered with animal signs and scat." Jamie continued. "Remember my field of study?"

"Forensic archaeology, right?" Jim said.

"Right. I could tell by the soil's color and texture that the debris was disturbed within the last few weeks. I've hypothesized that this cave was probably discovered about six weeks ago. And there was some kind of activity here as little as three weeks ago."

"What did you find inside?" Paul asked, his mouth slightly askew with wonder.

"I didn't want to disturb the cave any more than necessary, so I just cleared the entrance. Right inside the entry hole, I found partial footprints, so I stopped. You know the cardinal rules of crime scene investigation." Jim's eyes widened.

Flaunting his expertise, Jamie continued. "Protect all evidentiary materials, so they're not lost, destroyed, or altered. And anything and everything is evidence. Right, Lt. Higgins?" Jamie's bright eyes searched Jim's face for approval.

Jim gazed at Jamie with a growing sense of respect. He didn't smile, but his eyes twinkled. "Right. Absolutely right," he said quietly. He looked at Paul. *Jackpot.*

The rain had slowed to a steady pattering on the roof of the car. For a few moments, the three occupants sat deep in thought. Jim was amazed at the kid's tenacity and toughness. *Can't beat passion to keep a dream alive. He was determined to find the treasure no matter what the obstacles were. Think of all the discoveries throughout history. Passion was the slow burn that kept dreamers focused and determined. They absorbed disappointments and setbacks until their eureka moment arrived.*

Finally, Paul interrupted the silence. "What's the plan, Lt. Higgins?" A breeze ruffled the trees as the rain diminished, then stopped. Jim rolled down his window, and fresh air streamed in, clearing the foggy windshield.

"Let's get a crime scene crew out here as soon as possible." He glanced at his phone. "Secure the site and block it off so we can keep curiosity seekers at bay." The line of Jim's jaw hardened. "If we have to use a vacuum cleaner, I want every piece of possible evidence taken from this cave. We've got one dead person, and there may be others if we don't move on this. Someone out there discovered the cave and coins. It looks like they're willing to dispose of anyone who gets in their way." Jim said, his voice gritty. "I'll get Leslie out here, too. She can bring that information about the surveying."

Jim reached for his phone and began making calls. Paul sat hunched in the passenger seat. As he organized the CSI people, Paul gave the wonder kid a quizzical look. Quietly basking in his discovery, Jamie gently pounded his fists on his knees, muttering to himself. Jim finished his phone call and turned to face Jamie.

"Listen, this is a really important discovery. Leslie Brown, one of our CSI officers, will be bringing some information that I want you to compare to the map you used. Hopefully, we can figure out how this all fits together." Jim was frowning, but somehow he looked pleased.

"I can't believe I actually found the cave," Jamie said, his voice wobbling with energy. "Oh, and by the way, this place is called Rattlesnake Hill. That's what it was called on the old map."

"Rattlesnake Hill?" Jim repeated, his eyes widening. "Really? Huh. I've lived in its shadow for over ten years and didn't know that. Listen, we need you to stick around and direct the crew to the cave. Paul will wait with you in your Jeep. And could you possibly reconnect with the owner of the old map? I'd like to copy it, and I'll need his permission."

"Sure. Glad to help. The entry to the cave is very steep, and now it'll be really slippery, too," Jamie informed them.

Turning to Paul, he said, "I'm betting the cave is on Andy Straken's land."

"Andy who?" Paul asked, not recognizing the name.

"Andy Straken. The quarry's on his land, so I think the cave would be, too." Jim glanced at his phone. "It's only noon, and I'm sure Andy would be home. I'll run up to his farm and see what his reaction is to this," Jim finished. "We're going to need his permission, anyway."

While Paul waited with Jamie, Jim drove up the twisting road to the Straken farm. Andy and his kids were cleaning the barn and shoveling out stalls. Inside, the fermented aroma of ripe cow manure and sweet baled hay mingled in the air. Cows outside in the cowyard bellowed a welcome to Jim when he appeared at the open end of the barn.

Andy was pushing a manure scraper up and down the cement aisle. One of his kids was walking behind him, spreading barn lime to absorb odor. Looking up from his work, Andy said, "Higgins. What brings you back here?"

"I was wondering if you were aware of any caves south of the quarry that would be on your land?" Jim asked, getting right to it.

"Caves? On my land?" he repeated, leaning on the scraper. He placed his hand on his chest as if to say, "Who me?"

"Yeah, caves," Jim restated.

Andy's brow wrinkled. *Was that an expression of worry or confusion?* Jim thought.

"I remember hearing stories about a cave over the bluff from my grandparents, but we were never allowed to explore on those cliffs. Too steep and dangerous," he answered.

"That doesn't necessarily mean you didn't investigate, does it?" Jim asked. "Kids do stuff they're not supposed to."

"Well, I never investigated anything over on the cliffs. I'm a chicken shit at heart. I have a terrible fear of heights. I get nervous just climbing my silos. I have three sisters, and if they would've found a cave, I think I'd have known about it. We were pretty close as kids," Andy said.

Jim continued to question him, coming at his story from different angles. Finally, he said, "Okay. I understand." And he did. He was 75 percent sure Andy was telling them the truth. Of course, he could be wrong. But he was glad he had come back and confirmed that the cave was located on Straken's land.

Shrugging, Jim said, "Well, maybe this news will surprise you. Maybe not. A treasure hunter has found a cave about three hundred feet south of the quarry over the bluff. We need to explore the cave. We think it may be important in relation to the death of Jorge Santana at the Chipmunk Quarry. Are you okay with that?"

"You mean will I give you permission to go on my land?" Andy asked.

"Yes, we need your permission," Jim said.

"Knock yourself out. You wouldn't catch me near that ledge. It's a long way down if you slip," Andy reminded them.

"Thanks. I appreciate it," Jim said, turning to go.

The crime scene crew arrived shortly after two o'clock just as Jim returned from the Straken farm. It wasn't until Jamie led them along a footpath above the mouth of the cave that they realized the entry was twenty feet below on a narrow ledge that jutted from the bluff.

One of the CSI crew members said, "Holy cow, getting to the entry of that cave will be pretty sketchy." He looked at Jamie. "You must be an experienced climber."

Jamie turned to him and nodded. "Approaching from the top is treacherous, and advancing from below is impossible."

Jim noticed the team was already slipping and sliding on the mud-slicked ground. He reconsidered his plan. If they weren't careful, someone would go over the edge to the sandstone bluffs and rocks below. After discussing several possible scenarios, they decided to call in a local firefighting unit known for its specialty in rock climbing and rescue. Their daring escapades rescuing overzealous climbers on Grandad's Bluff was well known.

They waited some more, the minutes ticking by. When the team finally arrived, Jim and Paul watched as Jamie and an expert guided two nervous CSI members over the edge as they rappelled onto the ledge outside the cave.

The work of collecting evidence began, but it was slow going. Mud, sharp jagged rocks, and thick undergrowth dripping with rain combined in a trifecta of endurance for the CSI crew.

About five o'clock, one of the crew let out a holler.

"Need Lt. Higgins for a minute," Les Riper said. "We found something interesting that he might want to see."

"Higgins is over there studying that old map with Paul," one of the crew said.

Les approached them holding a large plastic evidence bag and a smaller one. Paul rolled up the map and tucked it under his arm as Jim hovered over the large bag. They could clearly see a cloth sack through the plastic, now yellowed with age and dotted with holes from rot. Jim squinted at some faded lettering.

"What's it say?" Paul asked, moving his fingers over the bag to get a clearer view.

"First Natio … National, must be Bank of St. Paul," Jim recited.

"Some of the letters are faded, but they must have held the gold. How many were there?" He looked up at Les, waiting for an answer.

"So far, just this one. But we're just getting started," he answered.

"Good job. This is great. Let's hope we can find some other ones. But one will do," Jim said, grinning. "Excellent. We're getting somewhere."

"One other thing," Les Riper said. He held up the smaller bag. Jim and Paul took it and inspected the item inside.

"A button?" Paul asked.

Riper nodded. "Yeah, probably Civil War era. Proves humans were here quite a while ago," he said.

"Great. That's great," Jim said, smiling.

They visited a few more minutes, then Riper returned to the cave scene. In the early evening, Jim secured the cave with a couple of officers near the entrance to the footpath. As he drove off with Paul, he could see the halogen lamps glowing eerily in the early dusk as the moon rose over Rattlesnake Hill.

"We better put some surveillance on Maria," Paul suggested. "She's seen one of the coins, and she could be more involved than we think. Or the killer could be watching her, makin' some more plans."

"Yeah, she's got those two little kids, too," Jim said.

It was well after seven in the evening when he dropped Paul at his apartment. He drove back home and parked his Suburban in the garage. The rain had chilled him to the bone, so he headed for the shower. He dressed in jeans and a sweatshirt, slipped on his favorite boat shoes without socks, and opened the fridge. He dug out a Spotted Cow beer, humming under his breath. He cut a piece of pepper jack cheese and munched on it. He was leaning against the kitchen counter drinking his beer when his phone rang.

"Jim Higgins."

"Hey, I hear the Alberg kid turned in quite a performance, leading you seasoned cops to the famous lost cave," Carol said. Jim could imagine her smile on the other end of the line.

"Kid's no dummy, that's for sure. Plus, he got pretty doggone lucky," Jim commented. "But, I'll give him credit. He did use some good inductive reasoning. Saved us a lot of time and effort. But he could've been killed by some of those lightning bolts while he was hanging out so high on the bluffs. That's all I would've needed—a dead kid trapped in an unknown cave looking for lost gold. Can you imagine the headlines on that one? My butt would have been in the biggest sling ever invented." Jim took another swig of beer and a bite of cheese. "I suppose the whole department is blabbing about it."

"Oh, the hive is abuzz. I've got my sources, you know. Whoever discovered the gold has made some significant blunders already. Hard telling what else will turn up." She waited a moment. "What are you eating? I can hear you chomping on something."

Jim chuckled. "Yeah, just having a beer and some cheese." He thought for a minute, then said, "Hey, why don't you come over? I'll stir up some of my famous grilled nachos, and we can hang out on the back porch."

"Sounds good. I'll be over in an hour."

Jim drifted out to the back deck, lit the grill, and adjusted the vents, finishing his beer while he waited. He rooted around the kitchen, digging out his blackened cast iron frying pan. He layered corn chips, black beans, a little salsa, scallions, jalapenos, crumbled fried hamburger, and cheddar cheese in two alternating layers and then covered the skillet tightly with aluminum foil. When the grill was ready, he opened the cover and set the frying pan inside. He set the timer for twenty minutes. While the nachos grilled, he made salsa from cut up tomatoes, green pepper, cilantro, and lime juice. He was stirring the sour cream when he heard Carol's car coming down the driveway.

He waved her in from the kitchen window.

"Hi. Something smells good," she said, smiling as she walked into the kitchen.

Jim eased up to her and pecked her on the cheek. "I got soaked to the bone out there. I'm finally warming up."

When the nachos were done, Jim and Carol moved to the deck. A table was set with a couple of plates, condiments, and soda and wine coolers. They sat down.

"So, do you feel like you're any closer to catching the killer?" Carol asked, munching on her nachos. She got a dab of sour cream on her chin. Jim reached over and wiped it off.

"The things we're uncovering are helping us make connections. My team may be young, but that isn't stopping them. Still haven't formulated a theory, but we're getting closer."

He thought a minute and reached for his beer. Then he said, "Things have sure changed since I became a cop. With today's technology, things move so fast we can hardly keep up. Some criminal activity is very sophisticated, so we're constantly training our people about the latest advances. We have to be just as high tech as the cybercriminals, or we'll be on the short end of the stick.

"Does that include drug cartels?" Carol asked.

"Sure, but with them, it can be as simple as finding the right environment. Take Denver, for instance. Organized Cuban and Mexican drug cartels are renting and buying houses in upscale neighborhoods, gutting them, and growing pot all under the cover of "respectable" homes. Unless cops get tips from suspicious neighbors, the thugs are tough to catch." Jim sighed.

"Hope Wisconsin doesn't legalize marijuana. We better learn from Colorado's mistakes." Carol commented.

"That's the truth," Jim said.

They finished eating and talked some more about the case. Leaning back in their wicker chairs, they parked their feet on a footstool. The air stirred gently in the trees. Finally, Carol broke the silence.

"Don't you get jaded doing this kind of work? The good guys don't always win, do they? Must be hard to stay balanced and not get burned out," she said, looking at him with curiosity.

"Well, you probably experience some of the same things in your job," he replied. "It's easy to get discouraged and feel alone in the fight." Jim raised his eyebrows, shifted, and adjusted his shoulders.

"Keeping a balance is important in any job," he continued. "Everyone needs downtime and a regular life. I learned to confide in Margie. Some days require more endurance than others. It's good to know someone is there, ready to listen. I find my job interesting and challenging, and I have a good team. They're inexperienced, but we all were at one time or another." He paused a moment, thinking. "A sense of humor. Gotta have that."

"I have an advantage over you, though," Carol said seriously, her brown eyes locking on Jim's.

"Oh, yeah? What's that?"

"I work with the dead. They don't talk back or question my authority." Jim stared at her, and they both broke into a laugh.

"You've got a point there," he said, pointing his index finger at her.

"Just checking that sense of humor," Carol said, smiling, leaning back in her wicker chair.

"What about Luke? Must be hard to laugh somedays in his job," Jim said seriously.

"The last time I checked, the coroner was just fine. We just have our private jokes," said Carol, grinning. A few more minutes ticked by. "It's so beautiful here. Peaceful. Must be very rejuvenating," Carol said.

Jim reached over and took her hand in his. "There's something else here that's beautiful." He leaned over and placed a tender kiss on her lips, lingering for a little bit. "Not so sure about the nacho breath, but ..."

"Hey, speak for yourself, buddy."

They talked a while longer. Carol got ready to leave after they'd cleaned up the dishes and loaded them in the dishwasher. Jim walked her to her car. He pulled her into a brief but firm hug. "Remember our date Saturday night," he said, opening the driver's door. Carol slipped inside and rolled down the window.

"Looking forward to it." She looked up at him as he leaned down and softly kissed her.

SUE BERG

She started her car and drove down the driveway, beeping her horn briefly as she reached the main highway. Jim waved and thought about where he was going with Carol. Seemed to be a good direction. Leave it at that. ⊙

13

FRIDAY, JUNE 11

Leslie Brown woke to a slathering tongue on her face and a whole lot of dog breath.

"Paco, you old bum, you," she whispered, shifting from her stomach to her side, gently caressing his rich, velvety fur. Her blond hair fell across her eyes, and Paco nuzzled her under the arm, waiting for her to move. When Leslie threatened to doze off, he whined urgently.

Ever since she had returned from Iraq, Paco, her retired MWD (military working dog), had been her reliable friend and companion. He was a sleek black Lab with a keen intelligence, soft brown eyes, and an uncompromising sense of devotion. They ate together, slept together, and played together. Their deep, powerful bond had been forged on the missions they'd endured in the field, locating and detonating IEDs in combat zones frequented by U.S. troops and insurgents. Leslie and Paco were always in the lead on search and destroy missions where IEDs could be buried or hidden in roadside vehicles. Often, they were targets when disorder and chaos broke out.

Leslie struggled to completely trust her dog with her life when she began her handler training. How could a dog possibly save her or keep her from harm's way? But in Iraq, the dangers of combat, the

SUE BERG

grueling physical demands of the weather, the stark desert terrain, and the constant threat of firefights had taught her to trust the superior instincts of her canine partner. She had to. The lives of her company were at stake every day.

Paco understood his job. He had a vigilance that was otherworldly. He would never leave her. She belonged to him, and he belonged to her. Leslie had never experienced such an unconditional bond of love from another living being except for her parents. Someone had once told her that the bond between MWDs and their handlers was "the militarization of love." Yeah, she could agree with that.

They both had their issues. Paco had taken shrapnel in his hip once in a surprise firefight. He walked with a limp when he was tired, but his early morning jog and swim was the highlight of his day. Leslie had been injured twice in combat, receiving a Purple Heart. She struggled with the residual effects of combat, especially when she was physically tired and hungry. She had flashbacks now and then. She was learning to accept that her service had changed her, and now she understood she had to take good care of herself. Forgiving herself was a key component, too. Not everything she'd done was bronze star material. Being able to say, "It was the best I could do at the time," gave her emotional grace. It didn't solve everything, but it did give her a soft landing when she felt a crash coming on.

Leslie rose from her bed in one sleek, graceful movement. She used the bathroom while Paco huffed and whined a little, sitting at attention outside the door. He watched her change into her running gear, trading a nightie for leggings, a sports bra, and a T-shirt. She grabbed her apartment key from the hook by the door, put the lanyard around her neck, and tucked it inside her shirt. She tucked a plastic bag and glove in her pocket. By this time, Paco was on full alert, his eyes focused on Leslie, panting slightly. She grabbed his leash, hooked it on his collar, and closed the apartment door behind her.

"Okay, boy. Let's go," Leslie said.

They ran down the stairs, hitting their stride after warming up for a block or so. Leslie rented a duplex on La Crosse Street near the college campus. Myrick Park, a former petting zoo and playground, had been recently transformed into a center for environmental education. An extensive system of hiking and biking trails wound their way through the wetlands near the river. It was the perfect morning haunt for a run and swim.

Leslie and Paco picked up their pace as the world woke up. The morning was bright with sunshine, and a low scud hovered over much of the marsh. Birds high in the trees were calling to each other in a raucous chatter. An otter lifted his head and sniffed at them as they crossed one of the timber bridges. Then he slid silently into the dark water, only to reappear further downstream. Here and there, herons craned their necks, their beady eyes alert above their golden bills. Paco paused at random to investigate new sights and smells. His brown eyes scanned the terrain. His ears stood at attention as he picked up the morning sounds of an awakening world.

When they reached the La Crosse River, Leslie took off Paco's leash and let him jump in for his morning swim. She grinned as she watched him frolic and dive in the cool water. This was their daily routine, whether on this trail or another one in the area. Their run together each morning ordered her day and jump-started her motor, and Paco was in heaven.

Leslie found military regimentation hard to leave behind. She tried going home to Decorah, but the opportunities she was hoping to find in law enforcement hadn't materialized. In her more honest moments, she had to admit that being so close to family and friends seemed great at first, but then it grew stifling. Everyone was always thanking her for her service and asking her how she was doing. They meant well, and Leslie tried to appreciate it, but she struggled to put her life back together after her retirement. Missing the order and discipline of military life, she felt like a fish out of water. She felt the absence of her comrades deeply. Then, God had smiled down on her, and a CSI position had opened up in La Crosse. When she landed the job, she hoped it was the opportunity that would give her a chance to use her military experience and training to pull her civilian life together. It was early in the process, but she found the people friendly, the scenery gorgeous, and the job challenging so far.

She spent the last two years in the Army stateside after she was recruited to assist Dr. Rochelle Drummond in a new program developed to help soldiers recognize culturally important artifacts in combat areas. Under Dr. Drummond's direction, the soldiers were taught about local history and culture, which needed to be protected and appreciated if the U.S. military wanted to gain the locals' respect and cooperation.

Leslie had learned that real treasure existed. Protecting it from unscrupulous thugs and thieves was important work. Dr. Drummond, a preeminent archeologist from Rutgers University in New Jersey, had been guarding antiquities in war zones for years. The Department of Defense valued the curriculum she had developed. Leslie had been honored to work with her. During her years of service, she had developed an appreciation and knowledge of ancient art and treasure, particularly in the Middle East. Working with Higgins' team in a real mystery of the lost coins from Fort Crawford seemed tailor-made for her. That was an unbelievable coincidence—if you believe in coincidences.

Paco ran playfully up the steep riverbank, and Leslie reattached his leash. They finished their run arriving back at the apartment in time for Leslie's shower and a light breakfast. Paco retreated to the fenced backyard, and Leslie left for work.

Jim arrived at the office at seven-thirty, grabbed a cup of coffee, and headed to Leslie's work area. The CSI crew was at the cave site again this morning, continuing their search for evidence of human activity and the obscure gold coins. He was anxious to see what was being brought in from the cave. He found Leslie combing through a few bags of soil samples under a microscope, trying to identify particles that looked like metallic flakes. She continued separating and labeling other bits and pieces of material, storing it in baggies. Using a grid of the cave and notes from the crew, she recorded the location of the items she had identified.

"Morning," Jim said. "Looks like painstaking work." He was dressed in a pale yellow shirt with the cuffs rolled to the elbow, navy Dockers, and a tie that sported yellow, blue, and red paisley swirls. Subtle but in good taste.

"Morning, sir." She looked up from her task with a frown, ignoring Jim's pointed comment. A tiny tweezer poised in midair above her bright florescent lamp, and she had a look of intense concentration. "I've been thinking about this treasure and wondering if Jamie is the one who knows where the treasure is. Finding this cave with just an old prospector's map just doesn't sit right with me. Seems too easy. Had another thought after meeting with him at the cave."

She paused, studying Jim's reaction. He looked calmly at her and made a circular motion with his index finger.

"Keep goin'. I'm listening. Let's hear your theory," he said, "since we don't have one yet."

Leslie continued. "I learned a lot about treasure that disappeared in Iraq. Maybe Jamie already has the treasure socked away and is gradually unloading it to collectors. He could be taking us on some wild goose chase until everything settles down. These kids nowadays are very computer and internet savvy," she explained. Jim listened carefully.

"In the military, we were instructed to turn in any artifacts or cultural property to our superiors, but several times soldiers bragged about what they had taken. They unloaded the items online and put the profits in their pockets. Some of that stuff was very valuable. Keeping and selling it was illegal. And it also infuriated the Iraqis, making negotiations and tactical planning much more difficult. Maybe Jamie is doing something similar by keeping us close so he knows our next move. He might be selling the treasure to unscrupulous dealers online, then squirreling away the profits in some overseas bank account." She put the tweezers down next to her other tools.

Jim stood against the wall, arms crossed, watching Leslie. "Hadn't thought of that. He could be involved. Yesterday he seemed almost unhinged when he told us about his obsession with the coins. He's bright enough to carry out a complicated scheme, I'm sure." Looking at her, he said, "Don't know if he's capable of murder, but everyone could kill given circumstances that push them to the brink. If the treasure has been found, a ton of money is at stake. Millions, actually. Plenty of motive for murder. At this point, I'm still considering everyone connected with this case as a suspect, but nobody is standing out."

Leslie answered, "By the way, I contacted the people downstairs, and they're sending a drone out to get views of the surrounding area, including the gravel quarry and bluff this morning."

"Great," Jim said. "It'll be good evidence when this goes to trial."

Paul Saner came whistling down the hall and popped his head in the room.

"Is this where the meeting of the minds is happening?" he teased.

"Only people with thought-provoking, case solving theories are allowed to enter," Leslie piped back with a deadpan expression.

"Oooh. Well, in that case, what are you doing here?" Paul smiled. Leslie cocked her head and stuck out her tongue.

Jim sighed at the antics and rolled his eyes to the ceiling. "What's up?" he asked.

Paul put his hands on his hips and said, "Well, I thought Leslie and I could drive back up to the dairy and check in with Maria. Maybe we can—"

Jim interrupted him.

"Ahead of you. I stopped at Judge Benson's office and got a search warrant for her trailer and Jorge's truck. Been waitin' for you to get here. You two are with me. We're leaving right now." He turned and walked toward the door.

"Leslie, bring your kit and extra gloves," he said over his shoulder. Then he stopped and turned back, standing in the doorway. "We need to establish Maria's whereabouts for the last three weeks and especially this last week since her husband's death. We're going to take our time and go over every inch of that trailer and truck. We're looking for any evidence about their knowledge of the gold. Maybe we'll find something that gives us some ideas or will lead to some of their associates." Paul and Leslie followed him to the Suburban and piled in.

They fought through city traffic, climbing out of the river valley to the ridge above. The terrain leveled out. Wildfire Lane came up, and Jim negotiated his way around the puddles of rain from the previous night. The sagging blue trailer was still as decrepit as before. When Jim shut off the engine, the quiet was unnatural—eerie. The air smelled of ripe garbage, damp earth, and cow manure.

"Awfully quiet, sir," Leslie whispered, staring at the trailer. Her antennae were up, her senses on alert. "Didn't you say there are two little kids?"

"Yeah, there are two little kids. I'm getting a really bad feeling about this," Jim said, the hair standing up on his arms. He reached in his glove box for his holster and gun. Stepping outside the truck, keeping the open door between him and the trailer, he strapped on his police-issue revolver and slipped on a Kevlar vest. Paul and Leslie did the same. They got out of the truck, moving slowly and deliberately.

"I'll go to the door. You guys stay here," Jim quietly instructed. "Wait til I give you the all-clear." He moved out from behind the door.

"Maria. Maria," he shouted. No response. He walked carefully, placing his feet firmly in the grass squishing underfoot. "Maria, we're here to ask you a few questions," Jim said.

Stepping carefully on the rotting stairs, Jim stood on the landing and knocked on the battered, rusty door. Nothing. He noticed Santana's truck was missing. He knocked again—still nothing. The bad feeling was still gnawing at him. Finally, he lifted the handle and opened the door.

Jim went into the trailer and looked around. Scents of fried peppers and onions lingered in the air. He checked out the kitchen and living room areas, continuing cautiously down the narrow hallway, turning the corner into the back bedroom. Maria Santana was on the floor. He knelt beside her and snapped on a latex glove. No pulse. It was too late. She was gone.

Jim was not a cursing man, but he cursed now. He hung his head as if he were praying. This was as simple and complicated as it got. Maria was dead. From the looks of things, she'd been strangled, and she had put up a pretty good fight. Her neck had deep purple bruises from the ligature. Her arms were mottled with red welts, and her lip had been bleeding. One of her earrings was ripped from her earlobe. Jim swatted at a lonely fly hovering around his head, then stood. The tiny bedroom left him feeling claustrophobic. He unfolded his tall frame and glanced again at the vulnerable body of Maria. An overwhelming sadness mixed with a feeling of bitterness pervaded his thoughts. He swayed slightly. Then he walked from the room through the tiny hallway. His skin was crawling with the thought of the violence that had taken place in that tiny space. *God, you know this never gets any easier. Where are those two little kids? Please, Lord, let them be okay.*

Jim knew death was never easily explained or rationalized. Life was like the delicate thread in a tapestry. Cut the thread, and everything else comes undone. He groaned and walked to the door of the trailer. His blue eyes were dark with sorrow.

"Paul, call Luke. We'll need a couple guys. Maria's dead. Strangled. We need to find the kids and the truck. I'll call Sam Birkstein to come help Leslie. You're going with me over to the farm."

Leslie watched Jim step down the rickety stairs and walk dejectedly back toward the SUV. As a soldier, she had seen defeat before. One minute too late. One phone call you should have made. One person who didn't connect the dots. One decision waffled. Too late then. Too late now for Maria.

Paul and Leslie cordoned off the scrubby trailer site with yellow crime scene tape. A half an hour later, the crime scene crew arrived along with Luke Evers. Jim stood by the side of the bed in the tiny cramped bedroom watching Luke lean over the body. He seemed to hover uncomfortably close to the victim. The smells of rumpled sheets, sweat, and fear hung in the tiny cramped bedroom.

"I'd say she's been dead about eight to ten hours," Luke said. "So the murder probably happened around midnight, give or take an hour or two. Probably surprised her. She has superficial wounds on her upper body. She did her best to fight him off. We'll get her to the morgue and start the workup." He paused and glanced at Jim. "Sorry, Chief."

"Yeah, so am I." Jim's voice cracked, and his jaw hardened. His eyes were flecked with anger.

"Don't do this," Luke warned, looking up from his crouched position.

"Do what?" Jim snapped.

"Blame yourself. You deal with criminals every day. Sometimes they get ahead of you. Let it go. Slow and steady. That part of police work doesn't make the movies or TV." He locked eyes with Jim. "You'll figure it out."

Jim's shoulders sagged, but his anger continued to smolder like a glowing ember. "Maybe. I sure hope so," he added under his breath.

He turned and walked toward the front of the trailer. Paul and Leslie were taking the living room and kitchen apart inch by inch. The cramped quarters of the tiny trailer seemed even more stifling and oppressive as the three of them sifted through the personal effects of the young immigrant couple.

"Not a lot of paper," Paul said. "Found some drug paraphernalia. No coins, though."

Jim pulled out his phone and dialed Officer Sam Birkstein.

"Officer Birkstein."

"Sam. Jim Higgins here. Where are you?"

"Up on the north side looking for one of my informants. Not getting very far."

"Forget that. I need you to get up here to Middle Ridge right away." He informed him about the death of Maria Santana and gave him directions to the trailer. "I want you to help Leslie comb this trailer. We need to find out who Jorge's associates were. Hopefully, we'll find something that will send us in the right direction."

"Right. Be there in half an hour."

Jim pitched in, sorting through the detritus of a poverty-stricken mother. The fragments were a testimony to the destitution and poverty that had accumulated over the years. He glanced over at the refrigerator and noticed two hand-drawn children's pictures complete with smiling suns, colorful flowers, and a blue sky. *Oh, that life should be that simple,* he thought, closing his eyes for a brief moment.

When Sam arrived, Jim turned to Paul. "Come on. We're going over to the dairy farm."

"We've got this here, sir," Leslie answered. Her eyes met Jim's. "Just find those kids."

Jim and Paul jumped in the Suburban and headed down Highway 33 to Schoep's Dairy. Hiram Schoep was bent over the computer in his farm office, crunching numbers. He looked up as Jim knocked on the door.

"Hey, you're back," Hiram said, pushing his DeKalb's seed corn hat back on his head.

Paul and Jim found a couple of dusty chairs and sat down. "We've got more bad news, I'm afraid," Jim began. "We found Maria Santana murdered in her trailer this morning. It looks like she put up some resistance." He watched Hiram, gauging his reaction when he revealed that she'd been strangled.

Hiram turned pale, and a look of disbelief crossed his face. "Oh, boy. I knew Jorge had a history with gangs. Do you think this is some payback for a drug deal gone wrong?" Hiram asked.

"Could be, but I don't think so. Doesn't feel like that. Listen, I need to talk to your crew. Her two kids are missing. So is the truck that was parked there a couple of days ago. Any ideas where the kids might be?" Jim asked.

"We also want to know about anyone who might have visited the trailer in the last few days," Paul added.

"I've got enough trouble just keeping track of my crew here at work, let alone their wives and kids. Let's go to the milking parlor and ask around," he said, getting up from his chair. "Somebody might know something." He headed for the door, leading the way.

Paul and Jim spent the next hour interviewing and talking to the milking and feeding crew. Eventually, a Hispanic worker approached Hiram. In Spanish, he told him that his wife had taken the kids for a few days so Maria could make funeral arrangements for Jorge.

Hiram translated. He added, "Hace dos dias. That was two days ago."

Jim breathed a sigh of relief that the kids were safe. The innocence of children, broken and damaged by consequences they couldn't control, filled him with indignation.

"What about the truck? Anybody know anything about that?" Paul asked Hiram.

"It was a 95 or 96 red and white Ford F-350 dually. Pretty beat up. The front bumper was smashed. I think Jorge hit a deer with it. Probably uninsured," Hiram said, "and probably wasn't even licensed. Who'd want to steal that?"

Jim didn't respond. He noted the make and model in his notebook. "Thanks, Hiram. Here's my card if you think of anything else."

They continued to question the farmworkers until they were satisfied they'd covered their bases. One worker claimed he saw an SUV at the trailer a couple of nights ago, but his vehicle description was so vague, it was useless.

The rest of the day stretched out in a blur of phone calls. The collection of evidence from the trailer and cave continued. Jim called every junkyard up and down the river for thirty-five miles trying to locate the truck. He sent an email to all local law enforcement to be on the lookout for it. Most of the scrapyards only had an answering machine, so he left his name and number for a return call. By four o'clock, the team's energy was winding down, but they kept on until five. Jim scheduled a meeting for nine Monday morning.

Before he left, Paul popped his head in Jim's office, his jacket flung over his shoulder. Jim glanced up while he shut down his computer.

"What's up?" Jim asked.

"I'm playing at Diggers downtown on Saturday night. Just some champagne music. You know, Mancini, Sinatra, Lou Rawls, good stuff from back in the day. You might enjoy it."

"Saturday night?" Jim asked. "Maybe Carol and I will stop for a while."

Paul did a doubletake. "Carol? The Carol from downstairs?" he asked skeptically, pointing his finger at the floor.

"Yeah, the Carol from downstairs. Got a problem with that?"

"No, Chief. Heck, no. Go for it," Paul answered quickly, slightly embarrassed.

"Go for it? What am I going for?" he looked up at Paul, slightly irritated. *Kids nowadays.*

"Just a meaningless comment. She's nice. I'm glad for you." Paul held up his hands in a surrender gesture. "I'm leaving now. Maybe I'll catch you Saturday night."

"You might," Jim said, suppressing a grin.

As he walked to his car, Jim kicked at some loose walnuts that had fallen from the tree next to the parking lot. Every day when he left the building, he was always amazed that the world was still turning. The leaves were still brilliant green. Old Man River was still cold and flowing south. The weather dished out surprises while he struggled to keep evil at bay, making phone calls, chasing down leads, interviewing witnesses, and coming to dead ends. Good and evil advance side by side to the finish. He reviewed the day in his mind. *Well, I didn't lose my temper with anyone. And I didn't punch a hole in the nearest wall. Some days all I can do is thank God for the little things.*

Gordy Wilson cradled his head in his hands, wondering if he was having a stroke. His alcohol-induced pounding headache threatened to undo him. Lifting the coffee cup to his lips, his hands shook unsteadily, and coffee sloshed onto the table. He groaned when he thought about his unhealthy condition.

In his more honest moments, he was confounded that his life had slipped into such a downward spiral. Lately, he felt like he was spinning in his own lonely orbit around a planet that he didn't recognize. Suspended from his job as a cop with two failed marriages was depressing enough. Add multiple relationship disasters, a temper that jeopardized others' safety, and you had a bonafide catastrophe. He figured if he hadn't hit bottom yet, he was real close.

Regardless of his failures, Gordy still had a beef with Jim Higgins, especially since he'd horned in on Carol Olstad. She was supposed to be Gordy's new heartthrob, but like everything else, that had gone south, too. Higgins didn't play by the cops rulebook. To Higgins, a cop who didn't share his code of decency and moral uprightness was no better than some loser off the street.

Higgins could have covered for Gordy. Defended him. Given him the benefit of the doubt. Why couldn't he leave Carol alone so that Gordy could have another chance with her? Instead, he had betrayed the very code that cops were supposed to adhere to—defending and protecting their own.

He'd pay. Gordy would see to that. He flipped open his cell and punched in the number.

"Matt. Gordy here. I've got a little job for you if you're interested."

They talked a while.

"Yeah, I'm interested. Real interested," Matt Shafer replied, a reptilian smile creasing his face. ⊙

14

Saturday morning dawned warm and sultry. Earlier in the week, Jim had called his son, John, and they made plans to head to Timber Coulee on Saturday morning to fish the meandering creeks northeast of Coon Valley along Spring Coulee Road. The Coulee Region had become one of the premier flyfishing destinations in the United States. Rated Class 1, the trout streams in these valleys were stocked and managed by the Wisconsin Department of Natural Resources. Jim thought the trout streams were the sweetest slice of earth found anywhere. He was looking forward to a day of fishing and casting—cool, clear water, pristine surroundings, fat, healthy trout.

Jim puttered in his garage, gathering his fishing poles, tackles boxes, waders, vest, and a cooler filled with soda and beer. The sound of a truck on the gravel driveway followed by a familiar honk led Jim out of the garage into the warm sunshine. John jumped out of his Chevy Silverado with athletic ease. Built tall and lanky like his dad, he had darker features like Margie. He was the perfect combination of his parents. His easygoing demeanor hid a fiercely competitive streak that kept him busy playing golf in the summer and hockey during the winter. He strived to keep himself in top physical condition.

"Hey, Dad," John walked toward Jim and enclosed him in a bear hug. "I've been following that case about the gold coins you're working on. I've been over some of that terrain where that cave is located. Pretty rough country."

"Boy, you're not kidding. It took a raft of rescue personnel and a feat of engineering to get to the cave."

They loaded the truck with their gear and set off in the cool early morning light. John headed up over the hills and then dropped into Coon Valley. Woods and bluffs surrounded the sleepy little hamlet. They drove through town to County Trunk P toward Norskedalen, the Norwegian heritage center, then onto Spring Coulee Road.

John pulled off the road at a turnout and began unloading the truck while Jim assembled the fishing gear. The rippling waters of Spring Coulee Creek sparkled like elongated diamonds in the morning sunshine.

Gradually, the sun burned off the low-lying fog that had drifted through the hushed valleys. A rafter of turkeys with a newly hatched brood of chicks browsed in a hayfield nearby. Hay and cornfields bordered the streams. A red fox peeked out of her burrow in a limestone embankment while her kits played at her feet, nipping her mouth and nose. Wandering haphazardly in the open pastures, Holstein cows crunched on the grass. A few, having gotten their fill of forage, were lying under a huge cottonwood tree, chomping on their cuds, their eyes glazed with contentment. Occasionally, a tractor pulling a piece of machinery would putter by on the quiet country roads.

Jim waded into the stream. Donning his polarized sunglasses, he easily spotted the fish, their classic square tails swishing just beneath the surface. His mind drifted to his team.

With all the negative press about police brutality and overreach, it was a challenge to recruit dedicated, intelligent officers who have a heart for their community. Most of the time, detective work was a matter of citizen input, a spirit of teamwork, and a dogged determination to engage their working knowledge of the criminal mind and human nature.

Things were moving along in their current investigation. Leslie was a real asset, displaying a maturity beyond her years. Jim attributed her self-confidence to her military service. A pesky know-it-all, Jamie Alberg had provided crucial civilian assistance at just the right time. However, his continuing curiosity in the case could be a problem. Paul, as always, was steady and hardworking. Jim could count on him to have a balanced view of things. And then there was Sam with his goofy getups. A crazy combination of aloofness, intelligence, and a genuine interest in solving crimes.

The tale of hidden gold in the hills was pretty unbelievable to the team at the beginning. A criminal investigation can't be based on a myth. But that's what they'd done, although it made Jim cringe to think about it. The biggest surprise of the investigation to Jim had been finding the cave containing proof of the lost treasure.

Thanks to Jamie, discovering the cave had turned the whole case on its head. Now they found themselves continuing their line of investigation, zeroing in on the killer. Who was the killer? Didn't know yet. Who discovered and moved the gold? Didn't know yet. Would the killer become more desperate and kill again? Didn't know yet. Their progress was slow, but they were further down the road than they were last week.

Stepping carefully around rocks and avoiding holes, Jim found his new Sage Accel rod had a nice medium-fast action. He noticed John deftly casting further up the stream. His thoughts continued to swirl around the case, despite his promise to himself to chill out. The sun had climbed high in the sky. Jim cast his line with expertise form and his cap pulled low over his face. Concentrating on the deep shaded pools with rock walls and undercut banks, he landed several nice-sized fish in a few hours.

Toward noon, Jim and John took a break and stretched out under a low-branched maple tree on the banks of Coon Creek, enjoying some sandwiches and sodas.

The trout stream gurgled a few feet away as they sat in the shade of the overhanging branches. He paused, studying John's profile. He was so much like Margie. After a while, he said, "I'm glad we could get together today because I've been putting off talking to you about something. Sara came by the other night, and we discussed dating." Jim looked at John over his soda.

"You mean Sara is dating someone?" John asked, looking a little confused.

"No, no. I'm dating someone."

John held his sandwich in midair for a moment. "Whoa. Wait. You're dating someone?" He pointed a finger at Jim, which made him feel like the accused.

"Yeah, Carol Olstad." The creek spilled over the rocks, and the breeze rustled the leaves. White, puffy clouds floated in a brilliant blue sky overhead. Jim leaned back against the tree trunk and took a drink of soda. The silence went on, but he resisted the temptation to fill it with meaningless prattle. He waited a while. When John didn't respond, he asked, "So what do you think of that?"

John was quiet for a moment, then asked, "You mean what do I think of you dating Mom's friend? We've known her for a long time. How'd that happen?"

"Kind of a convoluted story, but let's just say I helped her out of a tough spot, and we hit it off. In fact, we're going to Leo and Leona's tonight for a concert."

John thought about that for a few minutes. "It's your life, Dad. I'm sure you know what you're doing. Carol's a great lady. We already know that."

"We're just good friends. It feels like the right thing."

"Sounds good to me."

After a while, John pulled out his phone and glanced at the time. "Speaking of dates, Jenny and I are heading to Rochester this afternoon to meet some friends for dinner. Hate to break this up, but

I gotta go." They began picking up the lunch and gathering their fishing gear together.

"Thanks, Dad," he said as they began trudging back to the truck.

"What a great day," Jim answered.

Meanwhile, Carol was considering the snacks she was bringing to Jim's for the evening. She decided on her standard grilled chicken tostadas with salsa and a nice variety of Wisconsin cheeses.

She'd spent the last year dating a few single guys from work, with only one slob in the mix, Gordy Wilson. *Sheesh. That was awful,* she thought. Now Carol realized she was deeply attracted to Jim. That was odd because Jim was so different from her former husband. Matt was capricious and spontaneous; Jim was steady and predictable. Creative and artistic, Matt could be self-absorbed and egotistical. In contrast, Jim was level-headed and analytical with a servant's heart and a humility that was touching. Jim was such a gentleman. Being a man of honor was not in vogue these days, but Carol found it disarmingly attractive. Thoughts about a relationship with him swirled in her mind. *Don't get ahead of yourself. Steady. Calm.*

She took a leisurely hot bath, thinking about the evening. They had never really been on a date, except for the boat trip on the river. Being rescued from an attacker and having nachos on Jim's back porch could not be classified as a date in anyone's book. Maybe that's why this night felt so important. Jim had seen her at her worst. Now she wanted him to see her at her best. She tamped down giddy feelings that could only be described as adolescent.

She opened her closet doors and stepped back, evaluating her clothes with a critical eye. It'd been a long time since she cared about a date. She finally decided on a pair of taupe pants with subtle embroidery down the side seams. A white tee and a multi-colored

Tuscan-style scarf added color. She wore comfortable cork sandals with ankle straps. A spritz of Sunflower perfume and she was set. Casual yet elegant.

A little before six, she packed her Jeep with the food and made the fifteen-minute drive to Chipmunk Coulee Road. Waiting in the car, she applied lipstick using her visor mirror until she heard the front screen door open. Jim stood on the steps.

"Come on in," he invited. "Drinks are on the back patio. Need help carrying anything?"

"Yes, I do," she said, getting out of the Jeep, walking to the hatchback, and opening it. She waved him over. Jim came around the fender.

"Wow! What a spread. Looks fantastic." He caught her eye, then said quietly, "You look fantastic, too. Very pretty."

"Thank you." Carol felt herself blushing, the pink color moving up her neck to her cheeks. "Come on. I need your help."

Glowing embers from the coals of a fire in the firepit on the back patio radiated a comfort and coziness to the outdoor setting. Sitting in Adirondack chairs, they feasted on the food and drinks. Laughter came easily, and the conversation was stimulating. By seven-thirty, they were in Jim's Suburban heading to Leo and Leona's.

"If it doesn't get too late, we can stop to hear Paul at Diggers," he said. Carol nodded.

Leo and Leona's Bar was located at the corner of County Road H and Highway 162 at Newburg's Corners. The official website listed Leo and Leona's as a historic bar that has the feel of a traditional roadhouse. The bar and ballroom had been the favorite haunt of the New Orleans Saints football team in the late 80s and 90s during training camp at the University of Wisconsin–La Crosse. The Saints loved the place because they could lose the press and let their guard down. Leo and Leona's borrowed a famous slogan from the TV show *Cheers*. "Where everybody knows your name, and they're always glad you came."

Jim drove up to the bar and found a random parking spot. The place was a two-story structure built in the late 40s. A green metal awning ran the length of the building with a white rectangular entry that seemed attached as an afterthought. It was decorated with a blue and red neon Old Style beer sign. Beat-up pickups and classic cars mixed with high-tech SUVs and trendy hybrids in the gravel parking lot. The vehicles reflected the eclectic make-up of the clientele.

Carol and Jim strolled into the bar, greeted a few acquaintances, and made their way to the renovated ballroom in the back. The bar had become a music mecca for local bands and soloists who performed everything from jazz to bluegrass. Strings of white lights flickered throughout the hall. The walls were festooned with humorous posters, sports memorabilia, a large U.S. flag, and beer signs of all kinds. Tables and chairs were scattered in an easy, relaxed arrangement.

"I've never been here," Carol said, sitting at a table, trying to get a sense of the place.

"Not much to look at, but it has atmosphere, great music, and great people," Jim answered, grinning happily. "It's one of a kind. You don't find places like this anymore."

By eight o'clock, the band The String Alongs had assembled their equipment onstage. Jim and Carol were soon tapping their feet and enjoying a great mix of bluegrass, country, and jazz. By the time the band's second set was over, they were making their way to the truck.

"That was great! Have you heard this band before?" Carol said as they walked through the parking lot.

"Yeah, at Riverfest and a couple of other times. Their Christmas concert is awesome. So how about a nightcap down at Diggers? Piano Man is entertaining, and I thought it'd be fun to end on a nostalgic note."

"Sounds good. A few oldies but goodies," Carol said as Jim opened her door.

Jim climbed in the SUV, reached over, and put his hand behind Carol's neck, gently pulling her toward him. "Thanks for everything," he whispered, kissing her firmly. He pulled away slowly, studied her face, and moved in again for another long, lingering kiss.

He pulled out of the parking lot, avoiding a group of revelers weaving toward their cars. Heading down Highway 33 toward La Crosse, he found Carol's hand and held it. He felt light and happy until he glanced in his mirror. A set of headlights was bearing down on him, coming way too fast. The vehicle quickly closed the gap and hung on his tail.

"Jim, what's going on?" Carol asked, her voice laced with anxiety.

"Don't know yet. Probably just somebody out for a joyride trying to get under an old man's skin," he said seriously.

Jim dropped Carol's hand and firmly gripped the steering wheel. Suddenly the pickup made a swerving move into the oncoming lane, accelerating while squeezing over toward the driver's side of Jim's SUV. Jim held his ground, giving none of the road. The pickup shot ahead and hit his brakes, sending Jim and Carol careening onto the shoulder of the road braking hard to avoid a collision. The pickup shot ahead again like a flying missile, but not before Jim noticed the missing license plates.

He stepped on it, studying the truck while he concentrated on stabilizing the Suburban. The threatening vehicle was a nondescript older model, a Chevy with an extended crew cab. Just as he was about to catch up, the truck bolted ahead and careened down a side road. Jim noticed a deep dent in the right rear fender and a yellow paint splotch near the back right taillight. He breathed a sigh of relief, but his anger bubbled over.

"Idiot!" he yelled, pounding his fist on the steering wheel. He pulled his cell phone out and called the sheriff's department, giving the road location and a description of the vehicle.

"… ran me off the road. I'm sure you won't find him, but I want you to try." More talking on the other end. "No, I think I was targeted." Jim listened some more, then clicked off.

Carol reached over and lightly placed her hand on his arm. "We're okay. It's okay," she said quietly. "Just some drunken bum getting a thrill."

They drove to Diggers downtown in silence. His enjoyment of the evening had ground to a halt. *Was the whole world filled with stupid jerks?* he thought. He found a parking spot, got out quickly, and helped Carol out of the SUV.

She squeezed his arm and tucked it under hers, sliding in close to him, sensing his mood change.

"Hey, don't worry about me. I've been lost in a swamp. Remember?" she said, smiling. She felt Jim's arm relax.

"Yeah, I remember," Jim said, feeling some of the tension dissipate. "You're something else, you know that?"

"People tell me that all the time," she joked. "Not."

Paul was at the baby grand in the corner of the bar, taking requests. He looked up, noticed Carol and Jim, and waved. Jim recognized a little Nat King Cole. He led Carol to the tiny dance floor and pulled her close. His hand rested lightly on her back. He was a good dancer. A little out of practice but with a smoothness just below the surface. Jim hummed the tune in her ear. *Unforgettable, that's what you are.*

"I really enjoyed tonight," Jim said softly in her ear.

"Me, too." She looked up at him. "Where'd you come from anyway?"

"What do you mean?" he asked, unsure of her question. Her brown eyes were very inviting. He felt a little zing when he looked at her so close.

"You're way too good to be true in this day and age. You must be from another planet."

"Just hang on. You ain't seen nothin' yet," he said, smiling, pulling her close. ⊙

15

MONDAY, JUNE 14

Jim stood in the meeting room on the third floor of the law enforcement center, waiting for his team to arrive. He glanced at his cell—8:42 a.m. The room was stuffy and smelled of magic markers, old coffee, and dust. He walked to the window, cranked the handle, and pushed it out. A puff of cool air rushed in, refreshing the stale room. In the back of his mind, he was still torqued about the crazy driver's attempt to run him off the road Saturday night. But he let it go. He had bigger fish to fry at the moment.

He had dressed carefully this morning in crisp navy slacks, a pale blue dress shirt, a vintage Swedish tie in reds, grays, and blues from his college days, and a lightweight navy blazer which hung smartly on his lean frame. His team began straggling in a little before nine. Jim greeted each one and picked up on the somber mood in the room. He wasn't sure whether the mood was from discouragement or lack of insight, or both. Maybe they were just hungover, although he hoped they'd had time to unwind over the weekend. With two murders and no real leads on the perpetrators, Jim knew things had to change. At the beginning of an investigation, his gut feelings weren't always the most reliable, although they were usually a good indicator of the difficulties ahead of them. For now, there were still too many unknowns to be certain of the outcome.

The whiteboard, that familiar harbinger of events and facts, stiff as a sentry, seemed to accuse them of incompetency and lack of progress. Peppered with paper litter and slips, scrawled notes taped here and there, and USGS maps with circled cave locations, the board was a hodgepodge of data and a wonder to behold. Jim stood in front of it, his head tipped, rereading the scribbled questions that vaguely hinted at a solution. Despite its inanimate nature, Jim felt taunted with annoyance at the items clinging to its surface. He had written a quote on a piece of cardboard and stuck it to the top of the board with duct tape: "To conquer frustration, one must remain intensely focused on the outcome, not the obstacles." It was a noble sentiment written on crude paper.

"Morning," Jim began. He was tempted to say, "Let's pray." He realized it probably wouldn't hurt, and it might even help. Instead, he went on. "Let's outline our focus for the next few days."

Sam was stationed at the board. He ran his slender fingers through his thick, wavy hair, picked up a marker, and waited for something to write.

"Nice quote, Chief," he said softly. Jim rolled his eyes.

Sam Birkstein was a study in contrasts—dark, swarthy good looks combined with a lean, muscular body. Jim didn't think he'd ever seen him dressed in anything but wrinkles. Wrinkled shirts, rumpled slacks, and mismatched socks gave him a waifish look. Whether it was intentional or not, Jim couldn't tell, but his innocent demeanor had the women in the secretarial pool fawning all over him. Despite Jim's disapproval, the women frequently fussed over him and tried to mother him. The kid's intellect and razor-sharp mind constantly surprised everyone, but he looked more like a homeless vagrant than a professional member of an investigative team. Lectures about the standard dress code had fallen on deaf ears. *Pick your battles,* Jim thought.

"As you might have seen in the news, we've released information about the death of Maria Santana. We need to focus on our outcome,"

Jim said, pointing to the quote, "which is to catch this murderer. We've got a slew of obstacles to overcome. The killer could have his eye on another victim, or he could be moving the gold out of state. Leslie pointed out the possibility of dumping the gold online."

Jim glanced her way, then continued his assessment. "We all need to crank up our observational skills. I'm not sure what the relevance of this is to this case, but I was run off the road Saturday night. I can't prove it was related, but it might have been. So be careful and be aware of your surroundings," he warned. The room stayed strangely quiet. Jim continued.

"Maria deserves an advocate, and right now, that's us." Jim's voice took on an intensity that made everyone sit up. "Those two little kids are going to want to know the history of what happened someday. They'll want to know that we did all we could to get her justice. I don't want to be the one who drops the ball on this," he finished, looking seriously at each member of his team.

His crew studied him, their eyes searching his face. Jim hoped he was getting through. He went on.

"That Walmart receipt in Jorge's pocket might give us information about his movements. Was he with someone? What did he buy? Do they have video surveillance of his purchase? Anybody have other thoughts?" Jim asked.

"I can check on the Walmart stuff," Sam said.

Jim nodded. "Okay. One other thing. Maria was strangled, but we didn't find the ligature or whatever was used that might give us the killer's DNA. This time, the killer was careful. If it's the same perpetrator, whoever murdered Maria is getting a little smarter. They probably used gloves. Maria's murder was planned and executed with cold-blooded intent, unlike the first one, which looks like it might have been an accident." He stopped, then started again. "We may be looking at one killer or two. Hard to tell at this point. Anybody else have anything?"

Leslie spoke up. "We're checking Maria's phone to see what calls she made in the last month and especially the last few days. Haven't found Jorge's cell, although Maria claims he had one. It seems to have disappeared. Maria told Paul there was some drug-dealing activity happening at the trailer, and we did find drug paraphernalia in the home. Identifying those who might have bought from him is harder, although Sam's been checking with his informants on the street. Maybe we'll get a lead from one of them. There has to be someone who knew him in the drug world. Maria was probably killed because she knew something about the gold and the drugs." Leslie stopped and hesitated. "I have the distinct feeling she knew her killer."

"I agree," Jim said. "Anything else?"

"Well, thanks to Jamie Alberg, we know the treasure exists. That was a surprise," Paul said. "With Leslie's coordinates from Fort Crawford and the old map Jamie found in Boscobel, the existence of the original treasure appears to be authentic. We found that old Bank of St. Paul bank bag, which makes the tale believable. What we really need to do is find that truck. It probably was used to transport the gold to another location. We're still sifting through all the cave stuff. There were traces of gold dust in the soil from the cave, and we did get a good partial footprint near the entrance, but it didn't match the shoes Jorge was wearing when he fell from the edge of the quarry. That doesn't mean he wasn't there, but it might match the shoes of the killer when we find him."

"Glad you said when and not if," Jim said, raising his eyebrows.

Paul kept on. "Like I said, the gold dust found near the wall of the cave seems to verify that the gold exists. Right now, we just don't know where it is or how much of it there is." Paul finished. "It would have been helpful to locate more of the coins."

Another interruption. "One more thing," Leslie said, holding up a small card. "I found a business card for Bargain Coins in Maria's garbage. There has to be a connection. We just have to find it. Sam and I already made one visit to that shop, but there's something else going on. That can't be accidental. We need to follow up on that."

"Good," Jim said, pointing to Leslie. "We'll run over there later."

Jim was perched on the edge of a tabletop, his arms crossed, listening carefully to the reports. "Okay, let's keep working. Follow your instincts," Jim emphasized.

"We got it, Chief," Sam said, laying down his marker.

Everyone ambled back to their cubicles. Paul followed Jim to his office, pulled a chair from the corner, and plopped down. They talked a while about the case, and gradually their conversation turned to fly fishing.

"Got down to Timber Coulee and did a little casting with John this weekend," Jim commented. "That new Accel rod that I got for my birthday from the kids was smooth. It worked great. Weather was perfect. I caught some nice rainbows."

"It was good to see you and Carol out together. You looked like you were enjoying each other," Paul commented.

"Yep. Had a nice weekend," Jim said tersely. Paul left it alone and moved down the hall to his office. *Higgins could be standoffish,* he thought. Sometimes he was hard to read, but you couldn't doubt his commitment to law enforcement. That's who he was.

Leslie Brown spent the morning sifting through the stuff they had removed from the trailer on Wildfire Lane. She peered through plastic evidence bags that contained paper of all kinds and sizes. Receipts, coupons, business cards, and other stuff that had been sorted at the trailer were piled on her counter. The contents of a locked metal box held the birth certificates of their children, Mexican citizenship papers, and two unfinished applications for American citizenship. All of it had to be listed and recorded as seized evidence. The business card from Bargain Coins irritated her like an itch she couldn't scratch. She walked down to Jim's office.

"Sir, when do you want to visit Bargain Coins?" she asked.

Jim looked up from his computer screen, then glanced at the clock. "How about one?"

"I'll be ready," she said.

Later, Sam strolled down the narrow hallway, knocking on Jim's office door.

"What now?" Jim asked, not unkindly.

"Talked to the manager at the Viroqua Walmart. He checked the video for the day of the receipt. He emailed a photo of Jorge at the self-checkout. He was alone. The image is clear and clean. What about releasing it to the evening news? See if someone in the area remembers seeing him around. Might lead us to some of his buddies." He leaned against the door frame.

"Good idea. Make a copy for distribution. Contact Jim Lauer downstairs in PR and have him release the image on tonight's broadcasts. Run it on the morning shows tomorrow, too. I'll send a press release down to go with the photo."

"Got it, Chief," Sam said, disappearing down the hall.

Before lunch, Jim heard a ruckus in the outer office as he worked at his desk. He hoisted himself out of his chair and stood in the hallway with his hands in his pants pockets. He watched Jamie Alberg arguing with Emily, his hands making choppy motions in the air. His communication skills left a lot to be desired.

"You have to let me see Lieutenant Higgins," he was saying. "I need to talk to him right now!" His voice was loud and insistent, bordering on disrespectful.

Emily caught Jim's eye as he mouthed, "It's okay." He motioned Jamie to come through, pointed him to a seat in his office, and asked, "So what's on your mind, Jamie?"

"Do you know who the killer is yet?" he asked anxiously, his eyes wandering to Jim's awards on the wall.

"No, we don't," Jim answered. "Do you?" Jim's cool blue eyes remained fixed on Jamie.

Jamie looked startled, his eyes darting around the room. He jiggled his leg nervously, then stopped when Jim noticed it. "Well, why would I know who the killer is?" he asked defensively, sitting forward in his chair.

Jim let the tension percolate. Finally, he said, "I don't know. Is there a reason you're asking about the killer? Could he be one of your treasure hunting buddies?"

Jamie hunched his shoulders and pulled the corners of his mouth down.

"How should I know?" he replied sarcastically. "Whoever he is, he's obviously desperate to keep the gold in his possession. Plus, he's murdered two people, which makes him pretty dangerous, I guess," Jamie concluded weakly, watching Jim's reaction.

"You guess? Yeah, that's pretty evident," Jim replied, trying not to sound impatient. "Was there anything else you needed, or you wanted to tell me?" Jim ran his hand through his graying hair. Didn't he have enough to do besides babysitting this kid?

"No, not really. I was just wondering if there's any other way I could help you." Jamie looked at Jim hopefully, like a kid who wants an ice cream cone right before supper.

"Yeah, there is one thing." Jim stopped, still standing behind his desk, making sure he had Jamie's attention. His mood turned a shade darker, and his voice took on an air of hard professionalism. "You need to understand the seriousness of this investigation. This isn't about you using your amateur sleuthing skills in forensic archaeology." Jim wrestled to keep the sarcasm out of his voice.

"We appreciate all your help, but you have to realize this killer will zero in on anyone. Did you get that? *Anyone* who is a threat. That could very well include you because you know quite a bit about the gold coins. And now you know about the cave. You need to be very careful and quiet about the discovery of the cave. I don't want to find you in trouble with someone who wouldn't hesitate to eliminate you and what you know." He stopped lecturing, noticing Jamie's raised eyebrows and pallid face. "Understand?" He adjusted his tie, waiting for Jamie's response.

Jamie stared wide-eyed. Seconds ticked by, the silence permeating the office.

"You look weird," Jim said. "What's the matter?" He groaned, and his shoulders slumped. "Who'd you talk to?" He waited. Jamie sat in stunned silence. "Tell me," he demanded.

"Well, I posted a video of the cave on Facebook this morning," he said, cringing. His body seemed to fold in on itself, shrinking until he was cowering in his chair. "I thought it might help." His voice petered out until it was barely a whisper.

Jim grappled with his anger, but he lost it. His clenched fists slammed the top of his desk. Pens jumped, and papers fluttered to the floor. Jamie flinched and jerked in his chair.

"Are you kidding me? You posted the cave on Facebook!" Jim snarled. Noticing Jamie's frightened expression, he forced himself to take a deep breath. In a calmer voice, he said, "Police investigations are confidential, Jamie. They have no place on social media unless someone in the department approves them. This could have some serious ramifications in our investigation. It could even put you in danger."

Suddenly Emily peeked her head around the door. "Is everything okay in here?"

He took a couple of deep breaths. "Yeah, we're fine."

He looked back at Jamie, and when he spoke, his voice was tight. "I don't have enough manpower to protect you, Jamie." He rolled his shoulders, giving himself time to gain control. "You're going to find yourself in a conundrum if you keep it up."

"I'm sorry, Lt. Higgins. Really, I am. You've got to believe me," Jamie responded weakly.

Jim waved him off, his anger still simmering. Finally, he said, "You need to stay holed up somewhere, preferably at your parents' residence for the next few days until we get a handle on where this is all going."

Calmly he added, "Listen, Jamie, you have my cell number. I want you to stay out of sight. You need to be accountable to someone at all times. If you get in trouble or get a threatening text or a phone call, contact me. Tell your parents what's going on, so they know where you are. All. The. Time. Deal?" There was a moment of hesitation.

"Deal," Jamie agreed, his voice soft with regret. He rose to leave, hanging his head like a whipped puppy. "I'll be okay, Lt. Higgins. I can take care of myself. Really, I can." He slowly backed out of Jim's office, turned, and dashed to the elevator. The eyes of the women in the office followed Jamie until the elevator door swished shut. Jim stood in the lobby, his tie askew and his face haggard. The women's eyes shifted back to Jim.

Emily gave him a puzzled look that said, *What in the world was that all about?* Jim shook his head and gave her a frustrated wave. Walking back to his office, he closed the door softly, leaned against it, feeling as if he were keeping the world out.

Jim took his phone out of his shirt pocket and went on Facebook to view the cave video. He sputtered in frustration and swore softly as he listened to Jamie give a blow by blow account of the cave's discovery. There was a quiet knocking on Jim's office door. He opened the door, and Leslie said, "One o'clock, sir. Remember? We're going down to Bargain Coins."

"Sure, sure," Jim answered distractedly. "Let's go." Looking pale, he slipped his phone into his pocket. His stomach growled loudly, and he realized he was starving.

"Are you all right, sir? I thought I heard some racket down this way," Leslie said, her face tight with tension.

"Remember that comment you made about Jamie the other day? About him being a little too interested in this case?" Jim asked.

"Yeah, I remember, and just for the record, I'm still kinda suspicious," Leslie replied.

"Wait til you hear what he's done now. I could kick myself in the butt for letting him get so involved." He scrunched up his face. "I'll explain on the way," he said, grabbing his jacket. "Come on."

On the way across town to the north side, they stopped at a McDonald's drive-through and grabbed sandwiches and drinks to go. Between bites of sandwich, Jim told Leslie about Jamie's latest caper.

"I haven't been that mad since my son John wrecked my car after a party in high school. Of all the stupid stunts he could have picked, he had to post that on Facebook! Let's tell the world everything we know and throw in a few untruths to boot." Jim waved a couple of fries in the air as he talked.

Although there was some truth in the video, the exaggerations and the grandstanding nature of it threatened to derail the progress they'd made in the investigation. It would wreak havoc on the facts the team had so carefully presented to the public. Relating the incident to Leslie had fired up his anger and frustration again. He was still simmering, but he was really more disappointed in himself. He'd had a slip in judgment when he let a civilian—no, a teenager—become entangled in the investigation. It had gotten out of hand.

"Well, that does sound bad, sir. Can't say as I blame you for being ticked," Leslie commented.

"Ah, it's my fault. I should have shown him the door a long time ago."

They pulled over and parked next to the curb on Gillette Street where Bargain Coins was located. It was a private residence with a back door office. A dilapidated sign hung precariously on a fading post near the driveway. Leslie and Jim walked to the front door of the house, but everything remained quiet as they rang the doorbell several times.

Jim eased down the driveway, his senses on high alert. He could feel the weight of his gun under his coat. Leslie walked quietly next to him, treading lightly.

"This reminds me of some of the missions I've been on. Everything's quiet until all hell breaks loose," she whispered, remembering the eerie sense she got when something suspicious unfolded.

Jim tapped on the office door despite the CLOSED sign that hung crookedly on the screen-door frame.

The place was in a severe state of neglect. The grass hadn't been mowed for weeks, the garbage cans near the garage in the back were overflowing and stinking in the summer heat, and weeds grew up between cracks in the cement driveway. A piece of cardboard from a potato chip box covered a cracked window pane near the back door. Emerging from beneath the steps, a scrawny calico cat meowed at

Leslie's feet, rubbing against her legs for attention.

"Think maybe they've flown the coop?" she whispered. Jim smiled at the barnyard euphemism.

"Looks that way," he said as he turned and continued walking toward the back of the lot. A forlorn sagging garage can sat at the end of the driveway. Jim and Leslie waded through knee-high weeds and grass that surrounded the perimeter of the garage. Jim stepped up to a window, peering into the structure.

"Well, look what we've got here," Jim said softly, tenting his hand over his forehead as he pressed his face up to the window. He recognized the Chevy extended crew cab by the dented fender and yellow paint splatter next to the taillight.

"I wasn't expecting this. This is the truck that tried to run me off the road Saturday night. That was no joy ride. It was a warning or payback of some kind." Jim glanced at Leslie. *Gordy,* he thought.

"What now?" she asked, her eyes wide.

Jim flipped out his phone and dialed Paul. "We found the truck that ran me off the road Saturday night," he said. "I need you to get over here to Bargain Coins at 507 Gillette Street as soon as you can."

"I'm not far away. Be there in ten minutes," Paul answered.

Jim returned to the rear entrance and began pounding aggressively on the back door without letting up.

"Sheriff's department. Open up! We have some questions," Jim yelled as he pounded.

After several minutes of continual beating, the CLOSED sign wiggled. A young woman with a disheveled curly mop of hair appeared in a tank top and pair of Spandex. Amy Bergholt frowned. Her sleepy eyes swept back and forth over Jim and Leslie. "What? Whaddya want?" she snarled, looking testy.

Jim flipped open his ID badge. "We need to find Matt Shafer."

"Matt! Matt!" the young girl yelled into the depths of the darkened house.

Jim turned to Leslie and ordered, "Cover the front entrance. He may try to run."

Just as Leslie sprinted to the street, the front door burst open. A dark-haired man cleared the front steps, hightailing it down the street with Leslie in pursuit. Jim began sprinting after Leslie, pumping his legs hard, his tie whisking in the wind until he caught up to her.

Paul had just turned on Gillette. As he approached the house, he noticed the chase. He accelerated down the street and hit the light bar. Twenty extra pounds and a smoking habit slowed the man considerably.

Within a minute, Leslie had tackled him to the ground, restraining him in somebody's front yard. Jim assisted in subduing him. The Coin Man resisted vehemently, sputtering off a string of profanities. Escorting the puffing man back to the squad car, Leslie placed him in the back seat, where he slumped in glowering silence. Amy, the girlfriend, watched the whole incident from the front yard of Bargain Coins. She stood in stunned silence as her live-in boyfriend was arrested.

Jim glanced over at her, still breathing hard, and said, "I need you to come down to the sheriff's department to answer some questions."

"Can I get some shoes first?" she asked timidly.

Jim looked down at her bare feet. "Sure, I'll wait," he said.

Paul drove the car down the street and stopped in front of the house, turning off his flashing lights. He rolled his window down and said, "I'll see you downtown with Happy Feet in a few minutes."

"Right. I'll bring the girlfriend," Jim answered.

Jim searched through his directory on his phone and found the A&P Auto Towing number. He talked to the dispatcher and gave orders to have the Chevy truck towed to the impound lot behind the sheriff's department. Then he and Leslie headed back downtown with Amy Bergholt in the back seat.

Downtown at the La Crosse jail, Matt Shafer, the owner of Bargain Coins, sat in an interrogation room. He fidgeted and sipped on a bottled water. He looked strung out, tired, and extremely irritated. He had a record of drug dealing, and he had spent several months in jail for traffic violations, the result of high-speed chases.

Jim and Paul entered the room and sat at a table across from Matt. Leslie stood by the wall and assumed a nonchalant pose. Matt's hostility toward them was evident in his hooded eyes and blazing defiance. He looked like a falcon ready to seize his prey. Rigid and tense, his eyes wandered from Paul to Jim, sizing them up. He crossed his muscular arms over his chest in a defiant attitude.

Throughout the interview, Matt denied any involvement in the murders of Jorge and Maria Santana. Disavowing any drug sales, he adamantly protested when Jim accused him of the road rage incident on Saturday night.

"Prove it," he snarled, his lip curling with disdain.

"Right now, I can't," Jim said calmly. "It's your word against mine, but I recognized the truck in your garage. It's the same one that forced me to take the shoulder on Saturday night up on Highway 33." Jim stared down the surly youth. "Where were you Saturday night?"

"I was home with my girlfriend."

Jim ignored his response. He was lying.

"Why were you trying to run me off the road? Who's behind this?" Jim asked. "Some drug buddy of yours? Or are you the gopher for the murderer? Did you help him move the stash of coins?"

"I don't know anything about murder or running cars off the road. Why would I want to do that?" he said. He flashed his angry eyes at Leslie, who remained calm, returning a cool stare. She'd had plenty of experience interviewing high-value detainees in Iraq. Matt's behavior didn't surprise her. She'd seen it before.

"Is that what your girlfriend, Amy, is going to tell us?" Paul asked casually, examining a fingernail.

"How would I know? She can answer for herself," Matt snapped, his eyes sparking with frustration.

"Do you know Jamie Alberg?" Jim questioned.

"No. Should I?"

"Have you recently had anyone come to your shop with an 1866 twenty-dollar gold coin?" Jim asked, keeping his voice flat and focused.

"They're pretty rare." Matt stopped himself. "No, I've never had one in my shop."

"What kind of clients come to your shop to sell and trade coins?" Paul inquired, his hands clasped calmly in front of him.

"My business is mostly locals. Collectors, antique dealers, numismatists—those types," he said, his arms still crossed in a hostile pose.

They continued hammering out questions, taking turns probing and interrogating. Finally, after an hour, Jim and Paul looked at each other. Jim chinned in the direction of the door, and all of them took a break, leaving Matt to stew.

Out in the hallway, Paul said, "We can let him go and get a search warrant to go through his place."

Jim shook his head. "No. Let's hold him for assaulting a police officer using a motor vehicle. That will give us another opportunity to question him if we need to go through his place," Jim said. Leslie listened carefully.

"Okay, we'll process him, and I'll get him in a cell," Paul said.

"Let's see what the girlfriend has to say. Leslie, you're with me on this one. Paul, you get going on Matt."

For the next hour, Jim and Paul informed Matt Shafer of the possible charges that could be filed against him. Then they secured him in a cell. Jim and Leslie interviewed his girlfriend, Amy Bergholt, but concluded that she was as strung out as Matt minus the attitude. She seemed to know little about his business associates, although she did admit he dealt drugs occasionally. After forty-five minutes, they decided the questioning was futile and let her go. They would keep Matt overnight until they could determine whether he knew anything about the murders or the Fort Crawford coins.

Jim called the district attorney about a search warrant. He explained Matt's suspected drug dealing based on the girlfriend's admissions during her interrogation. In addition, Jim told him about Matt's vehicle that had forced him off the highway. The district attorney told him his requests seemed reasonable. He'd talk to Judge Benson. He could pick up the warrant after eight the next morning.

Jim decided he'd done all he could do. He told Leslie and Paul to go home. He was bone tired, hungry, and needed a shower. He walked out into a beautiful, windless evening of warmth, the setting sun slipping behind the bluffs. The drive home left him feeling that something had shifted. He didn't know what was next, but evidence and suspects were lining up. More connections would come. ⊙

16

TUESDAY, JUNE 15

The killer listened to the rain steadily pattering on the roof in the early morning. His thoughts turned to Jamie Alberg. *That kid is a problem. He has superior tracking skills, and his broad knowledge base about treasure is impressive. But he's got an overconfident air of superiority. Thinks he knows everything. And he proved it when he discovered the cave and again when he'd posted that Facebook video. Well, I guess I'm not the only one who's made some stupid mistakes.*

Jamie was talented in archaeology, and when you were a treasure hunter, those skills transferred well to finding hidden things. But he sure didn't do anything to help me. Instead, he'd led the police to the cave. Now they'll never give up.

This whole affair was beginning to wear on him. He was exhausted from anxiety and sleeplessness. Not usually a drinker, he had been soaking up the booze every night. What everyone had forgotten, especially Jorge and Maria, was that the treasure was his and his alone. He discovered it. He was keeping it.

He had to make another decision. What should he do about Jamie? There were so many possibilities, weren't there? It was just a matter of choosing the most effective method. Getting those detectives involved had revealed that the gold wasn't just a legend—it was real. Things were getting complicated very quickly. But everything would soon be wrapped up. Then he could leave the country. South America was nice this time of year. Or maybe Spain. His passport was current. Yeah, Spain sounded like a very nice place for someone who was fabulously rich.

—◦O◦—

Paul Saner was still reeling from the news Ruby had given him last night. He'd tossed and turned, finally falling asleep sometime after three. Now he was awake. The numbers on his alarm clock glowed green in the early morning light of the bedroom. It was only five-thirty.

He got up, rolled quietly to his side of the bed, and stopped to listen for Ruby's breathing. Hearing her soft snores, he tiptoed to the bedroom door and closed it quietly behind him. The apartment was dark. He flipped on the kitchen light, then walked to the large living room windows and looked out at streaks of lightning as they flashed across the dark morning sky. A grumble of thunder rattled the window. More lightning crashed, and then the pelting rain began. Hunched along the shoreline, the bluffs were blue-black in the pervading thundershower. A few early commuters made their way across the big blue bridge, which arched majestically over the Mississippi. A good time for a freshly brewed pot of coffee. A good time to think.

Ruby. Pregnant. *How had that happened?* He'd just assumed she'd been protecting herself. He thought of Lt. Higgins' lecture on the word *assume*. "Remember what the first three letters of *assume* spell." He'd said it with his dry sense of humor. Somehow, it didn't seem so amusing now. He could still see Ruby's beautiful green eyes looking at him as he replayed the conversation in his mind.

"I need to tell you something, and I don't want you to go off on me," she said seriously.

He noticed the somber expression on her face. *What could this be about?* "Go ahead. I'm ready," he said. Now when he thought about his response, he must have sounded like the overconfident idiot he was.

"I'm pregnant," she said, watching his face carefully.

Paul sat there numb, unbelieving. The world shifted. His eyes searched her face as if he hadn't heard her.

"Paul, did you hear me?" Ruby repeated as she leaned forward. "I said, I'm pregnant." There was a moment in time, a silence that seemed to last forever.

His eyes widened, and his mouth hung open. "Pregnant?" Paul said incredulously. "How did that happen?"

"Well, if you don't know, that sex talk you had with your parents in junior high has fallen by the wayside," she said, a weak attempt at humor. Ruby looked at him, and her face collapsed. Tears began to flow.

"Hey, hey, hey. Come here," he said softly, scooping her into his arms. She cried even harder. "Shh, shh. We'll figure this out. I'm not going anywhere. Don't worry," he said as he rubbed her back. But his mind was racing with the ramifications. *Holy moly! This was huge.*

He held her as she cried and vented. He had an idea where this was going, but he wasn't ready for that yet. After a while, Ruby calmed down, and he made her some tea. He cracked open a Spotted Cow.

He thought about their strengths. They were both intelligent, had good jobs they enjoyed, and were committed to each other. *Didn't they tell each other "I love you" every day?* He hoped those words weren't just an empty platitude. *No, they're not. I love Ruby, and she loves me,* he thought.

But in the hard light of the morning, he had to admit he was terrified. He knew Ruby came from a traditional family—love, marriage, children, in that order. And frankly, playing house was fun, but it lacked commitment and stability. He was thirty-four, for Pete's sake! Maybe it was time to step up to the plate. Be responsible and own his decisions and actions.

He walked to the counter and poured a cup of strong fresh coffee. The warmth of the hot liquid comforted him and calmed the jitters in his stomach. *Wow! A baby.* Then a more serious thought. *Me, a dad. Unbelievable.*

He heard the toilet flush. Ruby stumbled into the kitchen straight into his arms.

"You up already?" she asked, her voice husky with sleep, snuggling into his neck.

"Yeah, didn't sleep too good. Thinking about this baby thing."

"I know. Me, too," she said. There was a pause. "We'll be all right, won't we?" she asked timidly, resting her head on his shoulder.

He set his cup down and took her face in his hands. Looking in her eyes, he kissed her tenderly. "We're going to be just fine," he said, brushing her hair from her face. "Just fine."

Jim woke early, heard the thunder and rain pounding on the roof and bedroom windows, and rolled over for more sleep. By eight-thirty, he was out the door driving down Chipmunk Coulee, the windshield wipers slapping in a rhythmic cadence. He stopped at the courthouse, picked up the search warrant for Bargain Coins, then continued on to his office. Emily sat at her desk, cheerful and perky, despite the pouring rain outside.

"Good morning," she said. "Paul's in your office already."

"Okay," Jim said, glancing down the hall. "Sorry about the ruckus yesterday with Jamie."

"Stubborn little twerp, isn't he?" she said, smiling at him.

"That's only the half of it. Thanks for your help." He flashed her a dimpled smile.

"Oh, I need to thank you. I haven't heard you yell like that for a long time. Shaped up the girls here in the outer office, I can tell you

SUE BERG

that. They were like little mice the rest of the day." Emily grinned at Jim and winked. Jim rolled his eyes and continued down the hall.

In his office, he found Paul comfortably slouched in a chair, his elbows perched on the armrests. His fingers were steepled in front of his chin, and he wore a serious, worried look on his tanned, sculpted face. Dark hair curled around the collar of his shirt.

"You're here early. What's up?" Jim asked, taking a good look at him. Always dressed professionally, Paul wore a clean, pressed plaid shirt, open at the collar. His slacks were casual, and a lightweight tan suit jacket completed the look. His usual grin and friendly manner were conspicuously absent. He seemed terribly sober. *Hmm, what's this all about?* Jim thought.

Paul unfolded himself from the chair without a word and quietly shut the door. He sat down again, then leaned forward and rested his elbows on his knees. Jim took a seat at his desk and turned to face Paul.

"I've got a problem," Paul said, looking up and locking eyes with Jim.

"About the case or something else?" Jim queried, returning his stare.

"Ohh, this is definitely something else," Paul moaned. He waited a moment. "Ruby's pregnant," he blurted, leaning back in his chair.

Jim swiveled toward the window and watched the trees twirling in the wind and rain. He waited a few minutes, then turned back. Paul was looking at him hopefully.

"Well, I'm getting the feeling this was not planned or expected?" Jim asked tentatively, taking a sip of coffee. His eyebrows arched like a question mark. The minutes ticked by.

Paul simply shook his head. He ran his hand through his hair and let out a sigh. Jim noticed the dark circles under his eyes. He looked rough. *The hard knocks of life,* Jim thought.

"Simple question. Are you in love with her?" Jim continued. He took another sip of coffee.

Without hesitation, Paul responded, "Yes, I am. Very much,

Chief."

"There's your answer."

"What answer would that be?" Paul asked, confused.

Although Jim knew about Paul's living arrangements, he refrained from getting too personally involved in his team's lives. Everyone was struggling with something. He was more than willing to lend a sympathetic ear now and then, but only when he was invited to do so. This seemed like an invitation.

"Love. You said you loved her," he repeated. "Now you have to do what you should have done in the first place. Give her a ring, have a wedding, build a home and a family, and quit playing house. Living together usually doesn't end well. I could quote some statistics, but I'll spare you the pain." He could hear himself lecturing.

"But I don't want you to think marriage will solve everything either. Marriage isn't easy. It takes a lot of communication and understanding. But with love, commitment, and forgiveness, it's really the best formula for a good life and happiness," Jim finished.

The office seemed stuffy and stifling. Jim walked to the window and cracked it open. He came back and sat down, his desk chair creaking under his weight. The rain-washed breeze lightened the atmosphere.

Turning to Paul, who looked pale and exhausted, he said in a gentle voice, "Look, it's a shock. But you're a smart guy. It's not the news you wanted to hear, but you'll figure it out as you go. Believe me, when you stand at the alter, you have no idea what life will throw at you. Nobody has all the answers." He paused, then went on in measured tones. "Life just threw you a curveball." he said, "A self-made one but still a curveball. Take a breath, be brave, and live your life the best way you know. You'll be fine," Jim stopped talking, thinking he'd already said too much. He always did that. Said too much, started lecturing, couldn't quit while he was ahead.

Paul sat for a moment absorbing everything Jim said. He stood. "Thanks, Chief. You're the best."

"Hey, I'm here whenever you need to unload," he said, giving Paul a sympathetic look.

"Yeah, I know," he said over his shoulder as he walked down the hall to his office.

Jim leaned back in his office chair. *Holy smokes, it's only nine o'clock. What else is going to come down the pike?*

—◦—O—◦—

Around noon, farther up the river, twenty-two miles north of La Crosse and another two miles north of the city of Trempealeau, the morning rain had stopped. The air was still heavy with humidity. The heat index, combined with the temperatures, would be pushed to intolerable levels.

Hush Perlotsky stood at the counter of his junkyard office. His business covered about five acres. Thousands of abandoned, rusted, and defunct cars and trucks sat in varying states of disrepair, flaking paint, and neglect. Dents, dings, missing wheels, crushed doors, and smashed windshields were the marks of his trade. Hush began the business when he returned from World War II. Now at age 92, he was still the hub of the wheel. His five children had all been involved at one time or another, but they had moved on and were employed elsewhere now. His grandson, Robbie, was the newest and most energetic family member of his small but talented staff.

Hush wore a quizzical expression as he reread the email from the La Crosse County Sheriff's Department. They were searching for a red and white dually 350 Ford pickup. He was pretty sure that the truck had come into the scrapyard about a week ago. But his inventory of vehicles numbered in the thousands, and hunting for it in ninety-five-degree heat at his age was not something he cared to do. The air-conditioned office was the only place he wanted to be today.

"Robbie!" he shouted, standing in the office door in his faded Oshkosh overalls. "Robbie!" he yelled again. He waved the young boy over.

Covered in a mixture of dirt, sweat, and grease, the tall, lanky teen asked politely, "What do you need, Grandpa?"

Hush puffed calmly on his pipe, the pungent smoke creating a drifting halo around his head. "Do you remember that red and white dually truck that came in a while ago? Like a week ago? Maybe ten days ago?" Hush asked. "A Ford."

"Kinda," Robbie said, squinting up into Hush's wrinkled face. "I can walk through the front lot and look."

Hush smiled down on him. "That'd be great. Let me know if you find it."

Hush went back to his counter in the office, writing receipts and checks for dead, beyond-repair vehicles. Stuffing envelopes with invoices, he placed stamps on them for mailing. Then he took the day's cash and checks thus far, tallied a subtotal, and slipped them into a zippered bank bag. Reaching below the counter, he opened the safe and slipped the bag inside. He'd finish the deposit slip later.

Who knew you could make a living collecting other people's junk? he thought. The metal market was all over the board, but averaging it out, he'd made a comfortable income. He was proud to provide jobs for guys with a minimal education who liked to work with their hands. He had high hopes for his grandson, Robbie. He had made straight A's in eighth grade this year. Maybe he'd become something better than a junkyard junkie.

As he looked through the receipts for the vehicle intake for the last month, he came across one that fit the police description, so he set it aside. Just then, Robbie came into the office.

"Yep, Grandpa, we've got that dually. It's sitting in the fifth row in the front lot. Now that I've seen it, I remember when it came in. It was early in the morning on a Saturday when we were just about to open. Remember? It was weird because it was parked by the gate with that note on it."

Hush snapped his fingers. "That's right. I forgot that. Now I know why I keep you around here. You've got an exceptional brain upstairs," he said, tapping his grandson's head. He puffed some more on his pipe. "Thanks, Robbie. You're a good boy." Robbie turned and left, letting the office door slam.

Hush grabbed his landline phone and dialed the number given in the email.

"Lt. Jim Higgins."

"Hi, this is Hush Perlotsky calling from the Trempealeau Salvage Yard."

"Yes, go ahead," Jim answered.

"Well, my grandson and I think we have that red and white Ford dually you're looking for." The line was quiet for a few seconds. "Are you there?" Hush asked. He heard a rustle of papers in the background.

"Yes, I'm here. I was just getting my description out. It's a Ford 350, red and white, with a smashed right front fender, in kinda bad shape, right?"

"Listen, all the cars I get are in bad shape. After all, I do own a junkyard," Hush wisecracked.

Jim chuckled. "Sure, sure I understand," he said. He could see the man smiling on the other end of the phone. Jim continued. "I'll send someone up that way to look at it. If it's the truck, it will have to be impounded since it was probably used in a crime. You'll be reimbursed for the vehicle." Jim paused, then continued. "By the way, does anyone there recall who delivered the truck? That's almost more important than the truck itself."

It was quiet on the other end of the line. Then Hush said, "Well, that's the strange thing. I'd forgotten this, but my grandson reminded me. Someone had parked it at the front gate before we opened. There was a slip of notebook paper under the windshield wiper that said FREE. We hauled it in and put it on the lot. We did a title search but didn't come up with a current owner. I tried calling the previous owner and left a message but didn't get a response. Probably a stolen vehicle somebody wanted to dump. Maybe their conscience was bothering them. I'll ask my crew about it. We'll be here until five tonight, and we open tomorrow at eight. Just call before you come, and we'll pull it out of the lot."

"Thanks so much. I appreciate it." After he hung up, Jim sat at his desk relishing the thought of recovering that truck. Hopefully, they would find fingerprints, DNA, or something in it that would help connect Santana to some of his drug buddies and possibly even the killer.

He walked down the hall to Paul's cubicle. Paul was frowning at his computer screen, looking a little better than he had this morning.

"Found the Santana truck. It was taken to the Trempealeau Salvage Yard," Jim told him. "We need to get up there and get that truck delivered down here, so we can go through it," Jim finished, grasping the door frame with one hand.

"All right. That's good news. You want me to go?"

"Yeah, and take Sam with you. There are some odd circumstances about its delivery to the yard." Jim explained its abandonment at the gate and the note. "Try to find out who delivered it, even though it might be a dead end. At least get the note if they still have it. We might be able to lift prints off it," Jim ordered. "Maybe they have surveillance cameras on the front gate. Check that out, too. It's worth a try."

"Got it, Chief. I'm outta here," Paul said. He grabbed his suit coat and went down the hall to collect Sam. He was thankful for something to do, like driving and interviewing, instead of being chained to his desk.

Paul drove up U.S. 35 north to the sleepy little village of Trempealeau located along the Mississippi River, home to Perrot State Park. As they entered the city, a nineteen-foot fiberglass catfish greeted them, reminding locals and tourists of their annual city Catfish Days held in mid-July each year.

"Ever been to Catfish Days?" Sam asked.

"Only once. They needed some extra cops, and I needed the extra money. It's pretty much your local city festival for tourists who like to drink beer and eat fried catfish. Your typical small-town Wisconsin celebration," Paul finished, preoccupied.

"I was here once in my college days. I don't remember much about it. Too much beer and not enough catfish, I guess."

Paul smiled and followed the GPS coordinates to the salvage yard.

The public complex of the junkyard was tidy. The front office was part of a pole shed where trucks and equipment were stored. In the back, a shop was used to tear down vehicles for their spare parts. A car crusher was front and center in the main yard. A couple of guys were looking at a Ford van, checking to see that all usable components had been salvaged before it bit the dust.

Paul and Sam got out of the truck and walked through the sweltering humidity to the office. Inside, a blast of icy air provided relief from the heatwave outside. An American flag hung stretched on the wall behind the counter. An airman's World War II jacket was tacked on the wall next to the flag, and a Purple Heart and a Silver Star were smartly encased in a gold frame. The smell of pipe tobacco lingered in the air. Hush Perlotsky looked up over his reading glasses and asked, "Can I help you guys?"

Paul made a quick assessment. He figured the guy was well into his upper eighties. He seemed sharp and attentive with ramrod straight posture.

"Officer Paul Saner," he said, holding out his police ID. "Officer Sam Birkstein. We're here about that Ford dually truck in our email alert."

Hush shook their hands and introduced himself. "A real honor to meet you boys. I'm the owner here, Hush Perlotsky. Yeah, I called about the truck. Let me get my grandson, and he can take you out to the lot." Hush limped to the door and waved Robbie over.

"Robbie, these policemen want to take a look at that Ford dually. Can you show it to them?" Hush asked.

Robbie escorted Paul and Sam to the truck in the fifth row. They looked it over carefully, comparing it to a photo Paul had taken on his phone. Robbie stood in the knee-high grass, carefully watching their procedures.

"Yeah, this is the truck," Paul said seriously, clicking more photos with his phone. "We'll have to arrange to have it towed down to the impound center."

When all the proper paperwork had been produced and signed in the office, Sam asked about a surveillance camera. Hush pointed to the porch outside and under the eave. "Installed a camera last year when we had a string of break-ins here and down the road amongst some of the neighbors. Only have it on at night and on the weekends. I wouldn't know how to use it, but Robbie knows about that. You know kids and this newfangled technology."

Sam knew how to use the machine, and within fifteen minutes, he had captured the video of the Ford dually. The image of the driver appeared grainy and unfocused in the early morning light. He replayed the video several times until Paul suddenly looked surprised.

"Hey, I know that guy. That's Matt Shafer, the owner of Bargain Coins," he said in a low intense voice.

"You mean the guy Leslie tackled—the one in jail right now?" Sam asked.

"That's the one," Paul turned to Hush. "By the way, do you still happen to have that note that was under the wiper that said FREE?"

"No, I'm sure that was thrown in the trash right away," Hush informed them.

"That's too bad, but the chief's gonna be happy about this," Paul smiled. "Really happy."

Paul called to fill him in on the image recorded on the surveillance camera. Jim was elated.

"Boy, that was lucky. Good work," Jim said. "When you get back here, I think another session with Mr. Shafer is in order."

"See you in an hour or so," Paul said, hanging up.

SUE BERG

Matt Shafer, the sole proprietor of Bargain Coins, did not have a new and improved attitude since his overnight stay in a jail cell. If anything, he was more belligerent and surly than yesterday. Jim stopped at the interrogation room door, turned to Paul, and said, "We need to rattle his cage. No cajoling. The nice guy stuff is over." His blue eyes bore into Paul's.

"No problem, Chief. After my news last night, I'm more than ready to tear into someone."

"That's my man," Jim said seriously, giving Paul a nod.

Jim entered the room and took stock of Matt. *Same surly kid as yesterday.* He pushed the button on the video camera and proceeded to recite the time, date, and participants in the interview.

After they were seated and Jim had read Matt his Miranda rights, he leaned forward. "Mr. Shafer," he began formally, "did you drive a 1996 Ford 350 red and white dually pickup to the Trempealeau Auto Salvage yard on Saturday morning, June 12 at about five?"

"So what if I did? It's not a crime, is it?" Matt's eyes wandered as he spoke.

"If the truck was stolen, it is a crime," Paul jumped in. "So you're admitting that you delivered the truck to the junkyard?"

"Yeah, I did it for a friend." Matt crossed his arms over his chest and stared Paul down, his eyes hard and uncompromising.

"Name?" Jim asked calmly, rubbing his chin.

"Someone who was a little down on their luck."

"Just answer the question. Who was the friend you delivered the truck for?" Jim repeated, his voice a little edgier.

"Maria Santana. I bought some dope from her, and she wanted a place to dump the truck. I said I'd help her out if she'd give me a deal on some pot."

"Why'd she want to get rid of the truck?" Jim continued.

"I don't know. Maybe she was sick of looking at it and wanted to get something better to drive. She's a woman. Go figure." Matt responded sarcastically.

"And this was Saturday, June 12?" Paul asked.

"Yeah, that sounds right."

Paul gave Jim a quick look out of the corner of his eye. "Do you want to revise that statement?" he said.

"Why would I?" snapped Matt, pulling on his earlobe and running a hand through his hair.

Jim leaned in on Matt, locking eyes with him. He felt the weight of the interview in his favor, the heat of anger starting. "Because Maria Santana was already dead by Saturday morning." Jim began tapping the table with his forefinger. "That's because you'd already strangled her and dumped the truck at Trempealeau." By now, he had notched up the intensity in his voice. "Isn't that right, Matt? You murdered Maria around midnight on Friday night, and you—"

"No! No! No! I didn't kill anyone!" Matt screamed. He stood suddenly, shoving his chair backward until it toppled over on the floor with a crash. He leaned over the table, his face pale, little beads of sweat forming along his hairline. For the first time during the interview, he looked scared. "Listen, I smoke some dope, but I would never kill anyone," he repeated, his voice intense with emotion.

Paul calmly stood up and walked around the table, replacing the chair. He pointed at Matt, then at the chair. Matt sat down and slumped forward, placing his head in his hands. The silence dragged on.

Finally, Jim spoke in quiet, measured tones. "I know you ran me off the road last Saturday night. Now we have evidence in the form of a surveillance video that you delivered a stolen vehicle belonging to Jorge Santana to a junkyard. More disturbing yet, you delivered the truck the morning after Maria was found strangled in her trailer." He paused for effect. "This isn't looking good for you, Matt. You need to come clean and cooperate, or you are looking at a murder charge."

Matt looked up, his face tear-stained. "You have to believe me. I did not kill Maria."

"Why should we believe you, Matt? You've been uncooperative and hostile," Paul explained. "You're going to have to tell the truth if you want to be believed. And right now, that doesn't seem to be happening."

Paul and Jim waited. The minutes ticked by.

"Could I have something to drink?" Matt asked in a quiet voice.

"We'll take a break and get you something," Jim replied. They exited the interrogation room and walked down the hall. Standing there, Jim turned to Paul and asked, "Whaddya think?" His blue eyes were intense with frustration.

"We're getting closer to the truth. Let's keep the pressure on. We'll tag team him and see if he gives up anything more," Paul said.

"I don't think he killed Maria, but I've got this sense that he's involved somehow. Maybe he knows the killer. Might be thinking he'll be the next one if he's not careful," Jim responded. "He was scared toward the end of the interview."

Paul continued down the hall, saying over his shoulder, "I'll get the guy a Coke and meet you back there in ten minutes."

Jim and Paul continued to question Matt over the next hour. He consistently denied his knowledge or participation in the murder of Maria Santana, falling back on his drug buying story instead. That seemed to be the only plausible part of his narrative.

Paul took over. "Matt, we know you're not giving us the whole story. You know more about Maria's death. Tell us what you know," he demanded, leaning forward in his chair. He hadn't expected what came next.

"Okay, this is the truth," Matt started saying. "I came to her trailer Saturday morning at about one and went in. But I swear, she was already dead. It freaked me out. I lost it when I saw her all curled up on the floor of her bedroom. I got out of there right away. I drove back to my house, and about three o'clock, my cell rang. Somebody told me to drive out to Maria's trailer, get the truck, and deliver it to Trempealeau. Otherwise, he'd see that the murder would be pinned on me. So I got my girlfriend to follow me. She picked me up after I delivered the truck. We got back to La Crosse about seven in the morning."

As Matt talked, Jim and Paul glanced at each other. Believable? Who knew.

"So, who was this mysterious caller?" Paul asked dubiously.

"I don't know. I was so shook up that I didn't recognize the voice, but it was a man. That's all I know."

Jim and Paul continued to rehash Matt's story, taking it apart bit by bit, but he stuck to it. They decided to continue to hold him for another seventy-two hours until he produced a list of drug contacts for Jorge and Maria Santana. The sooner he produced a credible list, the sooner his charges of intimidating an officer of the law with a vehicle could be dealt with. Jim informed him firmly that he was still a prime suspect in Maria Santana's murder.

The detectives took the elevator to the third floor. The secretarial staff had gone home, and it was eerily quiet. Paul threw his suitcoat over his shoulder.

"It's already six-thirty. Time flies when you're havin' fun. See you tomorrow, Chief," he said, turning to go. Then, "Thanks for this morning."

"Do the right thing," Jim reminded him, pointing his finger and winking.

Jim's phone rang.

"Higgins here."

"Hey, it's Carol. I'm still downstairs. I just finished processing a car accident. Hungry?"

"Starved."

"How does Rudy's Drive-In sound? Hotdogs and fries?" she asked.

"I'll be down in ten minutes."

Half an hour later, Jim and Carol pulled into the classic drive-in restaurant on the corner of Tenth and La Crosse Streets. The place came complete with rollerskating carhops. They ordered the standard fare: hotdogs, fries, and jumbo root beers. A young girl glided up to their window ten minutes later, carrying their order on a metal tray, which she deftly hooked on the window. Jim passed out the food and drinks.

"Man, I'm starving," he commented between bites of hotdog.

Carol dipped a fry in her ketchup. "Me, too. Sometimes it's just good to have some old-fashioned summer food in an old-fashioned summer place. I remember my dad and mom bringing us kids here every year for my birthday. It was such a big treat."

They caught up on their day. Jim filled her in on the progress of the case, and Carol regaled Jim with the latest mini-dramas of various courthouse employees. The air was filled with the smells of hot cooking grease and asphalt. In the cooling evening atmosphere, kids skateboarded through the drive-in parking lot, and a couple of teenagers sat necking next to the retaining wall. When Jim dropped Carol at her car at the Vine Street parking lot, the sun was setting behind the bluffs.

"Thanks for the invite. I'm stuffed," Jim said. He leaned over and planted a kiss on her cheek, catching a faint whiff of perfume, nuzzling her neck a little.

"No problem. See you later," she said as she exited the car. Jim waited until she was safely on the road.

On his drive home, he remembered the empty, aching feeling after Margie died. It was so real he could have bottled it. For a while, he thought he'd never recover his sense of well-being and balance. She had been the rock he relied on. That was no surprise to him. But the depth she had penetrated his soul was a revelation. When she died, he drifted, feeling useless and spent. Thank God for his kids. They had loved him through it. Now driving the backroads in the early evening dusk, he realized something else. The ache was fading, replaced with a small, delicious thing called hope. Hope to love, hope to live, hope to be happy again. ⊙

17

WEDNESDAY, JUNE 16

The desert sun beat down in unrelenting waves, creating sheets of white-hot shimmering mirages, blinding and unforgiving. Boots, clothing, hair, eyes, and teeth were permeated with the grit of sand. This was a world of harsh brutality, matched only by the danger of hidden IEDs and surprise ambushes.

Leslie felt parched like a dehydrated cracker. The desert road stretched for miles until it disappeared as a tiny white thread on the horizon. She heard the crunch of her boots in the desiccated sand and rocks. Paco walked next to her, panting, his eyes constantly roaming the landscape. His nose was on heightened alert to anything that might prove deadly. Leslie could feel her senses take on the same razor-sharp edge as her canine companion. The backpack cut into her shoulders, and her muscles ached from the weight of it. She licked her cracked lips and absently patted Paco's side. Everything here was reduced to its essence. Her primary goal was to survive for another minute, another hour, another day.

Suddenly Paco stopped. Nervous and whining, he looked up at Leslie. His muscles were taut and tense, ready for action. Leslie noticed the abandoned truck parked haphazardly along the route some fifty yards ahead. Paco's brown eyes were fixated on it. Leslie held up her hand, a signal for the company to come to a halt. Leslie and Paco continued to creep down the road alone.

"It's okay, boy. Come on. We'll be all right," she said quietly, trying to reassure her canine partner.

What she heard next wasn't really a blast, a bang, or even a crash. It was more a *whump*, a dull *thwacking* sound that entered her brain with sickening slow speed. She sensed artillery guns in the distance. More sounds, confusion behind her, her company returning fire. Paco whined and barked. Loud, persistent explosions rattled the atmosphere, sending sheets of sand rocketing into the air. Her feelings of safety and preparation abandoned her. She was rolling, instinctively reaching for cover, reaching for Paco—reaching, reaching.

Leslie squirmed and shouted. The sound of her own voice startled her. She sat upright in bed, the sheets twisted around her torso. Paco whined and nudged her arm for cover. She was sweating and shaking. She made a conscious effort to slow her breathing as her psychologist had taught her. Calming herself, she reached for Paco. His soft black fur and brown eyes provided comfort like a child might find in a well-loved teddy bear. Paco remained next to her, vigilant and focused, licking her hand and arm, whining and reassuring her. He seemed to say, "It's okay. We're okay. We're home."

Gradually, the light from the street that filtered into the bedroom reached Leslie's consciousness. She fell back on her pillow in a rush of gratitude and relief. Smells from her apartment—the scents of hamburger and fried onions and the cool night air—reminded her where she was. She breathed in and out, her tense muscles relaxing. Her system, a moment ago on high alert, began to normalize. The adrenaline stepped down until she began to think rationally.

"Just a bad dream, Paco," she whispered. "Just a bad dream."

She lay in the dark for a long time, turning thoughts over in her mind. Her companions were maimed and killed. Their faces and voices, their smiles, and tears. It was hard to shut off the flashback. But eventually, fear and confusion were replaced by the comfort of reality. She began to relax. Nestling her hand in Paco's fur, her eyes finally became heavy, and she slept.

—o—O—o—

Jim walked through the south side Kwik Trip, selecting a cinnamon crunch bagel and a Karuba Gold coffee. He paid and negotiated his way out of the crowded parking lot filled with gas-guzzling vehicles and caffeine-deprived customers. The traffic on Mormon Coulee Road seemed heavier than usual, but Jim made good time getting to the La Crosse law enforcement complex on Vine Street.

He booted up his computer in his office, organized and sent emails, and returned a few phone calls. Finally, he made his way to Paul's cubicle.

"Mornin', Paul," he said warmly. The padded dividing wall was covered with pictures of friends and family. He noticed a picture of Ruby, her red hair radiant in the sunshine.

Paul turned in his chair. He looked refreshed, like a huge weight had been lifted. "Yo, Chief. What's happenin'?"

"Have a good night?" Jim asked curiously. Then he reprimanded himself. *It's not my business.*

"Yeah, we talked until late. I think things'll be fine," Paul answered. He smiled, twiddling a pencil in his fingers, leaning back in his chair.

"Great. Listen, I had a thought last night. I need to talk to Matt Shafer again this morning. I need you to be there, but I don't want you to say anything. Just observe," Jim said.

"Can I ask why?"

"Well, I think when Matt ran me off the road Saturday night, it might not have been directed at me. It might have been aimed at Carol," he concluded. "I want to see what I can get out of Matt.

I know it's a long shot, but I have a gut feeling about this. Make sense?"

Paul had a dubious look. "Not really. Why Carol and why Matt?"

"Her in-house assault complaint against Gordy Wilson. Retaliation, payback. Gordy has been known to apply pressure to women who refuse his advances. Maybe Matt was paid off to shake Carol up."

Paul was quiet for a moment. Then he said, "I don't know, Chief. That seems kinda far-fetched. If you wanted to scare a woman, wouldn't it be more effective to hit her when she's alone? Besides, how would Gordy know Matt?"

"Gordy has policed the north side for years. Don't kid yourself. He has his share of shady contacts like we all do. I know from Matt's record that Gordy has hauled him in on occasion and questioned him. Maybe he'd been using Matt as an informant, and now he's hired him to carry out a personal vendetta against Carol."

"Or you? Really? Personally, I think it's a dead end. You better ask for his list of drug associates before you get into the road rage incident, or you might never get the names out of him."

"Good point. It's my call. You're off the hook," Jim explained.

"If you say so, Chief," Paul said, though he wore an expression of wary skepticism.

An hour later, in the interrogation room on the first floor, Matt Shafer had given up just seven names of drug contacts he'd seen or met at the Santana trailer. To Jim, it hadn't seemed worth the overnight detention he'd gone through to squeeze Matt for the names.

"So you're telling me that this," Jim held up the short list between his thumb and finger, "is the best you can do?" His voice had taken on a sarcastic tone.

"Those are the guys I've seen at the trailer. I didn't live there. I just picked up my dope there," Matt replied, hiding the hint of a grin. Jim let out a sigh of frustration.

"Okay, let me ask you this," Jim said, moving on. "Do you know Officer Gordy Wilson?"

Matt wondered where this line of questioning was going.

"Do you know Officer Gordy Wilson?" Jim repeated, his irritation just below the surface. Paul stood to one side, his hands in his pockets, observing the questions and answers.

"Must be a police officer, I guess, but I don't know him."

"Isn't it true that you've been a drug informant for Officer Wilson on occasion over the last few years? I know from your record that some of your activities have been reduced to a lesser charge for cooperating with police. So, you must have had some contact with someone on the force."

Jim waited, his leg crossed over the other, sitting back from the table, relaxed and casual.

"Didn't you just get a charge of trafficking in cocaine reduced to a misdemeanor when you gave up a bigger fish in the food chain?" More seconds ticked by. "Todd Sanborn might make life a little more dangerous for you when he gets back out on the street." Jim finished, his eyes boring into Matt's. "That's the price you pay for being a petty drug-dealing informant."

Matt stared contemptuously at Jim, his eyes lurking beneath partially closed lids. He weighed his options. All this wheeling and dealing with cops hadn't made his life any safer or easier. If anything, his life was more complicated now than it had ever been. He thought about it. Screw these guys.

"I don't know anything about Gordy Wilson," he said with a hard edge.

Jim waited, looked at Paul, who hunched his shoulders and gestured, "I don't know."

Jim picked up the defiance, questioned him another fifteen minutes, then stood and said, "Okay, we're done here."

"'Bout time," Matt muttered. Jim released him to the officer outside the door.

"Well, that went well," Paul said sarcastically after Matt left.

"Worth a try. Sometimes it's a wash. I still think the road rage was planned as retaliation against Carol," Jim said defensively.

"Well, you're not exactly Gordy Wilson's favorite person either, sir." Jim gave him a sideways look. "Maybe Gordy was targeting you both all along. Just saying."

"I hear ya," Jim said as they rode the elevator to the third floor.

Sharon Cross, Steve Stoner's reliable companion, usually didn't watch the local news, preferring CNN or FOX to keep up with national and world events. But she'd stayed up later tonight since tomorrow she was taking some time off to catch up on some household chores.

Listening with half-hearted enthusiasm, she turned up the volume when the Santana murder took the top spot headlining the ten o'clock report.

"The La Crosse Sheriff's Department is asking for citizen input into the Jorge Santana murder. Shown on your screen is a recent photo of Santana at the Viroqua Walmart making a purchase in mid-May. Lt. Detective Jim Higgins is asking if you recognize Santana or know of any of his associates to please call the number on your screen with information. You may remain anonymous by calling Crime Stoppers."

Sharon felt a chill. Santana looked an awful lot like the guy Steve had been hanging around with at that Mexican restaurant on the south side. She was sure she'd seen him there a number of times in the last six months. The establishment was one of her favorites in La Crosse, and she ate there frequently. But did she know enough about him to call it in? Probably not. Still, something about the familiarity of his face bothered her.

She flipped off the TV and began her nighttime routine. Her cat,

Taj Mahal, jumped on her bed, getting comfortable, purring loudly. Sharon turned out the lights. What did she know about Santana? Was it enough to even worry about? She'd have to think on it. ⊙

18

THURSDAY, JUNE 17

Jamie Alberg felt like a minor celebrity. He'd been stopped on campus by people he didn't even know who'd seen his post on Facebook. Professors in some of his classes had asked him questions about the case. Also, a couple of treasure hunting acquaintances had called to congratulate him on his discovery of the mysterious cave where the real Fort Crawford treasure had been hidden. Teenagers were tweeting and texting about their new interest in treasure hunting, driving up the demand for metal detectors. Maybe someday he could be as famous as Robert Ballard, Laura Grier, or Mel Fisher.

Now he was enjoying a Dairy Queen cake at MVAC in honor of his sleuthing skills. Becky, Jan, Mike, and Steve gathered around his desk. As they scooped up their melting ice cream cake, they hung on his every word.

"You have sent treasure hunting into a new realm, brother," Steve remarked. "It's the new hip sport. Ace Hardware said they've sold out of every small shovel and metal detector in the store. Can't keep the shelves stocked."

"Really?" Jamie exclaimed, wide-eyed. "Wow, I didn't know this discovery would have such a profound effect on the community."

"We've had kids registering for our archaeology classes because they want to find treasure," Becky added. "The interest in MVAC from ordinary people on the street has been phenomenal. People are calling to find out what we do here. We may have to hire more summer help if this keeps up," she concluded.

The small enthusiastic group continued their conversation until their supervisor peeked her head in the door. She suggested everyone get back to work. They split up reluctantly. Jamie drifted back to his workstation where he'd been cleaning a large Oneota pottery piece from the Brice Prairie time period. He brushed it gently using a small wooden tool to clean the zig-zag decoration on the body of the pot.

"Hey, Jamie. Some of us hunters are meeting tonight at Sloopy's. We'd love to hear all about your discovery of the cave. Can you come with us? About nine o'clock or so?" Steve asked.

Jamie paused, recalling the dressing down he'd received from Lt. Higgins about keeping a low profile. He'd been doing that, sort of. He hadn't told his parents about the conversation with Higgins, and frankly, he wasn't going to. He could take care of himself. He wasn't a twit. The killer had probably already left the area anyway. Too bad. Jamie would have loved to see the actual coins all together in one great big humongous pile.

"Jamie. Are you there, buddy?" Steve interrupted, waiting for a response.

"Oh, sorry. Yeah, count me in. I'll be there," Jamie said, smiling over the top of a dusty pot.

"Great. Don't forget. Nine o'clock at Sloopy's. See you there," Steve said as he turned and took the steps to the ground floor exit.

Becky Sanderson had worked as a supervisor of excavation at MVAC for over twenty years. The news about the discovery of the cave where the Fort Crawford gold was hidden was unsettling. How

SUE BERG

many other people were involved in the discovery? She knew that Steve had followed the news about the gold with intense curiosity, but that wasn't really surprising. He'd always been a treasure hunter. He didn't seem caught up in the hoopla of this lone incident. If anything, he seemed pleased with Jamie's current success.

Jamie, on the other hand, was something of an enigma. Curious, intelligent, and persistent were all worthy descriptors. But his other peculiarities were more worrisome—stubborn to a fault, intense, egotistical. And there were his mild autistic tendencies, which produced some very strange social situations. All of this would have to be monitored carefully so that no harm or shadow of impropriety would damage the stellular reputation of MVAC. *That will be easier said than done,* she thought.

•——○—◇—○——•

The phone rang twice, and then a voice recited, "La Crosse Sheriff's Department, Emily speaking. How may I help you?"

"I'd like to speak to someone about the man who was murdered— the one who was found in the quarry," the voice said politely.

"May I ask who's calling?" Emily asked.

"I'd like to remain anonymous," the voice replied with a little harder edge.

"Sure. I'll connect you with our chief investigator, Lt. Higgins. Just one moment."

The line was quiet, and then a voice said, "Jim Higgins."

"I saw the photo of the Santana man last night on the news. I've seen him a lot at that Mexican restaurant on the south side— Mexico La Fiesta. It's right on Mormon Coulee as you're coming into La Crosse."

"Yeah, I know where that is. Go on."

"I've seen him there with a couple of different guys. One guy is Steve, and the other is Matt. No last names. I had a drink with their group one night. That's all I know."

"Thanks. We'll run it down."

There was a click at the end of the line. Jim stared at the ceiling. The lead on Santana and the Mexican restaurant was another piece of information that needed to be checked out. He wondered if the Matt the caller mentioned was the drug-dealing punk, Matt Shafer. He just didn't seem to be able to keep his nose clean.

Jim was busy with some departmental paperwork that he had ignored far too long. He stayed at his desk the remainder of the morning, dispatching Leslie and Sam to check out the Mexican place lead.

While checking Maria's cell phone activity, Leslie had discovered calls to Mexico City, which was no surprise. Frequent calls to other Hispanic friends who worked at the dairy were no surprise either. The week before Maria was killed, she had made one call to Matt Shafer, but that only supported what Matt had already told them. He got his dope from Maria.

About eleven, Jim got up and walked to the conference room. He pulled up a chair in front of the board and studied what they had. To any outsider, it looked like a collage of paper scraps of various random dimensions. It might even be considered a work of art to those who had an eye for the expressive. To Jim, it held the key to the case. Someone on this board was probably the killer. Every piece of evidence, photographs, leads, and interviews were represented on the board. Now we needed insight and perceptive connections. Could all the information collected so far be developed into a workable theory that would lead them to the murderer? Who knew?

He thought back through the interviews they'd conducted. Faces and snippets of conversation came to mind. Steve Stoner had asked him what kind of coin he was looking for. Did he ask that before or after Jim told him about the murder? Jim referred back to his notes. Before. Interesting. Sometimes what people asked him was more important than the answers they gave him.

Jim thought about the treasure hunters meeting. He was

considering the possibility that the murderer was someone within the treasure hunting community. Who had contact or was known to Jorge and Maria Santana, Matt Shafer, and Jamie Alberg? What about that woman who'd asked questions at the treasure hunters meeting? Could she be someone they all knew? He thought about that for a while.

Finally, he heaved himself out of the chair and strolled out to the secretarial pool.

"I'm leaving for lunch. Be back in an hour or so," Jim said to Emily.

Emily was madly typing and taking calls on the Crime Stopper hotline about the Santana photo. She barely looked up. "Fine by me, Chief," she said.

Jim took the elevator to the first floor and pulled open the heavy glass door labeled La Crosse County Morgue. The narrow hallway was devoid of any artwork—just plain white walls. He stopped in front of the reception area at the desk. Carol was conversing with Luke, her back to Jim, their banter easy and light.

"... and she took a few steps, and now she's walkin' all over," Luke was saying.

"Funny how that one little milestone turns into a whole new chapter in life, isn't it?" Carol asked.

"Yeah, funny how that happens," Jim commented. He leaned over the counter, his tie askew, his eyes bright with humor. "Time for lunch?" he asked as Carol turned in her chair.

"Hey, Chief, she's always got time for lunch. For once, we're not swamped," Luke said, lifting his eyebrows, a grin spreading across his face.

Carol's eyes brightened. "Let me grab my purse."

They ended up getting subs from Lindy's on Main Street. Walking to Riverside Park, they shared a bench on the quiet waterfront. Traffic on the river moved lazily, and sightseers gaped at the twenty-five-foot statue of Hiawatha standing at attention on the banks of the Mississippi. Pigeons strutted in the grass. A young man leaned against an old cottonwood and quietly strummed a guitar. Walking and running along the shaded streets, nearby office workers tried to keep their flesh corralled into culturally acceptable sizes. Obviously, many were failing.

"So, any progress on the case?" Carol asked, setting down her bottled water.

Jim let out a sigh and took a bite of his sandwich.

"That bad, huh?" she said.

"Pretty cerebral at the moment. Lots of unrelated facts that make no sense. It's frustrating waiting for something to break and hoping that someone else isn't going to get hurt or killed. On the brighter side, we got an anonymous call this morning that might turn into something." Jim shared the tip about Santana at the Mexico La Fiesta. "There's something I want to ask you." He looked over at her. She nodded, noticing his blue eyes.

"Go ahead."

"Do you know any women who got payback for not cooperating with Gordy Wilson? Mean stuff. Threats, like that?" Jim asked.

Carol stared out at the river, quiet and thoughtful. Jim was ready to move the conversation in another direction when she said, "I know of one gal who got a threatening text. Then she found her dog missing when she got home. After searching for hours, she found him again, but she couldn't necessarily tie the two things together. It really spooked her, though, and she was pretty sure the text was from Gordy, although caller ID didn't reveal his name or number.

She paused, and when she spoke, her voice had notched up a level. "I saw it and read it. It sounded just like him. Self-serving, conceited, arrogant bas—"

"Okay, I get the point," Jim said, touching Carol's arm lightly.

"Why are you asking?" She turned toward Jim, her brown eyes quizzical.

"I'm wondering if the car that forced us off the road Saturday night was intended to intimidate and scare you," Jim said as Carol's eyes widened.

"Do you think it might have been Gordy?" she asked, her voice hushed.

"It's a possibility, or he hired Matt Shafer to drive the truck. That's why I want you to be aware of your surroundings when you're out and about." Carol nodded. "Don't be scared. Just be the smart woman I know you are," Jim finished, smiling at her.

When Jim caught her hand, she said, "Oh, I'm well aware of guys who are attempting to get my attention. But thank you."

"See what happens when you hang around these law enforcement types. You might get a lecture once in a while."

She smiled and shrugged. *And you might get one, too,* she thought.

Jim continued, "By the way, thought I'd take the boat out on Saturday. The weather's supposed to be perfect. Interested?"

"Absolutely." She flashed a grin. "Wouldn't miss it. It'll be lovely."

Back at the office, Jim thought about weekends. He envisioned neat, square blocks labeled Saturday and Sunday on a calendar. Other people thought of weekends as bookends to their workdays, where planned events happened. His schedule did not lend itself to neatly devised events or blocks of time. His philosophy was more like "Que sera, sera. Whatever will be, will be."

For a cop, it had to be like that. People didn't plan and commit crimes within the parameters of the workweek. Solving cases often meant calls at inopportune times and trips to out-of-the-way places. He remembered many ruined dinners and family outings. Fortunately for him, Margie was the kind of woman who was understanding, patient, and independent. When things went south, she made a new plan or carried out the original plan alone with the kids.

Jim settled himself at his desk. The afternoon flew by. Leslie and Sam had a promising talk with the owner/manager of Mexico La Fiesta.

"The guy," Leslie said, as she referred to her clipboard, "a Juan Hernandez, said that Jorge came by the restaurant about twice a month. He identified Jorge from the photo I showed him. Said he frequently met with—guess who?—Matt Shafer for drinks and sometimes dinner."

"Why am I not surprised?" Jim said. "Our little drug dealer, Matt, does get around, doesn't he?" Jim leaned back in his chair, chewing on his lower lip.

Sam slouched in the corner chair in Jim's office. He sported a pair of cutoff shorts, wool hiking socks with a pair of blue Nike running shoes, and a brown Grand Teton National Park T-shirt. Jim glanced at him, taking in the homeless vibe, not even raising his eyebrows. He knew better than to lecture him about the dress code. His "look" did give him a certain status as an undercover cop. Was it worth another heated exchange that went nowhere? Probably not. Right now, Jim was more concerned with the facts of the case than with Sam's attire.

"What do you think, Sam?" Jim asked pointedly.

Sam looked coolly at Leslie, then Jim. A few seconds ticked by, everyone lost in their own thoughts.

Finally, Sam said, "Matt, Jorge, and Maria are all tied together with someone who's still in the shadows. Find the common acquaintance, and I think you'll have your killer."

Sam glanced at his notes, ticking off the points he'd made in his suppositions. Then Jim took over.

Regardless of his crazy persona, the kid had good analytical thinking skills, Jim thought

"Well, here's what I'm thinking," Jim began. "The person we're looking for is obsessive and impulsive." His voice filled the office. The Mexican's death at the quarry points to a lack of planning and an impulsivity in decision-making. Probably a loner, not willing to negotiate. He wants the treasure for himself. He's not inclined to share his tremendous good luck with anybody, even another treasure hunting buddy. Maybe the Mexican found out somehow about the treasure and wanted in. Our guy would have none of that, so he threw the Mexican over the cliff. Not a well-planned crime; it probably happened in a moment of rage. Or there might have been an argument. It also could have been a simple accident."

Sam gave him a circular wave. "Keep going. We're listening."

"Instead of making a quick exit to somewhere foreign like South America, I think he may still be in the area. He seems to have some sociopathic tendencies. If he killed both Jorge and Maria, he might be feeling some remorse, but not enough to stop him from eliminating anyone else who messes with him. He's dangerous right now, and Jamie probably made things worse with that Facebook post." Jim made a wry face.

The team watched him carefully, giving nods here and there. Paul had heard their conversation and joined them. Jim went on. "After he found the treasure, his obvious lack of criminal experience started showing in his inability to carry out a preconceived plan. So, I think the guy is definitely an amateur, not a career criminal. He's also a loner, but he must have some associations in the treasure hunting community. He probably keeps a low profile. When we catch him, he'll blame everyone from his mother to his dog for his sorry state of affairs."

Jim finished his spiel and took in the expressions on the team's faces. He wasn't telling them anything new, but he had summarized the main points of the investigation in his own inimitable style.

Jim noticed the depth of concentration that characterized Leslie's listening powers. She was used to taking orders, but she also had a lot to offer. While he was going through his theory of the crime, she had given him her full attention. Throughout his narrative, he'd noted her nonverbal cues. "Leslie, anything to add?" Jim asked.

"A couple of things," she said. "It's possible we've already talked to the killer. Maybe one of us already interviewed him, or maybe he was at the treasure hunters meeting in Stoddard. Who knows all the people involved in this crime?" She ticked them off on her fingers. "The Santanas, Matt Shafer, and Jamie Alberg? Find that person, and I think you'll find the murderer."

"That's what I just said," Sam reminded her, slouching in the corner.

"Great minds think alike," Leslie responded, smiling.

"Agreed," Jim said. Sam rolled his eyes.

"One more thing," Leslie continued. "I worry about Jamie. I've friended him on Facebook, and the responses to his video post are not going to discourage him. His followers have made him into something of a folk hero. He may not handle that too well."

"Yeah, our man Jamie is one more unpredictable part of this puzzle. I usually don't lose sleep over this stuff, but he does cause me some consternation." Jim groaned. Even as he said it, he wondered, *What's that kid up to now?* ⊙

19

EVE JUNE 17

The June evening had stretched out in a blur of heat and humidity. Ice cream scoop clouds reflected the orange cast of the setting sun, and the river was dotted with pontoons and speedboats taking advantage of the last rays of summer light. The city street lights hummed, and underneath them, groups of summer revelers dressed in tank tops and shorts languished in the tepid breeze.

A group of treasure hunters had gathered at Sloopy's Alma Mater on Copeland Avenue on the north side of La Crosse. In the not too distant past, Sloopy's had been a fixture in this community but fell on hard times and had to close. Now, under new management, the spruced-up bar had the feel of a friendly neighborhood hangout with good food and a great variety of beer. Locals and visitors found the atmosphere stimulating and genial. The Thursday night Trivia competition had put it back on the map in the city.

Jamie Alberg had been drinking for at least an hour. His MVAC buddies repeatedly asked about the cave and the treasure. Between recounting his bluff climbing experiences and cave haunts, he regaled them with the legend of the Fort Crawford payroll.

"And then I remembered this old treasure hunter and the map he showed me." He turned to Steve. "You know his granddaughter,

Amy. She was at that meeting in Stoddard."

Steve nodded. *Yeah, she was there.*

The drinks were piling up in front of him. It seemed like Mike and Jan kept proposing toasts and other listeners kept buying more rounds. What had started as a small group of friends and treasure hunters gathering to reminisce had now become an all-out hoopla involving everyone who walked into the place.

Another hour went by. The reality of the evening began to elude Jamie. He was having a hard time remembering how he got to the bar or how long he'd been here. *Where's my Jeep? Is this what it feels like to be really drunk? How am I going to drive home as drunk as I am?* Faces appeared as beheaded ghosts in front of him. The laughter and attention that had been so intoxicating just a while ago was losing its appeal. All he wanted was a nice soft bed. *Where are my friends?* They seemed to have left. *Who are these people anyway?*

Suddenly, someone appeared at his shoulder, steering him gently to the door.

"Come on, buddy. You've had enough for one night. Let me help you get home."

Jamie wasn't aware of his staggering walk to his Jeep. Although he was upright and moving physically, his mind had left the building. Someone tucked him into the passenger seat and buckled his seatbelt. The city lights zipped by, repeating themselves with sickening regularity as the car moved quickly through the streets. He dozed or passed out; he wasn't sure which. He'd never been drunk before. Boy, were his mom and dad going to be furious. More dozing. More nothingness until the car door opened, and a blast of fresh air revived his impaired senses.

"Oh, thanks for bringin' me home." Jamie weaved and squinted at his companion. "Do I know you? I don't think so," he slurred, tripping over the curb. "But I wan' you ta know I'm a surliberty."

"I think you mean a celebrity, Jamie. Right over here, buddy. We're almost there. Here we go. Just hang on to me. That's it," the voice cajoled.

"This was sure nice of you to bring me home," Jamie swooned, weaving like a reed blowing in the wind. "Let me give you a hug," he mumbled.

The shove would have caught him off guard had he been sober, but in his inebriated state, he didn't have a prayer. He landed in the river on his back with a tremendous splash. His clothes quickly soaked with water, pulling him down. He struggled to understand what was happening. Even in his drunken state, he realized he was in the river and in terrible danger. He wasn't a strong swimmer when he was sober, let alone when he was smashed.

The mighty current tugged at him, forcing him under and away from the shore. It wrapped itself around his legs like some kind of sea monster. Screaming for oxygen, his lungs were burning until they felt like they'd burst. He kicked and fought for air and finally made his way to the surface. Gulping, he tried to subdue the panic in his chest.

Swim! His mind screamed. *Swim!* He kicked off his shoes. Time seemed to stop. He felt suspended in a nightmare of water, darkness, and intoxication. Lt. Higgins' voice came to him then. "Take care of yourself. Don't do anything stupid. Let someone know where you are." Those thoughts alone seemed hysterically funny had it not been for the fact that he was drowning in the Mississippi River at night. Numbness enfolded him, and despite the coldness of the water, he just wanted to sleep. *Swim! Swim!* His brain screamed the command over and over until slowly the message and the muscles began to respond and work together.

Minutes passed. Jamie drifted in and out of a haze as if he were dreaming. He kicked and moved his arms, dog-paddling against the current. The cast on his arm felt like a dead weight, threatening to drag him below the surface. He continued flailing like a panicked first-time swimmer. That stupid childhood song came to him. "Inch by inch, row by row, gonna make your garden grow." Well, this was no garden, and inches was not going to cut it. Miles was more like it.

He noticed the big bridge coming up. He flipped on his back and floated silently under it, admiring the steel girders underneath—the tremendous workmanship that nobody ever saw from the top side. He heard the bang and thump of cars and trucks moving overhead across the bridge and smelled the exhaust of the vehicles mixed with the fishy smell of the river. Except for the traffic over it, the night was silent and black. The noises faded. Soon on his left, the neon blue and green Gundersen Lutheran Hospital sign lit up the night sky. Jamie was surprised at how brilliant the colors were against the darkness surrounding him.

He thought of his mom then. She was probably just getting home from her shift, kicking off her shoes, reading the paper in her scrubs with her Diet Coke on ice. He heard his voice hoarsely calling her name.

Suddenly, Jamie was angry and furious. His adrenaline kicked in, his rage feeding his determination to survive. *Kick! Swim! Kick! Swim!* His mind screamed the words until it became his mantra. *Kick! Swim! Kick! Swim!* He continued to the point of exhaustion. He began crying, sobbing convulsive gasps of horror. He was too tired. He couldn't do it. He was going to drown. It seemed unbelievable to him that his life could be snuffed out this easily. He was drifting, losing the battle. The shore seemed terribly far away. Still, he continued to kick and move his arms. He went to another place in his mind as the reality of the situation faded.

Jim read until eleven, when he finally began to feel sleepy. He had a lingering thought about Jamie then reflected on his relationship with Carol. Jim felt a surge of lust and tamped it down. Finally, he whispered a prayer for his kids and fell into a deep undisturbed sleep. At four o'clock in the morning, his cell phone buzzed on his nightstand.

"Jim Higgins," he said, his voice groggy from sleep.

"Lt. Higgins. This is Lydia Alberg. I'm very worried about Jamie. He hasn't come home yet, and that's just not like him. I was—"

"Wait a minute. How did you get my cell number?" Jim asked testily, turning on his bedside lamp. "What time is it anyway?"

"I rummaged around in Jamie's room and found it in some stuff on his desk. I'm very concerned that he might be in some kind of trouble."

Jim propped himself up on his elbows and leaned against his pillow, his eyes adjusting to the light. "It's four in the morning," he said, irritated. "Listen, Mrs. Alberg, I don't mean to be snarky, but what makes you think he's in trouble? He's a nineteen-year-old college student, after all. Trouble can come in many forms."

"Well, I'm sure by now you know Jamie has some social ineptitude, for lack of a better term. If he starts drinking, which he's never done that I know of, he might lose what little inhibition he does have and—"

Jim interrupted. "Listen, wait 'til morning. If he hasn't come home by then, call me back, and we'll make a plan. Do you have any idea where he went yesterday?"

"He was at work at MVAC, and then he mentioned something about Sloopy's. That's all I know," Lydia said.

"Maybe he met a girl?"

"Heaven forbid! I'll call you later. Sorry to disturb you." Lydia clicked off.

Oh boy, this can't be good, he thought. Jim laid his phone on his nightstand and wandered to the kitchen, flipping the lights on as he went. He shook his head. Parents of millennials—they practically lived their kids' lives for them. How were they supposed to become responsible when their parents tried to solve every problem for them?

He made himself a cup of tea. The phone call worried him, though. Jamie was so gullible. He would be susceptible to the wiles of a killer, and some of them could be quite charming. Even though his mom seemed more than a little protective, his supposed disappearance was disturbing. But like Jim had taught his kids; life is all about choices. Hopefully, Jamie hadn't chosen to do something stupid. Jim shook his head. Too late for that. He'd made poor choices already, and Jim had only known him less than two weeks. What next? He sighed and set his cup in the sink. *Can't save the world, but I can go back to bed.* He smiled and padded down the hall to his bedroom. After all, life was all about choices. ⊙

20

FRIDAY, JUNE 18

Jim slept late the next morning. After the strange phone call during the night from Lydia Alberg, he cut himself some slack. During his morning routine, he mulled over that conversation. Jamie's disappearance dredged up nothing that was remotely comforting. He tried to use his reason and what he knew about Jamie to get ahead of his imagination. It didn't work. Somehow he had a feeling this wasn't going to turn out well. The day was creating drama all on its own. His phone beeped while he was making a fresh pot of coffee, fixing his breakfast.

"Jim Higgins."

"Mornin', Jim. Emily here."

"Morning. Sorry," he said apologetically, preempting her questions. "I should have called you. I'll be there in about an hour. Don't send a posse out yet. Did you need something?"

"Well, no, not exactly." Her voice was laced with concern.

"So, what's going on?"

"Lydia Alberg is sitting in your office, and she says she's not leaving until she talks to you." There was a pause. "Is this a learned behavior, or does it come from some inherited gene?" She giggled. "Like mother, like son?"

"Oh, Lord." Jim rubbed his eyes and poured a cup of strong coffee. "Tell her she'll have to wait a while since her four o'clock phone call robbed me of sleep. That ought to give her something to think about until I get there," Jim responded sarcastically.

"Ten-four, sir," Emily said crisply. Jim could almost see her saluting.

"Anybody ever tell you that you don't get paid enough?" Jim asked grumpily.

"You're the first. See you in an hour."

Jim walked into the office an hour later with the *State Journal* tucked under his arm and a cup of Kwik Trip coffee in his hand. Emily rolled her eyes at him and flashed him a smile. He gave her an unenthusiastic salute, marched down the hall, walked into his office, and hung his coat on his chair. He turned to face Lydia Alberg, feeling like he was posing before a firing squad.

"So, any news from Jamie this morning?" he asked. He thought about generals who fired the first salvo of artillery. Now he understood how they felt.

Lydia had been crying, her eyes were red, and her temper primed and tuned for a fight. "I thought you cared about my son," she started in. *Oh, boy, this is not going to go well,* Jim thought. "What about the average common citizen who deserves and expects to get a prompt and appropriate response from law enforcement in an emergency? That would be me." She used her index finger to stab herself in the chest. "What about that, huh?" Her voice had escalated in volume. "What are your uniformed officers doing about this, anyway? My son is missing! This is an emergency!" she shouted, rising and pointing her finger at Jim. Her face was flushed and red. Her hair was hanging in loose tufts around her face.

"Whoa, whoa. Wait a minute," Jim said, holding up both hands. "I think you might be rushing to judgment. We don't consider people missing until they've been gone for at least forty-eight hours," Jim said calmly, although he could see that this conversation was heading south real quickly.

"I don't care! Why else would I be here? He's missing. What are you going to do about it?" she yelled, sitting on the edge of her chair. She looked like she was ready to launch out of it again and start throwing punches. Her face was crumpled with emotion, and her cheeks were wet with tears.

Jim took a deep breath and dived in. He was not happy about being screamed at, especially before ten o'clock in the morning. His anger was sitting in his throat just waiting for an opportunity to escape. Jim swiped two tissues from his Kleenex box on his desk and handed them to her.

In a well-modulated voice, he began. "Now, Mrs. Alberg, I'm going to inform you of a few things before this gets out of hand. Number one," Jim held up his index finger, his voice tight with restraint. "Jamie and I had a conversation a few days ago in which I specifically told him his activity and interest in this case of the missing gold could jeopardize his safety. We appreciate his help, but he has demonstrated a lack of ability to set boundaries for himself. I told him he had to back off and let us do our jobs." He stopped, surprised Lydia did not interrupt. She stared at him. Her eyes were big and wide, but her tears had stopped. She was dabbing her face dry with the tissues.

He continued, holding up a second finger. "Number two, I asked him to lay low after he used very poor judgment in posting a misleading and misguided Facebook video. At its worst, it could lead the killer, in this case, to kill again, and at the least, he made himself the center of attention. Hundreds of very gullible young people are always looking for a hero. Since he posted that video, the bluffs and hills around here are covered with wanna-be Jamie Albergs. The La Crosse Rescue Team has already had to retrieve two kids who got trapped on Grandad's Bluff searching for lost treasure." He took a breath and kept going before Lydia could interrupt.

"And third, I asked him to keep you informed at all times of his whereabouts, which he obviously ignored to his peril."

By this time, Jim's voice had risen a few notches. He straightened his necktie, a sure sign of frustration. His face was turning pink, and the grimace he gave her exposed the dimple in his right cheek.

"Are you telling me that this killer is out there and may have targeted my son?" she asked in disbelief and terror. Her hand found its way to her throat, where it remained.

Jim leaned forward, resting his hands on his desk. He lowered his voice, intentionally toning down his rhetoric. He felt that his anger was being held down like a lid on a wound-up jack-in-the-box. When he continued, he was satisfied that he once again sounded like a professional cop.

"Right now, we are actively investigating the crimes that have been committed surrounding the lost gold shipment. We don't know who the perpetrator is yet. It's our top priority, and my staff has been diligently collecting evidence and following leads." When the outburst he expected did not happen, he continued. "So, you can help us here. What kind of vehicle was Jamie driving?" he continued calmly, feeling in control again.

"A 2010 Jeep, dark blue," Lydia recited. "License number A1B879."

"Last seen?" Jim jotted the information on a sticky note.

"Well, he left yesterday for work at eight in the morning. I haven't seen him since." She began to cry quietly again.

"You mentioned Sloopy's."

"Yeah, when we talked at noon, he said there was a get-together there last evening."

"I'll either investigate this myself or have one of my officers do it this morning. Now, is there anything else you need help with?" Jim was thinking of things he could have suggested, but he bit his tongue.

Finally, she said in a contrite voice, "Thank you, Lt. Higgins. I'm sorry Jamie has been such a pest. I know his intentions are good. He's very intelligent, but he's just not very mature. I appreciate your patience with him." She stood to go. Jim stepped out from behind his desk and took her hand. "He's slightly autistic, you know," she said.

"I know," Jim said quietly. "Listen, kids do stupid things, especially boys. You know, the brain development isn't there for making good decisions until they're in their late twenties." He stopped and thought of Paul. In some instances, it's more like thirty. "We're on this. We'll check this out right away this morning, I promise you," Jim said gently.

"Okay, thank you again. I appreciate it. It's just that Jamie is such a regimented person. This behavior is unusual. He always calls when he's going to be late," Lydia said, lifting her tear-stained face to Jim. "You'll call when you know something?"

"Absolutely," Jim said. She slipped out quietly, closing the door softly behind her.

Jim strode to his desk, whipped out his phone, and dialed Leslie.

"Leslie, Jim here. We've got a problem. Come down to my office and grab Paul and Sam on the way. Right away, please," Jim ordered. He leaned back, thinking through his strategy. This is all we need right now—chasing a kid around La Crosse like a bunch of Keystone cops because he can't keep his mouth shut.

Paul noticed Jim's worried expression and flushed face wondering what had caused it. Usually, the chief was pretty stable and predictable. From the yelling and hollering that had just taken place, he knew he was frustrated. Something was up.

Crammed into the office, the team sat in stony silence, waiting for Jim to begin. It was like sitting in the principal's office when you had screwed up.

"I just finished calming a very hysterical Mrs. Alberg," Jim said brusquely. His team looked at him tentatively, then gave him a round of applause.

"Gee, Chief, we heard it all the way down the hall," Sam commented over the clapping.

"All in the line of duty," Jim said, suppressing a grin. Then he turned serious and explained Mrs. Alberg's concerns about her missing son. "Jamie did not come home after a night of drinking at Sloopy's with friends. Mrs. Alberg is concerned that Jamie has become a victim of foul play." He let that sit a moment. "I don't even want to tell you the thoughts I'm having right now," he said as he reviewed the details: the missing Jeep, the lack of communication, the probable drunken state of the young man. All of it was ominous, considering that the killer might still be in the area.

They made a plan to search the city for Jamie. Jim and Leslie would go in one car and Paul and Sam in another.

Jim called Sheriff Jones and La Crosse Chief of Police Tamara Pedretti. Alerting them about Jamie's missing vehicle, he gave them the license plate number. Both promised to dispatch the information out to the units on the street immediately.

Paul and Sam drove to Sloopy's and went around back to the kitchen area, where they found a prep chef just starting his day. After questioning him, they made a call to the bartender who had been on duty. The place was a madhouse for a Thursday night with all the trivia folks. But yeah, he remembered the geeky kid at one of the tables. Did he know anyone with Jamie? Honestly, he didn't have time to notice. He could barely keep up pouring beers and mixing drinks.

Jim and Leslie were en route to the university campus looking for the vehicle when Jim's cell rang. "Hey, Lt. Higgins. Officer Sanborn here. We found that Jeep. It's parked cockeyed on the sidewalk at Riverside International Friendship Gardens. The keys are still in it. We'll stay with it until you get here."

Leslie accelerated, flew down La Crosse Street, and turned right on Main to the gardens. Jim hopped out and approached the officers and the Jeep.

"Anything unusual?" he asked.

"Looks like the vehicle was abandoned. Keys are on the floor mat. Driver must have been drunk to park like that," the officer commented, pointing to the vehicle.

The Jeep's right front wheel was perched precariously on the sidewalk. The rear end of the vehicle stuck out into the traffic lane. *Knowing Jamie, he could have been completely sober and still parked like that,* Jim thought.

"Okay, we'll take it from here. Thanks, officer," Jim said. "Leslie, call the guys. Tell them we found the car. I'm going to walk over to the river and see if there's anything there."

Jim walked through the Chinese, German, and Russian gardens, stopping when he reached the banks of the La Crosse River. Its surface was dark and swirling. Whatever secrets it held wouldn't be given up easily. Was Jamie floating there just below the current? Only two hundred yards farther, it joined the Mississippi, where it picked up speed and power. Jim groaned, running a hand over his eyes. Birds sang and flew with great excitement in the cool morning air. Jim recognized the scent of lilies and roses. He met a few early morning walkers enjoying the beauty of this little corner treasure tucked behind the Pumphouse Art Center.

He didn't like the thoughts that were setting up in his mind. It brought back bad memories from 1997 when eleven male college students drowned in the Black and Mississippi Rivers. *I hope that's not starting again.* Despite a careful search along the banks, he saw nothing out of the ordinary. Jim looked for surveillance cameras among the structures of the park but didn't notice any.

Leslie, Paul, and Sam were waiting for him at Jamie's Jeep when he returned.

"Leslie, call Mrs. Alberg. Let her know we found the Jeep. Do what you can to reassure her, but man, I've got a bad feeling about this," Jim said through gritted teeth. He brought his fist down on the hood of the Jeep. "This kid is going to drive me nuts!" he shouted.

A pedestrian strolling by turned and stared at the commotion. Jim waved weakly and forced a smile.

"So much for positive interactions with the public," Sam commented.

"Coming from someone who looks like a homeless derelict, you aren't exactly Mr. Public Relations yourself," Jim snarled. Sam took a few steps backward, his eyes wide and wary. Jim took a deep breath. "All right, let's keep at it. We've got to try and find this kid. You guys head over to MVAC and talk to whoever was at work yesterday. Don't forget about volunteers. We're going back to Sloopy's to talk to that bartender."

They split up. Leslie stayed with Jim while Paul and Sam headed to MVAC on the university campus. They had to establish a timeline of last night's events and talk to anyone Jamie was with.

"What are you thinking, sir?" Leslie ventured, looking over at his profile as they drove across town.

"Lots of stuff, and none of it's good," Jim grumbled as he slumped in his seat and ran his fingers through his hair.

Jim and Leslie got the address of the bartender who lived a couple of blocks from Sloopy's in a second-floor apartment. They climbed the outside staircase and banged on the exterior steel door. It stayed quiet, so they banged some more. Finally, they heard the deadbolt slide, and the door opened. A tall, well-built man in a white T-shirt and plaid boxer shorts squinted at them. His hair was tousled, and he needed a shave.

"You better not be sellin somethin ," he growled. "You're not Jehovah's Witnesses, are you?"

Jim and Leslie held up their police IDs and introduced themselves.

"We believe a young man named Jamie Alberg was at Sloopy's last night. We found his vehicle this morning, but he seems to have disappeared. We're trying to find out who he was partying with. Could you tell us what you remember?" Jim asked.

"I already talked to a cop on the phone about that an hour ago," he complained, squinting in the bright morning sunlight.

"Yes, we know that," Leslie responded politely, "but this young man may be in some serious danger because of an investigation we're conducting. We really need to find him."

For the next half hour, Jim and Leslie sat at the kitchen table while the bartender recalled details about the evening. He said Jamie was celebrating with some friends. They were drinking a lot, getting noisy and wasted. About midnight, one of the guys from the group took the little geek out of the bar supposedly to give him a ride home.

"Can you describe the guy who took him home?" Jim asked.

"Yeah, I got a close-up look at him when he came to the bar earlier. Tall, about six-foot-two. His hair color was weird, sort of blond mixed with streaks of gray," his eyes traveled to Jim's hair, "kinda like yours. He had a mustache, sort of a biker type. Sturgis T-shirt, leather vest, biker boots. Seemed too old to be hanging around those young kids." Jim wrote the details in his memo pad.

"Any tattoos or other distinguishing features?" Leslie asked.

"None that I saw," he replied.

"You've got a good memory. Listen, if you think of anything else, here's my card. Just call," Jim finished.

"Sure. Hope you find the kid," the bartender said, walking them to the door.

Meanwhile, Paul and Sam hoofed it over to MVAC, where the news of Jamie's disappearance alarmed the staff. They huddled around Paul in the basement workroom. Sam remained on the edge of the group, watching reactions and recording facts and observations on his iPad.

An open wooden drawer filled with pottery shards and tools reminded Sam about the work that went on here. Gummed labels were affixed to all the drawers for easy identification. The smell of soil and musty paper drifted about the room. Dust motes floated in shafts of sunlight. Above the surface of the large plastic tables, employees cleaned, cataloged, and labeled artifacts. Fluorescent lighting gave a harsh cast to the pottery, and books stacked on wooden shelves were covered in a fine layer of grit.

"So you're telling me there were five staff members here in this area where Jamie was working," Paul said, waving his arm to indicate the area. Becky, the supervisor, filled in the details. She stepped closer to Paul.

"Jamie has his own station," she said, pointing to an adjacent table. "He's been working on the ceramic reconstruction of that Oneota pot sitting there." She pointed to the pottery. "He's been at it now for a couple of weeks. Jan and Mike were working down here, too. And Becky—another Becky—was doing some straightening and cleaning. I came in about three o'clock and broke up the DQ party and told everyone to get back to work."

"What about volunteers?" Sam asked from the edge of the group, looking up from his iPad screen.

Becky's fingers covered her mouth as she paused a moment. "Oh, I forgot. Steve Stoner was here. He's been a regular volunteer for quite a few years. He helps with excavation at new sites and sometimes sorts and cleans shards and other objects we find at digs," Becky explained.

"Were any of you present last night at Sloopy's for the celebration?" Sam asked.

Shaking heads in the crowd confirmed only a few had attended. "It was mostly the treasure hunting crowd," Becky said. She looked at her crew for confirmation. She hesitated, uncertainty hedging her features. "Oh, yeah, and Steve was there. He likes treasure hunting and seemed really excited about Jamie's cave find. In fact, he organized that get-together."

"We're going to need your names and addresses and where each of you was last night. We may have to contact you again," Paul explained. His phone chirped.

"Paul, what are you finding out?" Jim asked, on his way back to the office.

"Everything seemed pretty normal yesterday. Jamie had a regular day at work. Nothing out of the ordinary. We're getting the names and addresses of everybody and where they were last night. A few of them went to Sloopy's. They also mentioned a volunteer, Steve Stoner, who went to the bar. Why does that name sound familiar?" Paul asked, rubbing the back of his neck.

"Steve Stoner?" Jim said, surprised. "Really? Well, I interviewed him the first day we found the body in the quarry. He's a treasure enthusiast, but I didn't know he knew Jamie. The bartender gave the description of a guy who left with Jamie." There was a long moment of silence. "Stoner fits the description ..."

"Chief? You still there?"

"Yeah. I'm here. We need to talk to this Stoner guy. Maybe bring him in for questioning. I'll do some background. Let's meet back at my office," Jim said. *Stoner. Huh. Gotta think about that.*

The afternoon unwound slowly. Amy Bergholt had come in and posted the $1,000 bond for Matt Shafer, and he was freed on her recognizance. The impounded truck from the Trempealeau Auto Salvage had fingerprints of Jorge and Maria Santana as well as their children, which was no surprise to anyone. Matt Shafer's fingerprints were in the truck along with another unidentified person. Hair of varying colors had been placed in sealed bags, and other detritus found in the truck was being collected and analyzed.

The team reviewed the information from their morning interviews. Jim and Paul were convinced the person who offered to take Jamie home was probably the killer. Their only lead right now was Steve Stoner. They continued to review evidence, fine-tuning their assumptions.

"Well, theories are fine, but you can only theorize so long," Sam said. "I say we press this Stoner guy. Bring him in for questioning. See what comes of it."

"If he is the killer, we don't have enough evidence to hold him. Hauling him in too soon might spook him, and he might take off," Paul added.

"Which we don't want to happen," Jim continued that thought. "I, for one, want to nail the guy who did this. But, we could put a twenty-four-hour surveillance on him. Watch what he does. See if he makes another blunder. Maybe he'll lead us to Jamie," Jim proposed.

Jim's phone beeped.

"Higgins here." He listened, sat up straight, his blue eyes widening with surprise. "Yeah, we'll be there as soon as we can." He snapped his phone shut, then looked at his team and shook his head. "You're not going to believe it. Jamie just walked into the ER at Lutheran. Let's go." ☉

21

FRIDAY AFTERNOON, JUNE 18

Jamie woke briefly in the early morning with the worst splitting headache he'd ever had. His clothes felt damp and smelled fishy. He wondered where his shoes had gone. He sat up, felt dizzy, leaned over, and threw up in the weeds. He scratched his neck and batted at a cloud of mosquitoes. He took another look around. *Where am I anyway? The river? How did I get here? What day is it?*

Rational answers eluded him. His mind felt like a blank slate and a soggy sponge all at the same time. The most recent memory he could dredge up was walking out of MVAC and getting into his Jeep. He vaguely recalled some serious drinking. After that, nothing. Maybe it would come back to him. He attempted to stand up, but that produced an episode of sickening vertigo. He decided to lie back down. Gradually, the world quit spinning. Jamie curled up in the sun, closed his eyes, and slept the sleep of the dead.

He finally regained consciousness and entered the land of the living in the early afternoon. He was still sprawled on the bank of the Mississippi River. The sun was scorching. Although he felt woozy, his nausea had passed. He was able to scramble up the riverbank and get his bearings. An indescribable headache hammered in his brain. Using the hospital sign as a landmark, he wandered through an industrial park and a nearby residential area. A half-hour later, he stumbled into the Gundersen Lutheran Hospital emergency room.

He was a sight. His hair was matted and filthy. He was missing his shoes, and his clothes were mud-streaked. Focusing on the nurse in front of him was difficult. His speech was slurred, his face was pale and anemic. His face, neck, and hands were covered in ugly red welts. The disheveled appearance and disengaged look made another ER nurse pause in the hectic activity of the ER. She couldn't help but stare.

"Look what the cat dragged in," she whispered to another nurse. "Probably meth."

After being registered, Dr. and Mrs. Alberg were notified. Through a series of questions and a thorough physical examination, the ER doctor concluded that Jamie was suffering from alcohol poisoning. He had come close to death. The doctor ordered a blood draw to determine what else he might have ingested along the way. Jamie's inability to remember recent events was worrisome, the doctor said, but that would probably correct itself in the next twenty-four hours.

The tale of surviving a tumble in the river was so incredible it verged on the impossible. "All in all, you are one lucky drunk," the doctor told him. "Just surviving the level of alcohol in your blood is nothing short of a miracle, let alone swimming in the Mississippi at night. Why you didn't drown, I'll never know," he said glumly.

Completing his analysis, he tucked his clipboard under his arm and made his way out to the hallway. Rubbing a hand across his face, he released the anger and disbelief he'd been hiding in an audible sigh. That Jamie could not recall how he landed in the river didn't surprise the doctor at all. He was constantly amazed at the predicaments people found themselves in after drinking all day or all night.

By the time Jim and his team arrived, Jamie had been moved to a room on the second floor at his parents' request. He would stay for overnight observation. Jim talked to the floor nurse and got permission to see him.

"He may have information about a case we're working on," he explained to her, holding out his police credentials.

When Jim and Paul entered the hospital room, Jamie was sleeping soundly. His ashen face looked pathetic and childlike against a gown draped around his shoulders. His parents were seated by the window wearing expressions of exhaustion and worry.

"Looks like Jamie's had quite a night," Jim whispered as he walked over to the window.

"You have no idea," Dr. Alberg said, hissing furiously as he stood to his full six-foot-four height. His chambray shirt was wrinkled, and sweat stains bloomed under his arms. He'd thrown his tie on a coffee table nearby. Simultaneous expressions of relief and annoyance moved across his intelligent face.

"How did Jamie get from drinking in a local pub with friends to floating in the river in the middle of the night?" Dr. Alberg demanded.

Jim shrugged. "The impetuous nature of youth?"

Dr. Alberg continued his tirade. "This is just another unbelievable escapade piled on top of all the others," he finished, his rage just barely contained.

"Did Jamie mention how he found himself in the Mississippi?" Paul asked, surprised at the doctor's vehemence. His wife, Lydia, placed a cautionary hand on her husband's arm. He brushed it off.

"He doesn't remember much of anything. The toxicology report showed his blood alcohol levels were off the charts. Point two three, almost three times the legal limit. Plus, someone slipped an Ambien or some other sleep aid into one of his drinks. It's a miracle he's still alive," Dr. Alberg spat out angrily. "Stupid!"

At the sound of his father's voice, Jamie stirred and opened his eyes with difficulty. He recognized Jim. He lifted his arm, a weak attempt at a greeting of sorts. His arm flopped back down on the bed with a thud.

"Hey, Lt. Higgins. You won't believe the story I'm gonna tell you," he murmured, smiling weakly.

"I'm waiting," Jim said in a serious tone, turning and standing next to the hospital bed. The smell of disinfectant was diluted by a whiff of Lydia's Chanel No. 5. "What happened?"

Both men leaned in and rested their arms on the bed railing.

"Well, some of my friends wanted to celebrate finding the cave. So we met at Sloopy's over on Copeland. We got a little carried away with the drinking. I remember being in the bar until about eleven, and then everything after that is a blank. I just can't remember anything until the splash in the river," he told them. "That's when I kinda woke up."

"I'll bet," Paul said earnestly. "Do you remember if you drove your Jeep?"

"No, I don't remember," Jamie said hoarsely.

"Did someone else drive you to the International Gardens?" Jim asked, watching Jamie's reaction carefully.

"International Gardens? How'd I get there?" he asked, his eyes wide with surprise. His expression reminded Jim of a fish gulping oxygen, his mouth forming a little o.

"Well, if you don't know, I'm sure I don't either. Listen, Jamie," he continued, "we think the killer tried to eliminate you, too. So when you start to remember things, you need to call me right away, okay?"

Jamie nodded and closed his eyes. "I can't believe this," Jamie whispered under his breath.

"Neither can we," Paul said, shaking his head. He patted Jamie's shoulder.

Turning to the stunned parents, Jim instructed, "I need you to take him home when he's released and keep him there until I give you the all-clear. He survived this ordeal by the grace of God. He should not be here, but he is." His blue eyes darkened as he stared at the parents. He repeated, "Take him home. Keep him there. Understand?" Jim looked from one parent to the other. Paul felt sympathy for the Albergs. *I wouldn't want Higgins staring at me,* he thought.

Dr. Alberg recognized authority when he saw it. "Absolutely. Thank you," he whispered, taking his wife's hand in his. The anger had gone out of his sails, replaced by gratitude and humility.

"One more thing," Jim continued, holding up an index finger. "The fewer people who know Jamie has been found, the better. Keep him off Facebook and Twitter. Take away his phone. When people call and ask about him, always make the person calling identify himself. Do not give any information to anyone you don't know or to any of his treasure hunting buddies. Make a game plan and stick to it. Do not leave him alone. Someone needs to be with him twenty-four seven. Understand?" Jim's voice took on a hard edge. His blue eyes burned with anger.

"Yes, we understand," Lydia promised, her eyes reflecting apprehension and fear. The man in front of them was definitely in charge. No doubt about that.

"There's a killer out there, and he may try again if he finds out Jamie is still alive." Jim finished.

"We had no idea this was such a serious police matter," Dr. Alberg said in a somber tone.

"Well, your wife knew. We had an extended conversation about it the other day," Jim said.

Dr. Alberg looked at his wife standing next to him. "You knew about this and didn't tell me?" he asked in an accusing tone.

"Well, based on your reaction just now, was I right in not telling you? Especially when we weren't exactly sure of all the facts?" Lydia said, her eyes shifting from her husband to Jim.

"Never mind that now," Jim said impatiently, interrupting them. "We know what we're up against; that's the important point. Remember, keep Jamie out of sight." After a pause, he said, "I'm going to have the city guys patrol past your house for the next couple of days. They'll keep an eye on your place."

When he saw the terrified look on the parents' faces, he knew he'd made his point. He thought about apologizing but decided it was better they were terrified than finding their son dead. Dr. Alberg wrapped his arm around his wife and pulled her close.

Jim took one last look at the miracle kid who'd survived. "And

you, young man, had better start listening to the adults around you."
Jim pointed a finger at Jamie. "No more screwing around trying to be
the big hero." He waved to the Albergs and turned, walking briskly
from the hospital room.

—o—O—o—

Jim wrestled with the implications of the attempted murder of
Jamie Alberg. When he let the thoughts play out in his mind, shivers
of dread ran up and down his spine. He'd been given a reprieve,
and he couldn't afford to waste it. The responsibility of finding the
killer weighed him down until he felt his chest tighten with anxiety
and foreboding. *What do heart attacks feel like?* he wondered. He was
at a crossroads. The killer was still out there somewhere planning
something. Coldblooded. Greedy. Murderous. Would he make
another attempt on Jamie's life? *Over my dead body,* Jim thought.

Following the hospital visit, he set up a surveillance schedule
on Steve Stoner, recruiting La Crosse city police to tag team with the
sheriff's department. They began eight-hour shifts around the clock
for the next twenty-four hours and reevaluate tomorrow morning if
nothing broke overnight.

Jim propped his feet up on his desk, loosened his tie, and
reviewed what they knew so far. The physical description of the
man who had left Sloopy's with Jamie sounded like Steve Stoner.
Steve was a treasure hunter, which brought him into sharper focus.
Jim's recollection about him was that he was a loner, not exactly
antisocial but not very friendly either. Another tick on their checklist
of possible characteristics. Steve had a broad knowledge of treasure
and had been at the treasure hunters meeting in Stoddard. His vast
collection of treasure finds revealed his passion. He must have become
acquainted with Jamie when he volunteered at MVAC. Jim didn't
know how Stoner had come to know Jorge Santana except possibly
through drug sales. He transferred his mental list of connections to

his notebook, and a more complete picture of the suspect began to form. Jim felt like Stoner had walked into his office out of a fog. Things were getting clearer.

The implications of his suspicion about the murderer's identity left Jim with a feeling of dread mixed with an odd sense of excitement. This was the point in every investigation when he felt the most conflicted, like standing on the edge of a cliff preparing to jump.

He reached for his phone and called Carol. "Could you come up for a minute? I need to talk," Jim said wearily.

Fifteen minutes later, there was a quiet knock on his office door.

Carol poked her head around the door frame. Jim stayed where he was but waved her in, giving her an anemic smile.

"What's up?" Carol asked. Her brown eyes scanned his face. She didn't like what she saw. "You look like death warmed over, and that's coming from somebody who works in a morgue. More trouble with Jamie?" she said, taking a stab at a little humor.

Jim smiled, but the seriousness of his expression didn't change. His eyes held hers, and she could see some unresolved pain.

"Thanks for coming up. Jamie Alberg was thrown in the river last night and, fortunately, survived. How he survived only God knows, and he's not telling me."

"Whoa, that's serious business," Carol said.

"It brings back a lot of really bad memories when those kids drowned in the river back in 97." He looked up at the ceiling. "I'm angry that I didn't see this coming," he finished with a sigh. "I should have done more to protect him," he whispered, softly pounding the arm of his chair with a clenched fist. "Well, actually, I did warn him off, but that's like heading off a hound dog who's on the trail of a coon," he said. A shadow of a grin crossed his face.

"You're doing the best you can," Carol ordered soberly. "No pity parties allowed." Their eyes locked. "The parents' faces of those drowning victims will never be erased from my mind, either. I get it," Carol replied, her brown eyes moist with tears.

Empathy and poignancy filled her voice. She did get it. She'd

SUE BERG

worked the morgue during those nightmarish events. No one involved could ever forget the promising young men who were dragged from the river, cold and waxy white, cut down in the prime of life. Jim remembered the dark nights filled with flickering candlelight when vigils for the dead men were held by the river. Everyone holding hands, singing "Amazing Grace."

Jim leaned back in his chair. "What's that saying about death?" he said in a pensive tone, his hands clasped over his stomach. "'Death is as near to the young as to the old; here is all the difference: death stands behind the young man's back but before the old man's face.' Thomas Adams wrote that. He was known as the Shakespeare of the Puritans." The words filled the room, creating a somber, reflective mood. It was quiet for some moments.

Carol studied Jim's face, then said, "Yes, I guess you could say it's all in your perspective and what stage of life you're in. Those young men certainly didn't expect to die. They didn't see death stalking them behind their backs." She waited a moment. The solemn atmosphere in the office reminded her of a sanctuary.

"Listen," Carol said quietly, standing in front of Jim's desk, "You seem really down. I don't want you to go home alone tonight."

Jim looked up at her. She noticed the calm blue of his eyes. She knew she could get lost inside them, in the kindness she saw there.

"Is this a proposition?" Jim asked, suppressing a grin.

"No, no. Not that kind of proposition. We're not far enough down the road for that."

"Speak for yourself," Jim teased, his mood shifting, some invisible weight lifting.

"How about you come over for dinner? Nothing fancy. My place. Sevenish? I promise I won't keep you late. Just time to decompress." Her brown eyes looked serious. She wore the hint of a smile. She understood pressure and tension. Jim thought for a moment. *Might open some new doors*, he thought. His mood of the last few minutes seemed to change as if a breath of fresh air had fluttered in on a pair of gossamer wings.

"All right. I'll be there at seven. Thanks." This time his smile made it to his eyes.

Carol turned to go. She hesitated and then said, "What's done is done, Jim. You can't change that. You can only do your best today."

"Yeah, I know. See you tonight," he said, picking up a pencil and tapping his notebook. ☉

22

S am Birkstein and Paul Saner had only worked together for six months. Over time, Paul had warmed to Sam's personality and colorful, eclectic wardrobe. On arrival at the sheriff's department nine months ago, Sam seemed competent, having earned a degree in criminal justice with an emphasis in forensic criminology from the University of Wisconsin–Madison. Maybe that explained his quirky clothes and free spirit. Madison, aka Madtown, had rubbed off on him in a big way.

He'd originally been assigned to the investigative department doing undercover work in drug sales and dealing. But it was his clandestine activities in the world of prostitution that had distinguished him. His arrest record was unsurpassed. The problem was he wore his undercover getups whenever and wherever he pleased. This had gotten him into considerable trouble with Sheriff Davey Jones and Lt. Higgins. The hassles he endured from the department's upper echelons had been scathing and bitter, but it didn't seem to faze him.

Still, Lt. Higgins defended him, probably against his better judgment. Somehow, he believed in this kid. His cop instincts were there, and his arrest record alone put everyone else to shame. Couldn't we work with him on his decorum? Jim asked. With tongue in cheek, he asked if his drag persona wasn't the best they'd ever seen? The sheriff simply waved Jim from the room, shaking his head. Despite Sam's formidable record, it only put a dent in the drug traffic between the Twin Cities and Chicago. And prostitution showed no signs of slowing down, either.

Paul and Sam were sitting in Paul's Ford pickup just a couple of hundred feet from Steve Stoner's driveway on Monitor Street. The arching maple and oak trees gave it a throwback feeling to another time when security and stability were a reality, not just a description on a realtor's photocopied blurb. Their truck hung out at the edge of a trimmed arborvitae hedge, which partially hid them from direct view. Traffic was picking up as people finished work and came home with loaded grocery bags ready to start their evening meal.

"So where do you find the getups you wear when you're undercover?" Paul asked, turning toward Sam, laying his arm along the back of the seat. "Unique attire for a cop." He took a sip of water while scanning Sam's threads. Today he was decked out in a pair of gray jogging shorts, blue Adidas knee-high socks, an orange Wall Drug T-shirt, and Doc Marten boots.

"Well, I shop at Goodwill and Salvation Army, mostly from La Crosse to Rochester. Second-hand clothes shops are all the rage now with the millennials. They want to recycle everything and save the earth. I probably haven't spent more than three hundred dollars on my whole wardrobe since I started working as a cop. The only things I buy new are underwear and T-shirts."

"Thank God for that—the underwear, I mean," Paul said. He waited a few moments, then said, "I understand the drag stuff, but what about your work clothes? Why do you dress like that when you make a decent salary?" He shook his head. " In case you didn't notice, your clothes drive Lt. Higgins up a wall."

"Oh, I don't mean to piss anyone off," Sam sighed, his face lined with remorse. Paul believed him. "But I guess what I wear does upset the status quo. Nobody more than my parents, though."

"Well, hello. You're an adult now and a professional. So what do your parents have to do with it?" Paul asked, watching the foot and bike traffic on the quiet street. A couple of boys pedaled past, their backpacks loaded with baseball gear.

"Some would say I was rebellious. But I wasn't, not deep down," Sam continued. "See, I grew up a PK," as if that explained everything.

"A PK? What's that? Some new survivalist group I haven't heard about?"

"No, no. PK stands for pastor's kid. My dad is a Lutheran pastor. I grew up having to look the part of the perfect kid—good manners, polite, loving, obedient, and well-dressed with a minimum of dirt and mud. Always ready for Sunday church and Wednesday night Bible study. All very sterile." Sam looked over to see Paul grimace.

"Doesn't sound like much of a childhood, trying to be perfect for everyone," Paul remarked.

"It wasn't. But one thing it did was open my eyes to people who weren't like me at all. I was always dragging kids home whose parents were drunk or shacked up with someone they shouldn't be with. I brought home the school bully who was pounding somebody every day. Other times, it was the kid who was so shy it hurt them to smile, let alone talk. I remember bringing home Sammi Bolstad because he never wore underwear. I thought my mom should go right out and buy him some. I didn't realize that was his choice. He enjoyed going commando. It wasn't because he couldn't afford it. All of these problem kids drove my parents nuts."

"I'll bet," Paul said, looking at Sam with wonderment, breaking into a grin.

"And that was part of my motivation for going into law enforcement," Sam continued seriously. "Partly to thumb my nose at my parents and their perfect lifestyle and partly because my heart just broke for those kids. I wanted to make a difference. After all, wasn't that what Jesus did when he was on Earth? He hung out with people who were far from perfect, at least according to religious standards, the Pharisees being what they were."

Sam went silent, leaving Paul in a contemplative mood.

Paul thought, *What a unique mix of defiance, morality, and heartfelt compassion.* Funny what you could find out about someone when you just listened.

"So your clothes are a statement?" Paul asked after a few minutes.

"Not really. I just don't care about status and looking the part," Sam shrugged.

"Well, let me tell you this as a friend and coworker. Being in law enforcement comes with a certain standard and expectation. Now I know, and I'm sure Lt. Higgins knows, that you bring passion and intelligence to the job, but the general public can't see that because all they see are your weird getups. I know it's shallow, blah, blah, blah. But unfortunately, it's true. Your demeanor and dress sometimes speak louder than all the words you could say," Paul finished. He wondered when he started sounding like Higgins. "Just understand I'm not judging you. I'm just telling you the way it is."

"So you think I should invest in a suitcoat or two?" Sam asked, grinning.

"Wouldn't hurt," Paul said. "Can you get those at Salvation Army, too?" he asked, chuckling under his breath." And you've got to ditch that cut-off shorts look."

By six that evening, Jim had checked in with the surveillance teams and told them to call immediately if Steve Stoner moved so much as a big toe. He shut down his computer, grabbed his suitcoat, loosened his tie, and drove home under a perfectly cloudless sky. The river gave off diamond-like sparkles. Fishermen floated on the surface in colorful boats, their arms casting and retrieving their lures in one fluid motion. Eagles soared effortlessly on thermals of hot air above the shimmering bluffs, and a doe and her spotted fawn ran across the road as Jim turned into his driveway.

He showered and shaved, put on blue jeans, a casual shirt, and

SUE BERG

his well-worn leather sandals. Back in the Suburban, he headed back up U.S. 35 to Highway 14, turning southeast until he came to Firefly Lane. He pulled into Carol's driveway a few minutes before seven.

"Hey, feeling better?" Carol asked as she met Jim at the front door.

"Yeah, I'm okay." He grabbed her hand and kissed her. "Thanks for this. Something smells really good."

"Come on in," she said, waving him into the tiny kitchen.

The aromas of rich homemade spaghetti sauce and garlic bread filled the kitchen. Carol uncorked a chilled bottle of burgundy wine, and they talked and sipped while the pasta bubbled on the stove. Later, after dinner, they settled on the deck, which overlooked a grassy swale. The land rose gradually until it reached a wooded hill. The Shrine of Our Lady of Guadalupe, a Catholic edifice, was set against the rocky hillside. It was a miniature slice of Italy, complete with a domed ornate Italian-style sanctuary.

As the evening sun slid down below the brow of the hill, Jim could see the verdigris dome peeking out among the lush hills and bluffs. The scattered sunbeams gleamed and reflected off the roof, making it look like an ancient lighthouse in a sea of undulating green trees. The shrine had been built as a tribute to the Virgin Mary. Her message of love and mercy encouraged others to serve the spiritual needs of those who suffered in body and soul. In the hush of dusk, it wasn't hard to believe that the world needed someone to care for the damaged and hurting.

Carol noticed Jim studying the hillside shrine. She couldn't make her mind up about him. Was he really as good as he seemed? Where did that goodness come from? In Carol's experience, most people put on a good front, but their flaws became evident pretty quickly if you scratched deeply enough. "Do you believe in the message of the Virgin Mary?" she asked, watching his face, trying to spark some conversation.

"I believe people need the presence of God in their lives," he said. "There's no shortage of sin, that's for sure. In my job, disillusionment comes easily on the heels of grappling with the darker side of life. I fight that battle with my faith. Although sometimes it feels like I'm holding back the evil singlehandedly." He continued staring into the darkening dusk.

"Yeah, I'm sure it does. I've had that same experience. When you deal with death, the frailty of the human soul is obvious. Those are very vulnerable moments in life. It's easy to become calloused and miss opportunities to help people through a rough patch, as you did for me." A few moments slipped by. "You mentioned sin. Not many people believe in that anymore. What about you? Do you sin?" Carol asked.

In the gathering darkness, she caught a gentle smile on Jim's face. "People might say they don't believe in sin," he said. "But the reality of evil is with us all the time. Do I sin? Oh yeah. Every day. But I've been forgiven, and I believe forgiveness can change us. Shape us. Give us a fresh start and help us serve a greater good." His words sat between them for a while.

Carol watched whitetail deer tentatively emerging from the woods, browsing on the grasses at the edge of the tree line. Their ears perked up, their tails flicking uneasily, almost as if they knew they were being watched.

"Can I ask you something?" Carol said softly, her brown eyes scanning the bluffs.

"Sure. Go ahead."

"Where are we going, you and me?" She shifted to face him. Her eyes studied his face, and she placed her hand gently on his arm.

"That depends on where you want to end up, doesn't it?"

"What do you mean by that?" Carol asked, confused. Why did everything have to be a riddle?

Jim said, "Let's just continue down the road. It's a journey, and so far, it's been good for me. How about you?"

"Well, we've known each other a long time, but I think our relationship could easily slip into something more than just friendship."

Jim turned and looked at her, taking her hand and clasping it in his. He smiled, his eyes soft with emotion. A hint of his dimple creased his tanned cheek. "We're exploring unknown territory."

"What?" she asked, looking confused.

"Remember when we talked about having histories with other people?" Carol nodded. "You with Matt and me with Margie. Well, now we're writing our history, the one where you and I are the main characters. We get to decide how the story unfolds." He kissed her hand softly and held on.

"I think I'm falling in love with you," Carol whispered.

"Does that scare you?" he whispered back.

"No, I've never felt safer with anyone than when I'm with you."

Jim's heart was thudding in his chest, but he managed to smile and say, "Good, because something is happening to me, too." He leaned over and kissed her. "And it's good—really good."

Officers Mike Leland and Casey Thoreau sat hunched in a 2008 beige Toyota Camry. They had pulled surveillance duty and were watching the house of Steve Stoner, trying to be unobtrusive. It was 8:47 p.m., and the sunset had painted a riot of pink, orange, and purple hues in the western sky. Cottonball clouds had slipped up over the horizon, floating lazily, while the orange orb of the sun burned toward the horizon.

Steve Stoner's place on Monitor Street was quiet. Other than a run to the grocery store and the post office, Stoner remained holed up in his house. The neighborhood was settling down after a flurry of evening activities. Casey could smell meat cooking on a grill, and his stomach responded with sympathetic growls. They talked about women they'd known, their favorite computer simulation games, and law enforcement in the digital world between periods of sipping soda and bottled water.

About eleven, Steve Stoner's garage door banged up, and he climbed into his 2013 Chevy Silverado. He backed slowly out of his garage. Mike tapped Casey's arm.

"Looks like he's goin' for a drive."

"Yeah, don't lose him. I don't want to face Higgins if you do," Casey responded sourly.

Stoner backed into the street and drove through downtown La Crosse heading south out of town on U.S. Highway 35. He drove leisurely and seemed to be in no hurry. Mike stayed back as far as possible, keeping Stoner's taillights in view, not crowding him. Eventually, he turned left on Highway 14. Then a few miles down the road, he turned right on County MM. Heading toward the bluff, he finally pulled into an abandoned farmhouse just before the road began to curve and wind its way up to the top of the ridge. Officer Leland continued up the hill, found the nearest driveway, and turned around. He parked in the adjacent trailer court along a row of mobile homes where they could watch Stoner's truck.

"Call Lt. Higgins. Tell him what's going on," Mike said quietly.

Jim's phone rang. He was in bed reading and answered quickly.

"Lt. Higgins, this is Officer Casey Thoreau. We've followed Steve Stoner to an abandoned farmhouse on County MM at the bottom of the hill next to the Guadalupe Shrine."

"I know where that is. What's he doing?"

"Can't tell. From what we can see from the trailer park, nothing yet. He seems to be just sitting there."

"Can you get out of your vehicle and observe him on foot at closer range?" Jim asked.

"Maybe," Casey answered.

"Just one of you get out in case he starts to move. Watch him. Don't lose him," Jim ordered in a terse voice. "I'm heading out there now. I only live about five miles away. Hang on." His phone clicked off.

Jim ripped out of bed. He strapped on his shoulder holster and pistol. Buckling on a Kevlar vest and grabbing a sweatshirt from his closet, he pulled it over his head. He slipped into a pair of blue jeans and jammed his feet into running shoes minus socks. Fifteen minutes later, he was pulling up next to Officer Leland. He rolled down his window.

"Mike, what's up?" he said quietly.

"Nothing much yet. Casey's making his way down toward the road. There's some brush there, so he has good cover. Stoner's truck's still sitting in the driveway. No action."

In a few minutes, Mike's cell vibrated.

Casey whispered, "He's just sitting there like he's waiting for something, or someone." Just then, Stoner started the truck, and the taillights lit up. He backed out of the driveway, heading back to Highway 14. Casey ran up the bank and jumped in the Camry.

"Keep up with him, boys. Don't lose him. Keep me in the loop," Jim instructed.

After they left, Jim drove through the trailer park, his nerves jangling with the possibilities. What was the importance of the farmhouse? Why drive out to the country in the middle of the night and just sit in a driveway? Amateur criminals did dumb stuff. Go figure. Did he sense he was being watched or followed? It was possible. Maybe he was preparing to run and had come to the farmhouse for something important, like the gold. Well, he would be hemmed in by the two officers tonight and probably wouldn't go anywhere. If he did, they'd know about it. But Jim wondered about the abandoned farm.

During the night, a cold front moved in. The humidity in the air became saturated, and soon the distant thunder came rumbling over the bluffs like a herd of wild horses. Lightning cracked and hissed, sizzling and spitting giant arcs of light across the inky black sky. The wind picked up, and rain hammered the landscape. The trees swirled in wide loops, making the branches dance and the leaves scatter.

In the midst of the pounding storm, Jamie Alberg was lying in bed, the remnants of his headache a distant memory. He was beginning to recall a few details just like the ER doctor predicted. His night on the town. An unceremonial splash in the river. His view of the underside of the big bridge.

If only he could text or call someone or email his friends. Maybe they could help him remember. It was driving him crazy to be unplugged from the world of the internet, Facebook, Snapchat, and Twitter. Being banned from the technology grid sucked. He had argued vehemently and passionately with his parents to at least let him have his phone, but their resistance was immutable. He would not communicate with anyone, they said, until this crime involving murder and gold was solved. No further discussion. End of subject. Nada, nothing, zip.

Jamie moped around the house like the prisoner he was. He watched TV and read up on ancient treasure and archaeology. Junk food and soda were strewn around the house. He hadn't been able to settle into any productive activity.

He was having some serious flashbacks from his near-death experience in the river. At times, the memory of the dark swirling water chilled him to the bone. It was so real. He felt as if he had died and was buried in the cold black oblivion of a watery tomb. His grip on reality was weakening. More than once, he found himself in full panic mode, sweating and gripping the sides of the recliner.

He toyed with the idea of calling Lt. Higgins, but his mom had already tried that once to her peril. Jamie was not up for what would happen if he intruded on the lieutenant's sleep. Besides, what he had to tell him could wait until morning. He was starting to remember who was with him at Sloopy's, but the person who had shoved him in the river lay just beyond his grasp. But he'd been drunk out of his gourd, so it was no wonder the murderer's face and features remained out of Jamie's reach. Maybe by morning, things would be clearer. He could only hope. ☉

SUE BERG

23

SATURDAY, JUNE 19

The morning dawned crisp and clear, washed clean by the rain. Jim and Carol had planned to spend the day on the river, but developments with Stoner were looming on the horizon. Jim hated to scrap the trip, but he reluctantly called Carol.

"Sorry, but things are heating up, and I just have to be here," Jim apologized, frowning as he said it. "Do you understand?"

"If I don't understand that, I shouldn't be dating you. Law enforcement happens twenty-four seven. Criminals don't take vacations, do they?" Carol chuckled, but Jim could hear the disappointment in her voice.

"That's an understatement. We'll find another day to be on the river. I promise."

"I'll hold you to it. Take care. And don't get shot."

Jim decided to drive out to the abandoned farm on County MM for another look. He called Leslie to meet him there.

"I'd appreciate another set of eyes and ears," he explained.

"Right. I'll be there in half an hour. I'll bring Paco if that's okay."

"Absolutely. It's about time I met this dog you're always talking about. We've got to be careful, though. Let me explain my plan," Jim said.

For the next fifteen minutes, Jim explained where the property was located and what he had in mind. Paco would be great to have along, she said, in case any scary people showed up. That was a possibility.

Close to nine, Leslie parked her mid-size Toyota SUV in a shaded field road above the abandoned farmhouse. She parked behind Jim's Suburban. They were about seventy-five feet in on the road, and the trees provided good cover. They both stepped out of their vehicles. Jim was greeted by a pair of brown eyes, a sniff around his ankles, and finally, a wet kiss on his upturned hand. A wagging tail and a softness in Paco's eyes let him know he'd been accepted into the dog's circle of friendship.

They wandered down the bluff until they came to a place where the woods met an open field. They had a surreptitious view of the farmstead. They crouched down and observed the arrangement of the property. On the west side of the road, a white clapboard farmhouse stood like a sentinel watching the overgrown farm fields, dormant and uncultivated. A hundred yards or so to the northwest of the house, an ancient fieldstone flour mill leaned like a drunken derelict, its windows gone. A bank of weeds grew up around its perimeter.

"Why do you think Stoner came out here last night, sir?" Leslie whispered.

"Don't know, but it wasn't a random drive," Jim said softly. "It had a purpose. Maybe the gold's hidden here somewhere. Not sure. I think he was spooked last night, and whatever he planned to do, he ditched at the last minute. He must have sensed that something wasn't quite right, but I don't think he knew he was being tailed."

"When did you figure out he was the murderer?" she asked.

"I haven't. Yet. But he's a strong suspect. We haven't proven anything at this point, but lots of things point to his involvement. His presence at Sloopy's the other night was a give away. I'm taking a gamble that hiding Jamie will force him to be overconfident and take risks he normally wouldn't take. If he thinks that Jamie is truly out of the picture, he may make a run to leave the country." Jim looked at her sideways. Leslie nodded her head in agreement as she listened to Jim's reasoning. Using her field glasses, she continued to scope out the property.

Jim withdrew his memo pad in his pocket and sketched the layout of the place.

"What's that, sir?" asked Leslie, pointing across the road, her pair of binoculars held in the other hand.

A small wooden door was built into the hillside. It blended in with the dark red bricks that surrounded it. Brush and shrubbery had grown up around it, almost obscuring it from view. She handed her binoculars to Jim, who scanned the door. *Entrance to a cave,* he thought.

"Could be a cave entrance. The old-timers used some of the limestone caves in the area as a place to cool their milk and meat—a kind of natural refrigerator. I never noticed that before. Let's go have a look," he said, getting to his feet.

They walked along the road. A few cars passed. Crossing the road at a trot, they pushed brush back until they could see the thick boards and heavy iron hinges of a diminutive door. It had an impenetrable appearance.

Leslie leaned her hand against the abrasive brick wall and thought aloud. "Maybe this is where the gold is hidden."

Jim noticed the new heavy padlock that had been installed on the frame and door and said, "Somebody wants to keep us out. The padlock is probably here to keep out curious kids looking for adventure, or it'd be a great place to hide something."

He looked across the road. "Let's check out the farmhouse. Maybe it's open."

"Isn't that trespassing, sir?"

"Nobody lives there, and it's not posted. It's not a crime if we just look in the windows."

They recrossed the road. A weathered, peeling screen door hung on a sagging porch. Jim stepped up onto the porch. The ancient boards sagged a bit, creaking under his weight. He tried the front door, but it was locked. Leslie peeked in the nearest window of the house, but everything was quiet. No furniture. Some rotting curtains hung limply at the windows, drooping sadly as if in mourning. A ratty moth-eaten rug lay slung across the wide planks of the floor. The house had a feel of desolation and abandonment.

Jim walked up to Leslie, looking at the interior of the home. Paco ran in circles around the house, his nose to the ground, reveling in a world of unfamiliar scents and odors.

"Nothin' here that I can see. But I've got an idea. We're going to check out that stone mill," he said.

"We are?"

"Yup, we are."

To reach the mill, they had to cross a small creek that ran through the property. Leslie slipped and got her sneakers wet while Paco romped and played in the water, teasing a crayfish by the bank. Jim managed to step across using a flat rock that was exposed midstream. They waded through tangled weeds and brush toward the old, bleached-out building.

The time-worn mill had once been an important part of the surrounding community. Although solid limestone walls still stood firm, its main purpose for grinding flour had ceased long ago. They walked through an open doorway into the building's deserted skeleton, kicking up dust from a crumbling cement floor. A slight breeze blew through open windows. Barn swallows flew in and out of the building, coming to rest on old rafters. At regular intervals, they launched themselves into flight, dipping and diving for invisible insects.

"Too bad we couldn't put a surveillance camera here. But that's illegal," Jim said, looking around at the surrounding area.

Leslie scanned the neighborhood. "What about those two light poles near the road over there?" she asked, pointing in the distance. "They're on public property. Otherwise, they wouldn't be there. Could you mount a camera on that?"

"That's iffy. We don't want to go there yet. If I get Stoner on video admitting to crimes, I don't want to have it thrown out of court as inadmissible. We might be able to use the farm to lure Stoner out here, then get him to talk."

She nodded her head in agreement. "Good idea, but it needs to be done soon. If this Stoner guy is getting nervous and preparing for flight, we might miss him by tonight."

"You're right." Jim flipped open his phone and dialed Sam and Paul.

Leslie and Jim sat in the Suburban, waiting for them to arrive. The heat in the vehicle made them sleepy. Closing her eyes, Leslie sat back in her seat and dozed. The truck filled with the smell of wet dog fur as Paco panted in the back seat.

Half an hour later, Paul and Sam arrived. They looked over the farmstead.

"Yeah, I can see where this might work," Sam said.

"We just found out about this place last night," Jim explained. "The guys doing the surveillance on Stoner followed him out here."

"So what have you got in mind?" Paul asked.

For the next hour, the team discussed the ins and outs of a possible sting. They kicked around ideas and finally came up with a loose plan that would include minimal participation by Jamie Alberg. Jim would take care of discussing the plan with his parents. The team decided to meet at the Alberg's home late in the afternoon to prepare.

"So you're in agreement that we need to use Jamie?" Jim asked.

"Not in the actual sting. We just need him to send a text to lure Stoner in," Paul countered.

"I hate to think of him being involved in any capacity, but without the news that Jamie's still alive, Stoner isn't going to be motivated to meet with anyone," Jim said.

Jim drove home, still feeling ambivalent about Jamie's participation. He was just pulling into his garage when his cell rang.

"Lt. Higgins?" Jamie's voice came over the line.

"Hey, Jamie. I thought we agreed you were not to talk on your cell," Jim warned as he walked into his kitchen, his voice edged with a tinge of annoyance.

"I know. But my mom is standing right here, and this is her phone I'm talking on. I don't even know where mine is, and it's killin' me!" he rattled on, sounding defeated. *A typical teenage tirade,* Jim thought. Apparently, the battle Jamie had waged to thwart the plan of seclusion had not gone his way.

"Well, you should be glad your parents are following our plan. It's designed to keep you safe. So what's up now?" Jim asked.

"You told me to call you when I started remembering things."

"So what are you remembering?" Jim asked patiently.

Jamie began relating his recollections of Thursday night. "I was drinking with my buddies, Tom Shalat and Dave Driscoll from MVAC." Jim grabbed a pencil and jotted down their names on a scrap of paper. "I know some other people came a little later. I remember that. But I just can't remember who got in my Jeep with me. I've tried and tried, but it just isn't coming back to me. I feel like I've got Alzheimer's or something. It's so frustrating."

"Don't push it," Jim counseled. "The drug someone mixed with your drink was designed to make you forget anything that happened. Technically it's called induced amnesia. Sometimes people never remember the acts of violence committed against them when they're under the influence of these drugs even though they know it was real. Their bodies carry the scars. Rape, for instance."

"That must be what's happened to me. The forgetting, the amnesia."

"Listen, Jamie. We found out that Steve Stoner was one of the people in your drinking crowd at Sloopy's. A couple of different people have identified him as being there. Do you remember that?"

"Well, he was there early. But I don't remember seeing him there after about eleven or twelve. Those memories have vanished into thin air," Jamie commented.

"We think it might have been Steve who got you into your Jeep and then tried to kill you by pushing you into the river."

Silence. A few seconds later, Jamie asked, sounding confused, "Steve Stoner? Really? Why would he want to do that? We've been treasure buddies for years."

Jim waited. Then Jamie answered his own question. "Oh, I get it. You think he's the one who discovered the gold."

"Right," Jim said. "It's something we're following up on."

"Wow! That's wild." There was a significant pause in the conversation.

"I know that's a lot to take in," Jim said.

"Well, I guess you would know about that from your investigation. I'm sorry I can't tell you more." Jim heard some mumbling. Then Jamie said, "Oh, one more thing. Lt. Higgins, I'm sorry for all the trouble I've caused. I know I can be kind of a pain sometimes." His voice sounded contrite. Jim could imagine his mother standing next to him supervising his apology.

"Don't worry about it, Jamie. We're just glad you're safe. If you think of anything else, let me know. Now, would you put your mom on the phone?"

"I will," Jamie said. There was a rustling noise and then Lydia's voice.

"Yes, Lt. Higgins," Lydia said.

"Hi, Lydia. Listen, we're pretty sure we've nailed down the person who tried to murder Jamie, but we need to have your cooperation for our plan to work," Jim explained.

"Is it dangerous?"

"Not to Jamie. My team will take all the risks, but we need to use Jamie for part of the plan. I promise you it is minimal and just involves sending a text. Oh, and we need to come over and borrow some of Jamie's clothes."

"Okay. I guess we can do that," Lydia said hesitantly.

"Trust me. Jamie will be perfectly safe, and he will still be under twenty-four-hour lockdown until this is all over," Jim reassured her. "We'll see you about four o'clock."

Jim stood by his kitchen counter, leaning against it, thinking. He took a swig of Pepsi and crunched on a handful of tortilla chips. He hoped their idea would work. It was worth a try. ⊙

24

Jim Higgins looked at Sam Birkstein in the full-length mirror. He couldn't believe the transformation. The whole team, including Jamie, had gathered in his bedroom and stood staring wide-eyed at the new character standing before them. Even Sam seemed blown away by his uncanny resemblance to Jamie, their thorn in the flesh. All around them, wigs of various hues and styles and articles of clothing were scattered across the bed and floor.

"This is crazy, sir," Leslie commented, her mouth gaping slightly open, her eyes wide and gawking. "What made you think of it?"

"Well, whatever caused the thought, it's turned out pretty good, don't you think?" asked Paul.

"I'd say it's brilliant!" Jamie crowed loudly, pointing a finger into the air. He patted Sam's arm excitedly. "You bear an uncanny resemblance to me."

Jim stood shaking his head. "Unbelievable. You could literally pass for twins."

Sam had dug through his drag queen paraphernalia. He came up with a medium brown curly wig that Leslie had trimmed to imitate Jamie's naturally curly hairstyle. Dressed in Jamie's everyday clothes, Sam could pass for him in a heartbeat. He'd practiced his mannerisms until he had them down pat. The way he touched his hair, how he crinkled his nose when he disagreed, and especially the way he walked.

"You look virtually identical from a distance, and in the dead of night, he won't be able to tell until it's too late," Jim said seriously.

"Is this what you call a sting, sir?" Jamie asked with feigned innocence. Staring at his double in the mirror, he shifted his eyes to Jim.

"Yeah, buddy. If this works, it'll be the sting of the century," Paul interjected.

"All right then. Let's move on to the next phase of the operation," Jim said, suddenly all business. "Jamie, we need your phone. Can you get that, please?" Jim asked.

Jamie shot his fist in the air and pumped it excitedly. "Yes! I get my phone back!" he exclaimed. He took the stairs by twos and soon appeared at Jim's elbow, his cell clutched in his hand, bouncing on the balls of his feet. His mother trailed behind him with a look of panic plastered on her face.

"It's fine, Mrs. Alberg," Jim reassured her. "Jamie will be using his phone for a brief contact with one of the suspects in the case. He'll return it to you when the call is complete." She visibly relaxed, giving Jamie a look of triumph.

"What a ripoff!" Jamie grumbled, frowning at his mom.

"Here's the plan," Jim explained. As he spoke, the team remained hushed, listening intently as Jim divulged the parameters of the operation. When he was finished, Sam whispered, "I will be wearing a vest and my gun. Right, Chief?" he asked.

"Absolutely. Plus, you'll be wearing a mike to record the conversation. This guy has killed twice and attempted to kill Jamie. We'll have him surrounded with you in our sights at all times," Jim reassured him. "You know the risks. I'll understand if you decline this assignment. Nobody will think less of you."

"I'm all in, sir. Let's do it," Sam replied, touching the curls of his wig. His eyes gleamed with determination. There was a firmness in his jaw that aged him beyond his years. *He's such a kid,* Jim thought.

"Operation Gold Stinger is about to begin," Jamie said dramatically as he began to text on his phone. Jamie copied the text Paul had written verbatim.

Hi Steve. Followed you out to the MM farm. I really want to see the gold. Is that where you've hidden it? When can we meet? Jamie Alberg

Jim rolled his eyes and watched Jamie's thumbs fly over the keys of his phone.

Sitting in his recliner on Monitor Street, Steve Stoner glanced at his phone. He sat up straight. He couldn't believe it—a text from Jamie? First, he had to recover from his shock when Jamie's name appeared at the end of the text. Hadn't he drowned in the Mississippi? How had that gone wrong? It seemed so foolproof at the time. The kid was beyond drunk. And the Effexor Steve added should have guaranteed the kid was a goner. What were the chances of that? That kid just kept popping up, refusing to go away like some of those figures in a pinball arcade machine.

Maybe this was just a way of trapping him. He paused and thought about what he should do. Even if it was someone else posing as Jamie, they couldn't be allowed to blackmail him. If not Jamie, who could it be? Had someone followed him to the farm? He'd have to deal with it. He'd never be free to live his life otherwise. He'd always have a threat looming over his head.

This new proposition was so amateurish! What did Jamie think? That he was just going to hand over the gold and let him horn in on all his hard work? Never. But if Jamie wanted to meet him tonight and see the gold, fine by him. Quickly, he texted him back. *Good to hear from you, buddy. Sure. Eleven tonight at the farm on MM. Be there. Steve*

He wasn't worried. He outweighed the boy by seventy-five

pounds. Subduing him would be a piece of cake. He had decided it was time to leave town and move the gold anyway. This time Jamie would be out of the picture. He'd planned his route through the western U.S., heading south at Denver, driving through Texas until he came to Mexico. There he planned to sell his truck and pick up another vehicle. Then it'd be freedom and the open road.

He checked the time on the kitchen clock. Four hours. He sat back in his chair and smiled.

—o—O—o—

Jim's team sat around the gleaming granite island in the Alberg's kitchen, eating pizza and drinking sodas. At first, the conversation was jovial and upbeat, especially when Jamie had succeeded in texting Steve Stoner, arranging to meet him at the farmhouse on MM. They'd all crowded around Jamie and read Stoner's reply. That had felt like a major piece of the puzzle falling in place. Jim had to admit that Jamie had a certain bravado. But he sure didn't have any common sense, especially when it came to danger. People skills weren't his strong suit either. Reading nonverbal cues and noticing subtle changes in facial expressions were wasted on him. That partially explained the difficulties he'd found himself in lately. So in planning this sting, Jim knew a stand-in was the only option.

Over the years, Jim had discerned that everyone had a certain intuitive sense when things seemed hinky or out of the ordinary. The ability to recognize danger and then act to protect themselves was what kept people alive. Others tore through the red flags and found themselves raped, injured, or facing death at the hands of a demented criminal. Jim knew that instinct and that "small voice" were God-given gifts that could save your life only if you *listened*. Jamie seemed to lack the ability to sense when things were out of sync, and listening was becoming a lost art everywhere in modern culture, not just with Jamie.

SUE BERG

As the evening wore on, the team organized their gear and went over the plan. The jovial atmosphere evaporated, and everyone became serious and sober. Jim's worries increased as the minutes ticked by. Stings were notoriously hard to pull off. He thought about his young cohorts and their lack of experience. *Maybe I should scrap the idea,* he thought. He had carried on drug stings for months before making any arrests. Inexperienced officers. A plan thrown together at the last minute. No wonder he was anxious and his stomach was doing flip-flops. When Jim consulted with the sheriff, the only stipulation he'd had was to keep up surveillance on Stoner until he showed up at the farm.

"You're not having second thoughts, are you, Chief?" Paul asked quietly when they were in the hallway out of earshot.

"Of course, I am," Jim said seriously, concern reflected in his eyes. "There's so much that could go wrong. You're all so young. I've never attempted anything like this before, let alone ask a bunch of greenhorns to be involved."

Paul picked up on Jim's apprehension. "Hey! Give us a little credit!" Paul patted his chest with both hands. "We can do this. Look at Leslie. She's been in firefights and hardcore battle situations. I know Sam might look crazy most of the time, but he's sharp and obviously willing to put himself out there. Me? Well, I'm probably your biggest risk." He shrugged. "Besides, there's no time like the present. Things *can* go wrong, but we'll be fine, sir. We've got a good plan, and we're ready to go." His words failed to inspire the confidence Jim needed to hear.

"You're right, but it doesn't reduce the risk," Jim said. Jamie had eyed the two men in the hallway. He came and stood in front of Jim and Paul, planting his feet with determination.

"Can't I come along?" Jamie begged, his hands upturned. "After all, he did try to kill me. I should at least have the satisfaction of seeing the scumball get caught," he finished angrily.

"I understand your frustration, but this is standard procedure. No civilians! We'd be reckless and irresponsible to let you anywhere near the farm. I know you're disappointed, but when this is over, you'll have your day in court, believe me," Jim said firmly. "And I'll be counting on you to give the jury your version of Stoner's murder attempt. I'm sure you'll wow them."

"Please, Lt. Higgins, I'm begging you!" he complained loudly. Leslie looked up, hearing the heated argument in the hall. Jim waved her questioning look away. "We're just having a discussion," Jim said. He turned back to Jamie.

"Sorry, absolutely not happening, Jamie. It's too risky. And I would lose my job." Jim pivoted and signaled the team they were leaving. "Okay, everybody. We're heading out." He waved them toward the back door of the kitchen. It was 8:42 p.m.

By nine o'clock, dusk was fading fast, and full darkness descended. They gathered their gear in the Alberg's driveway, and the team strapped on their vests, mikes, and weapons. They adjusted their backpacks. Inside were first aid kits, water, energy bars, flashlights, knives, tactical rope, and night vision goggles. The car dashboard camera had been mounted inside on the roof of the Jeep's rear passenger side. Hopefully, it would go unnoticed by Stoner.

They drove out to MM. Jim parked his Suburban near one of the mobile homes in the trailer park across the road from the farm. He knocked on the door of the trailer and informed the owner that his truck would remain near his driveway well into the night.

"We're on official police business, so please do not call 911. If possible, stay in your home. We will give you the all-clear when the operation is over." Jim said, flashing his police ID to the middle-aged man.

In the dark, they stationed themselves at fifty-yard intervals in the woods surrounding the farmstead. Sam parked his Jeep in the farmhouse driveway. Squirming, he tried to get comfortable. Waiting made his nerves tingle with anticipation and anxiety. He was already sweating from the wig and itched all over from the unfamiliar clothes. He took some deep breaths to calm himself. Mentally, he practiced the mannerisms that distinguished Jamie's behavior. *Is this really going to work? Boy, I hope I don't get shot or strangled or thrown off a bluff.*

Jim sat in the woods that surrounded the farmstead. After clearing out the high weeds, he had a clear view of the farm. He sprayed himself with mosquito repellant. When he got settled, he checked with each team member to make sure their lines of communication were functioning and ready. When Sam responded, he sounded nervous and apprehensive.

"I'm ready, Chief. This wig is already drivin' me nuts. When Stoner arrives, I just hope I can engage him for a while so we can get more information about the gold. Do you think he's hidden it here somewhere on the farm?"

"Why else would he come here? Seems likely that it has something to do with the gold," Jim commented laconically. "Of course, he could just be jerking our chain. Or maybe he doesn't have a plan at all. Who knows? Listen, just don't worry. We'll back you up," Jim lectured. "Don't push him into a corner. You've surprised a lot of prostitutes and johns who never saw an arrest coming. Just be patient and see what happens. You can do this," Jim encouraged.

"Got it, Chief. I'll talk to you when it's all over," Sam said seriously.

The waiting began. The sounds of the night intruded. A rustling of leaves, the nocturnal chirping of crickets in the tall grass, and a gentle breeze threatened to lull them into a state of peaceful security. Far off in the hills, a pack of coyotes howled.

Paul leaned back against a protruding sandstone rock and fought the urge to sleep. Leslie felt like she was missing her right arm without Paco. Every operation she'd been involved in had included her canine companion. Jim dozed a little bit. During the snooze, his butt went numb. He wiggled, trying to stay awake. The scent of honeysuckle wafted on the breeze. The moon rose silently in the night sky and bathed the farm in a soft golden hue.

The moments ticked by and turned into hours. As eleven o'clock approached, the team felt their nerves tense. Everyone began to feel antsy, wanting to move around and stretch their legs. Jim's cell phone vibrated in his pocket.

He answered quietly. "Higgins."

"We're on our way, sir. Just heading down Losey, hanging back a little. But one thing is kinda crazy," Officer Leland said.

"What's that?" Jim asked, his voice tense.

"I think we're being followed," he said.

"What makes you think that?"

"We've had an older model Pontiac hanging on our tail. Trying not to be paranoid, but the car doesn't seem to be varying his route. He's stickin' right with us."

Matt Shafer, Jim thought.

"We're in position. Don't lose Stoner," Jim instructed. "Just walk him into us, then head up to the mobile home park. Wait for us there. We may need backup if things get wild."

"Yes, sir," Leland clicked off.

In a few minutes, the Chevy pickup turned on MM and rolled down the road. Stoner cautiously turned into the farm driveway. Sam looked in his rearview mirror, his heart pounding, his breathing shallow. *Relax. Breathe big. Confidence, man.*

The Chevy's lights went off. The truck door slamming sounded like the bell of a boxing match that was about to begin. Sam could hear the crunch of gravel under Stoner's boots as he approached the Jeep. Preparing to get in the vehicle with Sam, Stoner turned when he heard another car drive in.

The Pontiac that Officer Leland had described to Jim rolled in alongside the Chevy pickup. Matt Shafer emerged, ambling past the Jeep driver's door. He stopped and leaned over, resting his arms casually on the hood of the Jeep. Instead of getting in, Stoner strolled up the passenger side of the Jeep and positioned himself across the hood facing Matt. *Showdown at the O.K. Corral,* Sam thought.

Jim watched from the woods, the moon giving just enough ambient light to make out movement. Through his night-vision goggles, he sucked in a sharp breath at what he saw. Stoner and

Shafer. *Oh boy. Two desperados for the price of one? That might not work out so well. This is like a keg of dynamite waiting for a match.* Jim strained to hear the conversation, but the distance was too great. He hoped Sam had remembered to turn on the recorder. His anxiety ramped up.

"A meeting of the minds?" Sam chirped innocently, sticking his head out of the Jeep. A classic Jamie remark.

"Hardly," Steve said bitterly, his lips twisting in a cruel smile. "A meeting of criminals, maybe? Or drug dealers? Or killers?" He laughed crazily, the sound carrying into the woods.

"Speak for yourself, Stoner. I know you killed Maria Santana. So yeah, you are a killer." Matt pointed an accusing finger at Steve, jabbing the air for emphasis. "And Higgins tried to pin that on me. Thanks for nothin'."

"Prove it," Steve sneered.

"I intend to," Matt snarled back. He leaned over and cocked his head toward Sam, who was still inside the cab as if he'd just first noticed him. "Who's the kid in the car?" he asked, jerking his thumb toward Sam sitting in the Jeep. "Another little pawn to take the fall for you? Just like you tried to do to me?"

Sam smiled innocently, leaning his head out the window. "A pawn? If we're playing chess, I wanna be a knight."

Stoner's face was a mask of anger and fear. He suddenly turned his attention to Sam. "Well, Jamie, you screwed up the whole thing thanks to that stupid video you posted on Facebook," he sputtered furiously, bringing his fist down on the hood. "Thanks to you," he hissed, "Higgins started getting suspicious, especially when you survived your little dunk in the Mississippi."

"Well, excuse me. I do apologize. Now let's talk about the price you should pay for trying to kill me," Sam yelled. His eyes blazed with righteous anger, and he threw the driver's door open.

Matt, surprised at the move, hurried to the front of the Jeep. Now the three men formed a triangle around the vehicle's hood. The night air was charged with tension like the heat of a wildfire gone out of control.

"Why, you little snot-nosed brat! I could break both your arms in the time it took you to blow your nose and run to your mommy!" Stoner said, adding a string of obscenities.

Sam let him vent, then said, "All I want to know is where the gold is because I know you have it, Stoner. I just want to see it." His face looked like flint. "I've searched just as hard as you have. I want to know that I didn't waste eight years of my life chasing nothing."

"You want to see it?" Stoner said incredulously, backing up and thrusting out his chest. "You want to see it?" he repeated, ending with a barking laugh. "You lost that chance when you couldn't keep your big mouth shut." His words snapped off like dry twigs. In the moonlight, Sam could see the hatred in his eyes like blackened embers from a cold campfire.

"Well, I kind of agree with the kid," Matt interrupted cockily. "Let's see this big treasure you supposedly found. How do we know it really exists? Maybe you're making all this crap up. Where is it, huh?" he snapped as he glared at Stoner, baiting him. Silence followed. Matt spoke up. "Well, we're waitin'."

For a few seconds, Sam thought Stoner's resolve would crack. Maybe he'd be willing to cooperate and work out a deal. Or at least hint where the gold might be hidden. Everyone froze. The seconds seemed to drag by while the sense of danger increased like the tightening of a fiddle string. Stoner rocked back and forth from his toes to his heels like a crazed automaton, his demeanor becoming more threatening by the minute.

Unbeknownst to the team, Leslie had begun a quiet descent from the bank where she had been hiding. She began crawling on her stomach, propelling herself forward toward the Jeep. She'd move a foot or two, stop, and listen. She began advancing again only when she was sure she hadn't been heard or detected. She stopped when she was twenty yards from the arguing men. She waited on her belly in the tall grass. The darkness was penetrating, and the smell of damp earth filled her nostrils. The air pressed down on her until she felt like she was suffocating.

She could hardly hear the men's conversation, bits and pieces hovering in the air above her. But the expressions of anger, denial, and frustration were real. She remembered emotions like that from exchanges when questioning captured insurgents. That tone was universal no matter what language was spoken. Her heart pounding, she willed herself to remain calm and alert.

Suddenly, there was a shout. Jim caught a swift gesture by Stoner. A flurry of short outbursts and exchanges filled the night air, then more loud shouting. Through his goggles, he could see Stoner desperately pulling a pistol from his jacket.

"No! No!" Matt yelled, his hands waving wildly in front of him. "Don't shoot me!" he begged as he backed away from the Jeep. "Don't kill me!" He continued backing up until he was twenty feet away. He waved his hands in panic.

Jim and Paul stood up where they were and began trotting from the edge of the woods to the farmhouse. Leslie kneeled from her prone position. The clear, calm voice of Jim Higgins carried through the darkness.

"Everyone drop your weapons. This is Lt. Jim Higgins, La Crosse Sheriff's Department. Stoner, drop the gun! Now! It's not worth—"

Jim never got to finish. Stoner raised his pistol, pointing it at Matt. He pulled the trigger multiple times, aiming haphazardly. Bursts of gunfire boomed over the valley, making sounds like a small cannon. Sam ducked, then ran behind the Jeep. He dived at Stoner's legs, tackling him in one athletic arc, bringing him to the ground with a loud *boof!* Shots continued firing wildly. Bullets ricocheted off the Chevy's fender, and the windshield of the Jeep exploded, sending splinters of glass raining down on Sam and Stoner.

Sam grabbed Stoner's wrist in the scuffle and torqued the empty gun from his grip, sending it flying into the high grass next to the Jeep. Sam scrambled to get on top of Stoner, but he was fast and strong. He curled his large hands around Sam's throat. They felt like ribbons of steel, cutting off his oxygen. Sam beat him with his fists, but he felt himself going away somewhere else. *This must be how Maria felt,* he thought. He began blacking out.

Jim stumbled in the dark, but his legs churned down the hill. His heart hammered in his chest like a gong. He came around the Jeep and piled on Stoner. Fists flew, muscle on muscle. Grunts and the sounds of blows finding flesh punctuated the night air along with a few choice words. Sam and Jim continued pummeling Stoner until they were able to overpower him. Handcuffed, Stoner lay subdued and fully spent facedown on the ground next to the Jeep.

At the same time, Leslie had come in at a low crouch until she reached Matt Shafer. "I'm shot. I'm shot," he whimpered, a grimace of pain on his face.

"Okay, okay. We're here." Leslie switched on her Streamlight tactical flashlight and swept it over Matt's body. He was wounded superficially in the ribs, but a wound in his shoulder was bleeding profusely. She sensed Paul next to her, breathing hard, shouting into his cell. He called for an ambulance and backup. Leslie lowered her flashlight and tucked her gun back in its holster. "Easy, easy. Just breathe," Leslie said. She turned to Paul. "Need a couple of four-by-four bandages and some tape," she ordered, her hands shaking. "Let's get him stabilized."

Paul rummaged through his backpack and found the first aid supplies. He ripped out some bandages and handed them to Leslie. Then she said to Matt, "I'm going to apply some pressure to your shoulder. It might hurt."

Matt screamed and pushed Leslie's hand away. He struggled to sit up then fainted into a heap in the grassy field. Leslie continued first aid, compressing the wound, trying to slow the bleeding.

"Hang in there, Matt. An ambulance is on its way," Paul said breathlessly. "You got this?" he asked. She nodded. He ran over to the Jeep and found Stoner cuffed and mute.

"You guys okay?" Paul asked, his eyes sweeping back and forth over them. His breathing was anxious and rapid.

Jim and Sam had recovered enough to lean against the Jeep. They were inhaling great gulps of the night air, sweat pouring from their faces and dripping off their chins. The adrenaline was still coursing through them, their faces tight with tension. Jim's chest and arms were starting to ache from the blows Stoner had landed. Sam nodded at Paul, who noticed that the Jeep seemed to be holding both men upright.

"Yeah, yeah, we're fine."

Sam whispered raggedly, his hands shaking. "Close call, Chief. Close call. Damn. I lost my wig." In the encompassing moonlight, Jim could hear the faint wail of an ambulance heading their way, the sound of its whining getting closer.

"We did good," Jim said, wrapping an arm around Sam's shoulders. He gave him a weak smile, his dimple barely visible. "We did good. We'll get you another wig." ⊙

25

SUNDAY, JUNE 20

Saturday night seemed like it would never end. Jim accompanied Steve Stoner to the La Crosse County Jail, where he was charged with the attempted murder of Matt Shafer. Jim was hopeful that other charges would follow as they uncovered more evidence.

Stoner sat sullenly in a holding cell, refusing to make eye contact with either Jim or Sam. Paul had accompanied Matt Shafer in the ambulance to the hospital. Leslie gathered shell casings at the farmstead with the help of the city cops, picked up weapons and backpacks, and took them back to the office. The city cops delivered Stoner's vehicle to the impound center.

Jim told Leslie, "Go home, sleep, and eat. You were great out there." *God, she's the same age as Sara,* he thought. "Snuggle up to Paco. We'll talk later," Jim said encouragingly.

"See you later, sir," Leslie said as she left the jail.

The hours had buzzed by. Now it was close to three in the morning. When all the paperwork was done, Jim and Sam walked into the cool air, the night crawling toward morning. They stood in the outer courtyard of the law enforcement center. A soft breeze ruffled the shadowed trees. In the early morning hours, the city had quieted to a whisper. Traffic was practically nonexistent.

"Tough guy, huh?" Sam commented.

"We'll both feel it later. He got in some good shots. We'll question him tomorrow. But he's not going to crack easily, especially when it comes to revealing where the gold is stashed," Jim commented. "Without the gold, the legend will remain and won't support our motive for murder."

"What about the farm? Didn't you mention some cave thing that was there?"

"Yeah, there is a cave right on MM. We'll get in there, and we'll tear his house apart, too. He couldn't have hidden it that well, not with all the mistakes he's made." They let that sit a while. Finally, Sam rolled his shoulders, stretched his arms over his head, and yawned.

"Well, Chief, I'm bushed." He was starting to decompress. Fatigue and exhaustion were pressing down on him like a ton of bricks. The red welt on his neck burned. Rubbing at it, he quit when the pain flared up again. He was sure by morning it would be black and blue. "I feel like I could sleep for a hundred years," he yawned. "I'm goin' home. See you later."

Jim slapped his back. "Go home. Get some sleep and eat something. You know the drill." Sam turned and waved. He ambled down the sidewalk under the enormous maple trees to the parking lot. Jim watched him fall into his car and drive out to the street. He beeped his horn as he passed.

Jim stood there for a moment, still thinking, his mind replaying the night sting. It had gone better than he anticipated, although it would have been best without the injuries. Matt Shafer was still in surgery. Jim walked to his Suburban and pointed it in the direction of Gundersen Lutheran.

He felt like he was on automatic pilot. Scenes from the incident at the farmhouse pulsed through his mind, and he felt his heart accelerate recalling the events. He was beginning to wind down. After twenty-four hours, exhaustion was bumping against his thoughts, making him feel like a tattered rag waving in a stiff breeze.

He parked his Suburban in front of the hospital entrance. Throwing his parking sign that said La Crosse Sheriff's Department on the dashboard, he climbed out and traipsed inside, stopping at the front desk to inquire about Matt Shafer.

"Who's asking?" the attendant asked brusquely.

Jim flashed his badge. "La Crosse Sheriff's Department. Mr. Shafer was injured in an incident this evening."

The attendant punched some keys on his computer. "He's still in surgery. It'll be another couple of hours, at least. Then he'll be transferred to the third floor. The waiting area is right up these stairs," he said, pointing to the staircase. "His number is 78621. The wall monitors will inform you as the surgery progresses." He wrote the number on a sticky note and handed it to Jim.

"Thanks," Jim said as he climbed the stairs. When he reached the top, he looked around at the number of people camped out. Some were on the chairs, and others sat on the floor and leaned against the wall with their feet kicked out in front of them. Others scrolled on their phones, the screens glowing blue in the dimmed overhead lights. Most of them were trying to find some kind of comfortable position so they could get some sleep. All of them looked exhausted. Worry creased their faces.

"Hey, Chief," Paul said, stepping up next to him. "Coffee, soda?" he asked.

Jim's eyes scanned Paul, looking for any signs of stress. He looked normal, his typical in-control self. "Yeah, I'll take a coffee—decaf if they have it."

"Be right back," he said, turning to the refreshment bar.

"You call Ruby yet?" Paul asked, as he handed the cup to his boss.

"Yup. Had some time while I was waiting for Matt to get prepped for surgery. She's fine."

"Well, don't minimize what you've gone through. And don't shut Ruby out. She's just as much your partner as I am." He stopped and looked over at Paul. That overconfidence of his was hard to penetrate.

Jim knew it could kick him in the butt if you weren't careful. Paul returned his gaze without flinching. Now when Jim looked at him closely, he could see the stress around his eyes and mouth. He wasn't as invincible as he thought.

"I hear you," Paul admitted grudgingly, looking away under Jim's scrutinizing gaze.

"I remember being a police officer during the first few years of my marriage," Jim said, staring into space. "It was pretty rough. Margie resented me when I was gone, and she resented me when I was home because I just couldn't unplug. I was always mentally on duty. I couldn't shut it off, so I shut her out. I didn't know if our relationship would last. It was pretty rocky."

By this time, Jim and Paul had found a couple of chairs in a quiet corner of the surgery waiting area. Jim studied Paul's face. His intensity and drive were his best assets, but they were also his greatest liabilities in a relationship. He hoped Paul could weather what would inevitably come in his work. The slaughter of innocent people, the evil that never gave in, the out-of-control drug problem; the list went on and on and seemed to get worse each year. The stress of the job could wreak havoc on health and relationships.

Jim had seen Paul's disposition level out since he'd become involved with Ruby. She was good for him. He hoped the relationship would continue, especially with a baby in the picture. But Jim knew that Ruby would be tempted to force Paul to choose between the work he loved and the home life he needed. Almost every couple in law enforcement that he knew had been through it. He'd learned through experience. It was always dangerous to coerce a choice from someone you loved—either this or that. Coercion was usually irreparable. Paul needed his job and a home life. He just didn't know it yet.

"So, what changed you?" Paul asked, glancing sideways at Jim.

"That's easy. Margie got pregnant. Twins no less. The first time I felt those babies kick, I knew how much I needed and loved her. But I still encouraged her to be independent. I wanted her to be her own person because I knew there would be times when I couldn't be there for her." Jim stretched out his legs and sighed.

"Truth be told, we both had to change. But everything shifted when a fellow police officer committed suicide when we lived in Blair. He went out into the woods during deer hunting and shot himself. That was really tough. It led us to a crossroad in our relationship," he said, his voice tight with emotion. His blue eyes seemed to darken, and he looked away, remembering that terrible moment. Paul stayed silent, not wanting to tread on Jim's emotional territory.

After a pause, Jim went on. "The night of the funeral, I came back to the house and cried like a baby. But that night was also a turning point in our marriage. Margie really came through for me. She let me vent, let me cry. She listened to my rantings and cursing. It was raw and real. But she empathized without smothering me and judging me. From then on, I knew I could count on her to have my back. She wasn't perfect. We had our share of arguments and fights, but she was a great wife and mother," he finished, his voice wistful.

"Yeah, everybody I know in the department talks about you."

"Really? Well, I hope it's good—what you hear."

"It's good, Chief. Very good."

The report on Matt came through about five o'clock in the morning. The doctor was tall and thin. He reminded Jim of a crane the way he stood at soldier-like attention in front of them. His eyes burned with intelligence above a beak-like nose. A superior self-confidence rolled off him as he sailed into the update. Articulating Matt's injuries, his voice was detached and professional, if somewhat impersonal.

"Mr. Shafer had extensive damage to his right shoulder. The bullet pulverized the rotator cuff and ball of the shoulder. It took us a while to remove the splintered bone and stabilize what was left. He had entry and exit wounds, and he suffered some significant blood loss. He will need additional surgery to reclaim the use of his shoulder. Recovery will be slow and require a lot of therapy. But he'll live," the surgeon said. "Any questions?" His bright eyes assessed the two exhausted men and dismissed them all in the same glance.

Jim shook his head and thanked him for the update. The doc turned and strode down the hall, his white coat billowing around his pants like bird wings, flying to his next crisis.

Jim touched base with the officer assigned to surveillance outside Matt's hospital room. Then he walked with Paul to the parking ramp. Reaching their vehicles, Jim reminded Paul to go home, sleep, and eat. "Don't come in before you've done that. Get some rest."

"Got it, Chief. See you later."

The weight of responsibility for his team lifted from Jim's shoulders. *They're all safe and in good shape.* He limped to his car, feeling old. He was so tired. *Fifty-two wasn't that old, was it?* Jim thought. The morning sky was beginning to glow above the bluffs. Everything was hushed and still. Dew glistened on the tall grasses and cattails next to the road, and a few birds were trumpeting their morning songs. Jim felt like he was in a bubble, in a place where he was just barely aware of his surroundings. He didn't remember the drive down U.S. 35 to Chipmunk Coulee Road.

When the garage door jolted up, he came out of his trance, drove in, and flicked the remote to bring the door down. Walking into the kitchen, he kicked off his shoes, plodded down the hall to his bedroom, stripped off his clothes, and fell into bed. He was asleep before he could pull the sheets over himself. ☉

26

SUNDAY, JUNE 20

Steve Stoner lay on his narrow thin cot in the La Crosse County Jail and tried to analyze where he'd made his mistakes. There were so many. Apparently, criminal activity required intelligence and higher-level thinking skills that he seemed to be lacking.

Since his arrest for attempted murder last night, he had run the gamut of emotions from anger, guilt, remorse, and then more anger. He knew that the murder of Jorge Santana would be hard to pin on him. There was little or no DNA evidence that would prove it. Santana's injuries were the result of a direct fall from 150 feet to the floor of a rock quarry. The only thing that tied him to the murder was the gold coin, but it was all conjecture on Higgins' part without the treasure.

Maria Santana was a different matter entirely. He'd been more careful, but he was sure his DNA was in the trailer. He could imagine it falling and collecting in drifts like snow during a snowstorm. He'd worn gloves and burned the scrap of clothesline he'd used to strangle her. But crime scene forensics was constantly improving, so who knew what they could pull out of the trailer as evidence. Still, in the final analysis, he could plead guilty to lesser drug charges and explain his DNA's presence in the trailer from the drug activity.

Jamie Alberg was a pain from the start. A snot-nosed kid with wealthy parents, Jamie had an inflated opinion of his intelligence and knowledge. Spoiled, cocky, and the center of his parents' world, he had no idea what it meant to do a hard day's work. The work at MVAC was a place for him to build his reputation and portfolio in forensic archaeology. Manipulating circumstances and looking for opportunities to build up his ego was something Jamie Alberg was good at. *Political BS,* Steve thought. Still, fate had been with him on the night at Sloopy's. When he pushed Jamie in the river, any DNA that was left had floated away in the current and was now a non-issue.

He didn't trust Higgins. That man was scary. His reputation as a determined, stubborn investigator preceded him and was well earned. Local media had followed the detective's career, and he had become something of a legend solving difficult cases when it seemed that evidence was lacking. He was willing to do the hard work of gathering and corroborating every piece of information. Despite overwhelming obstacles, Higgins had come out with charges that stuck. Many of those perpetrators were rotting in state and federal prisons.

He rolled on his side, facing the blank, white wall. Heaven forbid that anyone would notice his fear. As he lay in his orange jumpsuit, contemplating his bleak future, he couldn't help but shed a few tears at the unfairness of the whole ugly situation. *Things were going to become very difficult from here on out,* thought Steve.

Jim woke up about three in the afternoon feeling like he was hungover. He moved his legs and felt bruises on his chest, legs, and arms. His mouth was dry and cottony. He rolled out of bed with a grimace and used the bathroom, gulping down a couple of ibuprofen with a glass of water. Standing in front of the mirror, he took stock of the purple and red welts covering his body. The hot water of the shower relaxed muscles and nerves as suds rolled over him.

Later, he made eggs, sausage links, hash brown potatoes, and whole wheat toast. He sipped orange juice while he cooked and made a fresh pot of coffee. The smells permeated the kitchen. He was always overwhelmed by the normalcy of life, especially after some difficult policing situation. It was easy to take for granted the comfort of a bed, a hot shower, food in the refrigerator, or coffee brewing, but their absence would make life hell. That's what Margie had done for him. She'd given him a home, a safe place where he could unwind and regain a sense of peace.

He took his breakfast and phone out to the screened-in porch. Sleep, a shower, and good food began bringing him out of his funk. He noticed fifteen messages just since yesterday morning. He decided to answer them a little later. It didn't work. The phone vibrated on the table.

"Jim Higgins," he said, chewing on a piece of toast.

"Hey, how're you feeling?" Carol asked. "Heard your people did a bang-up job. My phone is buzzing with the news of your sting, but no gold was found?"

"No gold. And yes, they were great. Sam got a little beat up. Matt Shafer got shot. It'll take time, but he'll be fine. A slow recovery, though. Stoner's in the slammer, which he so richly deserves. So all in all, it's been a modest success," Jim explained unpretentiously.

"So are you feeling all right?

"Yep. I'm fine. A little sore, some bruises and stuff, but nothing that won't go away in a day or so."

"I'm glad your team is okay." Carol sounded relieved.

They talked about the confrontation with Matt Shafer and Steve Stoner. Carol listened carefully without interrupting, letting Jim divulge the sting at his own pace. He was confident some of the charges would stick but knew they didn't have enough evidence to convict Steve on all the murders.

"Any charges we file will center around the attempted murder of

SUE BERG

Matt Shafer at the farm. That conversation is recorded, so it should be a done deal. We had a dashcam inside the Jeep, but we haven't checked the clarity of the images yet."

"What about the gold?" Carol asked. "Are you sure Stoner has it somewhere?"

"Actually, no. We don't know that for sure. We're hoping it's true and that we can find it. That was part of the sting's purpose, but it got cut short when Stoner started shooting up the place. It was wild for a few minutes there. We'll question him tomorrow, but I doubt he'll tell us."

"So, what are your plans for today?" Carol asked tentatively.

"I don't know. Do you have something in mind?"

"You better be careful. I might surprise you one of these days."

Jim chuckled. "Well, I was just going to do some yard work around here for a few hours, lay low. How about this evening? Maybe we can go for a drive along the river and find someplace to eat," Jim suggested.

"Sounds good. Time?"

"Pick you up around six."

"Great. See you then." Carol clicked off.

Jim closed his phone. He worked his way through the messages, which took him half an hour. Then he loaded his John Deere ATV with some gardening tools and puttered around his property, pulling weeds and straightening fence posts. He thinned some overgrown and misshapen vegetation. Pruning back a lilac bush, he stopped, noticing the memory stone. *Margie Higgins, Always in our Memory, Always loved, X three. Jim, John, and Sara.*

Each time he had visited her stone in the past year, he'd been reminded of all his sorrow. The loneliness practically drowned him. The cathartic moments he'd spent here remembering their life together brought an ache in his chest along with tears. But now, he could sense a shift. He didn't know when he'd passed the milestone of self-pity. Standing here today, he felt privileged and honored to have known and loved her deeply. That described him and Margie. Real love. What had Paul said last night? "Everybody in the department talks about you two. And it's good."

Toward evening, he showered and changed his clothes. It was a perfect evening for a country drive.; balmy and warm with a cloudless blue sky and an open road.

Carol met him at the door of her condo, dressed in a pair of jeans that hugged her hips, a bright floral top, and strappy sandals. Her makeup was minimal, which Jim liked because it enhanced her naturally flawless skin and brunette hair.

"You look great," he said.

"Thanks. Where are we headed?" Carol asked, climbing into the Suburban.

"Well, I think it's the perfect time to head down toward Rockton and wander along the Kickapoo River and maybe see some sandhill cranes and deer. Sound good?"

"Love it." Carol gave him a high-wattage smile.

Jim drove leisurely, just under fifty. Taking Highway 14, he drove out of the La Crosse River Valley up onto the ridge. Just outside of Westby, he caught County Road P, where they wandered through the Amish countryside. The road along the Kickapoo River curved and wound its way through green valleys populated with lush stands of oaks, maples, birches, and white pines. Wild turkeys browsed in the fields and occasionally crossed the road in front of the Suburban. Rounding a sharp corner, a pair of Sandhill cranes gawked casually at them before scurrying off the road into the tall sedges, disappearing from view.

"Oh, look, Jim!" Carol whispered. "Aren't they something! They're huge. So majestic."

"Yeah, they are. They're probably one of the biggest birds around here, and to think just a couple of decades ago, they were on the verge of extinction." Jim reached across the seat and took Carol's hand.

Canoeists in bulky life vests paddled quietly under a bridge. A few late evening anglers stood in hip boots on the edge of the watery switchbacks, casting for trout. Black-eyed Susans, Queen Anne's lace, and tiger lilies bloomed in profusion in the ditches and roadsides along Highway 131. The sun was sinking in the western sky, painting hues of pink and lemon yellow.

The Rockton bridge came into view, aptly named by a local writer, "The Million Dollar Bridge to Nowhere" led across the valley. The bridge was part of a 1976 federally proposed man-made lake and dam project, which was halted due to a lack of federal funds. It carried tragic memories for the people who had their farms and homes confiscated, all in the name of eminent domain. Over the years, the original site had reverted to its natural habitat. Now the 7,300-acre area has been transformed into the Kickapoo Valley Reserve, featuring hiking trails, the Kickapoo River, and a nature center.

Jim crossed the bridge and stopped in front of the Rockton Bar, a hangout known for their wood-grilled chicken dinners. A huge fieldstone fireplace with a ceiling and walls constructed of peeled white pine logs created a casual, friendly ambiance that permeated the restaurant. Scattered throughout, canoeists, bikers, and hikers enjoyed beer and burgers.

Jim found a table, ordered a beer for himself, and Carol chose wine. They both ordered chicken dinners. While they waited for their meals, Jim studied Carol. She was chattering about the ride along the river and the wildlife they'd seen. Her face was animated, and in the tavern's low lighting, she was a lovely sight. Jim noticed other people looking at her.

"Weren't those sandhill cranes something?" she said. "Jim? Did you hear me?" She felt him studying her like she was passing some kind of test. She blushed. He was sitting with his elbow on the table, resting his chin on his hand, deep in thought.

"Yeah, I heard you. Beautiful," he said, but what he meant was she was beautiful.

An hour rolled by in relaxed conversation as twilight descended. They held hands while Jim drove north through the little town of

Ontario, cruised through the thickly wooded Wildcat State Park, and then tumbled along, the ride like a rollercoaster. Traveling over the ridge, they dropped down over the bluff into La Crosse. He felt thoroughly relaxed and rested. It was close to ten o'clock when he drove up to Carol's condo and parked the car.

"Come in for a nightcap," Carol said, moving her hand to his arm. "I'll make some coffee."

"Sure, but I won't stay long."

Carol bustled around the kitchen, filled the coffeepot, and found her gourmet coffees. "How does vanilla hazelnut sound?" she asked, slamming cupboard doors.

"Fine. Just fine," Jim commented, watching her get the coffee started. She kicked off her shoes. Setting out two mugs on the counter, she grabbed the non-dairy creamer from the cupboard.

Jim was standing by the counter, and she reached around him to open the drawer for spoons. Jim took her hand and pulled her to his chest. He touched her face and moved in for a long, deep kiss. She returned his kiss with an intensity that surprised them both. He pulled away after some time.

"Oh boy," he said, letting a groan escape. "This could be trouble."

"It's not trouble by me," she responded, laying her palms on his chest, looking up at him with her liquid brown eyes.

"I think I need to explain something," Jim said, taking Carol's hands in his.

"Has this got something to do with Margie? Because I can't compete with—"

Jim interrupted. "Shh, no, no. Just let me explain." He laid a finger across her lips, drew in a deep breath, and began. "I knew kissing you like that would lead to other things, but I couldn't resist. I think we've come to a tipping point in our relationship, don't you?"

"Jim, I'm fine making love with you. Who else will ever know? Besides, what's the big deal?"

He looked into her eyes, not knowing whether she would believe him when he told her.

SUE BERG

"God," he said. He felt her stiffen slightly, and she backed up about an inch.

Carol's eyes scanned his face. "Excuse me? God?" She looked confused.

He nodded his head, raising his eyebrows at the same time. "God will know," he repeated.

"Okay." There was more, she was sure.

"And my kids," he added carefully.

"They won't know unless you tell them," she countered. "Besides, they're adults."

"Sara knew we were on the boat together. I didn't tell her, did you?"

"No." She was disappointed. The sexual excitement that had been boiling a minute ago was reduced to a simmer. "Jim, this is ridiculous. We're two consenting adults. We can do what we want." A little spark of anger tinged her words.

"Not really," Jim said patiently. "When you have kids, you train them to believe a certain way. When you betray their trust and do something that goes against the code you've taught them, you lose your integrity. And they lose their faith in you. Sometimes they lose their faith in God. I can't afford to screw that up. My kids are very precious to me, and I treasure their respect." He pulled her back to him, holding her close. She didn't resist, but as he wrapped his arms around her, he could tell she was still confused.

"Listen to me. I love you," he said, holding her against his chest. She tipped her head back and stared at him. Her hair was slightly mussed, her eyes cautious.

"You do?" she asked. "Really?" Jim saw the start of a few tears.

"I do. Really." His blue eyes were intense and burning with emotion. "If what we have is as special as I think it is, it's worth waiting for." There was a long moment of silence.

Carol's stomach did a little flip. "What am I waiting for again? Remind me."

Jim smiled and kissed her forehead. "We're waiting to make love until we're married."

"This is the craziest thing I've ever heard of, like a throwback to another time," Carol said, shaking her head, her eyes round with wonderment. After a moment, she asked, "Are you asking me to marry you?"

"Yeah, I am," Jim said. When he thought about it, he didn't exactly know when he'd made the decision to ask her to marry him. At fifty-two, he had a feeling a love story would not come his way again. By now, Carol had wrapped her arms around his waist, and she was watching his face carefully.

"Listen," Jim said, "I could throw you over my shoulder right now and march you down the hall to your bedroom." Carol's eyebrows arched at the suggestion. "Don't mistake my refusal of lovemaking as something I don't want. It's just as tempting for me as it is for you. But I'm not interested in some intense sexual fling that's going to sputter and die after a couple of months. I want a life with you." He stroked her cheek with his finger.

Carol gave him an unfathomable look. He'd really thrown her a curveball this time. He kissed her tenderly on the mouth and untangled himself, turning to leave.

"Just think of it as character building," he said with a grin. "Delaying gratification now makes the surrender all that much sweeter when it happens. It'll all work out. Don't worry. And remember that I love you." He winked at her.

She sighed, standing in her kitchen. "I love you, too, but you're leaving me a very frustrated woman."

"You'll get over it. Nobody ever died from not having sex." He shut the door quietly and was gone.

"What about your coffee?" she said quietly to herself. ⊙

27

MONDAY, JUNE 21

The following day dawned cloudy and humid. A low front had moved in overnight, and the threat of rain lingered in the early morning air. Cars moved past the apartment. Their sounds were muffled as if covered with a blanket of fog.

Sam Birkstein rolled over on his side and looked at the time. He couldn't sleep any longer. He got up, strolling to the shower. His neck was sore, and the red welt from last night had turned purple and green. He grimaced as he touched it.

Hiking the trails under Grandad's Bluff in the shaded woods yesterday gave him time to reflect and process what had happened during the sting on Stoner. He tried to remember if Stoner had made any allusions to the hidden gold. He didn't think so, but he planned on listening to the tape again today to see if he could glean any hints from the conversation they had over the hood of the Jeep. Matt Shafer had to be interviewed again, too. It was hard to discern how much involvement he'd had in the stealing and hiding of the treasure and the murder of Maria Santana, if any. *He may be more involved than any of us realize,* Sam thought.

Toweling off, he pulled on a pair of pressed khakis, a light blue dress shirt, and a navy suitcoat, all bargain finds at the Goodwill

Store on Mormon Coulee. He finished the look with a used pair of hiking boots. He wasn't going to give up all his goofy outfits in one day. After all, a man had to have a certain pride about these things. He whipped a comb through his hair and thought about adding a necktie but decided the shock of his traditional dress would be enough for the girls in the office. He'd save the tie for another day. He could already imagine their oohs and aahs when they saw him looking so professional. Higgins was in for a shock, too. Sam smiled.

He gobbled down a carton of blueberry yogurt, a whole wheat raisin muffin, and a glass of orange juice. Fifteen minutes later, he slipped out the front entrance of the apartment and drove to the courthouse.

The elevator stopped at the third floor, and the door glided open. The girls turned when they heard the elevator arrive, anticipating some of the investigative team. Emily was sitting pert and cheerful at her desk. At the sight of Sam, the women stopped what they were doing, their eyes traveling over him from top to bottom.

"Is it really you?" one of them cooed.

Another asked, "What happened to your cool T-shirts?"

"What about those Adidas hightops?" someone else asked.

The rest of them began circling Sam like wolves stalking a deer.

"Here I am, in the flesh, dressed appropriately as a member of a crack investigation team." Sam grinned as he held his arms out from his sides and did a 360-degree spin in front of them. The girls gathered around him, touching his clothing, straightening the shirt collar, and fastening the single button on the suit jacket.

"My, you do look professional today," Emily remarked. *He certainly uses his charm and innocent demeanor to his advantage,* she thought, clearing her throat.

"Girls, we have work to do this morning," she warned, although a smile pulled at the corners of her mouth.

Sam turned toward the hallway, walking to his office. Jim was standing against the wall, arms crossed over his chest, grinning a wicked smile.

"Whoa! To what do we owe this honor?" he asked, eyes dancing with humor.

"Well, you know the pressure to conform constantly tests the bounds of my conscience. I finally cracked. I tried to resist, sir, but I caved," Sam said, a hint of sarcasm in his voice.

"You're lookin' good, buddy," Jim chuckled. Then he asked in a more serious tone, "How are you feeling?" His eyes drifted to the purple and green splotches around Sam's neck.

Sam fingered his bruise then said, "Fine, sir. Got a few ideas I want to discuss about Stoner." They strolled to the door of Jim's office.

"Good. We're meeting at ten. We need to process everything from the sting and line up our interrogation with Stoner. See you then," Jim finished. He turned, peeled off his coat, and rolled up his sleeves.

By nine-thirty, the investigative team was huddled in Jim's office, drinking coffee, and discussing the sting. Jim played the audiotape of the heated argument the men had around the Jeep.

"There's not even a hint of where the gold might be," Leslie said, in a tone that belied her frustration. She let out a long sigh. "Without the gold, our case will fall apart."

"I found out some other stuff this morning," Jim said, looking down at his notes on his desk.

"The deed to the farm on MM was transferred to Stoner in May of this year. His presence at the farmhouse is logical since it's his property, but it doesn't explain why he was there so late the other night unless he was just admiring his inheritance."

"Unlikely," said Sam. "He had to have some other motivation for going there. So are we getting a warrant to search the place?" Sam asked.

"Yep. Being processed as we speak—a warrant for both his city residence and the farm. Which reminds me, Paul, I need you to pick those up by eleven this morning," Jim ordered. He continued.

"Leslie, you and Paul are going to start ripping apart the farmhouse property. Don't forget to look for disturbances in the dirt. Maybe the gold is buried there somewhere." They looked at Jim skeptically. "Never know," Jim said, shrugging. "Also talk to some of the neighbors and see whether they've noticed how often Stoner visits there. They might have seen something. And don't forget the cave with the door."

"Sam, you're with me when we interrogate Stoner. I've had some more news from Luke about Maria Santana. The autopsy revealed that Maria had sexual relations with someone the night of her murder. We know it wasn't her husband; he'd been dead for a week already. So was this a secret lover? Was it an act of prostitution, or was it rape? Don't know, but we have two suspects: Matt Shafer and Steve Stoner. Of course, it could be some other random drug person." Jim looked at his team. "Once we get the DNA processed from Stoner, we'll know if the semen is a match." Everyone absorbed the news.

"Wow! That's a new development," Sam said.

"Well, the sex isn't really a surprise, is it?" asked Paul. "If you're dealing drugs, then other illicit activities go hand in hand with that."

"True," Jim said. "But the information gives us another angle with Stoner and Shafer. More leverage. Sexual assault and rape are not charges taken lightly." Not getting any responses, Jim moved on. "So, let's plan to interrogate Stoner about two this afternoon, Sam. Meet me here. Anything else?" He looked around, waited a minute. "If not, let's—"

"Ah, Chief, what about Stoner? Does he have a girlfriend? Someone he sees regularly? I know you said he was a loner, but everybody needs somebody now and then, if you get my meaning," Sam offered. A pink blush started at his neckline and grew until it settled on his cheeks. Leslie grinned, watching his discomfort.

"You mean a sexual partner?" Jim asked, unfazed by his embarrassment.

"Well, yeah," Sam said, tugging the collar of his shirt.

"Don't know. Why don't you see what you can dig up?" Jim asked. " If he does have someone, she might be able to tell us something about his recent movements. Let's get going."

The team shuffled out, and Jim called Emily into his office. He was sitting behind his desk, with an expression of satisfaction and a casual jauntiness.

"Close the door, will you?" he asked politely.

Emily obliged, her eyes wide with expectation. She grasped the door handle and swung the door shut until it clicked. Emily was the consummate professional. Jim rarely called her into his office unless it was something delicate or important. She mentally reviewed her recent performance and decided she'd done her best. Not to worry. Probably something about this case. Still, she thought of her girls in the secretarial pool fawning over Sam. Well, *that* might be an issue, or it could be Jamie Alberg and his antics in her office.

Jim looked up at her as he sat at his desk. She thought back to the days after Margie's death and the devastating effect it had on him. She'd listened then as a friend, not an employee. Apparently, Jim was counting on her again. He trusted her implicitly.

"What do you need, Chief?" she asked. She blinked hard, her pen poised above her notebook, her stomach fluttering a little bit. He could sometimes be intimidating when he took command. He reminded her of a general leading his battalion into war.

"I need you to do three things. These are all personal requests. I realize this is a favor to me. If you say no, it won't go any further, and I won't hold it against you. If you say yes, I'm trusting you to keep all of this to yourself. Understood?"

"Absolutely, sir. I'll do my very best."

"You always do your best, Emily. That's why I trust you." Jim beamed a big smile, a dimple denting his cheek. "First, I need you to order a bouquet of roses, sunflowers, delphiniums, and daylilies. Have it delivered downstairs to Carol Olstad with a note that says, 'I meant what I said. What about you?'" He paused a moment.

"Got it. That's easy," Emily said, smiling and writing down the specific flowers and the message. "Price range?" she asked, her eyebrows arching, tilting her head to the side.

"This needs to be a good-sized bouquet. Price is not a factor," he said businesslike. "Have them bill it to me. Use my address on

Chipmunk Coulee Road."

He leaned back, pulled out a side drawer in his desk, and withdrew a small book titled *Pocket Paris* by Rick Steves, the travel guru. "I want you to study this book and find a nice quiet hotel within walking distance of the Eiffel Tower. Don't book anything yet. I'll let you know the dates later."

Emily took the book from him and discreetly placed it within the notepad she was writing on. "Will do," she said. She looked at him expectantly.

Jim gave her a blank stare. He seemed to be somewhere else.

"You said three things, sir. You've only given me two," Emily informed him, her voice professional and crisp. She continued to hold his stare.

"Oh, right. Sorry." He seemed flustered for a moment. Then he reestablished his momentum. "I want you to go to that place downtown where women buy soap and lotion and all that stuff. Do you know that place? Down on Third?"

"You mean Le Lavender Boutique? They carry imported soaps and lotions made of natural oils and essences. Lovely stuff." Emily said, sighing, looking out the office window. She brought her eyes back to Jim. "That place?"

"Yeah, that's the one," he said, pointing his index finger at her. "I want you to go in there and have them put together a big basket of really nice stuff. You know, soaps, lotions, sponges, towels. All the stuff to make a woman feel special." He reached in his wallet, pulled out a one hundred dollar bill, rethought it, and added three twenties. He handed it to her without the least bit of embarrassment. *Margie loved that place*, he thought. A wistful look passed over his face.

"I'm on it, Chief," she said, giving him a conspiratorial wink.

He looked her in the eyes and gave her a thumbs up. "You're the best. Let me know how you fare." He turned to his computer and began typing. "Leave the door open, please."

"I will," she said as she quietly exited the room. As she walked back to her desk in the lobby, she was reminded of what she'd always known. Jim Higgins was domineering, demanding, and perfectionistic, but moments like this made her realize he was the best boss she'd ever worked for.

———o—O—o——

Jim and Sam stood outside the interrogation room. Jim scanned Sam's clothes. Apparently, he'd slipped home over lunch and changed. Now he was dressed in a red Berkley T-shirt, casual blue jeans with a few well-placed rips, and a pair of white Doc Marten slip-ons.

"I thought we had this dress code thing worked out," Jim said testily.

"I'm easing into it," Sam said defensively. "Besides, these Pressler Sex Pistol slip-ons are normally seventy-five bucks, but—"

"I know," Jim interrupted. "You got them at Goodwill. Don't tell me it was a steal," he said, irritated. *This is what I get for hiring non-conformists,* he thought.

"It was! Are you kidding? Seventy-five dollar shoes for fifteen? And Sex Pistol's to boot." Then turning serious, he said, "So what's the strategy, Chief?"

"I'll conduct the interrogation. Jump in if you feel inclined," Jim said brusquely as he opened the door.

Jim began the interrogation of Steve Stoner at 2:09 p.m. He'd checked the video and audio equipment earlier. The questioning proceeded without further delays.

Stoner was stoic and sullen, acting the part of the tough criminal, but Jim suspected it was an act. Underneath, he was probably insecure, immature, and narcissistic. In the world of criminal activity, Stoner had been a horrible failure for all those very reasons.

Jim spent time developing a rapport with him, asking about his family, cycle business, and treasure interests. After half an hour, Jim started to develop his theme.

"Now, Steve," Jim said in a quiet voice, "you don't mind if I call you Steve, do you?" Stoner shrugged, and Jim went on. "We know that you found the gold after a lot of hard work, studying topographical maps, hiking, and cave diving. Dirty, hard, physical work. Must have been quite a thrill coming across all those shining coins."

Jim watched for Steve's reaction, but he sat unmoved except to say intensely, "You have no proof of that."

"Oh, wait a minute. Now it's your turn to listen. No interruptions," Jim said casually, almost like a professor lecturing a student. His calm, smooth voice continued, reminding Sam of a father reading a bedtime story to his child. Sam sat back and found himself relaxing. He noticed Stoner listening raptly as the inflections of Jim's voice rose and fell, filling the small room. Jim stood and began walking back and forth in front of the small table. His voice and movements created a mesmerizing effect.

"You met Jamie Alberg at MVAC when you were a volunteer on a number of digs, and over the years, you got to know him pretty well. You discovered that you both had a passion for treasure hunting. Jamie was something of a know-it-all, but you put up with him because he knew his stuff. His knowledge of caves and the topography of the area was impressive. You decided to use his knowledge of the lost gold to find the treasure for yourself. You got lucky! You discovered it before Jamie did. A major accomplishment. How am I doing so far?" he asked Stoner, locking eyes with him.

Sam wondered why Jim hadn't studied law. He would be great in a courtroom—kind of an Atticus Finch.

Stoner fidgeted uncomfortably. Jim continued, using a professorial tone, inviting Steve into the story. Stoner slumped a little in his chair but continued listening intently. After all, the story was about him.

"Finding the gold was a dream come true." Stoner ran his hand through his short-cropped hair. Jim calmly continued. "But all that gold in a cave with such a tiny opening and on such a dangerous bluff was hard to move. That stuff is heavy. I figured it out. It must have been close to three hundred pounds of gold. You needed help, so you asked Jorge Santana if he'd help you remove the gold from the cave to a safer place. Although he was your drug dealer, you didn't have anyone else you could trust. But Jorge was a tough guy used to dealing with unsavory characters. He had survived dangerous gang situations by being a creative opportunist. When he agreed to help you and discovered what you were hiding, he wanted his cut. As you were hauling the gold out of the cave back to your truck, you argued, and in that argument, Mr. Santana was pushed over the bluff and fell to his death on the quarry floor. It all would have worked out, except for the gold coin in his pocket. A big, big mistake. Sound familiar so far?" Jim paused, his stare boring down on Stoner.

Stoner's eyes had turned to black steel, hatred emanating from them like radiant heat from a furnace.

"When Jorge died," Jim went on, toughening up his voice, working to a climax, "you had to make sure the discovery of the gold stayed hidden. You weren't going to share that with anyone. After all, you unearthed it. It was rightfully yours. The old finders keepers rule." Jim stopped, hoping Stoner would respond, but he stayed silent and imposing.

"Then Jamie got involved and began sharing with the police what he knew about the treasure." Stoner began to clasp and unclasp his huge fists, working them in his lap. Jim sent a warning glance to Sam. Stoner's rage was threatening to spill over.

"I'll admit that at first, the legend of the gold seemed farfetched to us—the stuff of fairytales. Hard to believe, but Jamie believed. He couldn't leave it alone, and he discovered the cave and proved that the treasure existed. Now that others knew, you had to ramp up your plan to eliminate those who threatened you. You visited Maria to see about her involvement. When she told you she didn't know about the gold, you weren't convinced. That made you furious. In a split second, in a fit of rage, you strangled her and left her lying on the bedroom floor." Jim paused. Stoner looked up at him. "But not before you had sex with her. We found semen on the bedclothes and in her body. That semen was yours."

By now, Jim's voice had crescendoed in volume. He stopped abruptly in front of Stoner, leaning over the table, his fists planted in front of him. "Did she consent to the sex to pacify you in a last desperate attempt to save her own life, or did you kill her and then rape her?" Jim snarled.

"Shut up! Shut up!" Stoner screamed, covering his ears. He collapsed on the table, hiding his head in his folded arms. "Shut up!" he said again, quieter.

After a few moments, he lifted his head and stared at Jim. "Everything I've worked for and planned for is over because of Jamie Alberg!" He spat his name into the air, ramming the table with his fist. "Don't you get it? He ruined everything," he whined. His voice had taken on the tone of a child. Silently, he sat in his chair, tears running down his face.

Watching the reaction, Jim thought, *"He really is a child—a stunted emotional adolescent who didn't get his way in the sandbox."*

Once Stoner began talking, the words were like sand trickling through an hourglass in a steady stream. Sam and Jim continued to listen as the confession poured out of him. After an hour or so, Stoner sat with a dull glassy stare, ragged with emotional exhaustion. It was as if he were finally cleansed, confessing the entire scheme, except where the gold was hidden. On that point, he refused to be moved. Jim called an end to the questioning and had Stoner returned to his cell.

Standing in the hallway, Sam said, "Wow, Chief. I can see there's an art to interrogations." He felt as if he had a caffeine buzz.

"He did cooperate pretty well, although I didn't think he'd give up so much the first time around," Jim said. "He'll be questioned some more. It's not over yet. Next time, you're up, buddy."

Jim and Sam tied up the bureaucratic requirements and paperwork linked to the confession. The workday was coming to a close. Jim thanked Emily again, winking at her as he strolled to the elevator. She gave him a thumbs up. He called Paul while he walked to his Suburban and broke the news of Stoner's confession.

"Good. We needed to nail that down," Paul said. He remembered other criminal investigations in the last two years that hadn't turned out so textbook perfect. Botched searches, faulty or weak evidence or no evidence that was admissible in court, mentally ill, incompetent witnesses who could not remember what they'd seen, let alone describe it. The list went on.

"The one thing we couldn't get out of him was where he'd stashed the gold," Jim said, disappointment in his voice.

"That's a problem since all the murders hinge on the existence of the gold. Without the coins, the motivation becomes questionable."

"Not really," Jim countered. "Stoner admitted to Maria's murder, and his hatred of Jamie for screwing up his great heist is palpable. We haven't questioned him about the attempted murder of Jamie yet. We'll get to that tomorrow. But we need to find the gold and put this legend to bed, once and for all."

"Well, we're just getting started on the house but haven't found anything significant yet," Paul informed him.

"I'll meet you there tomorrow, and we'll tear through it. Go home to Ruby." Jim glanced at his phone. It was already five-thirty. "She needs you, too."

"Right. I think you might be the first I've told this to, but Ruby and I have decided to get married, Chief," Paul announced.

"Well, congratulations. You're doing the right thing."

"I think so. Good night, sir." Paul clicked off.

Jim thought, *Why haven't I heard from Carol?* ⊙

28

EVENING, JUNE 21

Carol was sitting in her robe with her legs stretched out in her recliner, her hair still wet from a shower. The bouquet Jim had sent to her office sat accusing her until she looked away. What was the meaning of this extravagance? Adoration? Domination? What? The flowers were over the top and filled an entire corner in her living room. She'd had to rearrange the furniture just to find a place to put it. When Luke came out of his office and got a glimpse of the flowers, he said he'd never seen anything like it—even at a funeral—which earned him a withering gaze from Carol.

She valued her independence and opinions. She'd worked very hard to come out from beneath the shadow of her domineering father and be her own person. When she'd graduated from tech school and began working at the La Crosse County Law Enforcement Center, she regularly hid behind her pretty face and nice figure. Thinking she had nothing to offer, she avoided conversations in which people tried to elicit her opinions. *Just be the pretty wallflower,* she told herself, because that's what she'd been taught. *Look pretty but shut up. No one is interested in what you think.*

Then at a college bar downtown, she'd met Matt Donavon. He taught her to be self-reliant, enjoy her freedom, and gradually she realized she was more than just another pretty college coed. Matt asked for her opinions and valued her suggestions. Despite the failure of their marriage, she would always be grateful to him that he had encouraged her to be her own person. She'd decided long ago she would never be satisfied again to be just another pretty face.

"But I don't know what to do!" Carol said, her indecision sounding like defeat, her cell phone pressed to her ear.

"What do you mean? How can you not say yes to a proposal like that?" Vivian asked.

"Well, you're my big sister. You're supposed to give me advice," Carol chastised her. "I know this is not the time to be indecisive. Jim and I have known each other for a long time, but now it's different. Before, he was the husband of my best friend, and now he's someone I've fallen in love with. But we've only been dating a little over six months, and most of that was casual. It became intense very quickly. That's why I need to know what you think about what I told you he said."

"You mean the part about God or the part about the sex?"

"Both."

The line was silent for a moment. Then Vivian said, "Well, my dear sweet sister, if you remember, I gave you advice about Matt, but you didn't listen to me, and look what happened. You ended up divorced and hurt, and you've been gun shy about men ever since."

"I was young, stupid, and in love. What can I say?"

"Well, you can't use that as an excuse anymore. You're not young, and you're definitely not stupid. All I can tell you is that I have prayed for this day. You deserve someone who loves you for who you are. And from the sound of it, my prayers are being answered." She paused, then continued, her voice wavering with emotion. "Listen to your heart. It sounds like you're absolutely in love with him. From what you've told me about this guy, he's like the last of a dying breed. A man who will protect you and consider you precious and worth waiting for is an incredible find. It sounds almost too good to be true to me." Vivian sighed loudly. "We've been hashing this over for an hour, and you're no closer to a decision than you were when we started this conversation, are you?"

Carol fingered the card from the floral arrangement, turning it over and over, rereading the words. *I meant what I said. How about you?*

"Carol? Are you still there?" Vivian said, her voice pinched and frustrated.

"Yeah, I'm here. Well, if there's one thing I do know about Jim, it's that he's a straight shooter."

"He sounds like it. So what's the problem?" Vivian asked, exasperated. "Listen, here's what I want you to do. Get a sheet of notebook paper and make two columns. Label one column Good Things and the other column Not So Good Things. Then start filling it in with what you know about Jim. Be fair, though, and only put down the things you have observed or experienced. Then, go to bed, sleep on it, and read it again in the morning."

"Said like the true psychologist you are," Carol said. "And then what?"

"Make. A. Decision. It's either *yes* or *no*. *Maybe* is your worst option. I'm hanging up now because Craig is giving me a neck rub, and I want to go to bed with my husband. Bye, bye." And she was gone.

Carol shut her phone. She sat back in her recliner, her thoughts tumbling over themselves, jumbled and messy. Sighing, she got up from the chair and searched until she found a notebook. She had never really taken Vivian's advice about anything before. Maybe it was time to start. After all, Vivian was a happily married woman and had been for over twenty years. Carol sat down at the dining room table, drew a line down the center of a sheet, and began to write.

---◦O◦---

Meanwhile, Jim sat on his porch in the fading sunset eating a bowl of popcorn, the kernels crunching and crackling, his fingers greasy with butter. He licked the salt from his thumb and tried to ease the gnawing worry about Stoner and the missing gold. He absentmindedly picked up his cold beer and took a swig.

He was staring at nothing in particular, a faraway look about imagined things. It was at a time like this, when a case was beginning to gel, that he missed Margie and the way she always listened and asked questions to clarify his thinking. Now, without her counsel, he felt like his mind was a labyrinth of facts and information that twisted and turned. Even though the murderer was in the county jail, Jim still couldn't tamp down his nagging doubts that they'd ever find the lost gold shipment. He feared it would remain the stuff of legend. That wasn't going to happen if he could help it.

During the interrogation, Stoner had been taciturn and belligerent, refusing to even mention the gold coins. He admitted to the murder of Maria Santana, filling in the details they didn't know. Jim had trouble believing Stoner was delusional enough to think he would ever get out of prison in time to enjoy the gold. He was looking at a life sentence, possibly consecutive life sentences. Was he mute about the coins because they really didn't exist? But what about the coin they found on Santana? That was real. Why eliminate two people and try to kill two more if the treasure was a hoax? Was the legend of the treasure being used as a decoy for other illicit criminal activities? Drugs? Prostitution? Gang Activity? Human Trafficking? He didn't know, and it was worrying him.

What about Jamie Alberg and Matt Shafer? They'd never really eliminated Jamie as a suspect in the whole gold story, although his push into the river seemed to paint him as more of a target and victim than a perpetrator. Matt Shafer? A two-bit criminal with a drug problem. It was doubtful he knew the location of the gold. But over the years, Jim had learned that lowlifes could spin the truth into a good story to distract police from what was really happening.

He had the distinct feeling he was missing something or someone important that could turn the case on its head and lead them in a new direction. But who or what was it? The sun was sinking, and Jim was tired from the interrogations. They were usually a grinding down of stubborn individuals who had secrets to tell but refused to cooperate. In his exhaustion, his phone vibrated and startled him back to reality.

"Jim Higgins."

"Hey, Chief. It's Sam. I did some checking with some of Stoner's cycle customers who know him fairly well," he said. "Got the addresses when we got in his house with the search warrant. They all say he was a loner, but he did have a consistent friend he did things with—a Sharon Cross. They'd go motorcycling and go out to eat and socialize, that kind of thing.

I'm going to see her tomorrow. And another customer mentioned that he saw him a couple of times with Matt Shafer and Amy Bergholt. Amy seemed to be putting the moves on Steve. So that's a question mark, too."

"Amy who?" Jim asked, feeling stupid.

"Matt Shafer's stoned girlfriend, Amy. Remember? We interviewed her?" Sam reminded him.

"Oh yeah. I remember it now that you say it. Huh." Jim wished his mind would shut off, but the wheels kept spinning, and he supposed that was a good thing.

"Thanks, Sam," he said. "Jamie gave me the names of a couple of friends who were with him at Sloopy's. I made a few phone calls. One was to a Tom Shalat, who lives up by Holmen. The other was a Dave Driscoll in West Salem. They both remember Stoner being there, but they left about ten-thirty. We'll get statements from them tomorrow. Anything else?"

"No, that's all on my end," Sam finished.

Jim closed his phone. He'd no more than hung up when it beeped again.

"Jim Higgins."

"Hi, there," Carol's voice was soft, with an apologetic undertone.

Jim's stomach did a little lurch. Suddenly, he was anxious, and he didn't know why.

"Hi, what's up?" He tried to sound casual, but it came off as flippant.

"I wanted to thank you for those very special flowers," she said. Jim noticed that she avoided mentioning the message that went with the flowers.

"You're very welcome," he said in a kinder tone.

"The whole office is agog about this new developing romance between us. I got absolutely nothing done this afternoon. People were traipsing in and out of my office to see the bouquet. All thanks to you, big guy."

"You don't sound too unhappy about that."

"I'm not." She paused awkwardly. There was something of a more serious nature coming around the bend. Jim could feel it, kind of like when you could feel the rumbling of a train in the ground before you could see it. Carol went on.

"I want you to know that I'm in love with you, but I really need to consider everything before I commit."

"I understand."

"No, I don't think you do," Carol said assertively. "I've worked very hard at being a confident, independent woman, and I want you to know I'm not going to capitulate and lose everything I've worked for."

Where's this coming from? Jim thought. "Okay, I understand that. And you should consider it carefully because both of our lives will change, but I'm not planning on taking anything away from you. It's a big decision, so take your time. I'm a patient man—to a point," he said. *What happened between last night, the flowers, and today?* he thought.

"I just need to think things through. I'm not known for my strong decision-making skills, at least in my personal life, as my psychologist sister likes to remind me. So I'll need your patience."

"You've got it."

"Thanks, Jim. Good night."

"Night." Jim hunched farther down in his chair. He sighed and took a deep breath. Standing up, he thought over the conversation but decided his brain was shutting down. He needed to sleep. He'd have to deal with all this stuff later. He shuffled to his bedroom, undressed, turned down the covers, and crawled in. He reached for a Tony Hillerman novel, but fifteen minutes later, he woke with a start, the book resting on his chest. He turned off the light and drifted into a restless sleep filled with dreams of tunnels and caves, gold, and bouquets of flowers. ⊙

29

TUESDAY, JUNE 22

In the early morning light, Amy Bergholt sat on the broken-down couch. It smelled of pot and filth. She ran her slender fingers through her naturally curly mid-length hair. Her face was puffy from sleep, and her mind was racing with jumbled thoughts. She missed Matt, though her future plans did not include him. He had been fun for a while, but with the latest turn of events, she knew she had to get rid of him. Kind of like dogs needed to rid themselves of ticks. *Huh. He was kind of a blood-sucking parasite,* she thought.

The house on Gillette Street had been a working-class three-bedroom bungalow that someone had once taken pride in. Now it was a shell of its former self. She looked around the room, realizing she was living in a dump.

The living room carpet was filthy. Roach clips and other drug paraphernalia littered the floor beside Matt's secondhand recliner, along with empty beer bottles and cardboard pizza rounds. The roof had been leaking for some time. Large brown stains bloomed in profusion on the smoke-streaked ceiling tiles. The smell from the kitchen reeked of garbage, rotten meat, and stale coffee. If you walked across the kitchen floor, your shoes stuck to the gunk that had accumulated. You didn't dare open the refrigerator. It was ready to get up and walk out the door by itself. The bathroom was detestable. The shower was somewhat decent, but a disgusting black mold was beginning to grow in the corners of it. A crust of hard water soap scum covered the shower curtain. *This place isn't any better than a pigsty,* she thought, her nose turning up in revulsion.

Her thoughts shifted to Matt's latest predicament. She had visited him in the hospital last night. He was supposed to be released from the hospital later in the week, but he would be heading straight to the La Crosse County Jail. He was pale. Despite the Oxycontin, he was having a lot of pain. Even with the support of heavy bandages and a sling, he could barely move his arm and hand. The nurse told her that he had suffered a lot of nerve damage. In addition, the rotator cuff had been shattered, and the entry and exit gunshot wounds were far from healed. Matt was in a world of hurt.

Amy was surprised that despite all of her shortcomings, Matt still trusted her. She couldn't figure out why. She wasn't overly smart or good-looking. She wasn't even very sexually exciting. She was a hard worker, and to some extent, she had been loyal to Matt. But in the cold, hard light of day, Amy knew Matt had just used her to make himself comfortable and fend off the failures that came from being a two-bit drug dealer, deadbeat entrepreneur, and social misfit. It was Amy who paid the rent on time. On her measly salaries from Subway and the nursing home on St. Joseph's Ridge, she had kept the utilities turned on and the cupboards and refrigerator stocked with groceries. She used her money to maintain his lifestyle—if you could call the way he lived a lifestyle.

Now she had some decisions to make. Without Matt around, her thinking was becoming more focused, perhaps because the marijuana smoke had cleared out of the house with Matt's absence. She truly enjoyed her work at the nursing home, had good health care, and could work as many hours as she liked. Supporting herself was not a problem.

She started making plans. She was going to get her own place. Even a second-story one-bedroom walk-up with no garage would be better than this ramshackle, filthy affair. Then she needed to find a safe place to move the gold. Her position at the nursing home was going to come in real handy. She smiled to herself. With Matt in jail, this would be the beginning of a new life for her. She could hardly wait.

St. Theresa's Nursing Home and Care Facility was a sprawling seventy-acre complex situated on the ridge on State Highway 33 above La Crosse. It featured an eighty-five-bed nursing facility, of which twenty beds were designated for severe Alzheimer patients who needed round-the-clock care and assistance. The grounds were luxuriant and green. Twenty acres of mowed lawn, a gazebo, a raised bed garden, and two patios completed the comfortable outdoor grounds. Mature shade trees of oak, hickory, ash, and maple were interspersed throughout the property.

Amy Bergholt was working the three to eleven shift. It was particularly busy for a Tuesday night. Many children of the elderly patients liked to stop and visit on their way home from their jobs in La Crosse. They frequently stayed and ate dinner with their loved ones in the large, airy dining room. All of this added to Amy's workload.

In addition to the physical aspects of the job, Amy enjoyed the social time she spent with her patients. She had learned to appreciate their interesting personalities and their life histories. The wisdom they handed out so freely was something she'd never experienced in her young life. Older folks were so nonjudgmental; they accepted you for who you were. To Amy, who had struggled with an anemic self-image all her life, that was a precious gift. They made her feel important, as if she was a family member. When she revealed problems she'd had in her relationship with Matt, they smiled and gave her pithy and excellent advice. But now, she was about to take advantage of one of them, and she didn't like the ball of anxiety that had formed in her stomach. It made her feel little and nasty.

Tim Tostrud had been Amy's patient for the last seven months. A dairy farmer all his life, his hands were gnarled and arthritic with hard callouses, resulting from heavy manual labor. His round bald head was embellished with puffs of white cotton ball hair that stuck out from the sides as if electrified. Beneath a perpetual frown, perceptive hazel eyes took in his surroundings. A large red bulbous nose perched above a dainty mouth, but underneath his gruff appearance, he was really a marshmallow.

On nights when things quieted down, Amy would find herself sitting by Tim's bed, chatting with him about his life as a farmer. She liked it when she could make him smile, and she, in turn, would laugh at his barnyard jokes. Some of them were bawdy and risqué.

Tim felt good when he could lighten Amy's load a little. Over the months, she had shared some of her problems with Tim, including her childhood of neglect with alcoholic parents, her shyness in school and lack of friends, and now, her loser boyfriend. Matt seemed to be in a scrape with the law every other week.

"So how are things with that boyfriend of yours?" he asked, his eyes inquisitive beneath his bushy eyebrows.

Amy had a wary look, the way a rabbit freezes when it's startled. She noticed the kindness in Tim's hazel eyes.

"My boyfriend? You mean Matt?" she said, relaxing a little.

"Yeah, what kind of trouble is he in this week?" Tim asked, chuckling under his breath.

"Oh, things have gotten really bad. He was in a fight and got shot. He's at the hospital and
then he's going to jail."

Tim watched her. She didn't seem too upset by that.

"How's that make you feel?" he asked gruffly, but underneath the words, there was a tenderness.

"Really bad. But I've got a bigger problem." Amy felt like a weasel. She shyly looked up at Tim and made her eyes extra big. "I need to find another place to live. The police have gone through the house, and everything is turned upside down. My stuff is all mixed in with Matt's. It's a disaster. The problem is, I have nowhere to go." She said the last sentence softly, trying to fill her voice with neediness. She didn't have to try too hard—she *was* needy.

Tim eyed her carefully. He was old, but he wasn't stupid. This girl needs a break. *Somebody* should help her. Tim didn't have a wife and kids, but he wasn't oblivious to a need. It seemed to him that Amy had never gotten anything she wanted.

"Well," he drawled, "what about my farmhouse? Nobody's living there. It's not a palace. Furniture's kinda old, but it's pretty clean. And there's plenty of room there. Eventually, I'll sell it, but that might not happen for some time."

"Are you serious?" Amy tried to look surprised. She hoped Tim didn't notice her phony expression.

"Yeah, I'm serious. Just move in, and we'll talk about rent later."

"Oh, I don't know if I could. I'd be taking advantage of your good nature."

"Nah, don't be stubborn. Heck, I want to help you. Just accept it."

Amy waited an appropriate length of time before she answered, so it seemed like she was having a debate with herself. But inside, she was bursting with excitement and pleasure.

She looked up at Tim with a coy grin. "I accept your kindness. Thank you so much."

"Don't think about it, honey. I just want you to be safe," Tim said gruffly, his voice surprisingly authoritative.

Amy smiled and gave Tim a big innocent doe-eyed look. Things were working out so much better than she anticipated. Things were going to be fine. Just fine.

Jim Higgins sat at his desk the next morning thinking about the interviews that had to be conducted with Matt Shafer and his girlfriend, Amy Bergholt. Paul Saner sat opposite him, scrolling on his phone and texting with effortless dexterity. Watching him, Jim felt like a complete dinosaur. Despite his purchase of a new smartphone, his thumbs could never do *that*.

"So, who do you think is best suited to interview Amy Bergholt?" Jim asked.

"Easy. Sam," Paul said briskly, continuing his texting.

"Sam? Really? Why? Could you just stop texting for a minute?" His irritation was palpable.

"Oh. Sorry, Chief." Jim waved off his apology. Paul laid his phone in his lap. "There's a lot you don't know about Sam, Chief. He has an odd sense about the inner workings of people's minds and motives—almost like a sixth sense. For instance, did you know that he used to drag home needy kids to his religious parents and expect them to fix their problems? He could see what they needed. He just didn't have the resources to fix it."

"I didn't know that, but how does that translate to interviewing Amy?"

"Well, it does, sort of. He'll be able to get a sense of Amy's involvement in the crime."

"We're all supposed to be able to do that," Jim responded testily.

"Well, you had to be there when he explained it. It made perfect sense when he told me about it. Just take my word for it. I think he'd be the right choice to interview Amy. Sam has a lot of empathy for people in a tight spot."

"How does that help when dealing with criminals? I'm not sure they deserve too much empathy," Jim said, frowning, staring at Paul, wondering at the strange turn this conversation was taking.

"Amy's not necessarily a criminal, but she lives with one. She probably knows some stuff about Matt that we don't know. And Sam would be the best at finding that out. That's all I'm saying," Paul said.

"All right. I get that," Jim continued, "Anyway, I'd like you to take the lead with Matt. See if you can break him down. Maybe with his injury, he's rethinking his future behind bars. He might be willing to give up some information for a plea deal."

"Maybe," Paul said, but a skeptical tone had crept into his voice. "I'll get on it, Chief."

Jim was confident that the evidence they had on the audiotapes from the sting on MM would be the bedrock for conviction in the attempted murder of Matt Shafer. But that was for the district attorney to decide.

Some DNA belonging to Stoner and Shafer was found at Maria Santana's trailer, but their admitted drug activity at the mobile home explained that. It probably couldn't be used as conclusive evidence. However, Stoner's rambling confession was enough to convince a jury of the murder of Maria Santana. Jim still thought that Jorge's death was probably a freak accident. Stoner had admitted they argued, and Jorge fell from the cliff.

The team had thoroughly searched the farmhouse on MM and the padlocked cave to no avail. The gold wasn't there. But an interesting map tucked behind a storage cupboard in Stoner's garage had turned up in the search of his house. Jim retrieved it from the locked evidence room, and he and Leslie pored over it intently.

"I don't know, sir. This map just reiterates what we already know—that Stoner found the same cave as Jamie, just sooner. When he discovered the gold, he moved it and now refuses to give up its location. A kind of twisting of the knife in our collective gut, so to speak," she finished. "Too bad Jamie isn't here. He might be able to help." She cringed after she said it, realizing it might set Jim off.

"Are you kidding me right now?" He looked sideways at her. His face held a look of amazement and bafflement at such a suggestion. "I've had enough of that kid for a long, long time," he said with finality, the line of his jaw hardening.

"Where would Stoner have hidden it?" Leslie asked, quick to return to the subject of the missing treasure. "It's got to be someplace we should be able to figure out. Probably pretty obvious. After all, his planning was sloppy, and I'm sure that would translate to the gold as well. His financial records don't show large amounts of money deposited in his account. Of course, he could have traded them for other valuables like drugs and cash," Leslie theorized.

"Maybe, but then some of them should be surfacing somewhere. At shows or shops, like that. When we checked with our people in those fields, they hadn't seen any coins. Could he have melted them down and sold them as gold bullion online?" Jim asked.

"They would never be as valuable as the real coins, which are extremely rare." Leslie paused, then shook her head. "No, I think Stoner would have kept them as he found them. His schemes seem slipshod and haphazard, but he's not stupid. Melted down, they would have lost too much of their value."

"I don't know what to think right now. What about a rented storage shed? I know that doesn't seem very secure, but any place other than a museum or a bank vault is not safe enough to hold those coins," Jim speculated. "Maybe Shafer's got them hidden somewhere."

"Well, I did look through the stuff that came out of Matt's house," Leslie said. "His business records, if you can call them that, were a hodgepodge of receipts and incomplete customer information in shoeboxes." Jim gave her a puzzled look. "Yeah, shoeboxes of slips and bills that just tell us he was completely inept at operating a business of any kind. But I can look through the stuff this afternoon and see if anything pops out at me. We're still going through Steve's house and business. It's going to take a while."

"That'd be great," Jim replied, leaving the map and starting toward his office. "Thanks."

Leslie smiled and stood a little taller. "No problem."

He went into his office and plopped down at his desk. He checked online for storage rental units. There were twenty that came recommended, but he was sure there were more like thirty. He'd get Sam on it. He decided to take an early lunch, maybe catch a catnap in his truck, and do some thinking. He was just about to leave when he looked up to see Carol walk into his office and quietly shut the door.

She looked good. Well rested, and her eyes were glowing with an inward radiance Jim hadn't seen before. She was wearing casual clothes, a camisole with an embroidered shirt, and a pair of relaxed jeans that she'd rolled up slightly. She was the picture of carefree happiness. She stood there for a minute.

"Hi," Jim said weakly. She did have a strange effect on him, especially when he was feeling down.

"Yes," she said with a kind of conviction Jim hadn't heard from her before.

Jim frowned in confusion. "Yes?"

"Yes, I want to marry you," she said, her eyes suddenly flooding with tears.

Jim got up rather clumsily and walked around his desk, standing in front of her. He felt like the floor had fallen away, and he was suspended somewhere between reality and a dream.

"Say that again. It sounded awfully good," his voice husky with emotion.

Instead, she pulled his head toward her and kissed him long and slow and fervently. When she finally came up for air, she said, "Yes, I want to marry you."

Jim took a long, slow breath and then held up a finger. "One minute." He walked over to his laptop and shut the cover. Grabbing his jacket, he slipped Carol's hand in his and shut his office door. They walked together out to the reception area, where Jim informed Emily he was leaving for a few hours. She smiled, her eyes wide with surprise and excitement. *She knows,* Jim thought. The secretarial pool watched with bated breath as Carol and Jim stepped into the elevator. Jim would have given anything to hear the comments after the door slid shut.

Carol turned to Jim and kissed him again. "Wouldn't you just love to hear the gossip?" she asked. "How delicious would that be?"

"Can't even imagine," Jim said, grinning.

They took Jim's Suburban to Crescent Jewelers downtown near St. Joseph the Workman Cathedral. Jim led Carol into the store, and they began scrutinizing the rings in the diamond section. Carol finally picked a gold filigree band set with an emerald cut diamond bordered on each side by a diamond baguette. She tried it on her finger. Jim watched her face light up. She was so beautiful.

"Sir, will you be paying in total today, or would you like to use our installment plan?" the young blond assistant asked.

Jim smiled back. "I'm paying in total today," he said as he slid his debit card across the counter. "I'll take installments from her later," He grinned wickedly.

"Jim Higgins! You will make a dishonest woman out of me yet, but I can't wait for you to collect!" Carol said, giving him a subtle smile. She turned to the assistant and said seriously, "Don't listen to a word he says."

The young gal laughed. "You two are really cute. That's why I love my job."

When they climbed back in the truck, Jim turned and pulled Carol close. He looked into her brown eyes. That he could make her so happy filled him with a joy that made his chest hurt. "So, I hear there's a wedding that's happening. When's that going to be?" he asked, smiling like a drunken sailor.

"The sooner, the better," Carol whispered.

"Sounds good to me," Jim said.

Sam Birkstein had done his homework on Amy Bergholt. Abused and neglected as a child of alcoholic parents, she was put in foster care early in her life. She made the rounds from one family to another without ever bonding with anyone. Sam could understand how easy it would be for someone to take advantage of her with just a little insincere attention and flattery. A few compliments here and there, a little sexual activity to cement her neediness, and she would be hooked. Sam was sure that was what Matt Shafer had done.

He gritted his teeth, and his jaw tightened as he thought about the emotional abuse Shafer had visited on Amy, who was already damaged. He was pretty sure he had used her to commit crimes—delivering drugs, aiding him in getting rid of the Santana truck at Trempealeau Salvage. Her money probably paid for his broken-down home and put food on the table. Sam's job now was to find out if Amy knew anything about the missing gold. That would be uncomfortable for her. He hated it when people who were mistreated ended up paying the price for crimes their partners committed. But there was always the possibility that Amy wasn't as innocent as she appeared. He reminded himself that her naivete and simple-mindedness could be a great cover for her involvement with the hidden treasure.

The day had turned cloudy after a brilliant morning of sun and heat. The humidity made the air heavy. Now dark clouds were churning and piling high in the southern sky in familiar thunderhead shapes. Sam crested the bluff and headed toward St. Theresa's Nursing Home. He enjoyed the last few miles of his trip, glancing at the neat farms and woods that bordered the fields. He could see the nursing facility in the distance, which looked like a small city that even had a water tower. But despite the neatness and outward appeal, Sam had the same feeling of dread he had when he visited the state prison at Boscobel. Irrational as it was, nursing homes scared him. He'd take convicted drug dealers and prostitutes over this any day.

Amy had agreed to talk to him during her lunch hour. On the phone, her voice sounded casual, not suspicious. Still, he had a feeling this would be a tough interview.

Pulling his Toyota into the parking lot, he climbed out and locked the car. Dressed in a tan suit coat, new slim-fit blue jeans, and a button-down blue dress shirt, he looked the part of an investigator.

Sam found the main entrance and wandered into the building. A large counter was manned by a slightly overweight nurse in pink and gray scrubs who gave him a friendly smile.

"Good morning," she said cheerfully.

"Hi. I'm Sam Birkstein," he said as he flashed his ID. "I'm supposed to meet Amy Bergholt here somewhere."

"Just a moment. I think she's on her lunch break. I'll locate her if you want to have a seat," she said. Her smile diminished a little bit when she looked at his ID.

Sam chose a chair near the window so he could watch the weather developing while he waited. A streak of white-hot lightning shot across the dark gray sky. The resounding thunder echoed throughout the building, bouncing off the hard surfaces of the floors and ceilings. A sudden burst of rain dumped on the parking lot like someone pouring out a pail of water. The torrent flooded the sidewalks and inundated the surrounding green landscape until it smudged into bluish-gray indiscriminate shapes.

"Hello," a quiet voice startled him.

Sam jumped up, surprised. "Wow, you snuck up on me there. Sorry. I'm Detective Sam Birkstein from the La Crosse Sheriff's Department," he said, shaking her hand. "We met earlier at Bargain Coins, but I still have a few questions," he said.

"Sure. Should we sit down?" Amy asked. Her hair was pulled away from her face making her look vulnerable. She wore gray scrubs, and a name tag dangled from a lanyard that hung around her neck. Crossing her hands in her lap, she focused her green eyes on Sam.

"Will this work for you? I thought they said you were on your lunch break?" Sam asked.

"It's fine. I already ate my protein bar."

They settled on a hard plastic couch near a large window. Sam balanced his clipboard on his lap, turned toward her, and smiled.

"So what's this about anyway?" she asked, a slight frown forming.

"Would you tell me about your relationship with Matt Shafer?"

Sam asked, businesslike, his smile fading.

"Let's see, I met him in one of the college bars on Third Street about a year ago, and pretty soon after that, he asked me to move in with him," she said quietly. "We've been living together ever since."

"What month was that, would you say?" Sam asked.

"Mmmm, probably around January. After Christmas sometime."

"So you were in a sexual relationship with him?"

"Yes."

"Were you aware of Matt's drug dealing?"

"Oh, yeah. That was obvious from the beginning. People were coming to the house all hours of the day and night."

"Did you ever deliver drugs for him?"

She hesitated, her eyes traveling to the rain outside. "I'm not sure. He did ask me to deliver a couple of packages for him."

"Who was the customer?"

"Somebody named Steve who lived on the northside," she said, her nose crinkling slightly.

"Steve Stoner?" Sam asked, feeling a slight chill run along his arms.

"Yeah, he has a bike shop in his garage."

Amy was very careful about her responses, tiptoeing around her answers. She gave off an innocent vibe, but Sam realized she was smarter than he'd thought.

"What do you know about the murder of Maria Santana?" he asked, his voice harder.

For an instant, a look of panic passed over her face. Then she recovered, feigning innocence. "I just know what I've heard on the TV news," she said, looking down into her lap. When she looked back up at Sam, her demeanor had hardened.

"I don't believe you, Amy," Sam said softly. Her shoulders tightened. "Matt told us you helped him deliver the Santana truck to the Trempealeau Salvage yard. We know that's true because we have footage of you on the surveillance camera. You were waiting in the car behind the truck. We could clearly see it was you."

The silence dragged on. Sam waited. This was always the hardest part for him, being patient, letting the suspect reveal themselves. Most people couldn't resist filling in the gaps of silence. Seconds ticked by. Amy finally filled the void.

"I did help him with that," she confessed, "but I swear I didn't know anything about why he was doing it. I was suspicious about the whole deal. Matt knows a lot of dirtballs." Her voice was rougher now, her simple-mindedness evaporating as she recalled the incident. Sam could see the years of neglect and abuse in the way she held herself. Making herself small and insignificant, she hunched her shoulders and pulled in her feet. "He threatened to throw me out of the house if I didn't go along with it," she finished quietly.

Sam had no doubt Matt roughed her up. Intimidation would be easy with someone as wounded as Amy. He continued, inching toward the subject of the hidden gold.

"Have you visited Matt since he was injured in the shootout?" he asked.

"Yes, just once to tell him I was moving out. I knew he couldn't hurt me since his shoulder is out of commission. He'll probably be in jail for a long time. I thought it was a good time to wash my hands of the whole thing." Her eyes had hardened a bit, and she seemed more defensive. Sam wondered was she meant by *the whole thing*.

"What do you mean by that?"

"Just everything. The dump we live in, the constant trouble with police, the drugs, always begging me for money," she grumbled, her hand making a sweeping motion.

"So, where are you living now?" Sam asked nonchalantly.

There was a pause. "At a friend's house out in the country. I had enough of city life," Amy said in a soft voice. "Besides, it's closer to my work at St. Theresa's."

"Amy, Matt was involved with Steve Stoner and the murder of Maria Santana. We think he has information about the gold that everyone, including the police, is looking for. You know about that, don't you?" asked Sam. He watched her carefully, modulating his voice into a gentle prodding.

"I overheard Steve and Matt talking about some business venture," she did air quotes, "but since I don't know anything about business, I didn't think too much about it. What's this treasure you're talking about?" Amy asked innocently, her eyes blinking rapidly.

Sam knew she was lying. How could she know about Maria Santana's murder and *not* know about the gold? She even used the word *treasure*. It had been all over the news, from the *Tribune* to radio, from the internet to all the local TV stations. She knew a whole lot more than she was admitting.

Sam played along. "The treasure is a gold shipment from Fort Crawford that was hidden in the bluffs above the Mississippi River and was never found—until recently. We know it exists. We just can't find it." Sam stopped talking, looking casually out the window. The rain was still falling steadily, and it made a comforting kind of rhythm on the roof as they talked.

"Sounds interesting, but I don't know anything about it," Amy said. This time she held Sam's gaze with one of her own. *You're going to have to be a lot tougher than that, bud,* she thought.

"Amy, do you know what an accessory is?" Sam asked pointedly. He tried to keep his face neutral.

She noticed Sam's mouth was set in a serious expression, and his eyes were carefully studying her. She cleared her throat. "Well, I think it means someone who helps someone else commit a crime," she answered. By now, her expression was immutable. She sat transfixed, her face a mask.

"I hope you realize if you have knowledge or a connection to the gold and you don't share that information with us, the charges against you will be very serious. You will be looking at some significant prison time. I assure you, we will find the gold." Sam paused for emphasis. "I think you know where the gold is hidden, Amy." Sam stopped, realizing he had taken a huge gamble that she would crack and confess.

Sam could feel the weight of the moments ticking by. As the time passed, he had a sinking feeling he'd bet and lost. The girl at the front desk answered the phone, then cupped the receiver in her hand and said loudly, "Amy, they're wondering when you're going to get back on the floor. They needed you, like fifteen minutes ago."

"Tell them I'll be there right away." She stood and faced Sam, her eyes hard and glittering. "I think we're done here." She turned and walked briskly past the reception desk, disappearing through a pair of swinging doors.

Sam slammed his fist on the plastic couch. The chief was not going to be happy about this. So close and yet so far. ⊙

30

WEDNESDAY, JUNE 23

The next day, when Jim returned to his office after lunch with Carol, Emily motioned him over to her desk with a wiggling finger. "Sam is waiting for you, and he's as ornery as I've ever seen him," she said, worry etched on her face.

"Sam? Ornery? I've never seen him like that," Jim said, concerned, although nothing was going to rock his boat after yesterday. He stared off somewhere above the clock on the wall, remembering how Carol glowed when he had slipped the ring on her finger.

Emily noticed. "Chief?"

His attention drifted back to her. He gave her a dimpled smile. "Yeah. I heard you," he said quietly. "I'll see what's going on."

Boy, oh boy, is he in love, thought Emily. "Forewarned is forearmed," she said curtly.

"Thanks," Jim replied. He strolled down the hall, got a cup of coffee in the break room, and came back to his office. Sam was hunched down in the corner chair. Lately, that chair seemed to be the place where everyone dumped their anxieties and problems—on him. Sam's face was shut down, his expression frozen in a frown.

"What's up, Sam?" Jim asked casually as he lifted his cup to his lips.

"Amy Bergholt knows where the gold is," he declared in a hard voice.

"Well, that's great!" Jim said, setting his cup down and taking off his suitcoat. "Isn't it?" He waited, noticing the look of frustration on Sam's face. "Oh, I get it. She knows, but she's not telling us."

"She's up to her ... neck," he said with obvious restraint. "She knows where it is!" Sam punched the air with his index finger to make his point. His face had turned red, and he was puffing, taking small breaths.

"Well then, let's figure it out. That's what detectives do, after all," Jim advised patiently. "I appreciate your passion, by the way."

"I want to follow her and see if I can find out where she might have hidden it. I found out where she's living," Sam said, calming down.

"Yeah, at Matt's over on Gillette, right?" Jim looked up as he held his coffee cup.

"No, no. She moved out of there," he blurted impatiently, waving his hand at Jim. "She's living at a friend's place in the country," Sam recited, referring to his notes. "Somewhere over by Chaseburg on Dodson Hollow Road."

"How did you find that out?" Jim asked.

"I leaned on the girl at the front desk, telling her I'd forgotten Amy's address and needed it for official police business." Sam grinned slyly.

Jim cocked his eyebrow. "That was clever. So do you know who this guy is?" he asked, placing one hand on his hip.

"Yeah. He's actually one of her patients," Sam explained, wrinkling up his nose. "If she's living at his place rent-free, that's unethical, isn't it?"

"Probably, but let's play along. We can use that to our advantage. So what's the rest of your plan?" Jim asked as he stood sorting papers on his desk, looking up at Sam now and then.

"I bet she's going to move the gold to this farm and hide it in some of the farm buildings. I drove by there today, and there are plenty of places she could stash it." Sam leaned back in his chair, relaxing, putting his theory out there. He was good at constructing theories, but frequently they lacked evidence.

"What proof do you have that she has the gold, or at least that she knows where it's hidden?"

"None. But to quote you, sir, it's a gut feeling," Sam said, loosening up a little, raising his eyebrows, and returning Jim's stare. "I've heard you say it."

"True. Do you want some backup?"

"Yeah, I thought maybe Leslie could help me stake out the place."

"Night or daytime operation?"

"Well, I don't know yet. I'm going to try and find out Amy's work schedule, so I'll have some idea when she'll be home."

"How're you going to do that?"

"Leave it to me, Chief. I've got a plan." Sam winked at Jim, his foul mood lightening with the prospect of catching Amy with the gold.

"Atta boy. Use the brain God gave you."

That evening, Amy Bergholt took her time getting dressed for her clandestine activities. She had a big night ahead of her. She wore black capris, a black turtleneck, black stocking hat pulled down low with her hair tucked up under it, and black Sketchers in case she had to run. In the back seat of her red Nova, she had twenty shoeboxes from Matt's office, duct tape, a heavy-duty flashlight, and a BB gun to shoot out the security light at the storage shed. Alongside her in the front seat was her Ruger Mini-14 Ranch rifle, muzzle pointed to the floor, that she'd purchased at a gun show in Rochester, Minnesota, over a month ago. Technically, the gun was illegal because it wasn't above the window line and in full view, but she wasn't going to worry about that in the dark. She'd taken firearm safety lessons at Dick's

Sporting Goods and felt fairly confident in handling the gun. The key to Tim Tostrud's farmhouse was secure in her pocket. She was set for phase two of her plan.

When Detective Sam Birkstein came by the nursing home questioning her about the lost gold shipment, she had no choice but to step up the timetable to safely move the gold to a more secure location. No one would have guessed that the gold was in a storage unit in Barre Mills. In a year or two, after she'd done her research, she could take the gold and leave the country. During the week, she had driven by the storage facility and checked it out at almost every hour of the night, from ten to five in the morning. Traffic on County B in Barre Mills was light, particularly during the week. Tonight, a Wednesday, should be perfect.

It had all worked out far better than she planned. Matt and Steve had gotten drunk together more than once. Conversations flowed, and eventually, Steve had revealed his possession of the gold coins to Matt. But he refused to tell him where he'd hidden them.

Convincing Matt to tell her about the gold had been easy. He loved to hear himself talk about his plans for the future while smoking a big Havana cigar. *What an idiot.* He lay in bed at night, puffing on his big stogie, building air castles in the sky while the house around him was literally falling apart. Common sense and a good work ethic did not exist in his world. Well, it was easy to see how far his dreaming had gotten him—the county jail. So much for dreams.

Steve Stoner, on the other hand, was not stupid. It had taken her a while to gain his trust. She couldn't count the evenings she had pumped him about treasure hunting down at Sloopy's and Mexico La Fiesta. It was all so boring to her, but she had fabricated an interest to get what she wanted. When the conversation dragged, she'd fed him another question. Off he'd go, revealing more and more about his treasure adventures until one night, he'd spilled the beans. Her insincere attention had paid off. Once they had sex, his guard came down. With a couple of joints in his system and a few shots of

J Bavet brandy, he'd passed out. She'd been able to get the key to the storage unit that night. She made a copy and began planning the final phase of the gold heist.

But before the gold could be hidden in a new location, she had a difficult job that would be thoroughly unpleasant. It required her immediate attention. *Tonight.* She sighed, started her car, and pulled out of Tim's driveway on Dodson Hollow Road into the cool night air. Amy was finding out how strenuous the life of a criminal could be.

—o-O-o—

Carol sat on Jim's couch, her legs tucked up under her, cuddling into his shoulder, both of them sipping on glasses of red wine.

"So, when are we going to tell John and Sara the news?" Jim asked, burying his nose in her hair.

"Today's Wednesday. So how does Saturday night look?" She sat up and leaned her head back against his arm.

"Fine by me. I can grill steaks if you make some sides. Our news can be dessert."

"All right. We should talk about a date. You know, when we're going to actually tie the knot. I'm sure you've got people you want to invite, and I'll have to do some—"

Jim interrupted. "Babe, I did a big wedding once, and so did you." Carol let out a pent-up sigh. He thought again about her independent nature. *Suggest, don't dominate.* "Think about this—a small affair at the courthouse or a church if you want. Something quiet and intimate?" He studied her, still learning to read her moods.

Carol liked being asked her opinion. She nodded her head in agreement.

"Well, it would be easier to plan if it's just a few people. The twins, my sister. That's pretty small. We can go out afterward to someplace nice for dinner," she said, pursing her lips. She sighed and looked at him. "We could have a little party for friends at Piggy's later on, right?"

"Sure. Sounds great. Let's do it." He kissed her, playing with her hair, kissing her again.

They wandered to the dining room table, talking and planning. Carol wrote down specifics about dates, marriage licenses, and places for a special dinner until well past eight.

"Listen, I've got to work tomorrow, and I'm tired. But oh, this ring. It's really beautiful. Thank you, Jim," Carol said dreamily, holding her hand up to gape at the stone.

Jim took her hand and studied the ring, too. "Yeah, it is beautiful and fit for someone who deserves all the happiness I can give her."

"Enough. I'm going now before we get ourselves in trouble," Carol said. She pecked him on the cheek and was gone.

Jim was glad the wedding was a short wait. He'd been alone quite a while, and although solitude was still important to him, he wouldn't miss the loneliness.

He realized in all the excitement of the day that he hadn't had anything to eat. He rifled through the fridge, found fixings for a sandwich, popped open a Pepsi, and took his plate out to the porch. The night was turning velvety. He sat in the darkness, listening to the cadence of crickets, watching the moon peeking out from behind a cloud bank like a shy child playing peek-a-boo with a favorite blanket. The stars were hard and glittering, washing the sky in waves of pinprick light.

He was just about to get up when the hairs on the back of his neck stood up. He glanced into the still darkness. A feeling of uneasiness spread over him, causing his stomach to contract. He thought he heard something, maybe a rock falling. *Probably a deer.*

The next instant, the patio door behind him imploded in a blast of glass splinters, the shards flying in every direction. Jim rolled onto the floor, crawling on his belly to the entrance of the living room. He cursed. Staying low, he crab-walked across the living room carpet. As he jumped up to escape to the hallway and the bedrooms, another shot blasted through the living room bay window, the bullet striking him in his right calf. He managed to limp into his bedroom, his heart pounding in his chest. The burning pain in his leg caused his breath to come in ragged gasps. He stayed away from the windows, keeping the house dark, feeling for his phone. Finding it on his nightstand, he tucked himself in the floor of his closet, opened his phone, and dialed 911.

"What is your emergency?" a calm voice answered.

"This is Jim Higgins with the La Crosse Sheriff's Department. There is a shooting in progress at my home at 7690 Chipmunk Coulee Road. I need backup immediately! The shooter appears to be in the rocks at the back of my property. Somebody is blasting the windows out of my house! I'm going after them! Repeat: an active shooter at 7690 Chipmunk Coulee Road. Need support and backup immediately."

Jim slammed his phone shut before they could encourage him to stay put. Grimacing from the throbbing pain in his calf, warm blood streaming down his leg, he decided he didn't have time to think about it. He crawled to his nightstand and opened the drawer. Tucking his hand around his Glock 17 pistol, he felt the weight of it calming him, steadying his resolve. He limped down the hall and dashed through the kitchen to the garage. Once in the garage, he hobbled to the side entry door. He hunched behind a hydrangea bush, catching his breath, then ran toward the pole shed. Another shot rang out, spraying the gravel next to the garage. This time Jim guessed from the bullet's direction that the shooter was moving north toward the edge of his property and probably toward his car.

A few minutes later, he heard the faint sound of sirens screaming up the coulee, the sound pulsating along the low-lying valley floor. After a couple of minutes, cars and SUVs tore up Chipmunk Coulee Road, stopping just inside the perimeter of his property. He hugged the wall of the pole shed, staying quiet, listening, and waiting. He heard the cars and sirens go still, doors opening. Everyone stayed behind vehicles until they got organized. Jim recognized the muffled sounds of preparation—loading guns, putting on vests, getting ready for a firefight.

"Police! Police!" a voice called out from behind a squad car. "Put down your weapons!"

A couple of hundred yards up the road, Jim thought he heard the cough of a car engine. Probably the shooter leaving the scene.

"It's Jim Higgins! I'm down by the pole shed," he yelled. "I'm okay, but I heard a car engine up on the road." His voice carried well in the still night air.

"Stay down, Jim, til we know the zone is clear."

"Right. I can do that," Jim replied, sinking along the wall of the shed until his butt was cushioned in the grass. He stretched his legs out in front of him, willing his breath to slow and normalize. His leg was throbbing now with a dull ache, and when he moved it, the pain became sharp.

The cops worked their way down to the house, spreading out around the perimeter of his home. Shining their high wattage lamps, they moved in ever-widening circles throughout the property. Finally, after forty-five minutes, they yelled the all-clear. Jim got up, painfully hobbling to the house. Whoever had been there was gone. His shoe was squishing with the blood from his leg wound, and he felt lightheaded. As he limped toward the house, a ripple of chills coursed through his body.

The motion light next to the front door was on. Jim stood blinking in the brilliant brightness of it, shielding his face with his left hand. His Glock dangled unsteadily in his right hand.

"Jim! Are you hurt?" It was Paul Saner, walking swiftly toward him.

"Yeah. Just a flesh wound, but I'll need a few stitches."

Paul edged up to him. "Come on. We'll get you in my truck and get you to Gundersen," he said, throwing him a look of concern as he placed Jim's arm around his shoulder.

"I'll be fine," Jim muttered as they walked into the house. "Just grab a towel from the bathroom to wrap around my leg."

"Should I call someone? Your kids? Carol?"

"No. Not 'til I'm patched up, and we've got everything secured here," Jim said gruffly.

"Okay, Chief."

But it didn't work that way. Jim gave a brief statement of events to the officer in charge, who insisted that Jim be taken to the hospital immediately. Paul propped him on the seat of the truck. While he drove to the ER, Jim laid out his theory. His voice sounded raspy and clinical. Underneath it all, Paul could hear his aggravation.

"Whoever did this was inexperienced," Jim began. "Wasn't some deadbeat dad or lowlife drug punk. It had to be somebody entangled in this gold case. And the only other person who's on our radar right now is Amy Bergholt. She might be the shooter." His leg was throbbing now, and he grimaced in pain. He was beginning to feel woozy.

"Why would she do that, Chief? That doesn't make sense," Paul said, disbelieving. "That's not my impression of her. I can't believe a nurse's aide at a nursing home would even know how to load a gun, much less shoot it."

"Well, hear me out. Let me get you up to speed. Sam got a little too close for comfort in his interview today, and she's getting nervous." Jim was feeling indignation building. "His theories must have hit close to home. After the interview, Sam was convinced that she's not who she appears to be. The cops just told me they found two of the three casings. She used a small-caliber rifle, not sure exactly what kind. We'll know more after ballistics looks at them. Probably something a homeowner would use to shoot skunks and woodchucks. The shooter only fired three shots, and if she were serious about killing me, I would have expected her to be a better shot. When she missed, why didn't she keep shooting or try to hunt me down and finish me off? Anyway, I think she's inexperienced, and she's a pretty poor shot. I got the feeling that the shooting was more of a diversion meant to take attention away from something else."

"Moving the gold? Wanting to keep us away long enough to get it out of here?" Paul asked.

"Possibly. While I was behind my utility shed, I heard a car start up farther down Chipmunk Coulee Road and head up over the hill. It made me think of Amy. She's staying at a place about ten miles from me as the crow flies."

"What do you want me to do?" Paul asked.

"Call Leslie and Sam. Have them get over to Dodson Hollow tonight and watch Amy's place. See when she comes and goes."

"Will do," Paul said.

Over the next two hours, Jim sat in an ER room at Gundersen Lutheran Hospital while the nurses and doctor numbed his leg, cleaned the wound, did some minor surgery, and put twenty-two stitches in his leg. Fortunately, the bullet had passed cleanly through his right calf, missing bones and tendons. The doctor said there was a chance of developing blood clots, so he needed to come in if his leg got tender and hot. He was assured by a pretty nurse named Avery that his wound would heal fast.

"Good," he replied. "I'm getting married in a couple of weeks, and I don't want to limp down the aisle. Might give the wrong impression."

"Really?" she said wide-eyed. "You're getting married? I didn't know old people like you did stuff like that."

Jim gave her a disgusted look, and she collapsed in laughter. "Should I accuse you of age discrimination now or later?" he asked crabbily. He wasn't sure what she meant by "stuff like that," and he didn't ask.

But she smiled and said, "Gotcha, didn't I?" He grinned as he pulled out his cell phone.

Jim called Sara and John first but had to leave messages. They seemed to have shut off their phones. Then he dialed Carol. He looked at the clock and saw it was 1:12 a.m. He was about to hang up when she answered.

"Hello?" she said in a groggy voice.

"Hi."

"Jim, why are you calling me so late?" He could hear the

confusion in her voice.

"Don't panic. I'm okay, but I got shot." There was silence. "Carol, are you there?"

"What? When did this happen? Jim could hear the panic in her voice.

"Well, I'm talking to you, so it can't be too serious." He heard a sigh on the other end. "Listen, I'm just getting stitched up, and then I need to come to your house for a nightcap and maybe a spare bed. How does that sound?"

"Absolutely, but—"

"I'll explain when I get there in about twenty minutes." He tried to make his voice even and reasonable, but he was getting furious as he thought about the night. Questions were zinging around in his head, and none of the possibilities were providing much comfort.

"I'll be here," she said quietly.

Paul gave Jim a ride to Carol's condo, assuring Jim that he would board up the broken windows and secure his house. He walked beside Jim as he hobbled toward the apartment on a pair of aluminum crutches. Paul stayed while she settled Jim in her spare bedroom. Pulling back the sheets and quilt, Paul helped him out of his shoes, jeans, and T-shirt. The sedatives and Novocaine were starting to wear off, so Carol rummaged through the bathroom for some Tylenol. She mouthed "Thank you" to Paul as he hurried out the front door.

"What's this?" Jim asked as she handed him a glass of water and two blue tablets. She sat down on the side of the bed.

"Two Tylenol PM with codeine. So you can sleep."

Jim waved at her. "I don't need that. I'm fine," he said impatiently, feeling the slow burn of frustration in his chest. But he swallowed the pills and a few gulps of water when Carol insisted. Trying to puzzle through the whys of the shooting had left him confused and foggy.

Noticing her wounded look, he quickly apologized. "Sorry, honey. It's just a flesh wound. I'll heal fast." He pulled her down to him, looking squarely in her brown eyes. While she perched on his chest, he explained. "This is part of who I am. If you're going to be my wife, you'll have to accept that I sometimes deal with some dangerous people. And occasionally, getting shot is part of the package. This time I got hit. I've been hit before. Nothing too serious, thank God."

Carol made a wry face, and Jim smiled weakly. "Your phone call scared me so bad," Carol said. "I guess in all the excitement of the wedding, I forgot how dangerous your job could be."

She paused a minute, looking him over. A smile teased her lips. "You're looking mighty sexy, barechested and all. Couldn't blame me if I took advantage of you in your condition." She kissed him softly.

"You have no shame," he said. "Is this your idea of a proposition? Waiting until I'm wounded and vulnerable and have no willpower to resist?" But his eyes were laughing. He started to explain what had happened, but his story and the meds met in the middle. His eyes began drooping, and his words seemed to be drifting off a cliff somewhere. The pounding in his leg was finally backing off. "I'll be fine in a few days." His hands flopped on the quilt and his eyes closed. He rolled over, and soon he was snoring.

Carol kissed him lightly, turned off the light, and tiptoed to her bed.

Meanwhile, Sam Birkstein and Leslie Brown were huffing and puffing in the dark through thick undergrowth and a patch of prickly blackberry bushes that surrounded a cow pasture. They were hiking to Tim Tostrud's dairy farm on Dodson Hollow Road. They'd hidden their car in some brush along a field road a half-mile back. The velvet night was intensely black. Leslie was familiar with night reconnaissance, and tonight she felt energized. Earlier, as they passed the farm, they noticed Amy's car was gone. But that wasn't unusual. She'd told Sam she worked all shifts and picked up extra hours whenever she could.

They wormed their way through a three-strand barbed wire fence and ambled through a hayfield, occasionally stumbling until their eyes adjusted to the ambient light. The moon hung in the hazy night sky, and wispy clouds moved across the golden orb with the stealth of a burglar. The hip-roofed barn sat to the left of the clapboard farmhouse, which was surprisingly close to the road. A smattering of other small buildings, including a tool shed, chicken coop, and small modern steel-sided pole shed filled in the picturesque farmstead.

Leslie stopped in front of him, holding up her hand. She knelt down. Sam followed, kneeling beside her. A slight rise in the land gave them a good vantage point. They could easily see Amy's movements anywhere near the farm buildings.

"This looks like a pretty good spot to me," Leslie whispered. She was dressed in black, a slight bulge under her fleece jacket where her weapon was holstered. Her blond hair was tied back and pushed under a black Wisconsin Badgers stocking hat. "Think this spot's okay?"

"Yeah. Looks good. Better hunker down and get comfortable."

Leslie and Sam laid on their stomachs in the foot-high grass at the edge of the field, placing their binoculars and night vision goggles beside them within quick reach. The hours wore on. They counted six cars and two pickups on the road. Sam ate a Snickers candy bar, and they took turns dozing for brief intervals. Soon the horizon began glowing lemon yellow. Then a pink blush spread over the hills as the sun worked its way toward morning. Birds began their first early warbles, and other small creatures started coming out of their burrows.

Leslie stirred. "Whaddya think? Should we stick around?"

"Let's wait a little longer. I'd like to stay until she gets home from wherever she's been," Sam whispered.

Another fifteen minutes passed, and a little red Nova turned into the driveway, coming to a stop in front of the house. For a while, nothing moved. Leslie had a deja vu moment, thinking about when she was in Iraq walking a dusty road on patrol, trying to figure out who the good guys were. She had a bad feeling about Amy.

The car door clicked open. Amy placed her feet on the driveway and sat there for a few minutes. She stood and began walking wearily toward the house. Sam gripped Leslie's arm.

"Look. She's wearing all black," he whispered close to her ear. "Not your typical nursing home clothes, ya think?"

"When she gets in the house, let's sneak up to the car and take a look inside. See if we can figure out where she's been." Leslie put her index finger up her lips. "Stay down," she mouthed to Sam.

They waited for half an hour, thinking Amy might be sleeping. Then they ran crouched over to the side of the pole shed and checked again for movement. Nothing stirred. They ran to the side of the car and peered inside. A Ruger Ranch rifle lay across the front seat along with a black hat. About five shoeboxes, a cardboard box filled with kitchen utensils, and a crockpot were sitting on the back seat.

Leslie made a gesture, her palms face up like, *What's up with that?* Sam pointed toward the barn. They sprinted, staying low until they were crouched in the shade of the barn.

They talked it over and decided Sam would make the arrest. Leslie thought they'd need backup, but Sam said as long as Amy wasn't armed, they could take her in.

Sam's knock on the farmhouse door seemed to echo across the gravel driveway. He felt like the sound came up and hit him on the back. He knocked again louder.

"Amy, it's Sam Birkstein. I need to talk to you."

There was a rustling in the entryway. Amy opened the door, still in her black clothes. A look of recognition was slowly replaced with a look of utter despair in her hazel eyes.

Sam said, "Amy, I'm taking you in for questioning. Get your things. We're going down to the law enforcement center."

SUE BERG

Leslie and Sam hunched together in the hallway outside of the interrogation room in the lower level of the La Crosse County Jail.

"So you want to take the lead in her questioning, right?" Leslie asked.

"Right. I had a pretty good rapport with her in my other interview," Sam said, scrunching up his face. "Although, it didn't end the way I thought it would." He paused. "But we have more circumstantial evidence now. We have the rifle, the black clothes which were probably intended to conceal something, and of course, her close association with Matt Shafer."

"Sounds good. Looks like you've thought this through," Leslie said. "Let's do it."

Leslie and Sam entered the room where Amy Bergholt sat mute and shriveled. Her hair was disheveled, her black clothes a testimony to possible covert activities. An odd combination of regret, angst, and suspicion clouded her facial features. She looked up expectantly when the two detectives came into the room. When they completed the preliminary formalities of the interrogation, Sam began.

"Okay, Amy. Can you tell us where you were last night between the hours of eight o'clock and seven this morning when you were taken in for questioning at the La Crosse Sheriff's Department?

Amy leaned back in her chair. She seemed to be weighing her options.

"Well, I wasn't at St. Theresa's."

Sam groaned inwardly. He didn't want to have to spend an inordinate amount of time squeezing a confession out of Amy. *Just cooperate,* he thought.

"Yes, we could see that from your clothes. So where were you last evening?" Sam asked, looking patiently at Amy.

"I went for a drive," she answered, tipping her head back, looking down her nose.

"Where?" Sam's patience was already wearing thin, and they'd hardly gotten started. "Must have been a long drive. You were gone all night."

"Listen, Amy," Leslie counseled, "we are aware of the Ruger rifle in your car. Your clothing suggests some kind of nighttime activities. It's beyond the bounds of normal reasoning to think that you were taking a country drive in the dark that took ten hours."

Sam could see Amy was debating with herself. Confess? Hold out? A few minutes of silence ensued.

"What do you know about the shooting incident that happened at Lt. Jim Higgins home last evening?"

"You told me he was shot," Amy declared defiantly. "I didn't say I knew anything about it."

"Do you know anything about it?" Sam asked.

Amy looked up at the ceiling, an inward dispute raging in her mind.

Sam's phone beeped. The impound center. He shut off the recorder and motioned to Leslie to step out of the room. Amy was left sitting at the table, a look of anxiety washing over her face.

"Sam Birkstein."

"Sam, this is Jack Lang down at the impound center. We've got this little red Nova here. You mentioned those shoeboxes. Did you happen to take a look in them?"

"No, we were busy getting Amy locked up. We thought she probably had a penchant for shoes and that she was moving them to the farmhouse. Why?"

"Did I hear you were looking for a bunch of gold coins? Something about some heist that took place more than a hundred years ago?"

"Yeah. We are looking for some coins." Sam felt a chill run up his back. *It's not possible.*

"Well, buddy, they're here. Piled very meticulously in twenty-one shoeboxes in the back seat and trunk. I mean, this is friggin' unbelievable."

"Don't move. Leslie and I will be right down." Sam suddenly turned very pale.

"Sam? You don't look so good. What's wrong?" Leslie said, grabbing his arm.

Sam did a once-over glance at Leslie. "You'll never believe it," he whispered.

After returning from the viewing of the ancient coins, they reentered the interrogation room. Amy had been pacing in the room for over forty-five minutes, her irritation and impatience unmistakable.

"Amy, what was in the shoeboxes in your car?" Sam asked, his eyes boring down on her.

"You found the boxes?"

"Yes. What do you know about the gold coins?" Sam continued. "If I remember right, the last time we talked, you claimed you didn't know anything about that."

Amy let out a sigh, covered her face with her hands, and went silent. Finally, her hands dropped in her lap, and she began to talk.

"I should have planned more carefully," she began. ⊙

31

THURSDAY, JUNE 24

The early morning light was just creeping into Carol's apartment windows as she began to brew coffee. She sat on the back deck in her nightgown, sipping her hazelnut concoction, her hair tousled and uncombed. The low-lying valleys were filled with fog, drifting in ethereal mists, swirling and twisting in surreal patterns. A doe and her fawns munched timidly at the edge of the woods, alert and wary. The doe's ears and tail twitched nervously.

Carol thought about her future as a cop's wife. She wondered if she was up to the expectations that the job would place on her once she said her vows. Thinking about last night, she tried to discern whether she was ready or not. The phone call from Jim in the hospital had made her panic, but she'd recovered. *I can do this.* Then another thought. *I'm already doing this.*

She heard a thump inside. Jim appeared at the patio door with one crutch under his arm.

"Coffee?" Carol asked.

"That'd be great. And maybe a few regular Tylenol." Jim's face was pale. He grimaced as he lowered himself into a chair. "Mmm, you look beautiful all mussed up."

Carol bent down and kissed the top of his head. "If you think this is beautiful, we need to work on your concept of beauty. Back in a minute." When she returned, Jim was on his phone, intense and focused.

"She's in custody?" He listened. "I'll be down this afternoon. I've got to go look at my house." More listening. "See ya then."

"What's up?" Carol asked, handing Jim coffee.

"That was Paul. He's still at home, but he's coming to the center in about an hour. Once I get this pain under control, I need you to go with me over to the house, and then I'm going to the office. Sam and Leslie staked out Amy Bergholt last night, and they have her in custody. Found a Ruger Ranch rifle in her front seat. She's in jail, and they're going through her car as we speak." Jim looked satisfied, leaning back in the patio chair.

"Oh, so that's who took the potshots at you and wrecked your house," Carol said with an undertone of anger. "Well, she deserves to be in jail if she did that. You want a shower first?"

"Yeah, and breakfast?"

"Sure. Oh, by the way, Sara and John both called. I guess Paul got through to them early this morning and filled them in. I invited them here Saturday night. Hope that was okay," Carol explained. "But they want you to call as soon as you can."

"Got it," Jim said tersely.

"How are you doing, really?" Carol asked anxiously.

Jim's face softened. "I'll be fine. I just feel a lot older than fifty-two today."

"I can believe that." She held out her hand and pulled him up. "Let's go. Duty calls."

Jim and Carol drove out to Chipmunk Coulee Road after breakfast and surveyed the damage to the house. The patio door and large living room window were shattered but had been boarded up by Paul. The insurance adjuster met Jim and told him that his homeowner's policy would cover everything. Jim spent some time on his cell, locating his building contractor and arranging for the windows and bloody carpet to be replaced. In the meantime, Carol strolled through the house, making mental notes on improvements she wanted to make. The contractor promised he'd get the work done in the next week.

They drove downtown to Jim's office. They were just getting off the elevator when Jim's phone buzzed. "Jim Higgins."

"Chief, you're never going to believe this." Sam's voice was higher than usual, and he was talking rapidly. He sounded like a ten-year-old who'd inhaled helium from a balloon.

"What's wrong with you? You sound weird," Jim said, standing by Emily's counter, leaning on his crutches.

"We found the gold. Well, Leslie and I didn't really find it. Jack Lang at the impound center did. It was in shoeboxes in Amy's car. Can you believe that? Shoeboxes. Go figure. You know how we wondered if it even existed. Well, it's real," Sam said, his words tumbling out. "I'm standing here looking at a huge pile of gold coins worth millions. Unbelievable. You've got to get down here and see this. It's incredible." Abruptly, his rapid account stopped, and then he said, "Are you there, Chief?"

"I'll be right down." Jim grabbed Carol's arm. "We've gotta get down to the impound. I'll tell you about it in the car." Jim chinned Carol toward the elevator as he hobbled across the reception area.

Emily raised her hand in a wave. "Jim, I've got some messages for—"

"Later," Jim shouted as the elevator door closed. ☉

32

TWO WEEKS LATER

In the end, federal officials from the FBI, U.S. Treasury offices, representatives from the Wisconsin Division of Criminal Investigation, the Department of Justice, and Andy Straken, converged on the La Crosse Sheriff's Department, and the infighting and arguments about jurisdiction and ownership of the lost treasure began. Jim was sure it would take years before it would be completely and adequately resolved. Threats of lawsuits and the recitation of laws pertaining to ownership were volleyed back and forth between each branch's lawyers. Andy Straken shrilly claimed the gold was his since it was found on his land. The war had begun. In the meantime, the coins were secured at a Madison Wells Fargo branch and would be kept there until a decision could be reached between the combative parties.

Jim and his team conducted interviews with the *La Crosse Tribune*. Persistent local TV personalities continually called Jim's office about the gold coins. The discovery created headlines throughout the country. Eventually, *Gold Rush* on the Discovery Channel and another reality show called *Cooper's Treasure* picked up the story. Jamie Alberg gained more notoriety and fame when he sold the rights to his story of attempted murder by Steve Stoner to the *History Detectives* on PBS.

Jamie's story was becoming a legend in its own right.

About a week after finding the gold, Jim heard Jamie's familiar voice echoing down the hall. "Listen, Emily. I need to see the chief and congratulate him. Is he here?"

Jim couldn't hear Emily's reply, although he heard a quiet murmuring. His cell beeped.

"Jim, your favorite amateur sleuth is here. Can I send him in?" Emily questioned.

"Send him down. And by the way, how are the plans going for the Paris honeymoon trip?"

"As soon as you give me a firm date, I'm on it," she said cheerily.

Jim leaned back in his chair, his hands folded across his stomach, legs outstretched. In a moment, Jamie appeared at Jim's door. He looked older—more settled and confident.

"Hey, Chief. I just wanted to tell you how excited I was that you found the gold. Cha-ching!" He pumped his arm in the air. "The pundits and talking heads are calling it the find of the century, ranking right up there with Robert Ballard's discovery of the *Titanic*." He stopped, waiting for Jim's reaction.

"Really? Well, I have to be honest that I never thought we'd find it. It seemed like too many people had their fingers in the pie. I really thought it had already been moved overseas or maybe even to Canada."

"It's just an incredible accomplishment, Chief. You should be very proud of your team."

"I am very proud of them. But that's what we're paid to do." Jim felt embarrassed by all the lauds Jamie was heaping on. *After all, the coins were hidden in cardboard shoeboxes in the back of a beat-up Nova,* he thought.

"I got a grant to study abroad in Egypt for six months next year under Dr. David Levinson, who is the head of the archaeology department at Rutgers. It's a very prestigious university in the field of forensic archaeology. The opportunities that this might open up for me are endless," Jamie prattled on, sounding like a professor himself.

"That's great, Jamie." Jim smiled. He leaned over his desk to shake Jamie's hand. "Keep us informed about your studies."

"I will, sir. You know what the great race car driver Bobby Unser said, don't you?"

"No idea, Jamie, but I'm sure you're going to tell me." Jim crossed his arms across his chest and tipped his head as Jamie pointed a finger at the ceiling.

"Success is where preparation and opportunity meet."

"Well, there you go. Good luck, Jamie. I'm sure you'll be a success."

"Thanks, Chief, for everything."

And with that, Jamie Alberg turned and sauntered down the hall and out of the building. *He'll be back. Just wait and see,* Jim thought.

The sunshine outside was brilliant and filled Jamie with a renewed sense of purpose. He stood on the sidewalk, thinking back to the moment he'd heard the news report about the lost gold. Cautiously, he caressed a gold coin in his pocket. He dug it out, turning it over in the light. *What Lt. Higgins doesn't know won't hurt him,* Jamie thought, a sly grin spreading over his cherubic face.

Lying in jail awaiting trial, Steve Stoner lay on his narrow bed reading the latest update of the discovery of the gold coins in the *La Crosse Tribune.* He'd assumed that his treasure would remain hidden as long as he kept paying the rental fee on the storage unit. Reading about the discovery of the coins in Amy's car, he sputtered and threw the paper on the cement floor of his cell. Groaning at his stupidity, he regretted getting involved with Amy Bergholt. Amy hadn't been interested in him at all; she just wanted the gold. Who knew she was that smart? ☉

33

SATURDAY, SEPTEMBER 23

All the well-made plans for Jim and Carol's wedding crumbled in the wake of the gold discovery. Jim was swamped with meetings, interviews, and the documentation of evidence. But finally, on a crisp September day when the trees were aflame with red, orange, and gold, Jim and Carol were married in a late afternoon ceremony in the gazebo at the International Friendship Gardens in La Crosse.

The gazebo at the park had been decorated with corn shocks, pumpkins, and sunflowers. Twinkling white lights flittered like fireflies set loose in the autumn dusk. Pastor Berge, Jim's Lutheran pastor from Hamburg Ridge, conducted the ceremony. Vivian was Carol's maid of honor, and John stood up for his dad. Carol had twisted Jim's arm to include a few more people besides family. Sam, Leslie, Paul with a very pregnant Ruby, Emily Warehauser, and Luke Evers and his family were all in attendance. And, of course, Jamie and Dr. and Lydia Alberg had wormed an invitation out of Carol despite Jim's protests.

Jim's feelings bumped up against each other, giving the moment a surreal quality. He could hear Margie's voice urging him on and giving her approval. Glancing over, his eyes found Sara, so much a picture of her mom. John stood tall and proud next to him, his eyes rimmed in tears. He thought about the phone conversation he'd had with Carol after her attack and how vulnerable she had been, how comfortable he felt with her from the beginning, and then how their loved bloomed so unexpectedly. His own eyes shimmered with tears, and he blinked as they spilled on his cheeks.

In a strong, calm voice, Jim repeated his vows. "I believe in you, the person you will grow to be. With an undivided heart, I take you as my wife, acknowledging and accepting your faults and strengths as you do mine. I promise to be faithful and always make our love my priority. I will be yours in plenty and want, in sickness and in health, in failure and triumph. I will dream with you, celebrate with you, and walk beside you through whatever our lives may bring. You are my person, my love, and my life, today and always."

Carol was radiant in a knee-length azure blue dress that featured a crochet-trimmed bodice, shoulder-baring sleeves, and a skirt that fell in soft gathers around her hips. She carried a simple bouquet of white roses and baby's breath. Carol repeated her vows with a strong, clear voice. She was never so sure of anything in her life. Jim was all she wanted.

The reception was simple but elegant with trays of finger food, glasses of sparkling champagne, and of course, a beautiful wedding cake. Paul played James Taylor's "How Sweet It Is to be Loved by You" for Carol and Jim's first dance. By ten o'clock, the bridal couple was ready to go home.

"Hey, beautiful," Jim said as he caught her hand and pulled her away from Lydia Alberg. "Whaddya say we get outta here and go home?" he whispered seductively in her ear.

"Mmm, sounds like everything I've been dreaming about."

"Oh, that's just the beginning. I've got a couple more surprises up my sleeve." Jim's smile hinted at something out of the ordinary, revealing the happiness he felt.

"Jim Higgins. I can't imagine what you've been up to," she whispered back.

"Oh, baby, you've no idea." He kissed her.

It took them a full hour to say their goodbyes, but finally, they were speeding toward Chipmunk Coulee Road and their first night together. Driving into the garage, they climbed out of the car. Carol had packed her suitcases, and Jim carried them into the bedroom.

"Just wait, sweetheart, for one minute," he said from the master bedroom. Carol plopped on the couch and wiggled her way out of her heels. She leaned back with a sigh, reviewing all the special moments of the day.

Before Margie had passed away, Jim had designed a spa suite off the master bedroom. Now, after two years without a feminine presence, the suite was ready for Carol's wedding night. Jim ran the soaking tub full of warm water with lots of bubbles and French soaps. He lit twinkling votive lights along the windowsills and the vanity and turned the lights down low. Anna, Jim's housekeeper, had laid out luxurious towels and a white velour bathrobe for Carol. Atop the towels, Jim had laid copies of their airline tickets to Paris and a confirmation of their hotel room. A large bouquet of lavender sat on the vanity along with a huge basket of exquisite French lotions and eau de colognes. Jim stood back to admire the effect. *Lovely. This is going to be great.* He closed the door and stepped into the hallway.

"Jim, what are you doing back there?" Carol asked with exasperation.

"Okay, babe, come on back. I have something for you."

Carol walked up to Jim, melting into his arms. "You know what I want. Don't tease me," she said seriously, kissing him

He opened the door. Carol gasped in wonder.

"Oh, Jim, this is absolutely a dream!" Her hand traveled to her throat, where it stayed. The fragrance in the room was divine, and the flickering candlelight heightened the romance of the evening. Carol felt like a princess, and at forty-two, that was something. "I can't believe this." She turned back to him. "Did you do all of this for me?"

"With a little help from Emily and Anna," he admitted shyly. He gently pushed her into the bathroom and said, "Take your time. You know where I'll be."

An hour later, Jim had turned down the sheets on the bed and was characteristically reading a little Tony Hillerman, but he wasn't really reading. He'd read the same page about fifty times. The light from the lamp was low when he heard a rustling. He looked up, and Carol was standing by the bed in her robe.

"Are you ready for this?" she said demurely as the robe dropped to the floor.

Jim spent a moment taking her in—all of her.

"I've never been more ready. You are beautiful. Come here, love." And she did. ☉

THE END

ABOUT THE AUTHOR

"Stay faithful to the stories in your head."
Paula Hawkins—author of *Into the Writer*

Sue Berg grew up with family stories; stories about hunting and fishing adventures, slightly irreverent relatives, and family sagas of immigrant descendants. Growing up with four brothers in the little Wisconsin town of Glenwood City, she tagged along as the odd-girl out and participated in wild risk-taking and saucy adventure—all at the hands of her daring siblings. Later, after a career in teaching and the trials and eventual successes of raising four children to adulthood, the smoke cleared. Through all the ups and downs, Sue continued to read a variety of literature. Completely by accident, she came across the book, *Shut Up and Write!* by Judy Bridges, founder of Red Bird Studio in Milwaukee. The advice struck a chord in her. She sat down at her computer five years ago and began writing. *Driftless Gold* is the story that wouldn't leave her alone and Judy's sage wisdom that launched her career as a writer.

Driftless Gold is Sue's first novel. Previously in 2011, she published a family memoir entitled *Solid Roots and Strong Wings*.

Sue lives with her husband in the Driftless area. When she's not writing, she enjoys quilting, watercolor painting, camping, gardening, hiking, and sitting around campfires with her four children and eight grandchildren. ☉

THE DRIFTLESS SERIES

Coming in December 2021.
Turn the page for an excerpt
from *Driftless Treasure*

When stolen Iraqi treasures show up in a La Crosse
antiques store, Detective Jim Higgins becomes suspicious.
But that's just the beginning. A delivery truck is bombed
and the discovery of its surprising cargo is the beginning
of a deepening sinister mystery. Higgins and his
team must untangle the source of ancient
stolen antiquities and a murderer
with a dark, evil secret.

1

BAGHDAD, IRAQ

APRIL 2003

The Baghdad National Museum's doors were flung open like a gaping, toothless mouth in the cool desert dawn. It was eerily quiet after the fierce firefight a few days ago between Saddam Hussein's rebels and U.S. occupation forces. Inside the museum, a few citizens and employees wandered stupified at the destruction that had taken place within its walls.

In the early morning light on April 12, a convoy of three jeeps, led by U.S. Army Colonel Michael Bogdonavich, kicked up a dust trail on the main road as they drove rapidly toward Baghdad. They were on a mission to safeguard and protect what was left at the museum after the firefight between the hostile forces. Approaching the building, U.S. Army Sniper Wade Bennett pointed upward to the main entrance gate where a crude sign flapped in the wind "Death to Americans and Zionist Pigs." Bogdonavich shuddered and ordered his troops into the museum.

Inside the museum, the insurgents had looted the contents. The havoc that ensued was jaw-dropping in its ramifications, and the raid on the museum had shocked the art world. Thousands of Middle

Eastern antiquities had been destroyed and carried away. Precious vases lay crushed and broken. Discarded uniforms from fleeing Iraqi soldiers were strewn in careless abandon, and the acrid smell of gasoline rag torches filled the air. Ancient statues lay decapitated on the marble floors where they had tumbled from their pedestals in the mayhem. The shattered glass of overturned showcases crunched underfoot. Ancient gold jewelry, amulets, cylinder seals, and coins littered the floor. The museum offices were in disarray. Desert air currents filtered through the vast structure, creating tornadoes of paper documents that floated in the air. Smashed during the hysterical chaos, computers and office equipment lay in desolate heaps.

Noticing a man sitting on a pile of rubble, Colonel Bogdonavich approached him cautiously. The man held his head in his hands, his soft sobs barely audible. His traditional long white gown pooled at his feet like a marble statue. Around his feet, fragments of plaster and pottery had been swept into haphazard piles.

"Sir, could you tell us who is in charge?" Bogdonavich asked the distressed man, leaning down to speak to him as he absorbed the anguish on his face.

At the sound of a human voice, the Iraqi lifted his head. His eyes were pools of profound sadness. Tears stained his cheeks, and despair was imprinted on his regal features.

"They hauled our treasures out in handcarts and wheelbarrows. They jeered and cackled like hyenas," he said through muffled sobs. "We can never replace what was lost. Never. The world will be less civilized because of what was done here," he said with finality. His emotions swelled, and he began to sob again.

Colonel Bogdonavich straightened himself to his full height. It was worse than anything he could have imagined. The National Museum was in utter shambles, and no one was in charge. The museum was unguarded, abandoned, and deserted. Worst of all, thousands of precious treasures had vanished.

PRESENT DAY—WEDNESDAY, OCTOBER 17

Wade Bennett sat on the peak of his barn roof in Rockland, Wisconsin, enjoying the warm October sunshine. He tipped his face toward the sun, worshipping its warmth. Since his retirement from the U.S. Army in January 2017, he'd changed his appearance from military garb to eclectic hippie.

His buzz cut was gone. He now sported a short brown ponytail. He'd splurged on a U.S. flag tattoo on his left bicep. His deep-set gray eyes looked out from a sculpted face. His trimmed beard and mustache were all that remained of his tough ex-soldier image. Blue jeans and Carhartt shirts and jackets were his favorite clothes now. His six-foot frame was hard and chiseled thanks to his jogging and weightlifting regimen.

Coming back to Wisconsin, Wade purchased a twenty-acre farmette near Rockland, about fifteen miles northeast of La Crosse, Wisconsin. Sitting on the barn rooftop, he gazed with pride at the changes he'd already made to his property. When he'd purchased it, the place was dilapidated and needed serious repairs. He dove into the remodeling with enthusiasm.

The broken-down fences were replaced with four-strand barbed wire and steel fence posts. To replenish the depleted soil, he bought five beef heifers who grazed and cleaned up the overgrown weeds and pasture, enriching it with their manure.

The clapboard farmhouse was a classic two-story affair. The driveway curved through the property dotted with large soft maples and a few pin oaks. The kitchen and bathroom would need updating, but Wade could get by for now. After all, he'd lived out of a pack in the desert and mountains of Iraq and Afghanistan. Having a house was a privilege compared with life in military barracks and tents.

The barn was the next improvement project on his list. Carrying a tool belt and hammer, he expertly removed the old shingles, throwing them down to a flat rack wagon below. He wouldn't be a very savvy businessman if he let the treasures stored in the barn become wet and moldy. After all, some of them were as old as civilization itself. Getting them out of the Middle East had been a long, difficult process, fraught with danger, intrigue, and lots of money.

He recalled the day in 2003 when his military unit had rolled into Baghdad and driven up to the National Museum with Bogdonavich in command. During the restoration of security at the museum, he'd made invaluable friendships that introduced him to the lucrative antiquities black market. Those relationships had made him a very rich man. And now, he intended to capitalize on it.

Once he had the barn fixed, he was going to get reacquainted with his old girlfriend. He let out a contemplative sigh. His beautiful Nordic dream girl, Leslie Brown, was as intelligent as she was beautiful. They'd parted on uneasy terms, but that was about to change. He'd done his homework. Leslie worked for the La Crosse Sheriff's Department now. He could imagine the shock on her face when she saw him on her doorstep. As Gomer Pyle used to say: "Surprise, surprise, surprise!" ⊙

2

WEDNESDAY, OCTOBER 17

Jim Higgins, chief investigator for the La Crosse Sheriff's Department, stood in his bedroom at the foot of his bed in the early dawn, admiring the shapely legs of his wife, Carol. As if she knew he was watching her, she stirred. Rolling over, Carol stretched her hands over her head in a catlike pose.

"Mornin'. What time is it?" she asked sleepily.

"Five-thirty."

"Ugh. I'm still on Paris time," she mumbled. She buried her head in her pillow again, her dark brunette hair falling gently over her face.

"In that case, I'm just getting started," Jim said. He scooted her over and pulled her on top of him. Kissing her, he ran his hands down her back.

"At some point, we're going to have to rejoin the human race," Carol whispered, studying Jim's face, running her fingers through his graying hair. "You do know that, don't you, honey?" His blue eyes sparkled with humor. She gave him a long, languid kiss.

"Yeah, I know, but don't remind me now," he said. He buried his hand in her mussed hair and nuzzled her neck. Carol's breath quickened, and she kissed him eagerly again.

Later, while Carol showered and Jim shaved, he reminisced about their ten-day honeymoon in Paris. Leisurely breakfasts on the hotel balcony with quiche, croissants, and generous cups of latte. Hours lazing on a blanket in shady parks and lunching on baguettes, cheese, and wine. Jim's memory was flooded with the romance of Paris nightlife in small, dimly lit cafes accompanied by wine and intimate conversation. He visualized the Eiffel Tower brilliantly illuminated at night. Their days in Paris were filled with investigations at the Rodin Museum, strolls down the Rue Cler exploring quaint little shops, bike rides along the Seine River, and watching the constant parade of Parisians ambling nonchalantly down the Champs-Élysées. They also enjoyed exploring every inch of each other in their charming suite at Hotel Relais Bosquet. *How could it be over so quickly?* Jim mused. Now they were back home, adjusting to the reality of domestic life on Chipmunk Coulee Road in the house Jim had lived in for over twenty years.

Carol stepped from the shower and wrapped herself in a thick towel.

"Remembering Paris?" she asked saucily. She watched Jim in the bathroom mirror.

"Uh-huh. Remembering every moment with you," Jim said, his intense blue eyes traveling over her bare shoulders to her warm brown eyes. "From now on, Paris is my go-to happy place." He held his razor mid-air, his face still partially covered in shaving cream.

"Me, too," Carol answered coyly, giving his butt a little slap as she headed for the bedroom.

After breakfast and coffee, Jim turned his Suburban out of the driveway. The air had that brisk autumn snap that he loved. As he turned onto U.S. Highway 35 toward La Crosse, Wisconsin, he noticed the scarlet sumac at the edge of the woods, gracious and balanced. Deciduous trees blazed in a riot of crimson, pumpkin orange, and gold, their trunks standing like dark brown sentinels along the river road. Leaves floated to the pavement and fluttered in the air. A bald eagle perched in a dead oak tree and watched the river with hooded yellow eyes. Floating just above the surface of the Mississippi, wispy currents of fog created eerie columns and otherworldly shapes. Later the sun would burn it off, leaving the river's surface like a mirror, reflecting a million glittering sparkles.

The harbor at Genoa, Stoddard, and Pettibone Park was still busy with fishermen getting in their last days of casting and trolling before the winter season began. Jim wished he could join them. It was a perfect day for a boat trip on the Mississippi in the *Little Eddy,* the craft he'd inherited from his dad.

He dismissed thoughts of cruising on the river and maneuvered his car into the south side Kwik Trip on Mormon Coulee Road to purchase a coffee and a cinnamon crunch bagel. He cruised through town and turned on Vine Street, where he parked in the La Crosse Law Enforcement lot. Inside the complex, long-time friends and colleagues shouted "Congratulations!" and "How was the honeymoon?" Stepping out of the elevator on the third floor, Jim heard the jangling of phones and the gentle hum of secretarial duties. Had he been gone just two weeks? It seemed like a lot longer, but it felt good to be back.

Jim's secretary, Emily Warehauser, sat behind her desk, the picture of efficiency and competence. Emily had been with him for over ten years. Consistent, dependable, and loyal, Jim had complete confidence in her ability to keep the administrative side of his investigative team running on all cylinders. She had also been a faithful friend during his first wife Margie's illness and death from breast cancer. Jim couldn't count the times Emily had been there when his world was falling apart.

At fifty-two, he was still relishing his recent marriage to Carol Olstad, secretary of the La Crosse County Morgue and personal assistant to Luke Evers, the coroner and medical examiner. Their whirlwind romance had been the fodder of law enforcement gossip for the past three months. When he walked off the elevator this morning, he felt the pool of secretaries pause in their activities as if they were inhaling a big breath of air. Although they weren't looking at Jim, he knew they were listening intently to his conversation with Emily.

"Good morning, Chief!" Emily chirped enthusiastically. "How was Paris?"

Leaning over the counter, he said softly, "Paris was fabulous, thanks to all of our planning and preparation." Jim smiled, his dimple denting his cheek. "I owe you big time. You'll have to come to my office later, and I'll give you all the juicy details." He winked conspiratorially.

"I'd love to!" Emily flashed a dazzling smile.

"Any news while I was away?" Jim asked, glancing at his office door.

"Oh, yes. I almost forgot," Emily remarked. "Paul and Ruby had their baby, Melody Ann Saner, six pounds, seven ounces on September 28. Everything went fine. Paul is on paternity leave for a few weeks until they get a schedule going." Emily looked up at Jim and shrugged. "You know, bonding and all of that." She paused briefly. "You look good, Chief," she said enthusiastically.

"I feel great." Jim turned toward his office, balancing his coffee cup and bagel.

"Your mail's on your desk," she informed him, swiveling back to her computer.

"Got it," Jim said. He walked down the hall. Opening the office door, he hung his coat on the peg behind the door, sat down at the computer, logged on, and began perusing emails.

Carol wasn't back to work yet. She was redecorating the home that he'd shared for twenty-six years with his first wife, Margie. Replacing some furnishings with new pieces and painting rooms to reflect her style occupied her days since their return from Paris. The contents of her condo had been moved and transferred to Chipmunk Coulee Road. After consolidating all their stuff, they took a huge load to Goodwill and The Salvation Army. Their recent conversation reminded him of the adjustments coming down the pike.

"Jim, are you sure you're okay with the changes I'm making?"

she asked, frowning. "I know it's a lot to deal with."

Jim lowered *The Wisconsin State Journal* a few inches, his blue eyes peering at her. "I'm fine with it. You want to make this house your own and put your stamp on it. Go for it, sweetheart. The only thing you can't touch is my study, but you already know that." He raised the paper again and continued reading.

"Yeah, I'll be sure to leave that alone," she said smiling, holding up the paint samples with an outstretched arm in the evening light. "There might be a few more boxes to go through in the garage," she finished in a distracted tone.

"Probably won't get to it 'til the weekend," said Jim, his voice muffled behind the paper.

A faint tapping on his office door startled him, bringing him back to the present. Sam Berkstein and Leslie Brown were timidly standing outside in the hallway, leaning around the door frame. New investigators in Jim's department, their boundless enthusiasm more than made up for their inexperience. Jim waved them in.

Leslie was dressed in black slacks with a burnt orange pullover sweater and a fashionable scarf draped around her neck. *Elegant,* Jim thought. Her minimal makeup and blond, shimmering hair hinted at her Nordic genetics.

His eyes shifted to Sam, and he scanned him from head to toe. Red sneakers hid beneath a pair of saggy gray sweatpants. A red and black hoodie that read "Pike's Peak—Only Real Men Do It" completed the look. Dark, curly hair fell over his forehead. A pair of curious hazel eyes punctuated his handsome features.

"I see you've fallen into your old habits while I've been gone," Jim commented, glancing at Sam's latest getup. "Our officers shouldn't look like they just spent the night under a bridge somewhere."

"I'm doing some undercover stuff up on the north side today," explained Sam.

Trying to redirect Jim's attention away from Sam's homeless vibe, Leslie said, "It's good to have you back, sir. You look rested. Just ignore him."

"You don't have to apologize for me," Sam said grumpily to Leslie.

"I didn't, did I?" Leslie asked, looking surprised.

"Sounded like it," Sam said peevishly.

Jim looked from Sam back to Leslie, wondering at the barbed exchange.

Leslie noticed how refreshed Jim looked. Contented happiness radiated from him. *Must be his new haircut,* Leslie thought. His blond hair, streaked with gray, was styled in a casual, messy, uncombed look that set him apart from other men his age. His face was accented by piercing blue eyes, which radiated self-confidence. Leslie couldn't remember seeing Jim so relaxed. When she joined the staff six months ago, he was still reeling from the death of his wife, Margie. *This might be the first time I've ever seen him truly happy,* she thought.

"Well, it's nice to be back, bickering aside. Carol and I had a fabulous time in Paris. It's definitely a city that caters to lovers." he said frankly, looking over at them.

"That's great, sir," Leslie said, embarrassed, looking at her shoes. "We'll just leave it at that."

When he left for Paris after his wedding in late September, Steve Stoner had been arrested after confessing to the murders of two local migrant workers and the attempted murder of Jamie Alberg, a forensic archeology student who had become involved in the case. It all started with the discovery of an 1866 cache of gold coins stolen from Fort Crawford in Prairie du Chien and hidden in a cave along the bluffs above the Mississippi River for over one hundred years. The discovery of the coins led to other criminal activities.

Jim pointed Sam and Leslie to chairs. "So, how are our felons doing in the La Crosse Jail?" he asked in a brisk tone.

"Well, they've lawyered up, sir. We're hoping that all of our evidence will stand up in court," Leslie answered.

"You can never have enough evidence," Jim said seriously.

"On another note," Sam interrupted, "we arrested a ring of prostitutes operating out of an apartment complex on 25th Street over by the bluffs. You should have seen my drag outfit. I was even invited to a party and propositioned. The sting was a classic. You should have been there."

As Sam rehashed his story, Leslie watched him carefully, her expression a curious mix of disapproval and admiration.

"What?" Sam said, staring at Leslie.

"Don't brag. It isn't becoming to your so-called Christian image," she said, crossing her arms and tipping her nose in the air.

"Boy, are you snarky today," Sam complained.

"What about the charges facing Amy?" Jim asked, trying to steer the conversation back on track. Amy Bergholt, another perpetrator in the gold coin mystery, tried to derail the investigation when she'd shot up Jim's house, wounding him weeks before his wedding.

"She's toast," Sam recited. "Her innocence disappeared when she stood before Judge Benson in the preliminary hearing. She's facing some serious charges that will land her in state prison. You should have been there, Chief. You would have enjoyed it." There was a moment of silence as Jim stared at Sam, his blue eyes penetrating and serious.

"FYI. I never enjoy seeing people end up in jail," Jim said sternly. "But the alternative of perps wandering free after committing crimes shouldn't happen either. I would prefer that they didn't commit crimes in the first place," he finished, slitting open envelopes as he stood behind the desk. "But you can't get away from our depraved human nature."

"Right, Chief. 'The heart is deceitful above all things and desperately wicked. Who can know it? Jeremiah 17:9.'" Jim looked taken aback. Sam shrugged. "Well, that's something my dad would say, being a Lutheran pastor and all," Sam said, cocking his head.

"Well, dealing with criminals every day, it's a truth all of us should remember." Jim looked up from his mail and said, "Listen, I have a ton of emails and other paperwork to catch up on, so you're going to have to make yourselves scarce while I catch up." He made a shooing motion toward the door.

"Right," Sam said, getting up and walking into the hallway. "Later, Chief."

Jim noticed Leslie lingering, standing near his desk.

"Did you need something, Leslie?" he asked, noticing her rigid posture. *At ease, soldier,* he thought.

"Well, I spotted some genuine Iraqi vases downtown at the Antique Emporium on Third Street while you were away," she said. "At least, I think they're genuine." Jim gave her a curious glance. She hurried on. "You know I like antiques, so I went in the Emporium out of curiosity, and there they were. Are you familiar with that place down on Third Street?" she asked.

Jim nodded. "Yeah, Margie and I used to go there looking for Indian arrowheads and stuff like that. She bought some Native American baskets there once. It seems unusual to see Middle Eastern antiquities in La Crosse. What makes you think these vases are real?" he asked, slitting another envelope open.

"I'm not positive they are," she said, shaking her head. "I looked through my materials at home that list the stolen items from the National Museum in Baghdad. I was stationed in Fallujah when our troops were rushed to Baghdad in 2003 to save what was left at the National Museum after the looting. Saddam's insurgents and our troops decided to fight it out using the museum as their battleground. Some of the guys texted me pictures of the damage. It was horrible. Over 7,000 Mesopotamian pieces had been stored there. It was a great loss for the Iraqi people and the world." She glanced at Jim. "Sorry, didn't mean to get on my high horse. Anyway, these vases downtown look very similar to a pair listed in a reference catalog I have."

Besides being a working dog handler in the Army, Leslie had been trained as an Army antiquities specialist by Dr. Rachel Drummond. Dr. Drummond developed a program in conjunction with the Department of Defense designed to sensitize enlisted soldiers to the cultural and historical artifacts of countries where they served. Leslie had assisted Dr. Drummond in expanding the program, and in the process, she had become something of an expert on Middle Eastern antiquities and treasure.

"So, how valuable are these vases?" Jim asked, his curiosity sparked. He stopped rifling through his mail.

"They're worth several thousand dollars each, but they were marked at $6,500 in the shop. It's typical for sellers of these antiquities to lowball the price. Most dealers assume they're replicas. Copies sell very well on the decorative market. But if these vases are authentic, which I think they are, then their value is cultural and historic. Plus, they're stolen property, and they need to be returned to the National Museum in Baghdad. Some of those pieces date back to biblical times and have their origins in Mesopotamia," she said passionately, her eyebrows arching. "The Fertile Crescent. Remember your world history lessons, sir?" she asked skeptically, crossing her arms over her chest.

"Absolutely. I'm old, but I'm not *that* old. You mean Ur of the Chaldees where Abraham lived? The Cradle of Civilization, Hammurabi's Code? The birthplace of Islam, Judaism, and Christianity?" Jim responded, a satisfied look crossing his face. "That Mesopotamia?"

Leslie's eyes twinkled with surprise. "Very good, sir. I'm impressed."

"So if you think something's hinky about these vases, what's your plan?" Jim asked. He leaned back in his chair and clasped his hands behind his head. He watched her carefully, feeling a little glow that he'd remembered his history.

"I thought I'd keep checking at area antique and art galleries to see if any other missing items start appearing. Like everything else, the antiquities market fluctuates. The price on this stuff has gone down recently. Dealers may try to dump what they have before it completely crashes. I'd like to keep an eye on the situation," she proposed.

"Sounds good. Use your knowledge, and keep me informed. If you need help, let me know," Jim advised, turning toward his computer.

"Yes, sir, I will." Leslie turned to leave.

"One more thing," Jim said, holding up an index finger, rotating in his chair to face her.

Leslie stopped and turned. "Yes, sir?"

"Remember. Treasure can have strange effects on people. If the wrong person gets hold of these artifacts, things could go south real fast. We've already had that happen once before. Be careful." Jim's eyes locked on Leslie. There was no mistaking his serious tone.

"Yes, I'll remember, sir," she stammered. "Good to have you back."

Jim turned to his computer again. "Good to be back. Nice work, by the way."

Leslie nodded briefly, turned, and left Jim's office.

Paul Saner worked with Jim Higgins as a detective at the La Crosse Sheriff's Department. He was on paternity leave, and he'd never been so stressed. He stood by the baby bassinet in his living room, listening to his newborn daughter wailing again. He groaned. He'd worked stakeouts and long hours apprehending criminals without much sleep, but tired didn't come close to describing how he felt right now.

He leaned over the tiny bed. Grasping Melody under her small flailing arms, a little fist connected with his chin when he kissed her tiny cheek. Her pint-sized legs pedaled furiously as she worked herself into a full-blown meltdown. The quietness of the apartment was inundated with her piercing cries.

Carrying her to the couch, Paul changed her diaper and dressed his tiny daughter in a warm cuddly jacket, placing her in a stroller in the hallway. Paul knew he needed a change of scenery. Riverside Park would do them both a world of good this morning.

The crisp morning air filled Paul's lungs with optimism as he breathed deeply. Ripe woodlands, the flowing river, and the aroma of fresh bread from a downtown bakery wafted on a gentle breeze. He craved these morning outings where so many other young parents took their little ones. Paul exchanged ideas and experiences with them about parenting, which he found comforting and helpful. His cell beeped.

"Paul Saner."

"Congratulations, Daddy!" The familiar sound of Jim Higgins' baritone voice was loud and clear. "I hear Melody is just like her old man. Up all night partyin' and loves to sleep on the job during the day," Jim joked.

"Did Emily tell you that?" Paul heard Jim chuckle into the phone. "Well, it's good to hear from you, Chief. When did you get back?" Paul asked.

"A couple of days ago."

"That's great. Can't wait to hear about Paris," Paul joked.

"You won't hear about everything," Jim reminded him. "So how's it feel to be a parent?"

"Wow! It's crazy. One day you're this independent, confident person, doin' your own thing, and the next minute you're responsible for this tiny baby who depends on you for everything. Like. Everything. She can throw a wrench in the best-laid plans," Paul sighed.

"Been there, done that. Times two," Jim replied. "Listen, Carol wants to stop over with a gift for the baby."

"That's fine. Ruby and I are trying to make sure we each get enough sleep, so a call first would be great."

"Okay, then. I'll have her call. Talk to you later." Jim clicked off.

Paul had only been gone two weeks, but he already missed his colleagues and the frenetic activity of police investigations. Once Melody got her schedule settled, he could return to work. He leaned over the stroller and gazed at the sleeping face of the newborn. He couldn't believe he had such a beautiful baby girl. Then he felt a pang of guilt. It wasn't that he didn't want to help Ruby with the baby. He did, and he loved it. But his Type A personality was better suited to investigations. He sighed as he turned the stroller back toward the apartment. A battle waged inside him—guilt at being gone from work and guilt about having to go to work.

He was sure of one thing. He was doubly blessed with his beautiful wife, Ruby, and now his daughter, Melody and to have work he loved. What more could a man ask for?

THURSDAY, OCTOBER 18, MID-MORNING

Leslie parked her Toyota Prius on Third Street in front of Antique Emporium. She joined Sam on the sidewalk, zipped her insulated blue jacket, and wound a gold scarf around her neck. The October air was invigorating, and held a hint of frosty weather that would soon come in November. Cars and trucks rumbled by, the sound of tires amplified in the cold air. Bundled in warm jackets and scarves, people hurried around them like water flowing around a rock in a stream.

Leslie thought back to her conversation with Sam yesterday.

"Tomorrow, wear normal clothes–not your homeless, orphan, destitute look. You need to wear a nice pair of jeans, a dress shirt and a suit coat." Her blue-eyed stare made Sam stop and reconsider his objections. "I have something planned, and I need your help," she finished succinctly. She turned and headed down the hall to her office. Sometimes she had a strange effect on Sam, especially with her tough talk. *Nobody else seems to care what I wear, except Higgins. Why should she?* Sam thought.

"Wait a minute!" Sam yelled after her, upending the water bottle on his desk. "Crap!" he hissed under his breath, grabbing a handful of Kleenex to mop up the mess. He hurried out into the hall.

"What are we doing tomorrow?" he asked, standing in the hallway. The wet Kleenex in his hand dripped in a puddle on the floor. Leslie stopped and pivoted to face him.

"A little undercover assignment," she explained, tilting her head, her eyebrows arched. "Right up your alley." She grinned shyly.

Sam's eyes widened, and he grinned back. "Ooo, undercover. All right, I'm all in."

Now standing outside the antiques shop, Sam wondered what he'd gotten himself into.

"So here's the plan," Leslie explained. "There are a couple of vases in here that I think are stolen booty from Iraq. We're going to pose as a couple who are looking for decorative items for our new apartment. That way I can examine the vases up close to determine their authenticity." There was an uncomfortable silence. Sam had an odd look on his face.

"Wait a minute. Let me get this straight. I'm posing as your husband?" Sam said quietly.

Leslie shrugged casually. "Husband, lover, whatever. You're missing the point. Posing as a couple will make us look believable. We don't want to tip them off that we're cops. We need to have our story straight so we can look around, and get the ay of the land." She reached in her jacket pocket, pulled out two rings, and handed him one.

Sam nodded, slipping the ring on his finger. "OK, let's do it." Leslie tipped her head. Sam blushed and held up his hands. "Oh, sorry. I didn't mean *that.*"

"Will you get serious? Sheesh!" she said angrily. She took a deep breath. "Now, did you do your homework last night?"

"Yeah. I did," Sam replied sarcastically. "*The Treasure from the Royal Tombs of Ur* was stupendous." He rolled his eyes, parroting her serious tone. "I know as much now about Middle Eastern antiquities as I did two years ago. And that ain't much." Frowning, he shifted on his feet and his eyes brightened. "But I'll be a bang-up husband." He grimaced again. "Sorry."

"Are you always this much of a nerd?" Leslie asked. She sidled up to him, entwined her arm in his, and walked toward the emporium. "Come on. Let's get this over with. And by the way, you need to look like you're enjoying this," she lectured, glancing at him sideways. Sam's insolence left her feeling irritated like fingernails scraping a chalkboard.

"You better take your own advice. You're lookin' pretty damn ornery." He smiled disarmingly as he kissed her on the cheek. Her shocked expression gave him a sense of satisfaction. "Just playin' the part," he said, gaining confidence about the ruse. *Two can play this game,* he thought.

"What a putz," Leslie said. She tried to control a chuckle, but it escaped.

Located in the downtown Historical Development District of La Crosse, the Antique Emporium was a 20,000 square foot building with tall, oblong windows that faced the street. Originally, the building had housed the Galletin furniture store, and it was recognized as a landmark in the city of La Crosse. Inside, three floors and seventy-five booths were packed with collectibles and antiques. A black walnut handcarved staircase led to the second floor.

Walking into the building, Sam and Leslie strolled arm in arm and began meandering around each floor. A musty smell circulated in the old structure when the furnace kicked in. A couple of booths displayed antiquities like copper scrolls, late eighteenth century vases, Chinese sculptures from the Ming dynasty, and fourteenth century Iranian tapestries.

"Is there something I can help you with?" A clerk with frizzled gray hair approached them. Within her wrinkled face, two bright bird-like eyes peered at them, a pair of half-moon glasses perched on her bulbous nose. Her frumpy clothes were supposed to hide the bumps and lumps of an aging body, but the woman was obviously overweight and seemed to be arthritic.

She looks like an antique, Sam thought.

"Actually, I brought my husband with me today to see those two unique vases you had here last week." Leslie pointed toward the back of the store. "You know, the ones that looked Middle Eastern?" she ventured. "We're looking for some interesting pieces for our apartment, and I wanted Sam to see them."

"Oh, yes, dear. Come with me. They're in a locked showcase," she explained, hobbling into the depths of the store. "I'll have to get the key in the back."

They waited at the glass showcase. Sam studied the vases. They about ten inches high. Cast in a dark ocher color, the vases had panels of stylized deer and women decorating the sides. They were exquisite if you liked a dull, earthenware look. Sam was no expert, but their patina looked authentic to him.

"I've seen similar vases at the Smithsonian in Washington from the Abbasid period around the 10th century. Look at that surface! Aren't they wonderful?" she exclaimed quietly, glancing at Sam.

"Wow. You really do know about all this stuff, don't you?"

"Oh, I don't know everything," she said modestly, "but I've learned to really love Middle Eastern art and artifacts. It's such a splendid culture, and what was done to the treasures at the National Museum in Baghdad is a national shame," she whispered. She looked over at him, and Sam was surprised to see tears misting at the edge of her eyes. *I'd save my tears for something other than pottery,* he thought skeptically.

There was a rustling of fabric and footsteps behind the glass display case. They looked up and saw the clerk approaching the showcase carrying a ring of keys.

"Would you like to examine the vases?" she asked politely. A faint scent of violets hovered in the air, and her perceptive gaze stopped briefly at Sam's wedding ring.

"We certainly would, wouldn't we, honey?" Leslie cooed.

Just play along, thought Sam.

"Yes, my wife just loves this stuff. Me? I'm just starting to learn about it," Sam said, looking over for Leslie's approval.

Leslie's eyes softened as the clerk carefully set the vases on the counter. She ran her fingers over the surface decorations, tipping them over, and inspecting the marks underneath. To her professional eye, she had no doubt about the legitimacy of the vases. They were the real deal.

"May I take a few photos with my cell?" she asked.

The clerk's eyes hardened for a second. Then smiling she said, "Only if you're very serious about purchasing them."

"Oh, we are. Aren't we, Sam?" Leslie said looking over at him.

"Whatever makes you happy, darlin'," said Sam, smiling disarmingly. *I'd like to make you happy,* he thought.

Leslie began snapping photos before the clerk could object or change her mind. When she finished taking the photos, she said, "We'll be in touch in the next few days. Do you take debit or credit cards?"

"Either is just fine," the clerk smiled, but her eyes had become wary with suspicion.

They exited the store and walked energetically to the car. Leslie rubbed her hands together rapidly after starting the engine. Whether from the cold or excitement, Sam wasn't sure.

"Did you notice the change in her attitude when you started examining the vases?" Sam asked.

"Oh, yeah. A definite blast of cold air came rushing in, didn't it? She was suspicious, or at least protective. I wonder what she knows about them."

"Any other places you want to investigate?" He looked over at Leslie's silhouette. *She is lovely.*

"Yeah. There's an art gallery on Pearl Street—Rossellini's. Let's take a look there, too, while we're at it. I'm going to send these photos of the vases in a text to Dr. Drummond and get her professional opinion."

Later in the afternoon over in Rockland, Wade Bennett's phone chirped.

"Hello, this is Wade," he answered brusquely, taking a break from pounding shingles to his barn roof. Despite the cool October temperatures, the sun was hot, and he was sweating from the physical activity. He mopped his forehead with his sleeve while he listened.

"We've got a problem," an unfriendly voice said.

"Who is this?" Wade said, his stomach lurching with suspicion.

"You know who this is. Someone has looked at the Iraqi vases that are for sale down at Antique Emporium in La Crosse. They may be undercover police. You need to get over there and remove them. Immediately."

"I'm not removing them. I'm going to sell them. That's my business now, and I plan on making some good solid returns on my investment. Besides, unless you identify yourself, this conversation is over," he said sternly.

"Don't threaten me," the gravely voice barked. "Besides you know who this is, so don't pull that bullshit with me. I decide what antiquities are sold and where. I'm warning you for the last time. Remove them from the Emporium."

"Buzz off ..." but the line had gone dead. "Hello? Hello?" Wade repeated.

A cold thread of fear snaked up his back and sent chills over his body. He'd been afraid this might happen, but he had no one else to go to. He'd already burned all his bridges. He was truly out on a limb, and it felt like the limb was breaking. He began pounding more nails, attaching shingles to the roof. Despite the brilliant sunshine, a dread had fallen over him that he made him shiver with apprehension. ⊙

CPSIA information can be obtained
at www.ICGtesting.com
Printed in the USA
LVHW050850040222
710000LV00007B/17